THE TAILOR'S DUMMY

by

JACOB DARR

JBD PUBLISHING

First published 2021 by JBD Publishing

Copyright © 2021 Jacob Darr

Paperback ISBN: 978-1-8384531-0-7
eBook ISBN: 978-1-8384531-1-4

All rights reserved. No part of this publication may be reproduced, distributed, or transmitted in any form or by any means, including photocopying, recording, or other electronic or mechanical methods, without the prior written permission of the author, except in the case of brief quotations embodied in critical reviews and certain other non-commercial uses permitted by copyright law.

For permission requests, please email the author at jbd@jacobdarr.com

The majority of this work depicts a series of events which took place in the life of the author. Certain long-standing institutions, agencies, events, and public offices are mentioned. Some events and incidents in this book are the product of the author's imagination. Where this is the case, the resemblance to actual persons, living or dead, or actual events is purely coincidental.

Cover design by Creative Covers

For Nonnie, a couple of old saucepans & two grand saucepans.
Some might say, tablet time, others happy families.
With a nod to, The W's, RM, "Greenhouse one" and finally, Sibbo, the marathon man.
Das ist alles
Da

Chapter 1

Annoyed at being forced into arriving for work so early. It wasn't until I was nearing the CID office that the sound of all telephones' ringing made me realise I hadn't actually seen anyone on the way in. And parking at the back of the station had also been unusually easy. The floor deserted. Ordinarily at this time of day, there would at least be civilian staff and home beat officers readying themselves for lunch. Creatures of habit: lunching at the same time, with the same people, eating the same food for whatever day of the week it was, whether a pack-up or from the canteen's revolving menu. The only variation, the game of cards they played: whist, rummy or cribbage – it was the same throughout the Met., just not today.

Leaving the phones, I headed to the canteen to see if anyone was there, just a couple of traffic wardens looking lonely. They'd arrived early to avoid the queue, only there wasn't one. I then headed to the station office, which had to be manned. It too decidedly sparse, just the station officer and his assistant busy dealing with phone calls and the usual horde waiting to sign on. Complying with their bail conditions. All the lights on their mini switchboard flashing with incoming calls, at least they didn't have to put up with the noise. As the station officer finished a call, I covered the switches with my hand and said, "What's going on?"

"A body's been found on waste ground near Heckford Street and DCS Hampton's ordered all available staff; police and civilian to go to Arbour Square. He was adamant that all staff go, he must have said, 'All available staff' half a dozen times. Apart from the duty officer, I've been left with the area car and three PCs, and two of them are down at the scene."

I'd been at Leman Street for a couple of months, and it was without doubt the worst CID office I'd ever worked in. DCS Hampton, the area's senior detective, had seen to that. By sharing the main CID office with the home beat officers and civilian staff he'd created such a divisive atmosphere it was difficult to know who to trust. Something that was unheard of at other stations. The situation exacerbated by the fact that there were so few CID officers currently working at the station.

Not long after my arrival, Hampton had insisted on picking a team of officers mainly from our office to work on a very straight-forward domestic murder. Working out of one of two new incident suites at Arbour Square. They were now eking out the job for as long as they could, taking the mickey, trying to earn as much money as was humanly possible. In some quarters, their competency was now being called in to question, resulting in them being nicknamed 'The Muppets'.

I'd previously crossed paths with Hampton, one of many who had fallen foul and were not in his good books. Something which had been made abundantly clear by the actions of his lieutenants, trying to make my time at the station as unbearable as possible. Allocated all the rubbish – petty crimes, with lots of paperwork and little or no prospect of being solved. Being ordered to write off crimes, to get figures down, was another task I didn't like or agree with. I was spending so much time in the office; I felt more like an admin clerk than an operational detective.

Oddly, the only decent jobs came from Hampton's decision to appoint me as the Wapping Liaison Officer for the duration of my posting. Normally, the position would automatically pass to the newest arrival. Hampton, in his infinite wisdom, had decided it was mine until I moved on. There were two parts: firstly, dealing with all the major crimes emanating from

Thames Wapping. Mainly forged driving documents, MOTs and insurance certificates produced by individuals who'd been stopped by police and issued with a HORT/1. There was a perception amongst the locals they had a better chance of getting away with producing dodgy driving documents to river police than at a regular station. The truth was, they'd seen so many they were better at spotting forgeries than most. Secondly, you were the initial point of contact for dead bodies – or floaters as they were known. Found in the River Thames between Tower Bridge and The Isle of Dogs where the cause of death was either suspicious or unclear. The condition of some floaters made it impossible to tell and as a result I'd already been too five.

Bodies finding their way into the river would drift with the tide, and if not discovered, usually sink within the first few hours, depending on their size and the amount of clothing weighing them down. The water's temperature would determine how long a body remained underwater. The colder it was, the longer they stayed submerged. Eventually, a body would start to decompose, producing gases, increasing buoyancy, eventually rising to the surface – hence the term floater. Due to a combination of the skin breaking down and bloating, floaters could easily burst during recovery and being in their immediate vicinity was something to be avoided at all cost. The smell of putrefied human flesh alone was so unique it was not easily forgotten.

"Is Hampton dealing with it, then?" I asked. "He's already heading up one murder, isn't he?" Knowing that, with the other responsibilities, the district's senior detective had they were only meant to be actively involved in one murder or major incident at a time.

"Yeah, officers from the pool have been assigned. I know because I arranged for them to attend, having spoken to the commander. And, as far as I know they're still there but with Hampton you never know."

"Got time to tell me what's happened?"

"Sure, why not, they can wait," he said, wandering off to the nearby photocopying room while gesturing dismissively towards the flashing lights and punters at the counter. Ushering me in, he kicked away the dented wastepaper bin that normally wedged the door open, and as it closed, said, "It's all been a bit weird. During changeover, I took a call from IR. They had a caller on the line reporting the discovery of a dead body. The call had originally gone out over the radio, but as there were no takers and the location was on our ground, information room put the call through. Three dustmen had been given the job of clearing a patch of waste ground and, according to the guy on the phone, when they got there, they found that a lot of the rubbish had been collected up and burnt in the middle leaving this pile. Amongst the pile, was what they thought was a tailor's dummy. They had the shock of their lives when one of them went to pick it up, and at the last moment realising that it was a human being, with no head or hands."

The station officer hesitated, looking for my reaction, but I was already thinking about other possibilities and didn't respond. "Anyway," he continued, "having got the exact location, I sent a couple of PCs down to the scene and they've confirmed everything. After that, I tried to get hold of CID. But as night duty CID had already gone and none of the rostered senior officers answered their phones, I ended up calling the commander. He wasn't exactly chuffed at being woken, but at least he answered. He was even less pleased when I told him who I'd tried. Once I'd explained what had happened, he told me to get onto to the reserve at the yard and ask for someone from the pool to be appointed. He told me to emphasise that Hampton, sorry DCS Hampton, was already running one murder inquiry and to say that we were also helping those investigating the Curtain Road robbery. When I spoke to the reserve officer, and having explained the situation, he asked a couple of questions before telling me that a DCS Simmonds and his DI would be allocated the case and that they would be on scene within two hours. They arrived just before nine and as far as I know they're still there."

A couple of things struck me. The job had all the makings of a sticker; the name given to a murder investigation where there was no obvious suspect. Assuming Hampton wasn't involved. If I could somehow wangle my way onto the team, it would at least get me out of the office and away from him for a while. And, if the commander's comments were anything to go by, he didn't want Hampton running the case either. I didn't know why, but it was worth bearing in mind.

The other oddity was the commander's comments about the Curtain Road robbery, which were not true. That investigation was solely the domain of the Flying Squad, or 'Sweeney' as they were known. Who just happened to be using the other incident suite at Arbour Square. The robbery having taken place just three days ago, hitting the headlines as one of the biggest of its kind with an estimated six million pounds cash stolen.

The investigation was being run by Detective Superintendent Phil Saunders, or PeaSea as he was known. Somebody I knew both professionally and as a friend. We first met playing rugby when I was fourteen. My old school had an association with the local rugby club, where, because of my age, I used to get stuck on the wing for the B's or XB's. PeaSea skippered the B's. Then, having joined the police, our paths continued to cross. He was popular for a senior officer: open, approachable and relatively easy to get on with.

He did, however, have an Achilles heel. As part of his retirement plan, he'd gone into partnership with two others from the rugby club, becoming a silent partner in a new wine bar; something the job would never agree to. Any involvement with gambling, pubs or clubs was a complete no no, if discovered, would lead to dismissal.

A divisional reorganisation some time ago had meant that Arbour Square had been operating as a satellite station with limited uniform presence, creating lots of redundant office space. As it was more centrally located than Leman Street and had direct access to the magistrate's court next door. It had been identified as an ideal location for the new major incident suites. With the sudden influx of officers, it must have been pretty chaotic, and there certainly wasn't room for another major investigation.

"So, what makes you think Hampton's running the investigation and not the officers from the pool?" I asked.

"A few things. You've been upstairs; it's deserted. And, having spoken to the station officer at Arbour Square, he's convinced Hampton's looking to off-load the job he's currently got. By ordering everyone to Arbour Square, he's effectively cornered the market with regards to staffing. On top of which, he and some of his Muppets arrived on scene about twenty minutes ago."

"So, who's going to be dealing with all the day-to-day crap then?" I said, knowing he didn't know – it was a rhetorical question. It was just the sort of thing Hampton would do to keep the gravy train running. Never mind trying to solve a case; that wasn't his thing. He got a bigger kick out of disciplining officers. Ending the careers of others outside his sphere gave him a buzz. He could be such a vindictive so-and-so.

"Where's the office?" I asked.

"No idea, I'm not even sure there is one."

While the station officer had been speaking, I'd been trying to think of a plausible excuse to go to the scene. To find out what was really going on. If an incident room hadn't been allocated, neither had a telephone number. And advertising both, with a location other than Arbour Square, would, if nothing else, give Hampton a headache. Potentially providing me with the flimsiest of excuses to go down to the scene.

I needed to be sure an office hadn't already been allocated. A call from an external line to the local switchboard would tell me. If an office existed, they would put me through. If not, they would take a message. I popped next door to Mr Pickwick's, made a call, and was asked to leave a message.

Leman Street had its own major incident suite on the top floor. It was, however, derelict. The existence of the new suites at Arbour Square had resulted in all the fixtures and fittings disappearing; scavenged or stolen.

I made my way back to the DI's office, closing the door behind me to reduce the din. Freeing up a line, I made another call to the switchboard, this time using an internal line. Another operator answered, assuming I was the DI. I didn't dissuade her, saying that the incident suite at Leman Street was going to be used for the investigation and that I needed one of the suite's telephone numbers for publication. There was only one. The others disconnected some time ago. Armed with the information, I put a call into the press office, advising them of the incident room's location and public contact number. It sounded as though the press officer had fallen off his chair. Such was his reaction. A combination of astonishment, shock and euphoria. He couldn't quite believe that notifying the press office had been thought of at such an early stage of the investigation. Resulting in him promising to issue a press release for local radio within the hour, with the national and local newspapers being informed not long after. I couldn't have hoped for better.

Driving the mile or so along The Highway seemed to take longer than normal. As I got closer, I found out why. Some streets had been cordoned off by Special Patrol Group – a unit normally deployed to prevent riots and public disorder, although they were just as likely to be the catalyst for some. For some inexplicable reason, they'd been called out to set up checkpoints and diversions about a quarter of a mile from the scene, and apart from attracting the attention of passers-by and slowing traffic, appeared to serve no useful purpose. For a split second, I wondered who'd made the request. It had to be Hampton, another unnecessary attention seeking abuse of power. Having had to park so far away. It was only when I started walking towards the scene that I realised just how dark it had become, and that it wouldn't be long before it would begin to raining.

The area surrounding the waste ground was primarily made up of empty or derelict warehouses, with a few small terraced cottages dotted around and the occasional block of flats. As I reached Heckford Street, I could see one of the local uniformed officers standing by a gap in the corrugated iron fence, about half-way up, notebook in hand. Presumably logging the names, dates and times of those entering and exiting the scene. A little further along the street stood four men in deep discussion. DCS Hampton and DI Lambert, I recognised immediately, even with their backs to me. The other two had to be from the pool. You could tell they were senior detectives from New Scotland Yard by the way they dressed. I often thought it odd that senior detectives working in plain clothes effectively wore a uniform: dark blue knee-length Crombie, dark or navy-blue pinstripe suit, white shirt and black brogues. The only difference, the tie they wore, which would depend on where they'd served. One of the more unique and rarer ties I'd come across before being banned belonged to Stoke Newington's CID. It bore the mnemonic 'SYCUYA' in a half crescent below the station's code. The mnemonic stood for 'Stick your cock up your arse.' A real charmer, and probably not what Sir Richard Mayne had in mind when he defined 'The primary objects' of police in 1829: a passage of text that every officer in the Met. learnt verbatim when joining.

At the far end of the street, another group, The Muppets. Given their distance, and that the senior officers were in discussion, it looked as though whoever was running the case had yet to be decided. As I made my way towards the PC guarding the entrance, I could tell by Hampton's stance and the way he was gesticulating he wasn't happy. Making me warm to the officers from the pool. When I reached the uniformed officer and without being specific, I whispered, "I've got a message for the boss."

Just as quietly, he replied, "I'd hang fire if I were you. DCS Hampton's not happy. He's been shouting, even ranting. He didn't take kindly to one of others telling him they didn't like his attitude. That really got his goat."

"I can imagine, if it's all right, I'll wait with you?" He nodded. If nothing else, it gave me the opportunity of looking at the scene, albeit from a distance.

By the look of things, some time ago, someone had created an entrance to the waste ground by prising one of the corrugated fencing panels away from two weathered arris rails. Turning the waste ground into a play area for kids and a rubbish dump for others.

There were two people inside, a photographer and DS Philip Knight-Wells or PKW as he was known – the area's lab liaison officer. One of four serving police officers specifically trained in the forensic recovery of evidence. Better equipped and more experienced than the civilian Scenes of Crime Officers, or SOCOs as they were known. Called out to serious incidents such as this. PKW covered the north-east quadrant of London. The busiest of the four areas. And I'd worked with him in the past. The waste ground bigger than I had envisaged, about the half the size of an adult football pitch. A set of goalposts had been daubed on the fencing at one end. Although the lack of scuff marks around them suggested they were rarely used. An odd-looking track in the shape of a figure of eight had evolved. Where kids with their bikes had ridden over the rubble and earth, which had weathered and smoothed over time, forming an undulating circuit over which they would race. Amongst the mounds, rubbish, that by the look of it had also been discard overtime. The remnants of old kitchen equipment: a cooker, refrigerator, a couple of really old washing machines, bits of bicycles and the inevitable supermarket trolley. This, despite the fact there were no supermarkets nearby, that used trolleys. PKW was standing in the centre. The body, or what I could see of it, lay on the ground beside him. I was trying to take in as much as I could when I heard PKW say, "Don't just stand there, get in here and give me a hand, it'll be raining soon." Continuing to address the uniformed officer, he added, "Let DS Lomax in, would you, there's a good fellow?"

It was an offer I couldn't refuse and providing Hampton didn't end up running the show. It would put me in pole position for the role of exhibits officer. A key position on any murder enquiry and one I certainly wouldn't object to. Our uniform friend duly noted my name, the date and time, and I was allowed to enter. As I stepped between the two arris rails, none of the senior officers seemed to notice, continuing with their discussion. The Muppets had, but not having the bottle to say anything to their boss, only watched as I entered the scene.

PKW pointed to a route for me to follow. I consciously put my hands in my pockets and carefully made my way towards him. As I got closer, I got my first proper look at the body, or what was left of it. Naked, charred and lying face-up as it were, headless and handless. Surrounded by ash and odd pieces of wood which hadn't completely burnt. The remnants of odd bits of furniture and what looked like broken pallets, collected together to make a bonfire cum funeral pyre. It looked as though the pyre had initially been set on top of the mound. Subsiding as it burnt with the body slipping down the side, coming to rest where it now lay. The unmistakable smell of burnt human flesh lingered: sweet, sickly, and uniquely distinct. Occasionally interrupted by the whiff of an accelerant, probably petrol. Reminding me of the smell you occasionally got when refuelling a car. I assumed the body to be male, as I could see a lump of burnt tissue where the genitals would normally be, and there didn't appear to be any evidence of breast development. The lump vaguely reminding me of a parson's nose from an overcooked Christmas turkey. Apart from the body's overall charring, parts of the torso were distorted. The right foot, although discoloured, appeared to be the only part to have survived relatively unscathed. I found it impossible to determine the victim's ethnicity.

As I reached PKW, he extended his hand. He shook hands with everybody. It was one of his traits, along with the way he spoke. London born and bred. Putting on this posh voice when talking to people he was trying to impress or didn't know. The voice went with the bowtie and waistcoat he invariably wore. The Met. had more than its fair share of eccentrics.

"You with this lot then?" he said, speaking normally.

Not wishing to be overheard, I said, "That depends on who's in charge. Any ideas? If it's Hampton, the answer's no."

"They seem to have been arguing over who's going to be leading the investigation for some time. Initially, it was DCS Simmonds, who arrived with his DI not long after me. DCS Hampton turned up with his entourage about an hour ago, and they've been outside ever since."

PKW thrust a pair of rubber gloves in my direction, even though my hands were back in their pockets. I had no intention of touching anything unless he specifically told me to. As I took the gloves, he told me he'd examined the body, its immediate vicinity, along with the path I'd followed. The photographer had covered the same areas and was now getting more general shots. A cluster of small, sealed exhibit bags sat on one of PKW's metal cases. Small brown envelopes, all individually marked. Similar to those used by the taxman and other government departments. Utilised for bloodstained exhibits where the possibility of moisture within the exhibit remained.

"You can take a closer look if you want, just don't touch anything," he said, as a wicked little grin spread across his well-worn, weathered face.

Some of the remains looked as though they were ready to fall apart. The charred skin flaked and blistered in places. Moving the body without causing further damage wouldn't be easy. The more I looked, the more I realised just how badly burnt some parts were. Apart from being distorted, some of the lower ribs exposed, looking as though they might have become detached from the sternum. The head and most of the neck missing, having been severed close to the shoulders. The hands also missing along with the lower part of each forearm, charred stumps in their place. I leant over the body, getting as close as I felt comfortable with, looking for the remains of any identifying features – tattoos, marks or scars, anything that might help with identification. I couldn't see any. It was only then that I noticed what looked like incisions in the chest and thighs. Stab wounds masked by the flaking skin and blisters. Just how much this person had suffered was difficult to imagine.

"Find anything interesting around the entrance or along the path?" I asked.

"Not really. A few drops of blood near the entrance, that's all. You're welcome to have another look."

If PKW hadn't found anything, the chances of me doing so were negligible. "Maybe on the way out."

Two questions ran through my mind. Why burn the body, and why burn it bang smack in the middle of the waste ground? In a way, the two questions contradicted each other. I got that burning the body, along with the removal of the head and hands, would help to conceal the identity. But burning the body in the centre of the ground, where it could be seen from the flats overlooking the waste ground, was as if someone wanted to draw attention to the body and the pyre. Leaving the body in one of the derelict warehouses nearby would have been easier. There, the rats, cats, foxes and any other carrion-loving creatures would have made quick work of the flesh. Better still, they could have just dumped the body in the River Thames, which was less than two hundred yards from where we were standing. There, it would have simply drifted out to sea, never to be found. And even if it had, working out where it had come from would have been nigh impossible.

"Do you know whether the dustmen actually moved the body?" I asked.

"Not really. I haven't spoken to them. I was told that when one of them went to pick it up, he initially thought it was a tailor's dummy, getting the shock of his life, when he discovered it was a body."

From a distance, I could see how easy it would have been to make the mistake, and it must have been a real shock discovering the remains were human.

With his eyes flitting between the gap and sky, I could tell PKW was becoming increasingly agitated with the possibility of rain and the potential loss of evidence.

"I wish I knew what the hell was going on," he blurted. "We need to get the body moved and quickly, and where the hell are my undertakers? Buggers, I called for them ages ago."

In all the time I'd known him, I couldn't remember PKW swearing, and 'bugger' would definitely be swearing in PKW's eyes. The lack of information and deteriorating weather clearly getting to him.

"If I go and ask what's happening," PKW continued, "I'm bound to get embroiled in some long-drawn-out discussion, wasting more time. By the same token, I don't want to find that a dustman or someone else has said something I should be aware of, only to be told when it's too late and then getting blamed for missing or possibly losing vital evidence."

PKW knew that if things went wrong and Hampton was in charge, he could easily become the scapegoat.

"What else needs to be done?" I asked. "Have you looked around the rest of the ground?"

"Haven't had the chance."

"Do you want me to take a look, so you can carry on here?"

"That'll be good, I've got a bit more to do here, then it's just what's under the body, which'll get done when the body's been moved," said PKW.

The photographer came over, saying he was done and would wait in his van for further instructions.

Before PKW could speak, I asked him whether he'd taken any shots away from the body which would give those investigating an idea of which properties and which floors overlooked the waste ground.

"No, not so far."

"Better to do it," said PKW.

The photographer made a start.

"How long have you actually been here?" I asked PKW.

"Too flipping long. If you want to know, the officers from the pool weren't that far behind me. When they arrived, they introduced themselves, had a quick shufti, chatted to the photographer and divisional surgeon, and then went off to speak to the dustmen. I then saw them standing by the opening, as if to come in, when DCS Hampton and his crew turned up. They've been outside ever since. So, I've just got on with things. I've worked with the DI before," he said, "he was on the Flying Squad, working out of the Tower Bridge office, if I remember correctly. He's okay. The boss I don't know, never seen him before. He hasn't said much but seems pleasant enough."

"Hampton's here to take over?" I said.

"I guess so, he came with some of his team, which is a bit of a giveaway."

"But they haven't just handed it over, have they?"

"Not yet. Might have something to do with Hampton's oiks upsetting DI Clarke when they started wandering aimlessly around the ground. With the DI shouting at them to get out before they got too far. Getting our uniformed friend to stand by the entrance."

"Did you know that Hampton had ordered everyone from Leman Street to go to Arbour Square? CID, home beat officers, civilians, everyone. When I arrived, the first floor was completely empty."

"You're joking."

"Honestly."

I then told PKW what the station officer at Arbour Square had said.

"If Hampton gets this, the only way it will ever get solved is if someone walks in and confesses. He's bloody useless and his team are a bunch of wankers." I couldn't believe it, PKW was so incensed.

"Do you know, I did the initial examination for the domestic murder he's currently heading up. What a joke that was. Before I got there, the world and his wife had traipsed all over the place. No records of who'd been where. It would have been the same here if it hadn't been for DI. We even found Hampton's palm print on the doorjamb of the main bedroom. Most of them are complete imbeciles. More like the Keystone Cops if you ask me. Have you heard about the case?"

It didn't matter whether I had or not, he was going to tell me. "Do you want me to look around or not?" I said, glancing up at the sky.

"Yes, in a minute this won't take long."

Telling me about the murder was now a priority. It was as if PKW wanted to justify both his mood and the swearing.

"They've been working on that case for over six weeks now. It's a straight-forward husband and wife, and the evidence is overwhelming. She'd repeatedly stabbed him in the stomach and then cut his balls off. His blood was all over her clothing. Her fingerprints were on the knife. When she was arrested, his testes were found wrapped in a handkerchief in her pocket. On top of which, she's admitted it and made a statement under caution. You couldn't get much more evidence if you tried. The job was done and dusted in about five days, and they're still messing around."

"What made her do it?" I said, realising I might regret asking.

"Apparently, the old man hadn't satisfied her needs, and she'd sought solace elsewhere. It wasn't the first time she'd transgressed. Causing more than a few rows. But they'd managed to stay together. Anyway, they'd had another row, and she'd lost it. Her excuse was that she was suffering from an extreme bout of pre-menstrual tension, making her temporarily insane."

"So, what have The Muppets been doing for the past month?" I said.

"Taking the mickey and Hampton's letting them do it. He's the one authorising all the bloomin' overtime." PKW was really angry. I'd never seen him so wound up. It was obvious they were exploiting situation, earning as much money as they could. But there wasn't anything we could do, and it wasn't as if it was our money. It was the fact that Hampton was condoning, even encouraging what was going on that was getting to PKW. Normally, you would expect most of the work on a domestic murder to be completed within the first couple of weeks. After which the team would be reduced in size, with an initial report being submitted to solicitor's department within four weeks. Six weeks on, and as far as PKW was aware, neither had happened.

Hampton would know that even he wouldn't be able to justify the staffing levels and overtime with the current the case forever. Taking on a new job would keep both the team together and gravy train running. It was as if Hampton had completely lost sight of his primary role. Which was looking after the day-to-day running of all the districts' CID offices.

"It's a good job you turned up when you did," said PKW "but why exactly are you here?"

"To be honest, I wanted to know what was going on and whether the officers from the pool were running the show. If they were, I was going to try and get on the squad?"

Me helping PKW would not help Hampton's mood, not with our history. What experience you had counted for nothing and I, along with others, didn't fit his mould. There were a multitude of things he didn't like about me. One of which was having two registered informants. From his point of view, anyone who had any dealings with an informant had to be corrupt. He couldn't grasp the concept or the need for quality intelligence when it came to serious crime; admittedly, there were risks. But if you behaved yourself, the benefits outweighed the risks. I'd worked in east London for over eight years, having been involved, to varying degrees, in over thirty murder investigations, most of which had been solved. Which at the time wasn't that uncommon. But as far as Hampton was concerned, any experience you had counted for nothing. To stand any chance of getting on his team, you had to be a mason. Hampton's attitude infuriated others of the same persuasion.

Who, to be fair, didn't share his views? They felt he was giving the mason's a bad name. They were right.

PKW looked at me and then pointed to the exhibits. "You better check this lot and then move them over to the entrance, where the PC can keep an eye on them."

I began checking the bags, making sure they were signed, sealed and correctly entered in his exhibit book. Then, picking up as many as I could safely carry, I made my way over to the gap. As I arrived, I could see the senior officers making their way towards us. Hampton was leading, with DI Lambert a little way back, beckoning The Muppets to join them – Hampton had won. My enthusiasm instantly ebbed away. Having left the exhibits by the uniformed officer and not quite sure what to do, I made my way back to PKW. I hadn't got that far when I heard Hampton's booming voice.

"Lomax, what do you think you're doing, disobeying an order? You're supposed to be at Arbour Square, fool."

As I turned, I could see DI Lambert trying to attract Hampton's attention, coughing loudly, trying to catch up.

"I've had enough of you, you're suspended I'll have you sacked for this, disobeying a lawful order. I didn't give you fucking permission to..." DI Lambert grabbed an arm, drawing his attention to the officers from the pool who he'd obviously forgotten about.

I didn't deserve to be spoken to the way I had, and was about to give the uncouth, ill-tempered, jumped-up, over-promoted, power-mad prick a piece of my mind when PKW grabbed my wrist sensing I was about to say something I would later regret. Hampton, with his background in complaints, would know that swearing at a junior officer was completely unacceptable; his outburst could get him into hot water. PKW's intervention had prevented me from blurring the situation. Hampton hadn't given me the slightest opportunity to speak before going off on one. Biting my tongue, PKW and I slowly made our way to the entrance. By the time we arrived, Hampton had been flanked by DI Lambert and his Muppets. Looking more composed and in control, he said, "I didn't give you permission to enter the crime scene. You're not part of this team, you need to get back to Arbour Square. I will deal with this matter later, and that's an order. A lawful order."

"No, I did," said PKW. "I asked DS Lomax, I needed help."

"Who gave you the... what help?"

The way Hampton spoke, it was as if he'd forgotten or didn't know who PKW was.

"To stand any chance of finishing before it rains, I needed help. I've worked with DS Lomax before. He knows what he's doing, which is more than can be said for some." He said, looking towards The Muppets. PKW was still angry. Usually so easy-going, even placid. It just wasn't like him to make waves. Hampton's attitude had simply been too much. He'd sworn and was now being confrontational, even argumentative.

"I've been here for hours with no help, and from past experiences I wouldn't trust any of that lot as far as I could throw them." He said, waving a hand towards The Muppets. "Do you want evidence to be just washed away? Because that's what's likely to happen." PKW didn't wait for a reply. "With DS Lomax's help, I've managed to get a lot more done."

I was feeling more than a little embarrassed. In all honesty, I hadn't done much. PKW was protecting me.

"For the moment, we've done everything we can, we're just waiting for the undertakers. Then we'll be able to get the body moved. We'll be finished after that, unless, of course, there's something else you want us to do," PKW continued.

It wasn't registering with Hampton. He wasn't listening, agitated by something and wanting to have another go. Only the presence of the officers from the pool preventing him. Several times he'd started to speak, but either didn't quite know what to say or where to start.

"But you shouldn't... What are... Why aren't... How did you..." In the end settling for, "Why exactly are you here?"

Without realising, he'd opened a door and given me the chance of screwing him.

"Having been told about the murder and that you'd ordered everyone to Arbour Square. I was about to make my way over there, when the station officer asked if I could deliver a message on the way, which he'd been trying to send over the radio with no luck. Not wishing to interrupt any of you, I was waiting for an opportunity to pass it on when DS Knight-Wells asked for my help."

I could see the officers from the pool, who'd been standing at the back, look quizzically at each other, as if something I'd said didn't make sense.

Hampton then said, "And just what was this very important message?"

"I was to say that the incident room at Leman Street had been allocated for the investigation. Press office had been informed, and that they'd issued a press release calling for witnesses, which had been broadcast on local radio."

"Where did that come from? Who the hell has...? I didn't authorise... What the fuck is going on? This is my bloody investigation. I say what happens, nobody else. Go on, get out of my sight. Lomax, I don't want to see you again, you hear, go on bugger off."

I was trying to think of a suitable response when the older of the two officers from the pool spoke. A tall man, about six foot three, in his early fifties, with a full head of silvery white hair, which had a mind of its own. Taller than Hampton, but not as imposing. The other thing I'd noticed about him was how ungainly he'd looked when walking. Wearing what looked miniature versions of black clown's shoes, they were so big, which splayed outwards with every stride he took. Speaking with what I thought it was a relatively soft west country accent, he said, "DCS Hampton, I've heard enough. Clearly, you haven't been entirely truthful, and I find your behaviour and treatment of junior officers completely unacceptable. As a consequence, and in accordance with our original instructions, I am no longer prepared to hand over the investigation and will be assuming full control with immediate effect. Obviously, the investigation can be accommodated on district. Furthermore, it sounds as though the staff shortages you have alluded to, are in fact of your own making. I shall be speaking to the assistant chief constable regarding this matter, and I can assure you that your conduct will form a significant part of that conversation. Should you wish to take the matter up with him, please do? I'm sure he'll be very interested in what you have to say. Good day."

That had to be DCS Simmonds. He hadn't raised his voice, but his authority unquestionable. He'd made sure all those in the immediate vicinity could hear him clearly and unequivocally. At first, I had this sense of relief, closely followed by almost euphoric pleasure. Childishly, I wanted to chant while thumbing my nose and poking my tongue out at Hampton, who'd lost, but had to settle for imagining what it would be like. For a change, not only had he lost, but he'd been completely humiliated in front of others. Our uniformed friend, not used to witnessing such a dressing down and not wanting to appear to be gloating, had turned away.

Hampton and The Muppets slowly trudged back up the street to where they'd been standing. The man I assumed to be DCS Simmonds then turned and said, "You two better get a move on. Let's try and get things finished, preferably before it rains, there's good fellows."

Chaps, fellows, he was speaking PKW. We hurriedly made our way back to the centre of the ground.

"Thanks for that. I was just about to end my career," I said.

"No problem, it looks like you could be the exhibits officer after all."

Excited by the prospect, I carried on checking PKW's exhibits.

"Just how much longer are we going to have to wait for these undertakers?" PKW said.

I decided to try to find out, getting our uniformed friend to radio the station with a couple of messages. Firstly, to give the undertakers a hurry up and then to get a message to a DS Harrison, who I was meant to be working with later. He was the one person in the office I felt comfortable with. Taking some snaps of the comings and goings from a known fence's house. He'd been struggling to get hold of an official camera and knowing that photography was a hobby of mine was looking to use my kit. That job would now have to wait. Giving him a head's up and suggesting he collect messages from the switchboard while making a start on getting the incident suite operational should get him on the squad too, and was the least I could do.

Having checked the exhibits, I started to look around the rest of the waste ground for anything that might be relevant. We didn't have time for a proper search, and without using the Muppets, who I didn't trust, we didn't have the manpower. As I neared the corner where Hampton and The Muppets were on the other side of the fence. I could hear them talking – they hadn't given up.

"We need to make them look stupid, bugger them up," said one. "Misplace a few exhibits, make them disappear, or plant a few fakes. That could be good, it would make them look like twats," said another.

"They could still find themselves short-staffed, couldn't they? Then they'll have to use us," said a third.

"This needs to be thought through carefully. Whatever we do, we can't afford to get caught." It was Hampton. I recognised his voice immediately. "It can't be too obvious, or they'll guess which will only make things worse. I can't afford to upset the A.C.C. or the commander. So, I don't want any of you doing anything that might come back on us. Is that clear?"

"We could just wait. They still might need us, and we're a ready-made team with a dedicated office," said the third.

"Don't be stupid," said the first.

What was strange was the way they were talking. It was as if they were mates; I didn't hear anyone addressing Hampton or the DI as Sir, Guv or Boss.

Hampton then said, "Don't you think I've..." stopping. Thinking I'd been heard, I started to creep away. It was then that I heard DCS Simmonds's voice.

"Mr Hampton, I just wanted to confirm that we have decided to staff the investigation ourselves and will not be needing the services of those here. I also want to make it very clear that should it become apparent that anyone, particularly those here, attempt to obstruct or impede our investigation, I will have no hesitation in holding you personally responsible. And you can be sure that I will have no hesitation in taking the matter further. I do hope I have made myself clear?"

"Perfectly, can I assure you that none of my team would dream of hampering an investigation and I take issue with your insinuation? After all, we are all on the same side, aren't we?"

"Just one other thing. I also want to make it abundantly clear that, should I hear of any officers seconded to this enquiry being singled out or subjected to unfair pressures, duties or overbearing conduct, I shall again hold you responsible. I do hope, this too is clear?"

"Perfectly," said Hampton.

"Then, I can see no reason for either you or your officers to remain. I'm sure they have better things to do. I know I have, good day."

For a while, there was silence. I just had to wait and hear their reaction and provided PKW didn't call me, I should be okay. I didn't have to wait long before one of them said, "Who the hell does he think he is? Speaking to us like that, this is our manor, our ground. We run things here. He needs putting in his place, prick."

An unfamiliar voice then said, "He's a DCS, isn't he?"

"I know that. Pillock."

Hampton then said, "Look, I've already said, whatever we come up with can't come back on us and needs to be subtle. I don't want someone going off half-cocked, all right? Before doing anything, check with either DI Lambert or myself. Is that clear? We need to know what they're doing, and how they're getting on? Let's start with that. Come on, let's go."

I could hear the group moving off, their voices becoming more distant. It was time to get on with the search–I didn't find anything.

The immediate area, including drains, dustbins and a garden or two, now needed to be searched and until they were needed guarding. We didn't want to give Hampton, or anyone else, the chance of tampering with evidence.

It was spitting with rain when the undertakers finally arrived. Having done so, they didn't want to move the body. They didn't want to be held responsible for it falling apart. There wasn't time to argue. It would soon be too wet to do anything else. It was now up to us to move the body. Once we had it in a body bag, they were prepared to take over. As the body lay on the side of a slope, we were able to place a rubber mat the undertakers had just below it, and then gently nudge, nurdle and slide it on without causing any significant damage. Keeping everything together. The back of the body also burnt. Although, what I assumed to be stab wounds were more evident. I could also see what looked like small pieces of fabric and grit embedded in the skin near one of the shoulder blades. PKW made a note to get it photographed and recovered during the post-mortem. As rigor mortis had long since passed, moving the body had caused it to defecate, creating an unusual additional exhibit. We quickly checked where the body had lain and, with neither of us seeing anything of interest, it was time to call it a day and head back to the station. PKW led the way and, once through the gap, made his way over to DCS Simmonds and DI Clarke, where I joined them.

"We haven't been formally introduced, I'm DCS Simmonds, Paul Simmonds and this is DI Clarke, Bob Clarke," said the man who'd embarrassed Hampton with such ease. "As you will have no doubt realised, I, or should I say we," pointing to DI Clarke, "will be leading this investigation, and at present, whether you like it or not, you are the team. Popular with Mr Hampton, are we?"

"I'm not on his Christmas list if that's what you mean, Guv."

"Thought so. When we get back, you better ring any loved ones and tell them you may not be home for a while."

"I overheard you talking to DCS Hampton. I was on the other side of the fence," I said.

"Go on."

I then recounted what I'd heard, including them wanting to take over the investigation.

"Like hell they will, they've already pissed me off with their antics. If I get the chance, I'll have them, the bunch of idiots. They've got two chances. None, and—" said DI Clarke, stopping short of swearing.

"Are we going to get the SPG to secure the area? Just to make sure nothing's tampered with. After all, it was Mr Hampton who requested their presence," I said, feeling a little cheeky.

DCS Simmonds agreed, leaving it to DI Clarke to tell the SPG that no one, especially DCS Hampton or any of his cohorts, were allowed in the area, no matter what their rank. With PKW taking the boss's back to the station, I took the opportunity of mentioning DS Harrison and that hopefully; he'd made a start on getting the incident room operational.

Chapter 2

By the time I'd reached the station, the joy of having one over on Hampton had been replaced with trying to figure out how we were going to manage with so few. I found Alan queuing for drinks in the canteen, with PKW and the bosses sitting at a table in the far corner, where we sat for our first office meeting.

On the way back, PKW had spoken to the bosses. The net effect was that at least to start with Alan and I would be joint office managers. Although unusual, and provided nothing changed, we should be on the enquiry until the end. As the title suggested, normally an office manager would be office bound. Organising others, reading statements, creating and allocating actions. Making sure the actions were done properly, and that the investigation was going in the right direction. With joint managers, the potential to be actively involved in some operational elements existed – interviewing, even taking the occasional action, whilst also being out of Hampton's reach. And should there be anything untoward in that regard, we were to tell the bosses. After what they'd just witnessed, they were not about to let the investigation get derailed by Hampton, or anyone else. The boss wanted to know how operational the incident suite was. We decided to tell the truth. We needed at least twenty-four hours to get the basics sorted. Phone lines, power sockets and lighting all needed doing. The rest would have to follow. The boss then wanted a copy of the latest list of

CID officers on district, looking for potential candidates to join the team; assuming they weren't associated with Hampton.

The atmosphere had already changed, being asked for an opinion and feeling comfortable giving it. It was how most CID offices were, just not ours. Once we'd gone through the list, we were left with one DS, three DCs and the local crime squad, which consisted of five PCs and another DC. Twelve in all. With the house-to-house and local searches, let alone anything else, it wasn't enough. Hampton had at least that many still supposedly working on his shitty little job. I wasn't sure how the boss would deal with the need for more staff, or that none of those on the list jumped out at you and screamed 'exhibits officer'.

As the meeting continued, PKW politely excused himself. Some of his exhibits needed to be refrigerated and kept in a secure location. Leaving him, we headed upstairs so the bosses could see the suite for themselves.

It was while the boss was viewing what was likely to be his office that DI Clarke took us to one side, saying the office would be 'dry'. Alan and I looked at him in disbelief. No alcohol, it was unheard of? I could think of loads of office meetings where the odd bottle or two had led to new ideas, even cases being solved. All the DI would say was that alcohol had caused the boss problems in the past. Not long after, we were left to our own devices to make a start on getting the suite operational.

The station's top floor consisted of two suites. Our dilapidated thing at one end and Gold Control at the other. With most of the corridor's strip lights missing, there was hardly any light, and what there was came from one of Gold Control's doors being open and a little daylight, coming through the dust-covered transom windows that were fitted above most of the doors.

Gold Control was the operations room for major public order events and demonstrations. Bristling with the latest equipment, and except for the occasional Special Branch officer, was out of bounds to CID.

Our suite had five offices and two toilets, both with showers. Used soaps and toiletries told me that the Gent's was still in regular use. We needed to clean the rooms and sort out the lighting as a minimum. The suite hadn't been used for nearly two years, and pieces of grit had somehow become trapped under the doors, causing arced grooves to be scored into the floor tiles when pushed open. There was dust everywhere. Most of the vertical blinds had seized, and when we got a blind to work, there was so much crap on the reflective glass windows, it made little a difference. Getting the suite functional was going to be harder than expected.

We'd gained access to all the rooms except the one we presumed the phone was in. We'd tried the door handle, pushed at the door several times and were deciding what to do, when we heard noises, followed by this bad-tempered sounding voice saying, "Hang on, just a minute."

The door was then unlocked and partially opened by a half-dressed uniform inspector I didn't recognise. Initially, I thought he was from Gold Control.

Grumpily he said, "What are you doing? What do you want?"

"There's been a serious incident, a murder. We're going to be using the suite for the investigation and need to make a start on getting it operational," Alan said.

"Don't be daft. The suite's been decommissioned. Arbour Square is where you need to be. I suggest you toddle off over there." He said, closing the door.

"Not this one. The A.C.C. has instructed us to get this suite up and running as a matter of urgency. DCS Simmonds from the pool is running the case, he's downstairs if you want to check? Although he might want to know what you're doing here and why you need to know."

The inspector wasn't happy. It was only the threat of the boss that made him agree to vacate office. Although he needed time to sort things out. Given the number of trips he made to the lift, he could have been living there.

While we were waiting for him to leave, we had another look at the rooms. In terms of space, they were ideal, just derelict. The main office was about forty-five feet long, with two entrances. Next to it a smaller office, which would be perfect for the bosses. On the other side of the corridor, three rooms. The largest of which had obviously been used for exhibits. Evidenced by the lines of screw holes, all neatly spaced out along the walls where shelving had once existed. From a quick glimpse into the room the inspector had occupied, it looked as though it would be ideal for interviewing and report writing. With the third room looking as though it had been a locker room cum storeroom.

The one other thing that was immediately obvious was the layout of the main office. It was all wrong, and must have been a complete nightmare to work in. Presumably, with the new suites now at Arbour Square, no one had bothered to sort things out. For some reason, there was only one telephone point, conveniently located behind one of the doors. Resulting in the phone jack getting hit every time the door was opened, making it unusable. The only reason we could come up with for the placement was the telephone engineer saying it had to go there. Not because it was the best place for it, but because it suited him. Which was probably the same reason all the power points were at one end of the office. It was a dog's dinner.

Once we'd listed the physical changes, equipment and forms needed, I went to call stores from the office the inspector had vacated, only to find that the childish prick had taken nearly everything with him, including the phone. All that was left was a desk and two dodgy chairs. Having been down to stores, I found that Hampton had instructed stores not to keep dedicated major incident documentation. Statement and interview forms were the best they could do. On my way back, I liberated a telephone from the collator's office.

Having arranged for all the necessary documentation to be brought over from Arbour Square, we initiated our first action. Requesting the details of all missing persons who loosely fitted the description of our victim: male, aged between fifteen and twenty-five, reported missing in the last month within a radius of five miles of the scene. With the waste ground being so close to the river and about half-way between Tower Bridge and the Rotherhithe Tunnel, the possibility that the victim was from south of the water couldn't be ignored. We then made a start on getting the suite clean and functional.

Alan Harrison had only been at the station a month more than me. The new boys. He was in his mid to late thirties. Not a big man, quite quiet most of the time, although he didn't suffer fools gladly. Divorced. He swore a lot and had a wicked sense of humour. His slight build, gaunt face, deep-set dark eyes and pale complexion making him look almost ghostly. The look compounded by the light grey suits he frequently wore. His natural expression was to frown, making him look as though he was always in a bad mood. Anyone who didn't know him coming into the office seeking advice would always look to go elsewhere. We got on pretty well, considering the environment we were trying to work in. I often wondered whether his complexion had anything to do with all the café crème cigars he smoked. At least thirty a day, double that, if stressed or drinking. From north London, which was a bit of a novelty in the office, with most of the others being a mixture of northerners, jocks and taffs. His last posting had been on the Flying Squad, at Rigg Approach. It was his second tour, but had been cut short for some reason. He'd been there just over two years when four to five was the norm. He hadn't said why the tour had been cut short and I hadn't asked.

While scavenging, he'd managed to liberate a decent office chair from somewhere, which he'd placed in the centre of what would be the boss's office. Famished, we nipped out for doner kebabs. Returning fifteen minutes later, only to find the boss sitting alone in his new chair, gazing out of the dust-covered windows into total darkness. He must have heard us as we passed, but didn't move or say a word. A few minutes later, he popped in. Not interested in what we'd been doing, telling us to finish up and get some rest.

"We start in earnest in the morning. Office meeting, 8 a.m. sharp."

Just four of us, this will be interesting. I managed to get a couple of hours' rest in the only place I could find that was warm, unoccupied and where I couldn't hear phones ringing – the typing pool.

Making my way to the incident room, I could hear voices, lots of voices. There must have been twenty officers, all propping up walls waiting to be briefed. Roughly, a fifty-fifty split between uniform and plain clothes. Apart from Alan Harrison, there were two others I recognised.

DC Terry Weaver, 'The Vicar.' In his mid-thirties, thinning on top, with an egged-shape face. He wore those round glasses with fairly thick frames, the sort you immediately associated with a swot and frequently wore a dark green mottled blazer, with leather patches on the sleeves. He spoke so softly it was almost ecclesiastical; hypnotic – hence the nickname. The old girls just loved him; he was in his element, dealing with the victims of crime. I could just see him wearing a dog-collar and giving a sermon. Violent prisoners, however, were not his forte.

DC Ken Reeves the other. He hadn't worn well and looked as though he should have retired. Quite tall, slim, with a squarish face and dark greasy greying hair. A ruddy complexion and rosy cheeks. The few times I'd seen him, he'd always looked half asleep. If there was a phobia for irons and presses, his clothes had it. They were so crumpled. Having had no dealings with him, apart from being introduced at a rare office soiree where he'd ended up pissed.

It wasn't long before the bosses walked in. I did not know where they'd spent the night, but DI Clarke had somehow showered, shaved and changed his clothes. Now out of 'uniform' wearing a charcoal grey suit, pink shirt and maroon-coloured Flying Squad tie. Standing, as if he was modelling clothes, his right thumb hooked over the waist of his trousers, pushing the jacket back, revealing one of the latest pagers clipped to his belt. Dowsed in aftershave, his hair damp and combed back.

The room fell silent as they entered, the boss nodding and smiling at everyone with a general "Good morning" to all. We waited for him to start the briefing. I assumed he would be bringing everyone up to date, assigning responsibilities, possibly even mentioning Hampton's involvement. Instead, he just said, "Right, what's going on, where are we, what's happening then?"

Everyone looked a little perplexed. At first, I thought it was a joke but soon realised it wasn't when the DI said, "Perhaps we should introduce ourselves? For those who don't know, I'm Detective Inspector Clarke and this is Detective Chief Superintendent Simmonds. We're from C.1. and will be heading up the investigation. DS Lomax and DS Harrison are going to be joint office managers, with DC Reeves responsible for exhibits and DC Weaver house-to-house. When we've finished, the rest of you should give your names to the office managers who will allocate duties and actions accordingly. I suspect that some of you will have never worked on a major enquiry. It's different. Here we work as a team, no heroes apart from me of course." He said, waiting for a reaction to his attempt at humour. It didn't happen, not even a groan – those in uniform weren't used to quips or funnies from DIs. While those in plain clothes thought it not worthy.

"On a serious note, make sure you all know how the action book works. It is without doubt, one of the most important parts of any murder enquiry. Our Bible, a guide, possibly a panacea providing that magic bullet. Initially, many of you will be engaged with local searches and house-to-house enquiries. I can't emphasise just how important these are and that they need to be done properly. I know how laborious they can be, and that some of you may think they're a complete waste of time – they're not. One of you could easily come across something which leads to the entire case being solved. It only takes one tiny piece of information."

Pausing to emphasise the seriousness of what was being said, DCS Simmonds interrupted. "Right, let's get on with it, carry on." The DI's pep talk cut short.

"Shouldn't we tell them, what's happened so far, Guv?" said the DI.

"Leave that to the office managers, unless you have something specific you want to say. Oh, there is one thing. You will have noticed just how sparse these offices are. Workmen are due to arrive within the hour. To sort out power, phones and lighting. Office furniture will also be arriving throughout the day. Unless you want to be involved in humping stuff around, I suggest you make yourselves scarce." And with that, he left the office.

The DI went on to describe the condition of the body, how it had been found, saying that a post-mortem had been scheduled for 11 a.m. tomorrow. After which, he again tried to add a little humour, informing everyone that the cause of death had been from 'a lack of breathing'. Most, if not all, the plainclothes officers had heard it before, and again, most uniform troops didn't quite know what to make of it. I got the impression the DI was trying to say that he was approachable and wanted to be considered a team player.

Fourteen of the officers had never worked on a major enquiry. Alan Harrison took it upon himself to explain the significance of the action book. It was the one thing the DI hadn't been joking about. It was important for them to know they didn't write in the book. That was the sole domain of the office managers and OIC, using different coloured pens. Once an action had been allocated. It was their job to complete it as soon as practicably possible. It was also important for them to understand that they did nothing more. If they were tasked with taking a statement from an individual about a particular matter, that's where the action began and ended. Even if there was an obvious follow-up. It was imperative that they didn't go off-piste, trying to get ahead of the game, trying to score brownie points. Following up on to what might seem to be the next logical step without creating a new action would cause problems. As was just doing your own thing. It was completely taboo. Provided everyone stuck to the system, nothing should get missed and hopefully we would avoid duplications and other potential embarrassments or cock-ups. If anyone had any ideas, information or hunches, they were to either tell the office managers or write them in the suggestion book. Under no circumstances were they to go off on their own.

Chapter 3

Once the team had been split into groups with those doing the searches and house-to-house on their way, we started sifting through the pile of missing person reports, weeding out any obvious non-starters. Alan then grouped them into the stations from which they'd originally been reported missing.

"I can't believe it, there has to be more than a hundred 'mispers' and most of them are from around here, we'll just have to concentrate on those first." He then dealt out the missing person reports to the remaining officers, as if playing cards. We then got a call from the mortuary. The professor had found a window; the post-mortem had been brought forward to 1 p.m. that afternoon. Alan didn't fancy going, and as he hadn't seen the body, he didn't need to. To ensure the post-mortem could go ahead, someone who could positively identify the body as that from the waste ground would have to be there. Effectively, I would have to go. Having told the bosses, messages were left for the others. With just a few hours' notice, hopefully everyone would get there.

As we looked at other potential enquiries, a PC from the station office walked in. He'd come across another fifteen missing person reports, which had initially been placed in the wrong tray. If it hadn't been for him, they would have gone on a tour of the Met., ending up in a rubbish bin somewhere. Only one of the fifteen was local, a seventeen-year-old named Adam Pope. He'd been reported missing from a hostel in Whitehorse

Lane. It was a street I'd become familiar with. Part of a rat run I was now using to get to and from work. It was also on the way to the mortuary and if I left now, I could do it on the way.

The hostel was next to a playground, which had seen better days. It was one of many public areas that had fallen into disrepair. Weeds and grass had grown through the tarmac, and all that was left of the activities was the framework for the swings and a slide with no steps. Like the waste ground, it was still a meeting place for groups of teenagers and younger children with their chopper bikes.

As I arrived at the hostel, the door was immediately opened by a woman, who, before I had a chance to speak, said, "Follow me."

Immediately turning, she walked along a corridor to the manager's office. A 'Ms Nicola Saltmarsh' the name on the door. My escort didn't knock, she just walked in beckoning me to join her, saying "Fuzz" as she turned and left. The first thing to hit me was the smell of cannabis coming from a half-smoked reefer, sitting precariously on the side of an old mottle brown Bakelite ashtray. Next to which was a well-used tobacco tin, with Rizla papers and a box of Swan Vesta's on top.

The woman sitting behind the desk was flicking through an edition of The Socialist Worker. Slowly closing the paper, she pushed it to one side, glancing at the reefer as she did so. She then looked at me and I wondered whether it was some sort of test. With her sitting there, waiting for me to say something. Wanting to see what I was going to do. The answer was nothing. I had more important things to be getting on with other than the odd spliff and a bit of herbal. It was all a little strange. The woman I assumed to be Ms Saltmarsh was in her mid-thirties, quite slim. Not exactly mutton dressed as lamb but wearing stereotypical clothes of a radical student, she'd probably been ten to fifteen years ago. Denim dungarees, a multi-coloured tie-dye T-shirt and pumps. Her right nostril decorated with a large chromium stud, which appeared to droop. Hanging from her right ear, a very large CND motif drop earring; making her look lopsided. As soon as I went to speak, she launched into this monologue. A tirade about anti-establishment authoritarianism, whatever that was. The way she spoke, she could have been a contributor to the publication she'd been looking at. One way or another, I'd heard it all before and would likely hear it again. Amongst her topics; police brutality, the sus law, oppression and the constant harassment of 'her' precious residents. With an emphasis on 'her.' The only reason I was there was because one of 'her' residents had gone missing. Without taking a breath, she demanded to see a search warrant and my warrant card. Then continuing the soliloquy, went on to other subjects, including illegal searches and the planting of evidence. I didn't dare interrupt, for fear of prolonging the agony, justifying her continuance. Eventually, she slowed. Her final comment, or threat, was to complain to her local MP regarding my conduct. To say I was confused was an understatement. I was beginning to wonder whether I was in the right place? Ruing not checking the collator's records before leaving. She'd obviously complained to her MP before and knew the problems it would cause. As did any letter from the House of Commons sent to the commissioner's office. Its pure existence meant that not only would the complaint be prioritised, but it would also be allocated to an officer of superintendent level or above. Doubling, if not trebling, the paperwork. It was all very surreal, with her continually trying to provoke a reaction. I wasn't playing. As the words of one of my old training sergeants kept popping into my head, "Tact and diplomacy, tact and diplomacy..." he'd keep saying. Be a good boy and do nothing.

After a while, she sighed, as if giving up. The hackles on the back of her neck subsiding, providing me with a chance to speak. As calmly as I could, I introduced myself.

"I understand that one of your residents has gone missing, an Adam Pope?"

"I haven't reported anyone missing." The sound of her voice immediately aggressive, the hackles rising. The way she spoke, with the emphasis on 'I', reminded me of others, including Hampton. It was all very 'me, me and, I this and I that.' It was as if no one else was allowed or dare do anything without her permission.

Looking at my copy of the 'misper,' I then noticed that the bottom of the report, which included the name of the person making it, was missing. The carbonless paper forms notorious for not tearing in the right place. It was something else I hadn't noticed before leaving.

"We've received a report that an Adam Pope has gone missing. Is he a resident?"

"No one calls the Fuzz without me knowing, and no one is missing."

"Fuzz" – it was so dated. A throwback to her days as a student. She needed to get up to speed with the latest terminology.

"Look, I don't want to waste anyone's time. I just need to know if you have a resident by the name of Adam Pope, and if you do, whether he's missing? I'm not sure whether you're aware of this, but the body of a young man has been found near here, where the description appears to similar to what's on this missing person's report. You should also know that if I'm not able to get a satisfactory answer, my boss will have no hesitation arranging for periodic visits to be made by others, who will not be so understanding when it comes to the odd joint."

The message finally seemed to get through with her admitting that Adam Pope was a resident, agreeing to check with other members of staff. Ms Claire Laker, her deputy, had reported him missing. I passed on the opportunity to embarrass her; it would have been counterproductive. As a minimum, I needed to know the circumstances surrounding his disappearance. Get a good description and hopefully a photograph. Ms Laker told me that another resident had heard about the discovery of the body and thought it might be Adam. She either couldn't or wouldn't say why the resident was so concerned, just that this was the reason she'd reported him missing. Adding as an afterthought that, as yet, she hadn't had the opportunity of informing Ms Saltmarsh.

Ms Laker wouldn't tell me the entire story. I had to play twenty questions, being drip-fed information. It was as though Ms Laker was trying to redeem herself in the eyes of Ms Saltmarsh. The only thing I'd been able to establish with any certainty was that he'd been missing for three, possibly four, days. It was time to be a little more assertive. I repeated the threat of others returning if I didn't get any sensible answers. Adding that my boss would also look to get the place closed. He didn't take kindly to major investigations being hindered in this way, and would seek to have any funding, public or otherwise withdrawn. Something he was extremely good at. Realising they weren't doing themselves any favours, Ms Laker told me more.

It wasn't the first time Adam had gone missing. Three to four weeks ago he'd disappeared for a few days, turning up severely beaten. His face had been badly bruised, black eyes and his clothes were covered in blood. According to Ms Laker, it was this beating that had caused her to report Pope missing now. Seventeen, from a broken home. He'd been a resident at the hostel for about three months. His physical description roughly fitting that of the victim. When he'd been asked what had happened, he'd said that he'd gone home and ended up in a fight with his father. Fighting with his father was the reason he'd originally given the hostel for leaving home.

Residents could initially stay for up to six months, after which there would be a review. I again asked to speak to the other residents, including the person who'd brought Pope's absence to their attention. Ms Saltmarsh wasn't prepared to let that happen until she'd spoken to them personally. Promising that she would speak to the residents and pass on any meaningful information. It wasn't the answer I was looking for.

I then asked to see Adam's room, half expecting the request to be declined. I was pleasantly surprised when Ms Laker escorted me to a room at the end of a corridor. The door, however, was locked. Ms Laker asked me to wait while she went for a key. The longer I stood there, the more I wondered whether I was being messed with. I didn't want someone else rummaging through the room before we did, and neither did I want to risk being late for the post-mortem. One swift kick was all it took, and the door flew open. As a few wooden splinters and the lock's keep fell to the floor while a gust of body odour passed me by, leaving the room.

It was a typical teenager's room. A couple of posters promoting Rastafarian musicians on one wall. Clothes, including a bloodstained blue shirt; the sort that frequently formed part of a school uniform on the floor. Under the bed, a pair of well-worn trainers, forgotten and unused. An enormous spider having taken up residence in one. Against one wall a small free-standing wardrobe. Inside, a couple of empty coat hangers hooked on the rail. A bluey-grey duffle coat, sweatshirt and a pair of crumpled jeans hadn't made the hangers and were lying on the floor of the wardrobe along with a black T-shirt and underpants. A couple of pairs of socks and more underpants were in one of the drawers. Every pocket was empty. There were no photographs, and neither were there any personal effects. No money, keys, wallet, diary, library tickets, nothing – it was scant.

Having placed the bloodstained shirt on the bed, I was about to make the spider homeless when I heard Ms Laker angrily say.

"What the hell are you doing couldn't you wait?" The anger in her words seemed to dissipate as she caught sight of the shirt.

"Sorry, I couldn't wait any longer. I've got to go to the post-mortem. Look, we'll pay for any damage, and I can arrange for a carpenter to repair or replace the door later today." I said, hoping to appease her.

Expecting her to go running off to Ms Saltmarsh, I was surprised when she stayed, her eyes transfixed to the shirt. As if, considering its implications, whether for the hostel, herself or the wearer; I wasn't sure.

Not wishing to waste more time, I made the spider homeless. Taking the trainers and shirt, while repeating that I would arrange for the door to be repaired and that it would be preferable if no one else entered the room. I also asked her to make a list of any visitors Adam may have had, and to contact us immediately should he return.

Given Adam's description, his previous disappearance, the beatings and the proximity of the hostel to the waste ground; there was a real possibility this was our victim.

It was a five-minute drive to the hospital. On the way, I wondered what someone so young could have done to have met with such a grim death, and whether we'd been fortunate enough to identify the victim so early in the investigation. If we had, it would certainly hamper any ambitions Hampton might have of taking over.

The hospital was a vast complex. A mixture of old and new, cobbled together over time. A teaching hospital, which included a most unusual medical museum. Its most famous exhibit, the skeleton of Joseph Merrick, The Elephant Man.

Not surprisingly, the mortuary was in one of the older parts. Found at the end of a long, dimly lit, windowless, sloping Victorian corridor. A small sign hung above the swing doors. The closer you got to the entrance, the colder and damper it felt. Whether it really was or not was another matter, but it felt that way. The mortuary was split into three areas. The examining room, with three porcelain slabs, a writing desk and telephone. Doors led from there to a cold store and another office. The walls were covered with off-white tiles, which had somehow survived virtually undamaged during the blitz. As with all mortuaries, there was this unique aroma. The smell of decaying flesh which had become ingrained in the room as a result of the thousands of examinations that had taken place. Masked by a mixture of cleaning agents and stale air.

Professor Parker, Ken Reeves and a mortuary attendant were already there when I arrived. Paper cups and an empty bottle of whisky on the table. As I walked in Ken cleared the empties away, putting them in a bin under the table, saying, "Sorry, you're too late, the prof and I got the taste." Early afternoon, and a bottle of scotch done. Professor Parker was an internationally respected pathologist. Regarded as one of the world's best. Taking on high-profile cases from all over the world. We were fortunate that the teaching hospital had access to some of the most eminent individuals in their fields, and that we could get access to them. I knew the professor enjoyed a drink. I'd seen him give a presentation on pathology at the Detective Training School. During his introduction, he was presented with a bottle of malt to take home. Having graciously accepted the gift, he promptly opened it and drank the bottle while giving the lecture. It didn't seem to have the slightest effect. Five years on and despite his workload and eminence, he was still one of the go to pathologists; approachable and more than happy to give his all to both local and high-profile cases.

The mortuary attendant who'd been quietly sitting at the far end of the room was using the last slab for his lunch. Spread out in front of him, a stack of sandwiches sitting on crumpled aluminium foil, a thermos flask and mug on the side. I couldn't help myself, saying, "Anything good?"

"Liver pâté, the usual." his riposte. Grinning, he took a huge bite from one.

What else could it be, I didn't know whether he was telling the truth or not? The professor grinned, and I took it to be a lie.

Looking at Reeves I said, "Been here long?"

"Not that long, half an hour or so. I thought I would provide the prof with some company. I wasn't expecting you to bring a bottle too." He said, looking at the bag I was carrying.

"It's not a bottle, they're trainers to try on the victim. I've just picked them up from an address where a lad's gone missing. His description and the timing of his disappearance fit the victim, and he lives or lived not that far from where the body was found."

Just as Reeves was about to speak, we were interrupted by others joining us. Everyone except the photographer had made it. PKW would have to do the honours.

"Just like Cinders, get it? Burnt body – cinders. Cinderella – cinders." Those arriving looked bemused, and as I was about to explain when blabbermouth said, "Chris has brought a slipper. It's not glass, but he wants to try it on Cinders."

The boss, completely ignoring Reeves, introduced himself and the others to the professor. Then, after a few pleasantries, the professor nodded to the attendant who left his sandwiches, disappearing into the cold store. It wasn't long before he returned with our victim and a small white bowl on a trolley. Deftly transferring the remains on to the middle slab while placing the bowl near the sluice – it contained the faeces. Having removed the trolley, he nonchalantly returned to his sandwiches; for him, it was just another day in the office.

Within seconds, the unique aroma of the burnt human flesh filled the room. There was nothing like it. Thankfully, Ken Reeves had also brought along some Vicks, which he shared. Dabbing the ointment under our noses stung a little, but it certainly helped to mask the smell. I then formally identified the body as the one recovered from the waste ground, and the professor began his examination. Firstly, describing what he saw. Circling the slab while speaking into a Dictaphone in the breast pocket of his gown. Occasionally, he would point at parts of the body where close-up photographs were needed. The rest of us now spectators with nothing to do. As a distraction, I took to scribbling notes. Thankfully, we were going to be spared some of the more gruesome elements of a normal post-mortem. Such as the smell of burning skull, created when gaining access to the brain. Or the cracking open of the chest. These were the things which often caused officers to faint or leave the room. Delving into the stomach contents or squeezing a kidney to get a jet of urine were others. And, as these were missing or cooked, it wouldn't be that bad.

After a while, DI Clarke said, "Do you think you will be able to establish the exact cause of death?"

"Lack of breathing." Blabbermouth's response. He'd definitely had too much. He was reaching a point where he couldn't stop making quips and had already forgotten the DI trying the same joke earlier.

"Thank you," said the professor, smiling politely. "Several of the stab wounds look as though they would have been fatal in their own right. Given the condition of the body, it's unlikely we will be able to determine the order in which they were inflicted, if that's what you are referring to. From what I can see, there are at least twelve significant stab wounds, possibly more. I'll know more when we've completed further tests, some of which may help with a time of death. We'll do what tests we can and let you know as soon as. What I would say, is that more than one sharp implement appears to have been used. In relation to the stabbing; single-sided blades, possibly a carving knife or something similar. Regarding the dismemberment, decapitation, and removal of the hands, these are post mortem. The markings where the bone is chipped would suggest that an axe or cleaver of some kind has been used. Again, further tests may help." Pausing, he then pointed at some markings on his upper arms and legs which were barely visible, that he also wanted photographing.

"As you can see here, these markings would suggest the victim has been bound. I would need to do some further tests, but the marks appear to be ante-mortem. That is to say, he was tied up prior to death."

As the professor continued to talk, he carefully removed sections from the ends of both arms and what little neck there was. These he would keep for identification purposes. Used for a mechanical fit with a head and or hands, should they ever be recovered? Potentially allowing for the early release of what was left of the body, when identified and if appropriate.

"Any ideas on age, height, ethnic background?"

"Again, we need to do more tests for confirmation, but I would say. Male, around five foot six or seven, obviously slim build, and as you can see, not particularly well-nourished. I would hazard a guess at mid to late teens and of Caribbean extraction."

The boss then started making his way to the door, saying, "I think that will do for now. Thanks, Professor."

It was the first real opportunity I'd had to say anything without appearing rude. Stopping him, I told them about my visit to the hostel and Adam Pope.

"I told you, Cinders of Whitechapel," said Ken Reeves. I just looked at him and wondered whether he was going to be like this all the time.

The professor then took the right trainer from the bag, at which point PKW interrupted, insisting on taking swabs from both the foot and trainer before they came into contact with each other. Locard's principle of exchange in action. The trainer was a good fit.

"I'll take those," said PKW, placing each trainer into a separate bag. "I'll arrange to get a proper cast made and along with the swabs, see if the scientists can establish a connection. It will be interesting to see what they come up with. I've never actually done anything like this. It could be a first. Not sure how conclusive it will be, but it's worth trying. Anyway, it will give the boffins something to think about."

The boss agreed, saying little else. Not used to post-mortems he wanted to get back to the office. Leaving Ken Reeves and PKW with the professor, I drove both bosses back to the station. Surprised at the lack of conversation, I subjected them to a dose of Dire Straits.

Chapter 4

Chaos was the best way to describe what was going on in the incident suite, with workmen and cables everywhere. Six of the latest phones waiting to be installed. A new electronic typewriter and dedicated desk sat quietly in the middle of the room. Filing cabinets, desks, and chairs were just some of the other fixtures filling the corridor. Even some of the stationery had arrived. I was astonished at how quickly the boss had managed to get things sorted. Alan didn't seem that bothered by what had happened at the post-mortem. Distracted and excited by the arrival of new equipment. Especially the potential number of options offered by the new telephone system.

"If the boss is as good as an investigator as he is at admin, this job will be sorted in no time."

Having agreed, it gave me the chance to change the subject and tell him about my visit to the hostel and the possibility that Adam Pope was our victim.

"Cinders," his response.

"Don't you start. I've just had all that with Ken Reeves, who's pissed by the way. Just so you know, Pope's gone missing before. Disappearing for about four days, returning badly beaten. You should also know that most, if not all the staff, and most of the residents are female and anti-police or should I say 'Fuzz'. We'll need female officers to help."

"How's Ken Reeves got pissed?" said Alan.

"He took a bottle of scotch to the post-mortem and shared with the professor."

"The prof must have had a pretty big window, does the boss know?"

"They were both there, they haven't said anything. Not to me, anyway."

Later, the boss gave a quick briefing, bringing the others up to speed with the professor's findings. PKW also mentioned that after we'd left, the professor had found a small piece of burnt material in a wound on the victim's back. Which was being sent for analysis. His initial thoughts were that it was a natural fibre, possibly from something like a raincoat.

I was amazed at how quickly the emphasis of the investigation had changed. We were now solely focusing on Adam Pope and the hostel. The boss evidently convinced we'd identified our victim. A forensic examination of Pope's room now a priority. Closely followed by interviewing the staff and residents at the hostel. With most of the other actions, and missing person reports being put on the back burner. The one other decision to have been made was that now was not the right time to speak to Pope's parents. With the boss, hoping for a positive identification first.

As the meeting drew to a close, DCS Simmonds decided it was a good time to tell us a little of himself and DI Clarke, including how they came to be posted to the pool. He thought it best we hear from the horse's mouth. Hopefully preventing rumours circulating, pre-empting anything Hampton might insinuate. It was an unusual step to take, but one welcomed by the team. He knew that officers from the pool were looked upon with scepticism and suspicion. Often being posted there under a cloud, moving officers away from mainstream duties. A sort of punishment posting for senior detectives. If you considered having lots of time to improve your golf handicap a punishment.

Married with one daughter, who was hoping to go to university in the autumn. He'd lived most of his life in and around Epsom, which is where he'd also spent much of his service. The leafy suburbs of Epsom were a world away from the East End. Apart from that, he'd been posted to the Fraud Squad on three separate occasions during his career. Specialising in mortgage fraud, foreign land fraud, and public sector corruption. The biggest shock was that this was the first murder investigation he'd actually led. He'd been on other murder enquiries and been in charge of other successful major investigations; white-collar crime. It was also the first time he and the DI had worked together. His transgression, allowing officers under his control to consume excessive amounts of alcohol. Things had come to a head when one of his team went looking for their car in the underground car park, just as the commander was about to leave for an official function at the Guildhall, attended by members of the Royal Family. With the commander being delayed due to the officer vomiting all over the car. Resulting in the boss being given the option of transferring to the pool or being threatened with a disciplinary hearing – Hobson's choice.

DI Clarke was coy about his personal circumstances. He'd also spent much of his time south of the water, but in much busier areas, Brixton, Bermondsey, and Southwark. His transgression had occurred during a relatively recent posting at the Flying Squad's Tower Bridge office. A handgun seized during an operation, which had subsequently been linked to at least fifteen armed robberies, had gone missing. The fact only coming to light when it was required at Crown Court. Failure to produce the firearm resulted in the trial collapsing and several others having to be abandoned. An internal investigation failed to identify the person responsible. As a result, the entire team had been split up and transferred all over of the Met. Needless to say, the DI was adamant he wasn't responsible for the gun's disappearance.

At the end of the meeting, I called the hostel to get an update on Pope – he was still missing. Telling her that all the staff and residents would now need to be interviewed, and that Pope's room would also need to be forensically examined. Ms

Saltmarsh agreed without hesitation, as if she now wanted to be seen helping, and with PKW and Ken Reeves overhearing the conversation, they were on their way. I just hoped Ken Reeves didn't embarrass himself by talking too much. Alan Harrison told me he'd arranged for two WPCs who'd been helping with house-to-house to be assigned to the squad permanently, and that he'd asked for a dedicated typist too. All three would be there in the morning, but as he wouldn't be around, they'd been told to ask for me.

The following morning, WPCs Sally Bowers and Julia Meadows, along with a typist called Anne Buxton, were already waiting for me. Neither of the WPCs knew why they'd been re-assigned and neither had they any previous experience of major investigations. I told them they would initially be responsible for taking statements from those at the hostel. Mentioning the difficulties they might face, none of which seemed to faze them. The one thing they needed to do, though, before anything else, was to change out of their uniforms. It was an absolute certainty that turning up at the hostel in uniform wouldn't go down well. Having sent them home to change, I wondered how they would get on and whether they had anything in common. If the way they spoke was anything to go by, they were worlds apart.

Sally Bowers was born and bred in east London. She'd told all of us she was twenty-six, born in East Ham, and was now living in Beckton, having been a clerical worker for a while, before joining the job.

Julia Meadows sounded as if she'd been to finishing school, elocution lessons a minimum. A late joiner who'd previously worked as a personal assistant for someone in the building trade. Her place of birth and age, she kept to herself. At a guess, she was in her early thirties and from the home counties, Buckinghamshire, somewhere like that.

Anne Buxton was a diminutive soul. Who's demeanour gave the impression of a shy individual. With a soft voice, plainly dressed in subdued autumnal-coloured clothes. She was single, in her early forties and living in Sidcup with her mother, who she cared for. On the face of it quiet and very modest. She too had never worked on a major investigation and was surprised when the opportunity arose. When I asked her why, she said it was because Hampton didn't use dedicated typists, not even for confidential reports. All his work went into the typing pool where it was allocated on an ad hoc basis. He obviously didn't appreciate the value of a dedicated typist. I told her she would be solely responsible for all the murder squad's typing, which might necessitate looking at photographs. Some of which were likely to be graphic, possibly extreme in nature, even gory. She would also be expected to attend as many office meetings as was possible. She needed to understand that as one of the few individuals to read every document; she was an important part of the team who may very well be able to contribute to meetings. Given her demeanour, I was wondering whether she would cope and having explained everything, I said,

"Do you think you'll be okay with this?"

"Oh, yes, I'm looking forward to it – I volunteered."

I was surprised by both the enthusiasm in her voice and that she'd volunteered. It wasn't long before the electronic typewriter began to chatter.

When Sally Bowers and Julia Meadows returned, I couldn't believe they were the same people. Their transformation considerable, both much better looking. Appearing approachable and very different with their long hair not stuck up in buns. Julia looked the PA she once was, wearing a light bluey-grey dress suit, matching clutch bag and pearl necklace. While Sally had gone for a non-matching grey trouser suit and shirt – all very presentable.

The noise of the electronic typewriter brought Ken Reeves into the office. He had a load of lab forms that either needed typing or re-typing, which he now wanted Anne to do. Hoping to avoid any financial penalties the lab might impose. He was out of luck and would have to carry on doing them himself. After all, it was one of his jobs.

The police laboratory had a fine's system for incorrect submissions, which served two purposes. Firstly, preventing or minimising the risk of exhibits and their subsequent examination being called into question at court. Secondly, helping to raise money for worthwhile charities. In the past discrepancies had led to trials within trials, acquittals, and complaints against police, and trying to sort out exhibits while you were pissed wasn't a good idea.

The WPCs needed to get to the hostel and, with transport at a premium, I took them. Leaving Anne alone to take messages. At least I could introduce them while hopefully getting a list of Pope's visitors. The only thing that really worried me about the girls was their lack of experience. If things got difficult, it could lead to vital information being withheld. My staying wasn't an option, either. It would only make things worse with the staff, while potentially undermining the confidence of the WPCs. I just had to trust them.

If Adam Pope was still missing, we had to find out more. We hardly knew anything. The statements needed to cover the type of person he was, his movements, friends, enemies, relatives. Anything that might help in either finding him or those responsible for his murder. The one thing I had emphasised was that we didn't want to end up with collaborative statements. The witnesses needed to be interviewed separately. If they were found to be using the same or similar phrases, that needed to be explained.

When we arrived, I introduced the girls to Ms Saltmarsh, who was already waiting with three other ladies, including Claire Laker. The girls understood what was needed, and within a few minutes, I was making my way back to the office. By the time I'd arrived Alan was there, apologising for being late, saying he'd needed to attend to some business without elaborating. I told him about the WPCs, to which he said, "I'm told they're a bit of all right, are they single?"

"News travels fast, I've no idea."

"Didn't you ask?"

"No, I didn't, you'll have to do that yourself."

It was early evening before they returned. A number of us, including the bosses, had hung around to hear what they had to say.

"Everything go okay?" I asked.

"In the end, we didn't take any statements, we thought best not to," Julia said.

"What, no statements?" Alan said, jumping in. He'd been grumpy most of the day, and Julia's comment hadn't helped. Before he had the chance to say anything else, I said, "Okay, why don't you just tell us what happened."

Alan was itching to have a go. It was as if his bit of business was playing on his mind. Just then, the office door crashed open with Ken Reeves, lurching in, distracting everyone. Looking more than a little dishevelled, his 'Brylcreemed' hair sticking out at odd angles, tie half-way around his neck, and his shirt even more crumpled than usual, he'd obviously just woken up.

Seizing the opportunity, Sally Bowers jumped in and started going through what had happened. After an initial conversation with the staff, the girls had decided it would be a good idea to have an informal chat with the residents, starting with those who seemed to be the most important. The plan was to get an idea of what everyone was likely to say while hopefully putting them at ease. Catherine Kerwin was first. She'd become Pope's best friend at the hostel, admitting she had a soft spot for him. She was the one who'd initially reported Pope missing. Occasionally, Pope would stay out for the odd night and when she asked him where he'd been, he would always say that he'd stayed at his mother's place, sleeping on the couch. About three weeks ago, he'd been away for at least three days, something he'd never done before. Kerwin became so worried she spoke to Ms Laker, who initially told her not to worry, saying that she was sure he would turn up. Pope did in fact turn up the following day covered in blood and badly beaten. One of his eyes was completely closed. His arms and face both bruised and swollen, and he couldn't walk properly. Kerwin said she kept nagging him to find out what had happened? But he refused to say, wanting her to drop the subject and leave it. Adding that he didn't go out much after that. Kerwin said that she kept on at him to go to the police, threatening to go herself. Pope pleaded with her not to, eventually telling her he'd been caught 'Cracking an H'.

"What's 'Cracking an H' then?" said the boss.

Almost in unison everyone said, "A burglary, break-in, cracking a house."

"Alright, we don't all speak the lingo."

Alan Harrison then asked Sally to continue. The tone of his voice having eased considerably.

Kerwin said that over time Pope told her a story, which she didn't entirely believe. Saying he'd been out walking when he'd seen this house with louvre windows. It was on the corner of some street. He'd got in through a window, taking a video recorder. As it was daytime, he didn't want to be seen carrying it in the street, stashing it in a nearby lock-up. Then, when he went back to get the recorder, he couldn't find it, it had gone. A couple of days later, he went back for the television. Getting caught by the occupants who wanted their recorder back. Pope said they kept him tied up in the basement for a couple of days, taking in turns to beat him.

"Do we know where the house is?" the boss asked.

"No, just that it's a house with a cellar and louvre windows, near the corner of a street, with lock-up garages nearby."

"And what about his captors?"

"She didn't know much. Pope had said. They just kept asking about the recorder, wanting it back, and if they didn't get it back, they would kill him."

"So, why did they let him go?"

"Pope told Kerwin, that at one stage he really thought he was going to be killed, making him change his story. Instead of just saying, he didn't know where it was. He said he didn't know where it was, but he knew who had it. And that he could only get it back if they let him go, and the longer they kept him, the harder it would be. Eventually, they let him go, keeping his wallet, which had his mum's and the hostel's address in. They said they would give him a couple of days. Pope said there were nine or ten, boys and girls."

"Boys and girls!"

"Apparently, that's what Pope called them."

"Any descriptions?"

"Sorry."

"So, they carried out their threat," the DI suggested.

"Sounds like it," said the boss.

"What about friends or visitors, did you ask about them?"

"Pope didn't have any visitors. Occasionally, two or three lads would call and then wait for him in the playground nearby. Ms Laker thought she'd seen them together near shops in Salmon Lane. Ms Saltmarsh thought she may have seen them, too. The hostel's policy is for visitors to sign in and then stay in the common room. None of them knew any of their names and it was doubtful whether they would recognise them, either. Although, Ms Laker said that she thought that two of them could be brothers. The hostel had promised to let us know the moment anyone called for Adam. Their description – teenagers, a similar age to Pope, IC3s, jeans, hoodies, and trainers." A description that would fit most their age.

WPC Meadows went on to say that all members of staff had been interviewed briefly, and it was clear their accounts were an amalgamation with them frequently using the same terminology.

"So, what are we doing to get this in writing?" asked DS Harrison.

WPC Meadows said that arrangements had already been made to take statements at the station in the morning. Where they thought it would be easier. It would also give them an opportunity to show them some mugshots, hoping they might recognise some of those who'd called at the hostel.

Alan Harrison's attitude had changed. Under the circumstances, they'd done the right thing.

"Best get some mugshots together then," Alan said.

"We've already spoken to the collator, he'll have them ready for when we start," said Sally Bowers.

Alan smiled. Whatever had been troubling him forgotten, confirmed by him suggesting a small libation. If not in the office, then over the road in The Scarborough Arms. A pub at the back of the station that was not more than fifty yards away. The boss agreed, saying that it was about time we had some 'doins.' No one knew what that meant, but it sounded alcoholic. It wasn't long before the team had gravitated over the road. On the way, I asked Alan what had prompted him to risk suggesting going for a drink, when we'd been told the office was dry. He'd made a few calls to get some more background on the boss. To all intents and purposes, he was a good guy. Although he might disappear from time to time. Well liked. Staying loyal to his team had led to all his troubles. Very good at paperwork and admin. Not so good with practical operational matters, was how it was put. Most of the time he would just let you get on with things. But like most bosses, would have the occasional rush of blood and want to be more hands on. Going for a drink would hopefully help break the ice. 'Doins', it turned out, was the boss's name for scotch.

As soon as we got to the pub, it was obvious that both Alan and Bob Clarke had taken a fancy to the two WPCs, with the four of them forming a group of five along with the boss. As the evening continued, a lock-in seemed inevitable. With alcohol influencing the thinking of some. Who were now suggesting that it wouldn't be that long before the case was sorted. And that it would only a matter of time before the suspects were identified, arrested and charged, with the DI banging on about his 'domino' effect.

"When one piece topples, the rest will follow. Bish bash bosh, game over, job done, sorted." I'd become a spare wheel and didn't fancy ending up with Ken Reeves. Making my excuses, I took a circuitous route home to avoid the black rats from Bow, who'd been targeting CID. The bastards even had a league table. In the evenings, they would pick a station and park up close to where the people working there would park their private cars. Waiting for someone in plainclothes to turn up and drive off. With most civilians finishing work by seven, anyone leaving the station after that in civvies was likely to be CID, and I didn't fancy being one of their statistics.

The following morning Alan was reviewing the house-to-house, where there'd been a dramatic surge in the number completed. The occupants from a couple of flats had mentioned seeing a fire on the waste ground, but as they thought it was probably kids, was in the centre and didn't appear to be spreading, hadn't bothered calling anyone.

From the way the DI was speaking, last night's thoughts had continued. He still seemed to think that it was just a matter of time before he and the boss would be back at COCO, or New Scotland Yard, as it was known. Commissioner's Office Central Operations was such a mouthful. A couple of weeks at most, with a trial somewhere down the road, the DI's thoughts. It would be part of their redemption, a step on the road to recovery. It all seemed a little premature. We hadn't positively identified the victim yet, let alone arrested anyone. Adam Pope remained missing, and his parents still needed to be contacted. The boss was still hoping to identify the victim before having to speak to relatives. Wanting to avoid the possibility of any embarrassment or having to put anyone through an unnecessary ordeal. The problem was that they could have useful information, even know where he was. For all we knew, he could have gone home and not told anyone, which would be more than a little embarrassing.

The first of the witnesses from the hostel had arrived and were now waiting to be interviewed. For some reason, Sally Bowers hadn't. Nobody knew where she was, and neither had she called in. It looked as though Julia was going to have to make a start on her own. Introducing a male officer at his stage would be going back on a promise and wasn't worth the risk. Julia made a start; she'd been on her own for about an hour when Sally rang in, asking to speak to Alan. She sounded petrified. Alan listened for a while, saying, "Just take it easy, calm down, tell me slowly." I then heard him say, "Just wait there, I won't be long." Then turning to me he said, "Hold the fort, would you. Hopefully, I won't be long and if anyone asks, just say I've just popped out for cigars." Before I had the chance to ask what was going on, he'd gone.

It was more than an hour before he returned. The regular grumpy face replaced by an even bigger frown. Sterner, more intent, angry. Within a few seconds, he said, "Come on, we're going out... now. Come on, hurry up."

"Where we going?"

"Come on, get a move on, I'll tell you on the way." Without saying anymore, he grabbed my arm, pulling me out of the office. As we left, I could see Sally sitting in the small office opposite. She looked a mess. She'd been crying, her face flushed and blotchy. Dried rivers of mascara had run down her face onto the white shirt she was wearing.

"What on earth's the matter?" I asked. As she looked up, she looked scared.

"No time for that. Come on, we've got to get a move on. Sally, keep the door shut. We'll be as quick as we can," Alan said. When we got in the station yard; it was absolutely rammed with cars lumped anywhere. The CID car was at the back, parked amongst cars that had either been seized for examination or been reported as lost or stolen. The nearest car to the exit, and the primary culprit for the blockage, another GP car. Unlocked with keys in the ignition.

"I'll drive," Alan said, jumping into the driver's seat. We left the yard at such a rate that as the car grounded at the bottom of the ramp, I hit my head on the car's roof. Catching the radio's handset as it jumped out of its socket. We then hurtled off towards Cable Street.

"Take it easy. Do you mind telling me what's going on and where we're going?"

"Her old man's beaten her up. He's done that and we're going straighten things out."

"Do what?"

"He beat the crap out of her. Last night and again this morning, just as she was leaving for work. He doesn't believe she's on a murder investigation; dressing the way she has. Accusing her of going over the side."

"So why doesn't she report him, what's it got to do with us?"

"He's a skipper on the SPG. The Special Patrol Group."

"I know what it is. Have you've lost the plot? If Hampton finds out, we'll be in the shit. He'll stick me on for sure. He's already got it in for me."

It soon became clear that it didn't matter what I said. We were going. As we sped along the Mile End Road, Alan would occasionally ring the bell fitted to the car. I did not know why? It was useless. You couldn't hear the thing unless you were in the car or standing right next to it. We were about fifteen minutes into the journey, still bouncing around, when I heard Information Room calling over the radio.

"Hotel Lima One, Hotel Lima One, receiving?"

"I think they're calling us," I said.

"Who is?"

"Information room. Hotel Lima One, I think that's us. It's the call sign for the duty officer."

An entry in the car's logbook confirmed my suspicions.

"So technically, we've stolen the duty officer's car to drive to Beckton. Which is not on our district, let alone ground. So, you can give this bloke who just happens to be a skipper on the SPG, a piece of your mind and muggins is sitting next to you."

"Beckton. Who the hell's going to Beckton, we're going to his office. Ricketts – Sergeant John Ricketts, that's his name, do you know him?" said Alan.

"Barkingside. We're going to Barkingside. You've got a screw loose. Two of us against a team of trained thugs who spend most of their day looking for fights. This is crazy, there must be something else we can do."

It didn't matter, nothing was going to change his mind. He just drove. Information room was still calling and continuing to ignore them would only lead to more trouble. Changing channels, I gave them a rambling excuse for borrowing the car. Saying we would be back as soon as possible. If nothing else, it stopped calls coming over the main channel.

As we got closer, I decided to take my wedding ring and watch off, putting them in a jacket pocket. Then, having taken my jacket and tie off too, I put them on the back seat.

"What you doing?" asked Alan.

"Just in case. I don't want to tear my jacket, get strangled or scratch anything. If that's okay with you?" He grinned, knowing that despite my misgivings I would back him.

We got to Barkingside in record time and drove straight into the yard. Three SPG vans were parked in a line on the far side of the car park.

"Their offices are in the Portakabins," I said, pointing to a temporary two-storey structure close to the vans. Although temporary, the Portakabins had been there for as long as I could remember.

"I know, I've been here too."

"Okay, no need..."

Alan was still on a mission and, having abandoned the car, went straight into their briefing room. A PC was sitting by the door. "Sergeant Ricketts?" Alan grunted.

"Over there, the skipper with the dark hair," said the PC. Pointing to a table where three officers sat. Only one was a sergeant. As Alan got close to the table he said, "Ricketts, I want a word with you, outside now." Without saying another word or giving Ricketts the chance to react, Alan stretched over the desk, grabbing his shirt. Trying to drag him from the table. As Ricketts started to rise, he just got bigger and bigger. Typical

SPG. Fit, six foot plus, square jaw. The type of person who looked as though he had muscles on muscles, but not much between the ears. Alan quickly gave up trying to drag him and just took an almighty swing. Punching him in the face. Cutting his lip and in a very loud voice, saying, "Leave her alone, bastard. Do that again, and you'll regret it for the rest of your life. Nobody beats up my sister."

The speed at which everything had happened had taken them all by surprise. Only now were the others gathering themselves, with one of the PCs saying, "Just who the fuck are you?"

"Language, Timothy," I said as calmly as I could, trying to give the impression of being in total control.

"And how the hell did you get in here?" he continued.

Alan ignored him, saying, "You touch Sally again, I'll have your balls for breakfast, got it? Get a kick out of beating up defenceless women? Get off on it, or what? Just in case you morons haven't worked it out, I'm her brother."

The look on Ricketts' face told me he was trying to process not only what had just happened but what had been said. His knee jerk reaction was to reach for the truncheon in his pocket. His mates following the trigger movement. Their concentration broken by me saying as forcefully as possible, "I'd leave it if I were you. Unless, of course, you want to get hurt... badly? Back down and we'll leave."

Ricketts stopped drawing his truncheon. The others followed, like well-trained dogs.

Alan then said, "You best spend the rest of the day finding somewhere to live. Don't go back to Sally's. She doesn't want you anymore. If you do, I'll find you. I hear the section house has plenty of room."

As we backed out of the office, the PC we'd initially spoken to stood blocking our way. There was then the briefest of standoffs before he stood aside, allowing us to leave. It was all over within a couple of minutes. Ricketts made no attempt to stop us, threaten us or deny anything. Gawping out of a window as we drove off in what he would instantly recognise as an unmarked general-purpose police car.

"Brother, sister, where did that come from?" I said.

"It just popped into my head as I hit him. Thanks, by the way."

"Just don't make a habit of it," I said as we made our way back to the station.

When we arrived, all the operational cars had gone, including the CID car, and I wondered whether our radio message had got through or whether the relief was out looking for the car. If so, we could find ourselves in a spot of bother, especially if Hampton found out. We couldn't just leave the car in the yard; it would be a complete show out. On the way in, I'd seen what I thought was a space amongst the cars where officers on shift normally parked. As a precaution we parked there and made our way to the station office, where the station officer doing his best to cope.

"Where is everyone, I don't think I've ever seen the yard so empty?" I said.

"The duty officer's car's been stolen. Everyone's out looking for it. He thinks some locals have come round the back and nicked it. There's a bit of a flap on."

"What sort of car is it?"

"Maroon GP car."

"You know there's one parked out on the street, about a hundred yards up the road. We passed it on the way in. It's where the relief and home beat normally..."

I didn't get to finish. As the station officer ran out, giving me the opportunity to hide the keys amongst the spares on the board. I just hoped he didn't touch the bonnet.

By the time we'd got back upstairs, the girls were interviewing a resident I didn't know. The key witnesses were yet to be interviewed. Saltmarsh, Laker, and Kerwin were still at the hostel. It was as though leaving the most important until last was a uniform trait. The only thing that had been of any use were elimination prints. With the girls promising to get as many of the interviews that could be done by the end of the day, and although it was a distraction, the way Sally looked, I wasn't sure she was up to it.

Chapter 5

The local stations had all returned negative results, while looking for burglaries with a similar M.O. to ours. The only thing that had been discovered was that as part of a refurbishment programme, the local council had installed louvre windows in a large proportion of their properties. And that, flaws in the design had meant that the windows could easily be removed from the outside of the property.

The fact that the burglary hadn't been reported made the boss irritable. His frustration evident by his tone. It was another sign of the pressure he was under. Over the years the boss had lost touch with today's realities, with promotion automatically meaning more administrative duties. With postings in either the leafy suburbs of south-west London or the Fraud Squad skewing his perception of policing norms. If he'd ever worked in any of the deprived areas of London, he would know there were a myriad of reasons why crimes didn't get reported. A lack of trust, not caring or simply preferring to sort things out themselves, were just a few. Unfortunately, some of the pressure now coming to bear had been self-inflicted. Carrying on in the pub the way they had, where others could hear them, hadn't helped, and neither did not the results of the forensics. Irritable. The boss demanded an immediate update, wanting to know when exhibits had been submitted, whether they'd been examined and what the results were? As usual, Ken Reeves wasn't around and neither were the exhibit books, making it impossible to know. Which just made him even more tetchy. Everything was to be checked and double checked, now. The more the boss went on, the more desperate he sounded. As if he'd been given a deadline, and the clock was running.

A more comprehensive search of criminal records than was possible on the PNC had found a record of Adam Pope being arrested nearly two years ago. Stealing a pair of trainers, of all things, shoplifting. It was his first offence and because he'd admitted it and the property had been recovered, he'd been given a caution. As a result, his fingerprints hadn't been taken and what antecedents there were minimal. Something else that didn't help with the boss's mood. We were now relying on Ken Reeves to provide some positivity; he'd booked out to the lab first thing; nearly five hours ago.

Alan and I had already started looking at other ways of identifying the property Pope had been held in. Effectively trying to work in reverse. Identifying all the lock-up garages in the area, then identifying all the large houses with cellars, louvre windows and eight or more occupants close by. As most council flats had lock-ups, there wouldn't be a shortage.

When Ken did surface, the boss spotted him walking past his office. We could hear him calling his name, demanding an immediate update on submissions. I wasn't sure whether Ken had been startled or was just dithering? His voice sounding more than a little unsure. Everyone in the office heard him hurriedly make an excuse to go the toilet. Playing for time, trying to gather his thoughts. Moments later, both bosses entered the main office and slowly made their way over to the desk where Alan and I were sitting. Standing quietly, waiting for Ken. As if observing a minute's silence, as a mark of respect for someone passing. In doing so, the rest of the office subliminally joined the vigil, with the office falling into total silence. When Ken did arrive, he found himself standing at the other end of the desk, facing the bosses. I caught a whiff of minty toothpaste. On the way back to the office, he'd obviously stopped off at one of his many watering holes for more than just a snifter. With everyone now looking at Ken, the boss simply said, "Well get on with it then, what are you waiting for, what's the situation?"

Ken started mumbling, as if unsure of what to say. From his point of view, the most significant piece of information to come from the results was that the lab had been unable to establish whether the blood from the body was the same as the blood from Pope's shirt. It was the same group, but that was the best they could do.

Ken then rumbled through a load of outstanding tests he was waiting on. Amongst these, the result of an analysis of a small amount of stomach fluid the professor had recovered during the latter stages of the post-mortem. The analysis didn't identify any specific foodstuffs. But the volume of gastric acid was around ten thousand parts per million. According to Ken, this indicated that death had occurred some three to four days prior to the body's discovery. If nothing else, it was in line with when Kerwin last saw Pope. One set of fingerprints from Pope's room had not been identified. The assumption was that they were Pope's. But as we had nothing to compare them with, they would remain outstanding. The fibres found embedded in the victim's back were a thick canvas, covered with yellow plastic. Again, according to Ken, the lab thought they were most likely to come from a tent or possibly a sailing garment. As Ken continued to go through all the negatives, the boss, without saying anything, suddenly stomped out of the office. Leaving us to wonder what was going on? And although illegible, occasionally we could hear him talking to himself. When he returned, having apologised, he tried to explain that in his mind the results or lack of them, was evidence that Pope's captors were his killers. Having motive, means and opportunity. Their motive; wanting the video recorder back. Their means and opportunity, demonstrated by his capture, beating and subsequent imprisonment. Being held against his will while they administered gratuitous violence. Then threatening to kill him. A threat he took seriously, and one which the boss was now advocating. The more he went on, the more it sounded as though he was trying to convince himself as much as anyone else.

Obviously, these lines of enquiry needed to be followed. But I was reminded of when I first saw the body and the questions raised then. Which remained unanswered, and still didn't make any sense. There was now another question to add to that list. Where had the body been kept for the three or four days prior to being burnt? There weren't any lock-up garages or big houses near the waste ground. And, assuming Kerwin's version of events was broadly true, and Pope had been murdered by the kidnappers. Getting the body to the waste ground from the nearest big house would have been extremely risky. Which brought me back to. If the body had been moved that far, then why not go a few more yards and dump it in the river?

With all the dead ends, it was time to prod the boss about speaking to Pope's parents. We only had his mother's address. Assuming Adam wasn't there, she should be able to provide further information that would help with the investigation. It was a task we couldn't put off any longer. And neither was it the sort of thing you could delegate to a minion. After a while, the DI came in to get the address, saying the boss wanted another meeting arranged for 7 p.m.

We'd reached a stage where we could now redeploy some of those on house-to-house. Their first job was to go to the stations that were closest to the waste ground north of the Thames. To go through all the stations' records: crime books, stop books, parade books, collator's records, charge sheets, book 12a and book 66 entries. Going back at least six weeks from the discovery of the body. If the break-in had been in a property with eight or more occupants, we could be looking for a squat or some form of student accommodation. There would be lots of records to go through, looking for any incidents or individuals stopped at or near a location that could be en route to either the scene, the hostel or even the unidentified house. If the officers found anything, they were to seize the original, get the name of whoever had made the entry, their contact details and the date and time of when they were next on duty. As part of the same exercise, they needed to speak to all the home beat officers who covered any beats within a three-mile radius of the hostel north of the water. They were the officers who should be able to compile a detailed list of lock-up garages on their beats. They should also know whether they were close to any big houses with cellars. Finally, they were to spread the word. Making entries in the parade books. So that as many officers as was possible would know the sort of information we were looking for. We weren't exactly grabbing at straws, but because of the boss's demeanour it seemed a good idea.

On the off chance that a car had been used, we requested that all lost or stolen vehicles recovered on district be examined for blood.

We then spent the rest of the day checking handwritten statements against their typed versions. It was one of those necessary evils. Crucial both to the investigation and potential court proceedings. Making sure any typing errors or other mistakes were corrected and that every possible action arising from a statement had been identified. It was imperative that nothing was missed. The mistyped name of a person or location could really screw up an investigation.

I wondered whether it was worth mounting a surveillance operation at the hostel. If what we'd been told was true, visitors, either those looking to cause Adam serious harm or friends, should be calling anytime soon, and we needed to speak to both. The flip side was that if we were spotted, it would undoubtedly hinder things. Ms Saltmarsh had promised to call should anyone turn up, and the hostel's location didn't exactly lend itself to a static observation. In the end, I decided against it.

Everyone except PC Perkins had made it back for the boss's meeting, who began by outlining the visit to Mrs Pope. She didn't know where her son was. She hadn't seen him for about a month. He was an only child who'd become unruly during the break-up of her marriage. His father having moved out more than a year ago. Since then, he'd started playing truant, becoming harder to control, occasionally staying out overnight. When she asked where he'd been, he would just say he'd slept on a friend's sofa, refusing to say who the friend was. Then three or four months ago he told her he was leaving. He'd found somewhere else to stay but wouldn't say where. She said that she pleaded with him to stay. Saying she loved him and didn't want him to go. It didn't make any difference. Since then, she'd seen him once, about a month ago when he called by, to let her know he was okay, promising to keep in touch. His visit had made her feel a little better. It was true that he didn't get on with his father. He wouldn't stay there or be allowed to. She even doubted Adam knew where his father lived – she didn't. She had a school photograph of Adam taken about eighteen months ago. It was one of just a few, and now meant a lot to her. A typical school portrait picture, nothing remarkable, depicting a young adolescent with relatively short afro hair and a naturally happy smile. A picture of total innocence, well turned out and very presentable. The shirt in the photograph could easily be the one taken from the hostel. The fact that his mother hadn't seen Adam obviously increased the likelihood this was our victim. Having seen the photograph, I was now struggling to get my head around how something so horrific could have happened to such an innocent-looking lad. For those who'd seen the body, putting this happy smiling face on the carcass changed the dynamics. Giving the remains real identity. We got copies of the photograph made; twelve, the maximum number of colour photographs allowed. Others would have to be photocopies – budget restrictions.

The meeting then changed tack as the boss started thanking everyone for their efforts. He appreciated how hard everyone was working in what were difficult and challenging circumstances. It was either a prelude to cutting the squad or another apology for his behaviour earlier. He was definitely coming under more pressure than he was used to, some self-induced, some because the results were not going our way, and some Hampton undoubtedly had a hand in. Just as we were about to find out which, when PC Perkins burst in, distracting everyone. Puffing and panting, he'd run up the stairs. A station parade book in one hand and a load of loose sheets in the other.

Trying to catch his breath he said, "Sorry I'm late, Guv, but I might have found an address for the kidnappers." Instantly grabbing everyone's attention, but before he could say anything else, the boss told him to say nothing. A few moments later, everyone except the DI, Alan and I were ordered out, being told to get a drink and wait to be called, either in the canteen or over the road. Just the four of us were going to hear what PC Perkins had to say. Reluctantly, the others began to leave. Everyone except Ken Reeves. For some reason he didn't want to go, which was more than a little odd, given that he had never been known to turn down the opportunity for a drink. He was so reluctant, the DI ended up holding the office door open, prompting him to go, with Ken saying, "Are you sure you don't you want me to stay? It would save a lot of time if I knew where we were going."

"We'll make sure you've enough time and help to get ready. For now, I'd just do as the boss has asked," said DI Clarke, watching him all the way along the corridor.

The boss wasn't taking any chances, realising he might actually be able to deliver on a promise. He didn't want there to be any possibility of Hampton or any of his Muppets getting prior knowledge of an address we might be interested in. Finding it empty was the last thing any of us wanted. Once everyone had gone, PC Perkins said that Bow's collator had identified a possible lock-up, just off Lichfield Road, attached to a small block of flats. They were now part of an extensive redevelopment programme where tenancy agreements were not being renewed, the flats and lock-ups slowly emptying. Not far from there were half a dozen large Georgian houses, which were also part of the same redevelopment programme. They too were supposed to be empty, having been the subject of compulsory purchase orders. But according to the collator at least one was now a squat. The boss was urging PC Perkins to get on with it.

"Going through the parade book, I found several entries relating to complaints about noisy parties at one of the houses. The local home beat, a PC Edwards has been dealing. I've been told that he's been to the address on at least two occasions. According to the collator, the parties are well organised. Either starting on a Thursday or Friday and then carrying on through the weekend. Again, according to the collator, there could be up to a dozen or so people living there. All in their late teens or early twenties. He thinks the girls might be on the game."

"Toms in a squat, whatever next? We'd better find out if it's got louvre windows," said Alan.

"I did that on the way back, that's why I'm late. There are two groups of three houses with a small gap in between. The middle house in the first group is the one with the parties; it's got louvre windows on the ground floor. That are partly obscured by an overgrown hedge. There's an excellent view of the front of the house from the first floor of the flats opposite. Before leaving Bow, I tried contacting PC Edwards, but he's out at the moment. So, I've left a message with his missus."

"How far is this from the hostel?" asked the boss.

"By road, about three-quarters of a mile. Less on foot, there're some footpaths which cut across some of the roads, making the walk shorter," said PC Perkins.

"Come on, let's go. Get the troops. Let's do it," said the boss. Eager wasn't the word. No one moved. We all just looked at him.

"Okay, what have I said, why can't we go?"

"Guv, we need to wait. We need to speak to the home beat officer. He's been there, he can describe the layout. He might even be able to confirm the existence of a cellar. He should also be able to give us a better idea about the occupants. He might even have names we can check on before going. If we go now, how will we know who is and who isn't a resident? If they all deny living there, what are we going to do?" Alan said.

"Arrest the lot of them," the boss's reply.

"Alan's right, we need to wait for the PC. Similarly, we don't know how many people to expect and what they're like. We could have a riot on our hands," said DI Clarke.

Reluctantly, the boss agreed. Getting PC Perkins to make another call to PC Edwards. Again, speaking to his wife. She appreciated the urgency of the call, but all she could say was that she thought her husband would be back within the hour. The boss was adamant we were going tonight no matter what the time. I was then sent to get the others, the boss now wanting to brief them without specifying an address.

Making my way down to the canteen, I passed a couple of Hampton's Muppets heading towards the CID office. When they saw me, they went out of their way, avoiding any eye contact and looking decidedly sheepish. I wondered whether they'd finally been sent back to general duties. A little justice, I thought. The canteen's servery was closed, but the entire team was there. No one had ventured over to the pub, not even Ken Reeves.

Back in the office, the boss was eager to start the briefing. Only to be interrupted by Reeves arriving late.

"Sorry boss needed a piss," was all he said.

"So soon, you've only just been. So that's what happens when you get old?" Sally said jokingly.

Ken Reeves gave her a wicked look, really not appreciating the banter, muttering something inaudible.

PC Edwards rang in, confirming PC Perkins story. The boss ordered him back on duty. From what had been said, it sounded as though we were going to need more troops. Edwards was a career PC, with over twenty years' service, having been a home beat officer for over six. According to the collator, he wasn't typical of that ilk. One of the better home beats with his finger on the pulse. Engaging with the entire community, speaking to anyone and everyone, not just a favoured few. As opposed to the more typical home beat who just used up shoe leather, trying to avoid paperwork. Marking time, waiting for their pension.

On two occasions he'd been to the address about the noise, loud music. And on both occasions he'd been left speaking to the same young man who'd given his name as Jermaine Brown. The first time was late one evening about six weeks ago. Which again was unusual, as most home beats worked nine to five. On the second occasion, the noise abatement officer from the local council had accompanied him to measure sound levels. He hadn't been inside, but he had been to a break-in next door, when the houses were occupied and felt sure the properties were fairly similar. Originally built in more prosperous times for those responsible for managing the warehouses and businesses associated with the docks. From memory, he thought the house had a living room, dining room, breakfast room, kitchen, pantry and toilet downstairs. With a bathroom and four relatively large bedrooms upstairs. Along with a walk-in attic, cellar and small gardens, front and rear. Behind the properties, a parcel of land. Housing several derelict units, including a disused repair garage and an old factory of some kind, all overgrown with scrub. The land had also been acquired by the developers. His view was that should anyone get into that area, there were so many exits and places to hide, it was unlikely anyone would be found.

The lock-up garages were a short distance from there. PC Edwards thought we wouldn't be seen if we met up at the flats overlooking the houses. Armed with the information and at the boss's request, Alan made calls, trying to get more troops without any luck. Posing the question of whether the job should be put off until the morning when we could be sure of manpower. The boss was adamant there would be no delay. We were going as soon as we could and with whatever troops we had. A couple of uniform PCs and a dog unit were all we could muster. At least the dog handler could cover the rear of the property.

The DI split us into groups. The initial aim was to secure the main rooms, while preventing access to the toilets, bathroom and kitchen. Trying to prevent any evidence from being flushed away. It would then be a case of dealing with the occupants, confirming identities and making any arrests necessary. Once the place had been secured, we should be able to arrange for PKW to come and do his thing. The boss was also insisting that with any arrests, it would be a case of one prisoner per station. Splitting them up, making sure they wouldn't be able to communicate with anyone. Twenty of us, the dog handler and Sultan, made our way to the meeting point. As we were leaving, Ken could be seen heading off alone. He'd made a fuss of loading his car with what looked like the entire station's quota of exhibit paraphernalia.

From the first-floor balcony, I could see the houses and hear music coming from the house we were interested in. Four young men were standing outside, socialising, drinking, smoking, chatting. The house was in almost total darkness, just a faint glimmer coming from the open door. Alan Harrison handed out four working radios he'd got hold of. One for each of the teams and one for the boss. Having made such a spectacle of himself leaving the station, Ken was yet to arrive. The boss got one of the PCs to go down to the lock-up garages and see if he was there – no joy. The boss wasn't waiting. He gave the dog handler five minutes to get to the back of the property. After that, we would be on our way.

We wouldn't be knocking or waiting to be invited in. It would be plainclothes followed by uniform. Hoping that it would give us a better chance of getting in and securing the place without too much kerfuffle. With the door open, the four lads outside just looked as we passed. Getting in and securing the place was surprisingly easy. The music was loud, but not so loud you couldn't think. We did have a couple of other problems, though. The number of people was nearer to sixty, which was almost double what we'd anticipated. And not getting high on the cannabis smoke drifting around. A little more light wouldn't have gone a miss either.

Given the circumstances, everything was going reasonably well, even good natured. The layout was pretty much as PC

Edwards had described. The only differences were that the dining room and breakfast room were now bedrooms, as was the attic. Unfortunately for us, the conviviality quickly changed when PC Edwards, who'd been outside, came bounding in, announcing to all and sundry that he'd called for backup. The SPG now on their way. Immediately, the atmosphere changed. Becoming tense, almost aggressive. The partygoers readying themselves for their arrival. The SPG's reputation for gratuitous violence, racism, and fitting people up well known. And this was just the type of environment they would thrive in. I could see things getting out of hand if we weren't careful. To make matters worse, it then dawned on me that Ricketts could well be part of the crew. Which would really spice things up. Somehow, we had to stop them. Even if we tried calling them off, they would still turn up. And if we didn't let them in, the aggravating bastards would just park up close by. Stopping and searching everyone leaving with the message soon getting back to those still here, causing trouble. I got hold of PC Edwards, quietly taking him back outside, explaining the error of his ways. Making it his job to get rid of them. The last thing we wanted was for it all to kick off.

Leaving him, I then went to find Sally Bowers to let her know. As I passed the living room, I could see the bosses standing by a coffee table pushed against a wall, a television perched on top. The dusty outline of where a video recorder had once lived beside it. A twisted cable which looked to be connected to the back of the television at one end dangled under the table.

Sally Bowers was upstairs dealing with one of the female residents. When I told her there was a possibility of Ricketts showing up, she said she would stay upstairs where she felt safer.

Alan's response was, "Fuck him, he can do what he likes."

He just wanted to get on, suggesting we look in the cellar. The door was either locked or very stiff. A shoulder barge did the job. Once open, we got hold of PC Perkins to stand by the door, making sure no one, especially the boss, got in. If this was the scene of a murder, it needed to be preserved. Letting the bosses in would only increase the risk of contamination.

In almost total darkness, we ventured down a few steps, where with the help of Alan's cigarette lighter we found a light switch. A dust-covered bulb hanging from rudimentary wiring flickered into life. Just enough for the immediate area. Beyond that, shadows merged into the darkness. From what I could see, the cellar appeared to cover most of the house, supported by nine brick pillars. A concrete floor near the stairs, a relatively recent addition. Except for a cleared area close to the nearest pillar. The rest of the cellar looked to be littered with boxes and old household items, including an ironing board and mangle. Occasionally, the draft from the open door would cause cobwebs to give themselves away, swaying in and out of the shafts of light.

My eye was immediately drawn to a lone kitchen chair sitting in the cleared area. As we got closer, I could see pieces of knotted cord tied around the pillar, some of which looked to be bloodstained. Again, with the help of Alan's lighter, splatters of what again looked like blood were also visible on the floor. Not a vast amount, but certainly enough for testing. If this was where Pope was imprisoned, tortured, killed and then dismembered, there wasn't nearly enough blood. By the same token, if there had been any sort of cleaning up, there was too much. Our immediate impression was that this was not where Pope had been killed.

As the room needed to be examined, we left PC Perkins on guard, ensuring it would remain secure until PKW arrived.

By the time we left the cellar, both the residents and guests had been sorted. Fifteen bods arrested and in need of housing at different police stations. With the help of the ASO, we managed to get twelve of them into stations that were reasonably close. The others, miles away, Chadwell Heath, Waltham Abbey and Loughton. Getting them booked in was going to make it a long night. But the boss was insisting the prisoners be held separately and incommunicado. There wasn't another option. PKW couldn't get to the scene until the morning, but at least he would have better lighting. Thankfully, there had been no sign of the SPG. More worryingly, neither had there been any sign of Ken Reeves. PC Edwards radioed the station to see if they had any news, wondering whether he'd been involved in an accident or stopped by the black rats. They weren't aware of anything.

Assuming he was okay, not only would he have some explaining to do, but he would also have his work cut out collecting the prisoners' clothing from the various stations, along with helping PKW with the examination of the cellar.

Chapter 6

As we prepared for the interviews, there was an air of optimism, even excitement. Created by the boss, periodically making calls from the main office, updating whoever was on the other end of the line. Everyone could hear him fighting our corner, justifying the need for the team to stay together. In one of the earlier calls, he'd been heard to say that as large quantities of blood and rope being found in the cellar, he was confident of an early resolution. I had no idea where that nugget of information had come from. I hadn't said anything remotely close, and I very much doubted Alan had.

A couple of prisoners had previous convictions. Nothing serious – possessing cannabis, surprise, surprise. Shoplifting and an odd TDA or taking and driving away. There were no convictions for any forms of violence.

The boss had a plan for interviewing, which he couldn't be dissuaded from. Except for Ken Reeves, everyone else had been paired up and given two suspects to interview. With the bosses taking the one remaining prisoner, conveniently located at Arbour Square. Once the interviews had been completed and everyone was back in the office, the debriefing could begin. I could just imagine everyone sitting in silence, waiting for the last team to turn up. It was a bit daft, but the boss was adamant. Alan and I had been kept together and were fortunate enough to have been given two prisoners that weren't a million miles away. A Jermaine Brown and a David Lacey.

Being good at interviewing suspects was a real skill, an art form at which very few excelled. Working as a pair, you had to trust your partner, with one asking questions and the other writing. One of the hardest things to do was not to interrupt. Even if you thought something had been missed. I could think of many occasions where I was convinced a point had been missed, only to be proved wrong later. The best thing to do was make a note and wait until your partner had finished or had invited you to speak. The way police interviews were portrayed on television really wound me up. There were always exceptions, but the number of times you would see two cops taking it in turns to ask questions was daft. It could only do one thing, bugger up any train of thought you might have, and telling suspects what you were thinking was another no no. Why tell them, let them tell you? Letting someone know what you thought when you didn't have to wasn't smart. Open and closed questions along with some cognitive interviewing techniques didn't seem to exist on telly or make good entertainment. We both had previous experience of interviews getting completely screwed by idiots intervening at crucial points. That wouldn't be happening today. You had to be seeking the truth and if capable of corroboration, so much the better. I sometimes thought of myself as a salesman, looking to promote an all-inclusive stay at one of Her Majesty's fantastic locations for an indeterminate period, and all at very favourable rates – it was a tough ask.

Brown was first. From what had been said, he was one of the leaders. Twenty-two with no convictions recorded against the name he'd given. He'd been held incommunicado and the first thing I expected was for him to ask for a solicitor – he didn't. My initial impression was that he was quite a pleasant young man and having gone through the various formalities, I reminded him that others were being interviewed and that stories would obviously be compared. If he decided not to say anything or his story didn't match others, that may have consequences.

I then said, "We're investigating the murder of a young man whose body was found not that far from the squat. Part of the investigation has led us to your address. Any ideas why that might be?"

"I don't know anything about killing anyone, but I'm not surprised by the visit."

"Why's that?"

"I'm just not, that's all."

"Tell me, how long have you been living there?"

"I don't know exactly. Months, a year maybe."

"I understand the property is owned by a development company. Have they tried to evict you?"

"Not anymore, no."

"What do you mean, not anymore?"

"We have an agreement."

"An agreement?"

"Yeah, the deal is that we stay there and look after the empty properties. Making sure no one else moves in and then leave peacefully when the building work starts. Even finding somewhere else for us to look after when the time comes."

"Is this a written agreement?"

"No, shook on it, though."

"Who with?"

"The area manager."

"And, who did the negotiating?"

"Me, I did."

"When's the building work going to start?"

"Don't know."

"So, tell me about the parties, like last nights. How did they come about?"

"It became a way of making some money for the squat. Jobs are really hard to come by you know."

"Who's making money?"

"We all are."

"On what?"

"Everything, drinks, girls, weed, food, anything we can, really."

"Jermaine, do you realise what you're saying?"

"I think so. We never killed nobody and like you said, I don't know what the others are going to say, so I got no choice, it's bad."

"What's bad?"

"Killing's bad."

"Okay, let's back up a bit. Just so I'm clear, tell me how the parties started?"

"I can't remember exactly when it all started, but we used to have small parties, ten or twelve friends playing music on a sound system with a few beers. One of the guys had access to some videos. Blue films, which the others liked. I'm not sure who suggested it, but we started stocking cans. Sometimes some green and more films. Everyone was happy to contribute, it made it easy for them. They were happy to pay a bit for supplying the drinks and that. The parties became a regular. Got more organised with more friends, if you know what I mean. They started off as overnighters. Normally finishing around dawn, then one morning, one of the girls did breakfast, which then became a regular thing. After that, they wouldn't go home, just hanging around. Some might disappear for a few hours and then come back. It ended up being the whole weekend. We were just wasted, by Monday morning."

"How did others get to know?"

"Word of mouth. We weren't sticking up banners. To start with, there were about ten of us. Last week it was nearer to eighty. This week not so many. You got there before things really got going. To be honest, it was getting out of hand and we didn't know what to do."

"What about the girls, you mentioned them earlier? What were they up to?"

"Do I have to?"

"No, you don't, but I think we all know they contributed more than just breakfast."

There was a long pause and for the first time, he was really thinking about what to say. Giving Alan time to catch up, eventually he said, "I can't remember exactly who or when it was, but at one of the earlier parties everyone was sitting around. Happy. All was cool."

"Do you mean high?"

"Okay, everyone was high."

"And?"

"A video was on. It had become a bit of a thing and one of the guys, I'm not sure who, but it definitely wasn't me suggested the girls provide some live entertainment as their contribution."

"What do you mean live entertainment?"

"This is difficult, man. We were all sitting around, including the girls, and as I said, this video was on. It had two women doing each other, you know, sex. One of the guys wanted the girls to copy the video and started egging them on. The girls started giggling, whispering to one another. Then, after a while and with more drinks and green. They started carrying on, kissing each other at first, teasing themselves and us. Looking one another up and down and gently rubbing each other. They were copying the video. They just carried on, kissing, longer and longer getting more and more carried away. It was getting real, tongues everything. They started fondling each other more and more. We were all getting excited. I'd never seen them like it before. Not even close. I wondered just how far they would go. The other guys were enjoying the show, egging them on. It got to a point where I wasn't sure if I wanted to watch. I was getting embarrassed and excused myself, saying I was desperate for a piss. I disappeared for about ten minutes, when I got back the girls had gone. As had a couple of the guys. Turns out they'd gone to one of the girl's rooms, which is how things got started. With the rest of us ending up watching the video, again."

"Did this become a regular occurrence?"

"Not really, we had to stop showing the videos when more people started turning up."

"That's not what I meant. Did the girls start getting regular visitors, punters?"

"Oh, some of the guys would go to their rooms. Sometimes the girls would be together, sometimes alone."

"How often would they have visitors?"

"I don't really know. Over the weekend mainly."

"Just the weekend?"

"A few times, they had visitors during the week, but not that often. I don't know what they got, but they paid their way."

"So, what did you watch these videos on, I didn't see anything at the house?"

There was a momentary pause, as he hesitated before saying. "No, we used to have one, it got nicked."

"Tell us about that?"

There was another period of silence while we waited for Jermaine to say something. Eventually, he said.

"We had a break-in."

"When was this?"

"Not sure exactly, four or five weeks ago, maybe more."

"Did you report it?"

"Yeah right, just what we needed, the Babylon coming around."

"I'll take that as a no, so tell me what happened."

"Someone got in through a window, that's all I know."

For the first time, he seemed a little unsure of what to say or do. He wasn't a good liar. I needed to get him to tell the truth.

"Jermaine, you and I both know there is more to it than that. You know we've found blood in the cellar. If that matches our murder victim and you say nothing, what will that look like?"

It didn't take long for him to start talking so quickly, Alan couldn't keep up. He'd gone from being reticent to. I'm getting this off my chest. His version roughly mirrored Kerwin's. He didn't hold back. It was convincing, and in the end both Alan and I felt sure he was telling the truth about both the capture and the imprisonment of Adam Pope. Most importantly for us, was that he was the one who initially mentioned Adam's name. The only thing he'd refused to do was to name those involved. It was all "We did this, and we did that…" He didn't want to be seen blaming others.

They'd kept Pope locked in the cellar for a few of days. Pope told them he'd taken the video recorder, hiding it in a nearby lock-up, to collect later when it was dark, and that when he went back to get it, it had gone. Later, Pope changed his story, saying that he knew who had it. But that he could only get it back if they let him go. At first, they weren't sure what to do, but eventually agreed that keeping him wouldn't get the recorder back, and as this seemed to be their only chance to get it back, they gave him two to deliver. If he didn't, they said they would come after him. When asked how he knew Pope's name, he said it was in his wallet. He didn't know where the wallet was, and we hadn't found it. He was adamant that Pope left the squat alive and under his own steam. His description of Pope's clothing included what sounded like the bloodstained shirt recovered from the hostel.

In a way, it was a strange interview, with him declining a solicitor and yet willing to talk and sign the notes. Almost happy to confess to kidnapping, false imprisonment and assisting in running a brothel. Maybe it was a relief. He didn't seem to care what happened next, and was more than content to go back to his cell. Later he would be charged. His days of freedom over for now.

It was now Lacey's turn and, armed with Brown's confession, we made our way to Hackney Police Station, swapping roles. He too was content to be interviewed without a solicitor, which was almost unheard of. The interview with Lacey was also a little odd. He was okay with admitting his part in the kidnapping, the false imprisonment, even getting weed from a mate. His version of events pretty much identical to Jermaine Brown's. The only thing he wasn't having was anything to do with the pornographic videos and the girls being on the game. Hardly the most serious offences, given everything else. He was adamant that he didn't know anything, and wasn't admitting anything regarding those subjects. Whichever way you looked at their stories, they weren't Pope's killers.

By the time we'd returned to the incident room, those already there were comparing notes. It didn't seem that long before the only pair missing were the bosses. No one could understand what was taking them so long, considering they only had one prisoner. Causing rumours to start, suggesting that the reason they'd taken the prisoner at Arbour Square was so that they could secretly meet with Hampton, reneging on their word. If that was the case, then we would all soon be heading back to general duties. It was quite a while before they did eventually turn up, only adding to the speculation. Where they'd been was now more important than what the prisoners had or hadn't said. As the debriefing came to order, the bosses apologised for keeping everyone waiting, but didn't say why, only fuelling speculation.

We were then made to sit in our pairs, giving a resume of what each prisoner had or hadn't said. It was like being back at school. The boss's rationale was that there was a greater chance of identifying inconsistencies. We already knew there weren't any. Dutifully, we went around the room with everyone paraphrasing their interviews, providing observations on the validity and honesty of those interviewed. All the prisoners had answered questions. Some more reluctantly than others, and not everyone had been as forthcoming as Brown. Particularly when it came to what went on at the parties and how the girls had come to prostitute themselves. Their versions of events were, however, consistent when it came to the capture and false imprisonment of Adam Pope. Given the circumstances, the consensus was that they were telling the truth. They hadn't killed Adam Pope. It probably wasn't what the boss had wanted to hear, given the phone calls he'd made earlier.

Once we'd all had our say, the boss looked to change the subject, creating a clamour. We wanted to know what their prisoner had said, and whether that would provide any clues as to why they were late. The boss fumbled about, looking embarrassed while fiddling with papers. The two of them looking at each other without saying a word. They then just started laughing, with the DI saying, "I told you we wouldn't get away with it."

"Alright, I tried," said the boss.

The rest of us were puzzled until Alan Harrison piped up, saying, "He didn't say anything, did he?"

"No, he refused to answer every question. I've got six pages of unanswered questions. He said diddly squat. Not even no comment," said the DI.

Nobody else was laughing. They must have finished hours ago, and with the rumour that had been started, was there some truth in it. No one dare ask, then the boss said, "Okay, I'm making two executive decisions. From now on I'm not interviewing anyone else on this enquiry. I'm leaving it to you buggers. Someone get some glasses we're having a drink. Time for some doins, let's have a whip."

Ken Reeves, who'd been sitting quietly, having heard the boss mention a whip, was up and across the room like a whippet, volunteering to collect the money.

"I'll do that, Guvnor."

I was always suspicious of people who volunteered the way Reeves had. They had a habit of forgetting to contribute while making sure they got the drinks they wanted. Within a few minutes, a makeshift bar had been created at the end of the office with glasses, coffee mugs and a jug of water appearing. While we were waiting for Ken to return, PKW walked in laden with exhibits.

"Back from the lab, that's quick? We're having a little something. Care to join us, you're more than welcome?" said DI Clarke.

"Not at the moment, these need logging in. I've just got back from Tredegar Place."

"I don't understand, wasn't Ken with you?" asked the DI.

"Haven't seen him all day. I was running a little late, so I rang in and left a message to meet him there. As he didn't show up, I thought he must have been involved with the prisoners."

"Any joy?" I asked, changing the subject.

"I've got a load of fingerprints from various places in the cellar, which appear to be relatively fresh, given how little dust is on them. Some from around the TV and louvre windows. The stains on the cord look like blood and I've taken samples from some splodge patterns I've found near the chair and the pillar."

"Splodge patterns, what are they? I've never heard of those?" asked the DI.

"No, it's a name I've given to blood splatters where there's a minimal amount of lateral movement. More pronounced than passive stains or drips. But not as pronounced as projected impact stains, that you get from a flicking or stabbing movement. In my opinion, it's doubtful whether any of the blood found in the cellar, is there, as a result of any stabbing, decapitation or amputation, whether dead or alive. I've taken the pieces of cord from the pillar together with some I found on the floor. I've also taken a comprehensive set of photographs covering the whole of the squat. With an emphasis on the cellar, the splodges, the television, the dusty space beside the TV, cables and the louvre windows. Hopefully, I didn't forget anything."

"Sounds good to me, as always," said Alan.

"Is Ken around?" asked PKW.

"He is, but he's out at the moment. He volunteered to go and get the booze but shouldn't be long."

When Ken returned, he hadn't done himself any favours. Two bottles of gin and a cheap bottle of scotch, not the boss's favourite. A case of lager and some tonic. It didn't look much and wouldn't last long.

"It's about time we had a proper office meeting," Alan said.

DI Clarke agreed. "Look, the boss won't mind the odd drink in the office, but he doesn't want to make a habit of it or find himself in the shit again. Speaking of which, would you mind stepping into my office, Ken?"

Ken's facial expression quickly changed as they left. I could imagine what was being said. He'd been told to help PKW at the squat. God only knows where he'd been for most of the day. And it wasn't the first time he'd disappeared. With the DI personally witnessing this, Reeves could be history.

Ken Reeves was still being spoken to when a second whip took place. This time Notso was asked to do the honours. With the dry office becoming very damp, any doubts about the boss's allegiances seemed to ease.

Reeves eventually emerged, looking sheepish. Spending time grovelling and apologising to PKW. With the two of them, then disappearing into the exhibits room. To make a start on the exhibits PKW had brought back. Occasionally, they would come into the office for a few minutes, have a quick drink, and then carry on. The odd couple. PKW immaculate, with his blue and white gingham check shirt, cufflinks, polished shoes, burgundy polka-dot bow tie and tanned coloured herringbone waistcoat. Reeves, a ruddy-faced, dishevelled wreck. Who constantly wore creased clothes, typically, grey slacks with an off-white shirt and beer-stained Detective Training School tie, which refused to hang straight. The archetypal bag of shit tied up in the middle with a piece of string. It just showed how forgiving and easy going PKW was. I just hoped Ken Reeves didn't abuse his good nature.

We couldn't figure out how the commander recommended Reeves for exhibits officer, he just didn't fill you with confidence. The fact that he hadn't collected the prisoner's clothing, now possibly a blessing in disguise.

Later that evening, Alan and I were chatting when Sally Bowers came over, plonking herself on my lap, putting her arms around my shoulders. Not sure what was going on, she then kissed me on the cheek and whispered, "I just wanted to thank you for the other day."

"Sorry."

"Helping Alan with John. John Ricketts."

"Oh, that's okay. Don't worry about it. I didn't do that much, and I didn't exactly get a choice, did I?" I said, looking at Alan. "He did all the talking. I was just there for back up. Are you alright now?"

"I'm getting there, I'll be all right, but thank you anyway." Giving me another peck on the cheek, she then turned to Alan, while continuing to talk about Ricketts. From what she said, it sounded as though Ricketts had been bringing work home. Bloody SPG.

Chapter 7

As my head cleared, I realised that apart from a murder which still needed solving, we now had a bucket load of prisoners appearing at magistrate's court charged with kidnapping and false imprisonment. Where the victim was neither the complainant nor witness, which was more than a little unusual. The number of defendants and the serious nature of the offence would normally mean it would be a major enquiry in its own right. For us, it was a hindrance. More paperwork and another distraction, which Hampton might be able to exploit. Just preparing for and dealing with bail applications would be time-consuming. Let alone putting together the various bundles of statements and reports needed for solicitor's department. The only positive was that for the time being, the squad would remain together. We'd ended up charging nine of the fifteen while seeking advice on the others.

With office meetings becoming a daily occurrence, it didn't seem that long before the boss said that he was again being pressurised to cut numbers, despite the progress that had been made. We knew it would happen. It always did, but not normally so early in an investigation when there was so much to do. Apparently, one of the reasons given was that Hampton had been complaining about CID shortages, when the Muppets were the principal reason for the situation, the hypocrite. The boss had been sticking up for us as much as he could, but wanted to be open about what was happening. In short, we needed to make more progress, and soon.

During one of the many meetings, he asked everyone how they thought the investigation was going. Whether anyone had any other ideas and what else could be done? It all sounded a little desperate, and was greeted with total silence. He must have realised how it had come across. The DI certainly did. With no one saying anything, it was difficult to know whether anyone had any ideas or not. I did, but as no one else had said anything, I said nothing.

Given the precautions the boss had taken with the kidnapper's address and that it looked as though Hampton seemed to know what we were doing well before anyone else, there was a distinct possibility that someone was leaking information. Ken Reeves was top of my list. Somehow selected as the exhibits officer, a post he didn't seem capable of. Frequently pissed and constantly disappearing. The only thing that went against that was the way he was behaving, which was more likely to bring him to the attention of others, like the DI. Effectively, increasing the chances of him getting thrown off the case, which made little sense.

The more I thought, the more I kept thinking we really needed to be looking closer to the scene trying to find some of Pope's mates. Then, as the meeting ended and to everyone's amazement, despite everything that had been said about the need for progress, the boss ordered everyone to take the weekend off. It was as if he was working against himself.

The mood immediately changed, with everyone feeling more than a little disillusioned. With less time to make any progress, there didn't seem to be any desire to work. I mooched down to the CID office, wanting to get an idea of just how short-staffed the CID office was. And to find out how many of Hampton's Muppets had returned to normal duties. Peggy, the admin manageress, was on her own. A short, red-headed, bustling woman who didn't suffer fools gladly.

"Pegs, where is everyone?" I asked.

"What do you mean, everyone? This is it. The home beat officers are currently taking most of the major crimes. Burglaries, dippings, anything from the market."

"Really, what about…" I was about to say The Muppets, but stopped myself just in time, changing to, "the message book, Where's that? I need to check the messages."

"It's over by the duty sheets, where it normally is. Have you forgotten?" she said, pointing to a desk on the far side of the office.

I slowly scanned the message book while flicking through the past four days of the duty state. None of The Muppets were back. They were all still shown as being assigned to the longest running domestic murder the world had ever seen. After a brief social chat with Peggy, I headed back to the office to go over the statements from the hostel one more time. In particular, I wanted to pull together all the information relating to those who'd called for Pope. By the time I got back, Anne was on her own. The only other thing I noticed was the smell of the DI's aftershave. Before I could say anything, Anne said, "They've all gone for a drink." Pointing to one of the Nobo boards. "I'll be going too, just as soon as I've finished this interview."

"Who's they?"

"Nearly everyone I think." Anne started to list those she knew had gone, while pointing to a Nobo board where the words 'Annexe – All welcome' were written.

I sat down and made a start sifting through a bundle of typed statements. It didn't take long. It looked as though five people had possibly called for Pope or been seen hanging around the playground when someone else had. The descriptions weren't great. Three of them seemed to be of a similar height to Pope. The other two slightly taller. All had been described as wearing the same sort of clothing: jeans, T-shirts, hoodies and trainers. All mid to late teens. A couple, possibly older. All slim build and of Caribbean descent. There were no references to any facial hair or other distinguishing features. And with the vast majority of young men in London, possibly the whole of the UK, owning and wearing similar clothing. It wasn't great.

Just as I was finishing, Notso rang from one of the few telephone boxes in the area that hadn't been vandalised. He'd offered to finish the last of the house-to-house enquiries before going for a drink. He couldn't make out the number of one of the flats. Notso was the DC attached to the crime squad. His nickname had come about because of his surname, Bright. Notso Bright. Which to be fair wasn't true. While going through the lists, trying to work out the number he needed, he mentioned seeing a group of lads ambling along Cable Street near the scene. Having walked past Cranford Cottages, they'd turned and then walked back, looking down the street, which he thought odd. But by the time he got downstairs, they'd gone. His description, typical teenagers. Having found the number he was looking for, I wished him luck.

Then turning to Anne, I said that I would give the Annexe a miss, as I had a couple of personal errands to run. In truth, I wanted to have another look around the streets close to the waste ground. But I didn't want to be seen as not being a team player. While going through the list for Notso, I'd noticed that a lot of properties had been marked up as either unoccupied or derelict, including all the properties in Bere Street and Cranford Cottages. Cul-de-sacs which backed onto the waste ground.

By the time I parked up in Heckford Street, the early evening dusk had given way to near darkness. The dingy street desolate. Lit by a solitary lamppost which had somehow survived the constant target practice of kids with their air pistols and catapults. According to the collator's records, until recently, the cul-de-sacs had been a favoured spot for prostitutes plying their trade. To prevent this, the developers had strategically placed large boulders across the road. Walking into Cranford Cottages was as if I'd stepped back in time. Claustrophobic and eerie. Hemmed in by an old Victorian warehouse on one side and a high brick wall at the end. With damp cobblestones underfoot.

High up the wall of the warehouse, I could just make out a wooden stump protruding over what had once been an entrance to an upper floor. Now bricked up. What was left from a block and tackle used in times gone by when loading and unloading cargo emanating from sailing ships docked nearby. The tide would have dictated when goods moved to and from the warehouse. With horse-drawn wagons travelling along the cobblestoned streets at all times of day or night, carrying their cargo, the short distance. Struggling to turn in the confined space. It must have been oppressive. Now, the silence and emptiness added to the atmosphere. Eerie, even scary. All that was needed was a little fog, and Jack the Ripper could have easily been lurking in the shadows.

The other thing I'd forgotten was just how big some of the rats were: the size of a small cat. In the darkness and with the river so close, quite a few had already ventured on to the streets to scavenge. Their shadows making them look even bigger.

There were no doors to the front of the properties, making it difficult to determine exactly how many there were. Just boarded windows and the occasional pitch-black alcove or sideway, which I assumed led to the entrances. As I ventured to the end of the cul-de-sac, the sound of my footsteps seemed exaggerated, echoing in the confined space. Having bravely reached the end, I turned to make my way back and having taken just a couple of steps; I noticed a glimmer of light coming from a tiny hole in one of the boards covering a window. Stopping me dead in my tracks. Afraid to move, thinking I would be heard. Having gathered my thoughts, I went through the options; some of which were daft and plainly stupid. Bottling it, I crept away. Before we did anything, we needed to know more. We'd look pretty stupid turning the place over and finding it full of vagrants. On the far side of the waste ground was another disused warehouse. The upper floors of which looked as though it would make an ideal observation point. Assuming we could trace the owner and get permission to use it.

Looking at all the bleary eyes, it must have been a good night. So much so, the DI was still wearing yesterday's garb. Given all the sore heads, it was unlikely that I would be missed for a while, so I made myself scarce. Wanting to make a few calls without being overheard, I ended up in the witness interview room on the CID floor. It didn't take long to find the owner of the warehouse overlooking Cranford Cottages or to get their permission to use the property. I could even pick the keys up later that day. Armed with the information and before heads cleared, it seemed to be a good time to let Alan and the DI in on what I'd found.

Having mentioned the possibility of a leak as the main reason for not saying anything earlier, I was forgiven for not joining them in the pub. The new information seemed to galvanise the DI, who immediately looked to call in a few favours. Getting hold of some surveillance equipment, including a brand-new camera capable of automatically switching between day and night vision, fitted with a humongous 1600mm telephoto lens. Apparently, the lens cost sixteen grand alone. It was the only one the Met. had. He'd even managed to get an observation van from counterterrorism. An old post office van bought at auction and then modified. The alterations involved fitting a small control panel in the back of the van with a dead switch to stop the engine from starting. Although, I wasn't sure who would want to steal such a worn-out, dilapidated-looking piece of junk. The panel had switches to operate the windscreen wipers, screen washer and heater. If the heater was used, two things happened. It made a lot of noise, drawing attention to a supposedly empty van, while flattening the battery. A previous user had scratched the words "No No" under the switch. Presumably having found out the hard way.

Some surveillance operations you knew were a complete waste of time before they started. Often leading games being played on passers-by. Turning the washer jets outwards before arriving at the location, so you could squirt pedestrians as they passed, was always popular. If you'd parked on a yellow line, getting the windscreen wipers to work just as a traffic warden was about to issue a parking ticket was another. Surprised wardens would often look around, thinking they were being filmed for a TV show, like Candid Camera. Keeping quiet in the back of the van became the biggest problem. Other modifications included mirrored windows being installed in the rear doors, with numerous spy holes in a line along the sides of the van. To the average pedestrian they looked like large rivets. To a professional criminal, they were a complete show out. Some vans had a dedicated hole in the floor for peeing. I'd never come across one that had actually worked. They were always blocked, with milk bottles being used as a substitute. Number twos a complete no no. If you were on a long observation or mob-handed, the combination of smoke and ammonia could be overwhelming, making your eyes sting like crazy.

By mid-afternoon, the team was in place and for once radio communications were working. At the boss's request Alan and I had stayed in the office monitoring the radio, with him sitting in his office. We knew those in the warehouse had good visibility and with it being a cul-de-sac, the observation van could be parked a reasonable distance away. Spotters could then give the off, and direction of travel of anyone leaving. Those in the van would be able to identify anyone entering the street. Which would allow for the walkers to be parked up well out of sight, while still allowing them to get into position when needed.

Less than an hour had gone by when we heard radio chatter, movement. A young man who potentially looked as if could be one of those seen by Notso had emerged into Cable Street, coming from the direction of the properties. Who looked to be heading towards the city. But before the walkers had picked him up, he'd turned, heading back to the properties. No one had seen which entrance he'd used. It was another hour before there was more activity, this time two males of similar description entering the cul-de-sac. Those in the van had better descriptions but hadn't been able to get snaps, creating a lot of unnecessary chatter. With the boss hearing the noise, he came in for an update. He'd heard enough and wasn't prepared to wait any longer. He wanted the place hit with everyone arrested. Initially, those in the warehouse sounded reluctant, but with the boss re-affirming, his order had little choice.

Ten minutes later, it was all over.

The address was secured and three people roughly fitting our descriptions detained. PKW was at the scene of another murder and unable to attend. The search and seizure of evidence was now down to Ken Reeves and a local SOCO. Alan and I wanted to go, but the boss wouldn't allow it. Insisting we let the others get on with that, while we got ready to do the interviews.

All we could do was wait for them to be brought back to the station. When they arrived, we were told they hadn't said a thing. They hadn't given their names, complained, asked for a solicitor, asked why they were being arrested, nothing. The names we had were from correspondence in their possession.

Benjamin Ramadi aged twenty, Devon Parkes aged nineteen, and his brother Donovan, seventeen. CRO checks showed that both Ramadi and Devon Parkes had juvenile and adult convictions for various assaults, robbery, theft and burglary. Donovan Parkes didn't seem to have a record. From the limited amount of information available on the PNC, it wasn't possible to say whether any of offences had been committed together. One item worthy of note was that most of the station references showed the offences to be committed on "K" district. East Ham, West Ham and Barking. Those making the arrests thought the demeanour of those arrested suggested they were unlikely to talk, no matter how serious things were. The only thing Ramadi and Devon Parkes had done was to spit on the ground, through gaps in the middle of their teeth – a cultural sign of disdain.

With the boss's change of plan, Alan and I were likely to be the only ones doing interviews. Everyone else would help where they could. Making calls, checking information, whatever it took – assuming of course, those arrested said something. Alan asked the boss why he'd change his mind on interviewing. He wanted continuity. Having lots of officers interviewing hadn't been one of his better ideas. It was okay with frauds, where normally, there were lots of documents which would help prove or disprove a case, but not murders. Picking up and passing on any inferences drawn from body language was also difficult. On top of which, he'd decided that he didn't want prisoners going to other stations, especially Arbour Square. He didn't want the prisoners out of our control or anywhere near Hampton or The Muppets. Prisoners would now have to be housed at Leman Street, where we could post someone in the cell corridor, if needed.

Alan and I prepared for the interviews. Checking information, deciding on the order and approach we would initially adopt. We were still working things out when Ken Reeves and the SOCO walked in. Almost in unison, everyone said.

"That didn't take long?"

"It's such a tiny place, there's hardly anything there," said Reeves.

"Anything useful?"

"Upstairs there were some plastic bags with clothes in. Some could be bloodstained. Oh yes, and downstairs there were some plastic bags and in one of the other rooms, there were some plastic bags. Oh, did I forget to mention we found some plastic bags?"

Ask a sensible question, get a stupid answer – aggravating bugger. Ignoring Reeves, we spoke to the SOCO.

"Where were the bloodstained clothes?"

"Upstairs in one of the bedrooms."

"How many bedrooms?"

"Two."

"Both occupied?"

"Not sure. They both had sleeping bags. One was crumpled up, and the other laid out. If that means anything? There were clothes in both rooms, so I suppose so."

"What about the plastic bags?"

"Everywhere, clear plastic bags, shopping bags, refuse bags, they were all over the place."

"Any other blood?"

"Not that I saw."

"What about power?"

"Someone's bypassed the meter. There are some lights, but it's not great. As you know, all the windows are boarded, so there's no natural light, it's pretty dark." The SOCO went on to say that he hadn't found as many fingerprints as he would have anticipated, but what he had found, he thought, were fairly recent.

"Photos?"

"I've photographed everything DC Reeves asked me to. We lifted some prints and bagged up the clothes. That's all there was, really. Uniform are guarding the place."

"Can we get them to watch from the OP?" I asked.

"What for?" said Reeves.

"So, we can see if anyone else goes there. Leaving someone outside's a bit of a show out."

Donovan Parkes was the first to be interviewed. It would be a whole new experience for him and as such, he was the one most likely to talk. The boss having decided we would do the interviews, then gave us a lecture on doing everything by the book. No verbals or threats of violence would be tolerated. He still didn't get that the people and the environment we were dealing with was completely different to anything he'd previously encountered. This was the East End, where nobody blabbed. Well, hardly anyone, and if they did, they would say they'd been forced to; with the police being responsible for some form of coercion, blackmail or physical beating, irrespective of whether they had or not. I was frequently reminded of one of my early uniform arrests, where along with others I'd been called to an almighty punch up outside a pub. And having arrested and cautioned one of the assailants, his victim said,

"When they interview you, don't say anything, don't even say ouch when they hit you."

The criminal code was stronger in the East End than anywhere else I'd ever worked. If it involved any form of thievery, whether friend or foe, you didn't dob on them, well not to the old bill. And neither did the boss get that complaints against police were like confetti, they just went with the territory. There was a saying that if you hadn't had a complaint, you hadn't been working. When it came to trial. If a prisoner had made any form of admission, denial was the only way of saving face. You could almost tell what the thrust of the defence was likely to be by the firm of solicitors representing the defendant. Some specialised in finding loopholes in procedures as opposed to contesting the evidence, with fishing exercises becoming commonplace. Poring over station and exhibit records looking for the slightest anomaly, a prelude of what was to come. Others were frequently accusatorial; making allegations that the police had fitted up their client.

The trial process for the more serious cases was one big game, played out in three rounds. Round one. Magistrate's court, mostly just sparring. Round two. Committal proceedings. Depending on the offence and potential vulnerability of witnesses, the defence might try taking out some of the prosecution pieces having what was known as an old-style committal. Here, the witnesses they chose would have to attend, give oral evidence, and be cross-examined. Much like a full trial, doubling the ordeal. Proving there was a case to answer. Civilian witnesses were particularly vulnerable, and unfortunately, rape and sexual assault victims' prime targets for some of the more unscrupulous firms. Round three. Crown court, the final. Here, whoever played their cards best won. It wasn't just about the evidence; it was the way it was presented.

On the way down to get Donovan Parkes, Alan got into a right strop, moaning about the boss.

"What the fuck's going on with him, does he think we've never done this sort of thing? Why the fuck did he pick us?

We're not exactly probationers. And he got a blank with his fucking kidnapper. And what fucking planet is Ken Reeves on? Has he got a fucking screw loose? Or is he a complete wanker? He's always fucking pissed, he'll fucking cock this job up if he carries on the way he's going."

I didn't dare say anything and just listened, nodding in the right places as he carried on. Not wanting to set him off again.

The trend of not wanting a solicitor continued with 'Parkes the younger.' Given this was a whole new experience for him, it seemed worthwhile having a punt and simply asking him how he knew Adam Pope and then gauging his reaction. If he didn't know him, he was likely to say so and having gone through the procedures, I said, "Can you remember where you first met Adam Pope?"

"I think it was at the youth club."

He knew Adam Pope. At least that was a start.

"Did you ever go to the hostel he was living in?"

"Up near Mile End, a couple of times, yeah."

"When did you last see him?"

"Long times."

"How long?"

"Can't remember."

"Roughly?"

"I changed me mind, I'm not saying nothing else."

"Can you remember where you last saw him?"

No reply

"Was it at Cranford Cottages?"

No reply

I asked a couple more questions which weren't answered. Having finished, I asked him to sign the notes to say they were an accurate reflection of the interview – he refused. Maybe he wasn't going to be such a pushover, but at least he knew Adam Pope and had called for him. It was a start. The interviews with Ramadi and Devon Parkes were complete stonewalls. They didn't say a word the whole time, not even to acknowledge their name or request a solicitor.

It was Friday evening, and we could detain the three of them until Monday afternoon without too many questions being asked, and that was exactly what the boss did.

There were lots of things to be getting on with while they were still in custody, including getting PKW over to Cranford Cottages, checking nothing had been missed. The clothes the prisoners were wearing needed to be seized and, if possible, hair samples taken. These could then be compared with any fibres or hairs found during the investigation. The clothes in the bags themselves needed to be examined and everything photographed. Once that had been done, they could be shown to witnesses, particularly those at the hostel. We also needed to find out as much as we could about the prisoners. The boss's idea of a day off over the weekend looking increasingly unlikely.

It turned out that PKW's services were being used on two other murders and it was unlikely he would be able to get over until the middle of the next week. If we had nothing to charge the three of them with come Monday, they would have to be released.

Friday night and with the weekend ahead. We needed to find the owners of Cranford Cottages, confirming our prisoners were squatters. Assuming they were, we then needed to get control of the property. No one was answering calls. Not the rates office or anyone who could help at the local council. We even tried Land Registry with no joy – everyone had gone for the weekend. With no call-out, we would have to wait.

Since his return from the Cottages, Ken Reeves had spent most of his time in the exhibits room. Nobody really knew what he was doing. When he did eventually grace us with his presence, I said, "Any luck with the clothes?"

"Nope," he said, curtly.

"Any ideas who they belong to? Any names on them? Do you think they belong to the same person?"

"How would I know? I'm not a tailor."

"Well, are they all the same size? The same as any of the prisoners' clothes?"

"Dunno."

"For Christ's sake, Ken. What's up with you?" said Alan.

"What do you mean?"

"Are you pissed? You seem to have done fuck all. Where are the clothes?"

"They're all bagged up. Ready for the lab, why?"

"Because we need to know who they belong to. That's why. Whether they're Pope's or one of the prisoners. That's why? Stop fucking about and go and get them."

He returned with three sealed bags: brown paper sacks with a clear plastic gusset on one side. The gusset was to give you an idea of what the contents looked like. For some reason, Ken had double-bagged the exhibits, making it impossible to see anything. We just looked at each other in disbelief. It definitely wasn't the sort of thing an experienced exhibits officer would do. Unless, of course, he was doing it deliberately? As he hadn't seized the prisoner's clothing, we had nothing to compare them with. Here was a career detective, with over twenty years' service, who'd been recommended by the commander to be the exhibits officer who should know better. It was getting to the two of us, with Alan saying, "Ken, I'm not sure what's going on. You know what needs to be done, but you seem to be incapable of doing it. Get somebody to go down to the cells with you and examine all the prisoners' clothing. Get their sizes and bloody well make sure you know which size relates to which prisoner. Got that?"

"Yeah, yeah." It sounded as though he didn't care.

"After that. I want the clothes re-bagged so they can be seen, and then go with Sally to the hostel and see if any of the residents recognise the clothes. Have you got that? Or do I have to spell that out too?"

He left without saying a word. While he was gone, we took a look at the exhibit books for any obvious mistakes. It wasn't something I was really comfortable with, but was now a necessity. Skimming through the books, there were a number of errors. Which to be fair, Ken had spotted and properly corrected by putting a single line through the mistake, which he'd initialled. The bags he'd just brought back were yet to be entered. We then realised that what looked like the plastic bags the clothes had originally been in were now sitting in the rubbish bin, having not been exhibited. Fishing them out, we took them back into the main office. Notso felt sure they were the bags from the Cottages.

Alan just exploded. His voice so loud everyone on the floor must have heard him. We needed to keep a much closer eye on Ken. Which again raised questions, whether he was doing it deliberately, was incompetent or just plain stupid? As none of us had ever worked with him before, we didn't know. The obvious thing was to change the exhibits officer. However, without knowing more, it wasn't the sort of thing the boss was likely to do.

The only good thing was that as no entries had been made regarding the exhibits, we could get them re-bagged and documented without any fuss. When Ken returned, he went straight into the exhibits room, staying there for quite a while. It seemed to take him an age to realise that his exhibit books, the exhibits to be re-bagged and the plastic bags from the bin weren't there. When he did eventually make it into the main office, he just said.

"Sorry guys, I messed up – won't happen again." Ken hadn't noticed DI Clarke at the other end of the room.

"It's not the first time, is it? Any more lapses, and you won't make your pension. Take this a written warning," said the DI, sounding as though he meant it.

"Yes, Guv" was all Ken could say.

We then collectively re-bagged and documented the exhibits. As everything was bone dry, we could use clear plastic bags. Making it easier to see the whole exhibit. Ken and Sally then made their way to the hostel, taking the exhibits with them.

While we were waiting, I went to see if anything had been said between the prisoners – not a word. Donovan Parkes was sitting in his cell, gazing at a blank wall. Ramadi and Devon Parkes were lying on their beds, facing the wall. Making it impossible to tell whether they were awake or not – forcing you to enter the cell if you wanted to get their attention. They'd played before.

I also took the opportunity to see whether I could get a look at Ken Reeves' service record. There were two copies, one kept in central records; the other updated and kept by the local admin of wherever the officer was serving, following them from posting to posting. Having made an excuse to check my record, I looked for Ken's. Normally, when an officer transferred, local admin would create a temporary entry which was used until the travelling copy arrived. I couldn't find either and with Ken being on district the time he had; all I could think of was that his record had been removed.

His trip to the hostel had been a bit of a non-starter. With everyone apart from Ms Saltmarsh being out, who, according to Sally, when pushed, thought the blue hoodie might be Pope's? It was hardly convincing.

Despite having prisoners in the cells and buckets of work to do, the boss was sticking to his promise. We were having the weekend off; the prisoners would wait until Monday.

Chapter 8

Somehow, I'd managed to go most of the weekend without thinking too much about the case and felt quite refreshed arriving for work. It was a feeling that didn't last long. We'd just seven hours before the duty officer would be kicking off, and the prospect of the prisoners being released without charge loomed large. To justify their detention, they would have to be re-interviewed as a minimum.

It wasn't long after that Alan and Sally arrived, they'd obviously had an enjoyable weekend together and couldn't take their eyes off each other. I just hoped it didn't end in tears. And if it did, it wasn't while the investigation was going on.

Kerwin was willing to wait for Sally at the hostel so she could look at the clothes. Establishing they belonged to Pope before interviewing the prisoners would be useful. It was sod's law that when Sally went to get the clothes, the exhibits room was locked and with no keys we had to wait for Ken. But according to his wife, he'd been at work all weekend, having rung home Saturday morning saying there'd been a significant development on the enquiry he was working on, and that it was unlikely he would be home until either later that day or possibly tomorrow. Alan hadn't said he was part of the same team. Thanking her for the information, saying he would try to get hold of him at the station.

Over the weekend, the CRO files for Ramadi and Devon Parkes had arrived. Ramadi had been in prison until six months ago. Sentenced to three years' imprisonment for robbery and grievous bodily harm; a dipping gone wrong. While waiting at a bus stop, he'd seen an elderly lady with her purse in her handbag and had made a grab for it. The old biddy put up a fight, which ended up with her getting stabbed in the arm. Others at the bus stop, having seen what was going on, overpowered Ramadi. Holding him until the police arrived. He pleaded not guilty and had an old-style committal. Making the old lady and all the witnesses give evidence twice. The ploy hadn't worked. He'd ended up serving the full term with no remission. As a juvenile, he'd a string of convictions for burglary and possessing offensive weapons. Mainly knives. Apart from the dipping in Barking, the earlier offences had all taken place in and around Newham. Not once had he admitted or pleaded guilty to anything. Which meant that as a juvenile he'd never been cautioned. From the records there was no evidence of Ramadi and Parkes having been previously arrested together.

As a juvenile, Devon Parkes had been cautioned for an assault at school, resulting in his expulsion. There were two separate convictions for burglary. Where he'd been sentenced to a forty-eight-hour community service order and three months youth custody, suspended for two years. He also had an adult conviction for another burglary, where he'd been sentenced to one hundred-fifty-hours community service. When we called social services to get information about the community service, the jobsworth insisted we get a court order. Despite the urgency and serious nature of the offence, he wouldn't budge. I wondered just how long he would be able to dine out on this moment of power.

Enquiries with the rates office showed Cranford Cottages to be owned by a property development company associated with the newly formed London Docklands Development Corporation. A quango set up by the government to regenerate chunks of Docklands in the East End, including Cranford Cottages, the waste ground and swathes of disused mills and empty warehouses along the wharves by the riverbank. Their telephone number went straight to answerphone. As their offices were close to Limehouse Police Station, we got an officer from there to get the information we needed. As expected, they were squatting.

It was getting close to eleven before DI Clarke and Julia Meadows breezed in, hand in hand, not trying to hide their newfound relationship.

"Good weekend?" the DI said enthusiastically, looking around and then realising there weren't that many there.

"By the way, the boss won't be in, he's got some meeting at the big house. He wants picking up from his home in the morning. And before anyone asks, he wouldn't or couldn't say what the meeting was about. So, don't ask."

The DI wanted an update and, having briefly appraised him of where we were, Alan mentioned the need to get hold of Ken and the conversation with his wife. The DI thought he'd seen Ken's car outside. Notso went to look. It was there, and the engine was cold. Where the hell was he? We couldn't wait any longer. Alan then tried exhibit's room, where we could hear him banging at the door. Then calling out to say he could see a key on the inside of the lock. Joining him, we all started knocking, calling Ken's name louder and louder. Eventually we heard the key turn and the door open.

Reeves hadn't said anything or acknowledged our calls. "Sorry" was it. Standing in the doorway, he looked forlorn. The room reeked of body odour, takeaways, and booze. He'd been on a bender since Friday. Still wearing the same clothes. It stank. He was a bloody wreck.

"Ken, what's got into you, what a fucking state to get into," Alan said. "You've got to get yourself together, man. You need to get out for a while, get your head together. I want you to go with Sally to see Kerwin. To see if she can identify any of the clothes, got that?" Reeves nodded. "But first, you need to get cleaned up. Then when you get back, you can tidy this lot up."

Here we were looking at a sad old man whose life, for whatever reason, was falling apart. He needed help. We'd seen him pissed. Had heard stories of him sleeping on his desk. But nothing like this – three days drinking, alone. The DI had already threatened to discipline him. His job was on the line, and he seemed incapable of helping himself. Strangely, after everything he'd said and done, we found ourselves feeling sorry for him. Alan broke into Reeves' locker and found some old clothes he'd obviously forgotten about that he could wear once cleaned up. While that was happening, we made sure Sally knew to contact us as soon as Kerwin had looked at the clothes, and before making any statement. We needed to know whether she recognised them before any interviews started.

Amongst the squalor in the exhibits room. Covered in dried stains from the bottoms of wet glasses or bottles were the results of the fingerprint analysis from Cranford Cottages. Six sets of prints had been found. Ramadi and Devon Parkes were two. Another belonged to someone called Gabriel Baptiste, a name we didn't know. According to the PNC, he was nineteen with a conviction for criminal damage. His last known address, a flat near Watney Market, not that far from the scene. Assuming Donovan Parkes was another left two. We thought and hoped that one set would belong to Adam Pope. But as Ken had forgotten to request the prints from the hostel be compared with those from Cranford Cottages, we didn't know for certain. If that were the case, it left one set unaccounted for and unknown to police.

Sally Bowers called to say that both Claire Laker and Kerwin were fairly sure the hoodie belonged to Pope. Going on to say that since the body's discovery, no one had called for Adam.

The photographs of Cranford Cottages had also turned up. We decide to have a quick look before starting the interviews. The floor plan was of a small mid-terrace property. The area downstairs was divided into a kitchen and living space. Entry to the property was through a door in the kitchen area, next to which was a dustbin, the type you normally found outside. A roll of black refuse sacks and string sat on top. A countertop with a disconnected sink ran along the back wall. Covered with unwashed pots, pans, plates and the odd mug. Mixed in with this, a single camping gas stove and empty tins of baked beans, spam and sausages. Under the countertop, the framework for a couple of kitchen units, with no doors. Empty spaces existed where an oven and refrigerator would normally be. Lastly, a small drop-leaf table could be seen pushed up against a wall. The electricity meter had been bypassed. In the living space was a well-used two-seater sofa and two non-matching kitchen chairs. A battery-operated radio on the windowsill. Old newspapers and magazines were scattered on the floor. In one corner, more discarded empty tins of food. A staircase with a cupboard underneath led upstairs to two small bedrooms and a tiny bathroom. One of the bedrooms looked as though it contained mostly junk. Papers and magazines again strewn around, with a crumpled sleeping bag on the floor. This, we were told, was the room the bags of clothing had been found in. Unfortunately, and for some inexplicable reason, the bags and their contents had been removed prior to photographs being taken. The other bedroom had an unrolled sleeping bag, also on the floor, lying on top of more newspapers and magazines, which we assumed were being used as bedding. Reducing the draft coming through the floorboards while acting as a very thin mattress. Another pocket radio, similar to the one downstairs on the windowsill. There were no photographs of the bathroom or outside.

The time had come to have another go at interviewing. Again, we started with Donovan Parkes. If nothing was forthcoming, we would be forced into releasing them. We decided not to mention the name Gabriel Baptiste. While interviewing, the DI was going to sort out better security for the property. Donovan Parkes again declined a solicitor; a trait I was becoming more concerned with. The more it happened, the more I thought we were missing something, but didn't know what. Betting on a quick interview, Alan volunteered to write.

"On Friday, we started to talk about a friend of yours, Adam Pope. I would now like to carry on from where we left off. Is that okay?"

"Yeah, got it,"

"Tell me how you became friends?"

"We met at St George's, the youth club."

I was surprised he'd answered the question and wondered where it would lead.

"Where's that?"

"This end of Cable Street."

"When was this, roughly?"

"Not sure. I think it might have been Guy Fawkes Night. He knew one of the people I went with, and we ended up hanging."

"What were their names?"

"No names. If I tell you, they'll know I talked."

"Who will?"

"My brother and Ramadi, they told me not to say anything."

"So, how long have you been staying at the Cottages?"

"I don't live there."

"Do you sleep there?"

"Sometimes."

"Where do you sleep when you do?"

"Upstairs."

"In which room?"

"The one with all the shit in."

"They've all got stuff in."

"The one with the most in. Ramadi normally sleeps in the other room."

"Ramadi, just Ramadi?"

"Yes, just Ramadi."

"Do you use the sleeping bag?"

"No, on the floor, I sleep on the floor."

"What with no blankets, sleeping bag or pillow?"

"I've got a towel, and I wrap some of me spare clothes in it for a pillow. The other sleeping bag's Devon's. I'm not allowed to use it."

"Where does he sleep?"

"On the sofa thing."

"I've seen some plastic bags with clothes in. Are they yours?"

"One's mine, the others Adam's. His is the one with the hoodie, he left it when he stayed."

"In the same room as you?"

"Yes."

"How many times has Adam slept there?"

"Not many, two or three, maybe."

"And when was the last time?"

"I don't know. I said, I don't stay there all the time. He might have stayed when I didn't."

"When were you last there, together?"

"Three or four weeks, I suppose."

"Where else do you live?"

"Sometimes, I stay with different friends. I'm not saying who."

"You said Adam left a hoodie, did he leave anything else?"

"Dunno."

"Did he put the hoodie in that bag?"

"No, I did."

"Why did you do that?"

"I borrowed it and put it back."

"Do you wear his clothes often?"

"No, only the hoodie. I've worn it a couple of times, I suppose. I put it back, so?"

"Why did he leave it?"

"I think he just forgot it one time."

"How many times have you worn it?"

"A couple, I just told you."

"Why?"

"I was cold man, and I don't have anything else."

"Did he know, did he mind?"

"He was cool."

"Do you wear any other hoodies?"

"No, what's with the hoodies?"

"It wasn't just the hoodie. Did he leave anything else?"

"I can't remember."

"You've remembered everything else. Okay, let's change the subject and try something different. Having become friends, what sort of things did you and Adam talk about?"

"We didn't talk much, just hung around together, now and then."

"You must have talked about something, girls, maybe?"

"Girls, sometimes."

"What girls?"

"I've already said, I'm not naming nobody."

"Okay, sorry, so were these girls you wanted to go with?"

"Maybe."

"Like Cathy Kerwin?"

"Who?"

"Cathy Kerwin?"

"Never heard of her."

"So, how did he come to start sleeping over?"

"We were out late one night, and he said he wouldn't be able to get back in. So, we let him stay."

"Who's we?"

No reply

"Did you ever call for him at the hostel?"

"Sometimes, we would go."

"Who's we?"

No reply

"What was his room like?"

"Don't know, never been inside. Every time I went there I waited outside, because of 'miss bossy boots', the one in charge, I didn't like her much."

"I'm going to call it a day for now and ask you to go back to the cell, while I arrange to get this hoodie. Is that okay?"

"Do I have a choice?"

"Not really."

"Then, okay."

He then refused to sign the notes, becoming awkward. Saying he'd just made a lot of what he'd said up, saying what he thought we wanted to hear. As time was short, I decided to try a different tack. Going against conventional interviewing techniques, I said, "Donovan, we know the blood on the clothes is Adam's. We also know that he was killed at the Cottages and then burnt on the ground opposite. This is your one chance to give your side of the story."

He just stared, looking shocked, dumbfounded, uncoordinated. There was a disconnect, not knowing what to do, say, or where to look. His eyes glazed over, and he began to shake. It was as if we'd hit the bull's eye. His reaction said it all. He knew, and we weren't that far from the truth. Alan hadn't missed the reaction either. We just watched and waited, hoping he would say something. He just sat there, transfixed. He didn't move or say a word, just stared straight through us. We sat there in complete silence for what seemed an eternity. In the end I had no alternative other than to break the silence, saying, "Come on, why don't you just tell us what really happened?"

I wasn't sure whether it was my voice or the question which triggered a change. Almost in an instant, he'd gone from being a fairly lucid, coherent individual, through silence to a gibbering wreck, shaking erratically and seemingly unable to speak. When he did eventually look as though he was going to speak, nothing came out. Whether he'd actually committed the murder was hard to say. But from that moment. We all knew he knew about the murder. Getting him to say anything was a different matter. It took several minutes for him to regain any kind of composure. With the shaking slowing, he began to look around the room. I tried a couple more questions. He'd stopped talking. Unsure of himself or what to do or say. Having returned him to his cell and just before leaving him, I said, "What would your brother or Ramadi make of it. If I told them, you'd told us about

Adam? Repeating some of what I've just said as proof. What would they make of it?"

In an instant the shaking returned; he was scared, very scared. It was something he hadn't thought of. He knew what they would do. Brother or not, they would kill him. Finally, before closing the cell door, I reminded him of the alternatives, then for a while, I waited at the end of the cell corridor to see if any of them spoke – not a peep. When I went back to his cell to close the wicket gate, he looked dejected, as if he might cry. Then, on seeing me, he defiantly turned his back to hide his emotion.

While we'd been interviewing, DI Clarke had organised the changing of locks. With the owners promising to provide additional security to prevent further access to the cottage.

Ramadi and Devon Parkes again said absolutely nothing. And despite Donovan Parkes' reactions, the DI decided not to hold them any longer. They would be released on police bail, to return in a month's time. We told them there were conditions associated with their release. One of which was not to go to Cranford Cottages. It was a white lie. We couldn't impose conditions, but it was worth a try. They were also told the locks had been changed, and if they entered the property, they would be arrested and charged with burglary, under section 9 (1) (a) of the Theft Act and not (b), which was the norm.

Having been told they were being released, Ramadi and Devon Parkes became really cocky, strutting around the charge room, waiting for their property to be returned. Bragging to each other, showing off. It was as if they owned the station, the antagonistic bastards. The station officer didn't bother with trying to control them, he just wanted rid.

Once their property had been restored, Alan escorted Ramadi and Devon Parkes through to the front of the station. I deliberately held Donovan back, and by the time we'd reached the door to the public area, his brother and Ramadi were already outside. Being cantankerous, I let Donovan take a few steps across the foyer before calling him back. Slowly, he turned and trudged back, head bowed. As he got closer, Ramadi and his brother re-entered the station. The timing couldn't have been better. As Donovan reached me, I bent forward a little and whispered,

"Now, where would you have got to, if I hadn't called you back?"

Then, smiling pleasantly, I gently patted him on the shoulder while steering him back towards his brother, saying more loudly, "Thanks for that, much appreciated."

With his nerves getting the better of him, it was as if he'd crapped himself. He didn't know where to look or where to go. Prompting his brother to suddenly bark, "What are you doing, man? Come on, let's go. We've wasted enough time with these pigs."

Continuing to smile, I waved goodbye as Donovan trudged over to join his brother. I had no doubt they were responsible for Adam's death. Proving it was going to be the problem.

Later, during the obligatory office meeting, the boss told us he'd been summoned to a meeting with 'the gods', wanting an update. After which, he was initially asked to cut the team. Having refused, he'd then been ordered to. He had until the end of the week to decide who would stay and who would go. It was his impression that the decision had already been made and 'the meeting' was just to go through the motions. He'd been told that, if needed, the team would be given access to additional resources as and when required. With cover being provided by officers currently working out of Arbour Square – The Muppets. What a load of bollocks. It was pure lip service. At the end of the meeting the office quickly emptied, with everyone feeling so deflated, having got where we were. It was as if we'd been kicked in the stomach. I found myself aimlessly meandering around, ending up in the CID office, where the duty state told the same story. None of The Muppets had returned to general duties. It made little sense and had to be bent. While there, I noticed a sheet of paper tucked into the corner of the blotter on my desk. A handwritten message addressed to me, written on an old memo pad. The message hadn't made it into the official message book or upstairs to the incident room, it read.

DS Lomax – Meet usual 1 p.m. Mow too.

The message hadn't been signed or dated, and none of those in the CID office knew anything about it. It could have been there for days. It was from one of my informants. I decided to give Mo's number a call and, wanting a little privacy, went into the interview room, leaving the door slightly ajar, so that I could see anyone approaching.

While I was waiting for the call to be connected, I heard Ken Reeves' voice. I couldn't quite make out what he was saying, but from where I was sitting, I could just see him chatting to the two Muppets I'd seen in the canteen corridor. They were all heading for DI Lambert's office. What the hell was he doing talking to them? I couldn't think of a good reason and hung to see if I could hear what was being said, keeping the phone close to my ear, just in case I was seen. I couldn't make out what was being said. They were only together for two or three minutes before splitting up, going their own way. Wondering what to do and whether I should tell anyone, staying here I was until I was sure the coast was clear. The short answer was, say nothing for now. I didn't want to jeopardise my position, and I needed to be sure of my facts. I then went back to calling Mo, who wasn't answering.

With little enthusiasm to do any work, I took a walk down to Tower Hill. It was where we usually met and a ten-minute walk. Whether Mo would be there or not was another matter. Normally we met by the tube entrance close to the Roman ruins. From there we would head to one of the many pubs or bars in the area – it was his choice. I was always amazed at the number of tourists there were, irrespective of the time of year or weather. Every time I took the walk, it made me think about the huge diversity of cultures, lifestyles, wealth and poverty. All encompassed within the short walk. Leman Street's ground was truly unique. Roughly the shape of an obtuse triangle, with the station stuck in the tightest corner. It was close to the Tower of

London, Tower Hill and St. Katherine's dock. Taking the short walk, you went through a small business area where the head offices of financial institutions, banks and insurance companies were. Then within a matter of yards, an area of utter poverty around Dock Street. Followed by Tower Bridge and The Tower of London itself. The ground ran east along the River Thames as far as Limehouse and then north. Close to the infamous Blind Beggar Pub where Ronnie Kray shot George Cornell. Amazingly, his younger brother Charlie still had a little influence in the area. Primarily trading on the fear and notoriety his twin brothers had once created. Also included in the area, Petticoat Lane, a world-famous market. Brick Lane, an area taken over by the clothing trade with large groups of Asian families. Sydney Street, the location of a famous siege where a botched robbery led to the murder of three police officers, and a leading teaching hospital. The ground had it all – a complete melting pot of people and cultures with pockets of Africans, Bengalis, Indians, Jewish, West Indians. Even a few native East Enders. All living in close proximity and not always in harmony.

Making my way down to Tower Hill, I wondered what Mo wanted and whether I was too late. He wasn't usually a time waster and as far as I could recall, we'd only failed to meet on one occasion. Giving him his alias had aggravated him the most. It wasn't the name. It was the number which really wound him up. He wanted to be number one. Using an alias was to preserve his identity when registered. Being registered meant he could qualify for payments or rewards based on the information provided. Mo was the alias of my first informant. It was a daft play on words. Mo being an abbreviation of "Mow the grass" and "grass" being slang for an informant. When I tried to think of another name, I couldn't come up with anything sensible and ended up calling them "Mo One" and "Mo Two."

"Mo One" was just twenty-four. A professional car thief, he'd been an informant for a couple of years, which was quite a long time. We'd met because an elderly lady had lost control of her car and had an accident at a set of traffic lights. Where Mo was in one of the cars waiting to cross the lights. Also waiting at the lights was a uniform PC. When the PC came to get Mo's details for a witness statement. He couldn't remember the name on the forged driving licence he produced or the registration number of the car. Leading to him being arrested for TDA and possessing a forged document. The forged document necessitated CID involvement. Me.

He was quite affable, almost friendly. Although when we first met, he was in a bit of a pickle and looking at a stretch he didn't fancy. He was in breach of a suspended sentence for the second time. On top of this, his girlfriend was heavily pregnant with their first child, which he said he was committed to. He made me a simple proposition. If I could keep him out of prison, he would provide me with information. Normally, he stole to order. High-quality cars and lorries. He'd driven the odd getaway car and had recently been the chauffeur for an importer of large quantities of heroin. Part of his role included the following of shipments and couriers from a safe distance once they'd arrived and cleared customs. This was his main carrot. He knew the entire set up, including the address of the heroin factory in Sialkot, Pakistan. He'd been able to provide the details of previous couriers with consignments. Some, I'd been able to verify. He would know the details of future shipments he would be told to shadow. Keeping him out of prison had been very worthwhile. Having been achieved with an official letter written and endorsed by a high-ranking officer to the trial judge, emphasising the benefits to the Crown of a non-custodial sentence.

"Mo Two" was a completely different. Muscle, thirty-eight, a big man, not to be argued with, although some had. A good six feet four and just as wide. Ugly, bloody ugly. His nose had been spread all over his face more than once. With loads of scars. Some he was proud of, others not. Missing his left earlobe, bitten off in a prison fight. His arms and chest smothered with tattoos. He'd spent nearly two-thirds of his adult life in prison. Most of his work was as an enforcer. Racketeering, collecting money from clubs, pubs and the like. Ordered to cause misery and destruction to those who didn't pay. He'd also been on several armed robberies. Mainly controlling hostages on the plot. Making sure the punters didn't interfere. For a few years, he'd worked for Paddy Onions or Patrick O'Nione, to give him his real name. That was, until he was executed. The victim of a contract killing just six months ago. Shot in the back of the head while walking along Tower Hill Road on the south side of Tower Bridge.

O'Nione's had dabbled in a load of different schemes. Smuggling, robbery and protection his main earners. One of his last forays was to target street food vendors and their pitches. Crossing boundaries as he did so. Encroaching north of the Thames. He'd moved into new and dangerous territory. Treading on other people's toes. Until then, he'd operated solely south of the water. The area he was now targeting included London's west end. Theatres, landmarks north of the water, entrances to popular tube and train stations. He'd gone too far. And with O'Nione's execution, Mo two was now freelance. Working for whoever would pay, while trying to avoid getting involved in a turf war.

I hadn't walked very far when I realised that a slight detour would take me past St George's Church. And if there was anyone there who could tell me about the youth club, it would save some time.

Chapter 9

The church was open. A young priest named Brother Thomas was setting the altar. Having apologised for the intrusion and introduced myself, I explained why I was there. It turned out that the youth club was one of his responsibilities. Open to all young people, irrespective of race, religion or church attendance. One of the club's principal objectives was to get the younger generation from different ethnic groups to better integrate. Held every Wednesday for two hours from 6.30 p.m. There was no register or members list. Attendees came and went as they pleased. It was all very informal.

Brother Thomas immediately recognised the picture I had of Adam Pope as someone who attended the youth club from time to time. He only knew his first name and that he'd become part of a small group of about half a dozen. Matthew Peters, who occasionally attended the church's Sunday morning service with his parents, was also part of the group. Along with two girls, whose names he thought were Andrea and Georgina. One of the other boys' names was Gabriel. The name registering with him because of its biblical connotations. Having provided me with Mr and Mrs Peters address, I listened courteously for a while, as he talked more about the club's objectives. Thanking him for his help, I headed off to Tower Hill.

There were a couple of ways in and out of the tube station. I couldn't see Mo at either, ending up on the walkway above the

Roman ruins. Not wanting to go back to the office, I thought I would become a tourist for a while, taking a walk along the battlements and riverbank. Giving me a little more time to mull over everything that was going on. As I crossed to Trinity Square Gardens, I suddenly heard my name being called. Mo was standing by a pitch in Cooper's Row, selling fruit. I immediately thought of Paddy Onion's execution, which had taken place less than half a mile from where we were standing just six months ago. The pitch was in a prime location and as far as I knew Mo had never been involved with fruit stalls or racketeering north of the water. The only way I could see him being allowed to work the pitch was that it was some kind of reward. We greeted each other with usual the banter. Small talk, mickey taking. It looked as though I had some new material.

"Got any Ugli fruit?" I said.

"Yeah, just here." He said, grabbing his genitals "But they're not for sale, not to you, anyway."

"I didn't realise it was Halloween. Nice mask. Scared any customers?"

"Only the Ugli ones."

We were then interrupted by a young lady wanting to buy two red apples.

"Can you count that high or do you need to take a glove off?" I said, getting a grin from the lady.

Eventually, we got round to his message, which he'd left a couple of days ago. He'd been offered a berth on a job later in the week, taking out a post office van. He'd turned it down for now, as it wasn't the normal over-the-pavement job. A couple of things worried him. For a start, they had a bird driving and a dog on board, the four-legged kind. He'd never done a job with a dog or a bird and wasn't about to start now. In his mind, the combination was trouble. Too risky, even for him. He had visions of the dog getting too excited and jumping up at his sawn-off. His other worry was that the bird would simply bottle it and bugger off, leaving them high and dry. Although the target was quite tasty, a post office van full of old bank notes being taken for destruction. Close to half a million. Old, unmarked, and easy to use. He didn't know the exact location. Just somewhere in South Croydon. If he found out, it would be when the van's route had been approved. Which would only be a couple of hours before 'the off.' At which point, he would most likely have company, making it difficult to pass the information on.

While I was trying to figure out what was best, given the circumstances, he told me what he wanted. He wasn't looking for money. He wanted to keep the fruit stall and get another closer to the Tower of London's entrance, if he could. His own little empire. He said the rent for this pitch was sorted, and he didn't see another being a problem. Those whose turf he was on had given their blessing. His one problem was getting official permission. He needed a street trader's licence, which was proving difficult due to his previous convictions. It was more bloody writing, only this time to the Corporation of London. With the underworld's current power struggle going on, I wasn't sure who was currently running the show and didn't think it wise to ask. One rumour was that the turf was now controlled by the Adams' family or A-team. They were new to the scene, and had apparently stirred up all sorts of shit. Mo must have done something to get on the side of the angels. But wasn't about to tell me, even if I did ask.

I needed to see PeaSea, and having got back to the office, told Alan that I would be heading over to Arbour Square. Knowing PeaSea, Alan insisted on tagging along. I would have preferred to have gone alone, but couldn't dissuade him. The job Mo had put up was right up their street and PeaSea had access to better intelligence than we had on district. Through which we should be able to identify any other robberies involving female drivers and or dogs.

When we got there, PeaSea was in his office but could only spare a few minutes. I outlined the job, saying it was from a reliable source, standard jargon for an informant. PeaSea didn't bother asking how good. He knew I wouldn't have bothered him getting one of his DS's checking their intelligence records. He also said that with their current commitments, it was unlikely he could get a team together at short notice. But neither did he want the job being handed over to another department. If something happened, he would try to sort something. Possibly with one of the other squad offices. We were still waiting for the DS to return when PeaSea suddenly said, "Played recently?"

Alan looked puzzled.

"Rugby, he's not bad, is twinkle-toes. Surprisingly nimble, for someone his size." PeaSea continued.

"Twinkle-toes!" said Alan, laughing.

"Yeah, if he'd put up with training a little more. He could have played more representative stuff, even national level, who knows."

"I can hear you; I am here," I said.

"He always seems to be working these days. If you're interested, there's a French touring side. Sarcelles are coming down to the club in a few weeks. Fancy a run out? We could do with a decent centre."

"If it shuts you up and makes you happy, I'll play. Tell me, did you have anything to do with arranging the match? Through one of your wine contacts, perhaps?" PeaSea gave me look. It was just enough to remind him of what I knew. Not that it would go any further, and Alan wouldn't have cared, anyway.

"I'll pencil you in and let you know the exact details, as and when."

"You kept that quiet. If I'd have known when we were at Barkingside," Alan said.

It was PeaSea's turn to look puzzled.

"You don't need to know, Guvnor. Can we get back to why we're here?" Thankfully, the DS who'd been doing the searches returned saying, "Definitely no dogs, drivers or otherwise and no barking mad females."

I would just have to wait and see how things developed with Mo. Having again promised to turn out against the French, we made our way back to the office. On the way, Alan said that he thought Sally had recently done some work with the Corporation of London. And while it was fresh in my mind, I should ask her if she could get the name of someone to speak to regarding the licence.

The bosses were in their office, consoling themselves while consulting with a bottle of scotch. Raising their glasses and nodding as we passed their door. They didn't care where we'd been or what we been up to. Looking around, apart from the girls and Anne, the office was empty. And the only reason the girls were there was because they were waiting to go out with Alan and the DI.

By the time I got back to the office, most had already left, and it was as though everybody had given up caring about the investigation. An air of resignation clouding everyone's thoughts, subdued by the inevitability of how things would end, with Hampton finally getting his way. With everything that had gone on, I couldn't simply let go. I couldn't give in, not to that man.

With the collator's office being empty, it meant that I could go through whatever records I liked without being questioned. Brother Thomas's address for Mr and Mrs Peters was confirmed by the voter's register. And with no one else being shown as living at the address, it suggested a single-family residence. As opposed to flats, maisonettes, or bed-sits. I couldn't find any records for anyone linked to the address who'd either been stopped or had previous convictions. To all intents and purposes, a model family, if there was such a thing. According to the records I could get access to, Matthew Peters left school last summer, which would make him seventeen, possibly eighteen. An adult in the eyes of the law.

With the way things were in the office and not knowing who to trust, keeping the information I had regarding Matthew Peters to myself for now seemed the best thing to do. And, by the time I returned to the office, I was surprised to find others had too. The bosses then joined us, bringing a couple of bottles of scotch with them. Trying to raise spirits. When Ken Reeves appeared, I had to make a conscious effort not to stare. Not long after, a suggestion was made to make an evening of it by carrying on in The Scarborough Arms, followed by a nose bag in Musa's, a local Asian restaurant. When we got to the pub, Alan, Sally, Bob Clarke and Julia were like married couples. Sitting together with the boss. Somehow, I ended up in with Ken Reeves and a couple of off-duty officers from the station. Finding it hard not to ask leading questions, I left early.

Feeling a little more positive after last night, I was musing over what to do about Matthew Peters. What we really needed was proper surveillance on the address but didn't have the manpower, expertise, equipment or capabilities to mount an operation. There was also the small matter of trying to keep the whole thing quiet. I made a few calls to friends I knew who were on or had been on dedicated surveillance teams. They were all tied up, although one suggested I try the City of London Police, who had a dedicated team.

To have any chance of using them, I needed a link to the city. With nothing to lose, it was time to take a trip to Snowhill Police Station. To go through their crime reports on the pretext of looking for burglaries fitting a particular pattern. Similar to crimes we were investigating. Any old bullshit would do. I had a warrant card, and they wouldn't really care what I was looking at. What I needed was a hook. Something to get their surveillance team to follow Matthew Peters. An unsolved high-value crime, with a certain amount of planning, might do. It turned out they were getting hit with a series of van draggings and jump-ups, just as we were. High-value goods vehicles. Normally unmarked, containing alcohol or tobacco. Those responsible would target what they thought would be one of the lorries, leaving a depot in Stratford. Hoping it was heading for the city or East End. The type of thievery would depend on the number of stops and how the driver left the vehicle when making the delivery. If the driver left the tailgate down, they would jump up onto the back and steal as many crates as they dare. Being sure to be clear of the van in good time. Hoping the driver would at least make it to the next destination before discovering the theft. If that wasn't possible and they still fancied it, or the vehicle wasn't making many stops. They would follow it until it stopped at a junction or traffic lights. There, an armed member of the gang would then force their way into the cab, making the driver go to a predetermined destination. There the vehicle would be emptied, and the driver left tied up in the back. Matthew Peters had just become a suspect for these.

Both Mo One and Mo Two had pretty good track records when it came to providing information. It would be a simple matter of attributing the information to one of them. Which meant the source wouldn't be challenged and their identity would remain confidential. Anyone who had ever dealt with a real informant knew that not every job came off. This would just be one of those. All I had to do now was come up with a plausible story regarding his involvement. Keeping it simple seemed the best approach. Seeing where he went and who he contacted in the belief that this would lead to the identification of gang members, along with possible locations for the stolen property.

Keeping the surveillance job to myself was going to be impossible. So, I told Alan about Peters and what I thought we needed to do. He agreed to keep things quiet. We also needed a senior officer to make the formal request for assistance. It was getting complicated. We had a choice – PeaSea or the boss. With paperwork being his forte, we went with the boss. Making it clear that the request he would be making related to a possible cross-border crime and that it was nothing to do with our murder investigation, although it was. He got what was needed almost immediately. Even making a couple of suggestions on how to improve our chances, telling us to leave it with him. Later that afternoon, he called me into his office to say it was all sorted. I was to go to Snowhill for 10 a.m. the following day and brief a DS Morgan. I was curious to know how he'd sorted it out so quickly. He said, "Don't ask." Although a little later he put me out of my misery. I knew he'd spent a lot of time on the Fraud Squad. What I didn't know was the squad's full title: 'The Metropolitan and City Police Company Fraud Department.' It was the only unit which combined both forces, originally formed in 1946. As a result, he'd used their surveillance team in the past and knew who to speak to. Something he could have mentioned earlier.

It was going to be a busy couple of days. What with the kidnappers' due back in court. The possibility of the dog and bird robbery, and now the surveillance operation.

With the team still dealing with the kidnapping, Hampton would know how much work needed to be done and the additional pressure that would cause. He was making sure the kidnapping case couldn't be handed over. As a consequence, one of us would be heading off to court on Friday. We'd been informed by the defendants' solicitors that at the hearing they would all be making bail applications, which if granted, would reduce the chances of the defendants appearing together to zero. To offset the possibility, it made sense to get as much of the paperwork done as was possible. If we could demonstrate that progress had been made, and that the prosecution would be ready for an early committal. It would minimise many of the arguments the defence were likely to make. So, during the rest of the day, despite the mood, we all contributed to getting as much done as possible. Even the boss and DI helped with photocopying and the indexing of statements.

Chapter 10

Having got to Snowhill early, I was taken to the canteen, where I was asked to wait for DS Morgan. It wasn't long before he arrived, dressed in motorcycle leathers. Talk about eager, he'd already been out, scoped the address and found a location for a static observation point. DS Morgan asked a few questions about the address and potential occupants. As with the Met's surveillance teams. They used the same methodologies to ensure communications were coded and meaningless to anyone trying to listen in over the short distance signals were transmitted. DS Morgan offered to let me be a part of the team, following on at the rear. A sort of tail end Charlie with nothing to do. With other things on the go, I politely declined. He said he would update me when able, passing on logs and photographs, which were usually available within a couple of days.

As their suspects were white males in their late twenties and Matthew Peters was a teenage West Indian. I said that the information was that Peters was acting as a courier, passing information between the group. After all, it was the method used by drug runners who frequently used couriers a lot younger than Peters. And, as intermediaries had frequently been the starting point for operations, which DS Morgan readily accepted.

It was around 11.30 a.m. when a person believed to be Matthew Peters was seen leaving the house. He walked to a café in Watney Market, where he met a male and female of similar ages. They bought hot drinks and sat chatting for nearly an hour. After that, he returned home. Unfortunately, it wasn't long after this that the surveillance team got pulled off the job, being urgently redeployed on a case with much higher priority. All DS Morgan could do was apologise, saying he would let me know if, and when, they would be able to resume operations.

I hadn't heard from Mo and wanted to know whether the robbery he'd described had taken place. The police at Croydon weren't aware of any suggesting I try Surrey constabulary which bordered Croydon. Being smart, I thought that ringing their switchboard would give me a clue without showing out. The lady on the switchboard put me on hold, saying she would ask one of her colleagues. A few seconds later a voice said,

"Detective Superintendent Innis."

I hadn't been that smart after all and rather too cockily, said, "So, you have had a robbery?" Instantly regretting sounding so flippant. As soon as I'd said it, I knew it was a mistake. Then, trying to recover from the situation, I felt obliged to tell him who I really was. Resulting in him demanding to know what I knew about the incident. His manner, authoritarian and now condescending, put my back up immediately and instead of telling him, I said, "I'm assuming you've had a robbery involving a Post office van, where a woman and a dog were involved?"

"Tell me what you know, that's an order."

Obviously, they had. Mo was right. The more Innis went on, the angrier he sounded, continuing to make demands, ordering me to tell him what I knew. In the end, I said.

"All I can say at the moment is that I may be able to help. I just needed to know whether the information I'd been given was reliable, and as it is, I'll try and find out some more, and get back to you when I know."

It didn't seem to matter what I said. He didn't believe me. Becoming more threatening and official, reciting a gaggle of laws and procedures I was supposedly breaking. As he went on, he sounded more and more like a northern version of Hampton – Surrey's very own. For a moment I wondered if it was me. I just seemed to have this effect on some senior officers. His threats and demands wound me up even more. After all, I was the one ringing him, trying to help. His attitude pretty much ensured I wouldn't be telling him anything. However, in an effort to appease him and before hanging up, I reiterated that I would get back to him when I knew more, ending the call.

It was too risky trying to get hold of Mo. I would just have to wait for him to contact me, which wasn't until late afternoon. He still had company. They'd used his address to hold up for a while and then stayed. He'd been allowed out to pick up some booze and cigarettes. They were celebrating. He only had a few minutes to talk. After the blagging, they'd stashed most of the loot and dropped the dog off somewhere. They were now using his place to top up before going out on the town, using a few of the jollies they'd kept back. "Sweet as a nut" was how the job had been described. They'd changed cars on the way back and had another change of clothes stashed in another car parked up somewhere close to his flat for later. He said they were so pumped he'd no choice but to stay with them. Apparently, they kept saying, "Not one man and his dog, but one bird and a bitch." They, being Gerald Riley, Marshall Pavey and Amanda Storey – Mo, didn't know the dog's name. Riley was Mo's connection. He was the one who'd offered him a place on the team. Apparently, the dog had worked a treat, and 'Drives' the bird wasn't bad either. They were going clubbing. To have a little celebration and Mo was invited. He couldn't say no, as it would look strange. We agreed to speak later.

I then went and checked the names on the PNC. Gerald Riley's came up with a flashing warning, "WNTD RBRY, ATT MRDER, EXT CAU." There wasn't enough room to get the whole warning into the space provided. He was one of the UK's most wanted. Even the expanded version had been truncated. Wanted for a series of armed robberies and two attempted murders. From what was on the screen, he'd shot at police to avoid capture. Constantly carried ammonia, which again was used to evade capture. Was wanted by Essex, Surrey, Sussex and Kent constabularies, and most importantly for me, was also wanted by the Met's Flying Squad. A call to PeaSea would give me the name of someone to hand the job over to. Hopefully getting Innis off my back.

While I'd been out of the office, I'd been fitted up by some of my so-called mates, who'd volunteered me to hold the boss's hand at court with the kidnappers. There was no getting out of it.

The magistrate's court at Arbour Square sat from 10.30 a.m. With the lists following a pretty standard convention. Cases that were likely to be remands followed the overnight drunks and prostitutes. And dealing with those was the nearest thing the magistrate's court had to a production line. The court officer would get all the drunks lined up in list order, and once called they would trudge towards the dock in single file. With the court officer saying something like:

"Fred Bloggs drunk and incapable, your worship."

The clerk of the court would then briefly read out the charge and ask how the individual pleaded, which was invariably guilty. The court officer would then give the briefest of facts, something like:

"On Thursday, 12th March 1983, at 12.30 a.m., Outside the Prospect of Whitby public house, found drunk and incapable, your worship. No trouble, police transport used."

The magistrate would then sentence them to a fine of £5 or one day. By the time they'd all made it into the dock, it was time to turn around and head back to the tank. Where they would remain until 1 p.m., which counted for one day. Providing just enough time for the tank to be made ready for the next batch. Prostitutes were dealt with in much the same way. The only difference being the number of kerb-crawlers approached and the fines, which typically ranged between ten and fifteen pounds. Our case was likely to get called just after they'd finished.

When I arrived to pick up the papers, the boss was already there, coughing loudly as I passed his door, beckoning me in.

"What have you been up to?" he said quietly.

"Not sure what you mean, boss."

"We've got visitors, a Detective Superintendent Innis and a DI, from Redhill. Apparently, they've been here since seven-thirty. They won't tell me why, not without you being present and they don't seem very happy either."

"They must have been up really early and they've had a wasted journey. Superintendent Innis is here regarding some information I have about an armed robbery. I phoned Surrey yesterday, to see if they'd had a robbery and got put through to him. At the time, I didn't know the identity of the robbers. Just an approximate location and M.O., which was more than a little unusual, because it involved a female and a dog. The information was obviously accurate, otherwise they wouldn't be here. During the conversation, he threatened me with all sorts of things, and now he's going to be even more pissed off, because the job's going to the Flying Squad, or it will do as soon as I get someone's name."

"What robbery? You'd better tell me what's going on, shut the door."

I then told him about the job and Mo. On reflection I'd cocked-up by calling Surrey. I then reminded the boss as diplomatically as I could, just how important it was to keep Mo's identity confidential. Innis would undoubtedly demand to know his details along with everything else, and I didn't want to tell him anything.

"You better try and get hold of someone before going next door," said the boss.

Thankfully, PeaSea was in and having explained what had happened, he began bollocking me about calling Surrey, but as soon as I mentioned the name, Gerry Riley... he said, "Stop there, don't say anything else, we'll do it. That bastard shot at two of my guys, as well as trying to blind others – he's ours, I'll find someone."

He then gave me another contact number I was to give Innis. Under no circumstances was I to tell him anything. While PeaSea was on the phone, the boss also had a brief conversation, after which he accompanied me into the main office where they were waiting.

The older of the two men was sitting at the desk Alan and I used. By the way he was dressed, he had to be Innis. Wearing a blue blazer, with a light pink silk handkerchief poking from the breast pocket, grey slacks, with what looked like some kind of regimental tie. Greying hair, which had been subjected to a severe comb-over, in an attempt to cover an obvious bald patch. Combed and greased into position with precision. Finished off with a military-style pencil moustache, similarly groomed. I could imagine him wearing something similar on his days off. Possibly swapping the tie for a nifty paisley-patterned cravat and fedora. Drinking pink gin or mint juleps on the veranda with milady on sunny evenings. The other individual, I assumed to be the DI, had his back to us. He was gazing out of the window at our concrete jungle. He had dark hair and was wearing a dark grey suit. Lying on the desk were the investigation's current action, suggestion and message books, which normally leant up against the two triple stack in-trays at either end of the desk and had obviously been gone through. Along with these were a few envelopes containing correspondence delivered overnight through the dispatch system. One of those on top I could see was addressed to me. The boss introduced me and as he did so, the man by the window turned. Innis stayed sitting, making no attempt to acknowledge either of us despite the boss's higher rank. Extending his right arm out across the desk, he started drumming his fingers on the overnight dispatch, looking me up and down. His mannerisms and demeanour again reminding me of Hampton. How well they would go together. As yet, he hadn't said a word. But if someone had asked me to describe the person from yesterday's telephone conversation, he could well be it. Yet another over-promoted wanker. It didn't just happen in the Met. Continuing to drum his fingers, he just stared at me, presumably thinking I would say something. I then realised that the A4 envelope addressed to me he was drumming his fingers on was in fact from criminal records; Riley's CRO file. The envelopes were designed for re-use and were never sealed. Innis can't have noticed my name on the envelope. If he had, he would have been waving the contents at me. Innis broke the silence. Starting with my insubordination, total disregard for rank, and my failure to disclose information when ordered to do so. As he continued to drone on, I rudely turned away, wandering off to the desks at the other end of the office. Angering him even more, forcing him to turn in the chair. The DI was preparing to take notes. Having finished his general bollocking, Innis continued.

"More specifically, with reference to yesterday's telephone conversation. It is my duty to directly order you to disclose all relevant information appertaining to, and pertinent to identifying those responsible for undertaking a heinous crime I am currently charged with investigating. Namely, the larcenous depredation of a Royal Mail post office van on the thirteenth instance of this month at Noke Drive, Redhill, Surrey. Within the jurisdiction of the Crown. My enquiries in relation to this offence have led me to believe that you, Detective Sergeant Lomax, have material information relevant to the said investigation. And that you are currently withholding the said information without lawful authority or reasonable excuse. I should advise you that this may constitute the commission of a criminal offence, do you understand?"

He stopped short of actually cautioning me, and for a moment I wondered if he was being serious. He'd gone back in time with the phraseology. It was almost gibberish and unless he always spoke like that, it must have taken ages to formulate. Initially, I wasn't sure what to make of it and from the boss's facial expressions, neither did he. Although it soon became clear

Innis didn't think it was a joke. At first, I didn't get why he was saying that his enquiries had led him to me when I'd initiated the call. I then realised he'd said it because of the notes the DI was taking. A glory seeker looking for a quick result, wanting to take advantage of others for his own benefit. If I did pass any information on, you could be sure I wouldn't be getting any credit. Feeling malevolent, I wondered if I could get him to repeat what he'd said, saying, "Sorry, Guvnor, I'm not with you. Could you run that by me again?"

Like a flash, the DI interjected, saying, "Can you tell us what you know about the post office van robbery, that took place in Redhill, yesterday morning?" Innis scowled at the DI for jumping in.

Having listened as politely as I could, it was now my opportunity to tell them I'd been ordered not to say anything. And that he was to call Det. Supt. Saunders from the Flying Squad on the number PeaSea had provided. Innis continued to remonstrate and make demands, while I dialled the number on one of the phones at my end of the office, holding it out when I had. Begrudgingly, he got up and made his way over, snatching the phone and waving me away. I sauntered back to the boss. Innis then found himself doing most of the listening, in what was a very one-sided conversation. Giving me the opportunity to slip the envelope from CRO under the others. I needn't have bothered. Innis suddenly slammed the phone down and stormed out of the office without saying a word, leaving his DI to follow.

There was just time for a quick coffee before heading off to court with the boss. His fee for being with me when I saw Innis was for him to be a spectator. He was leaving the remand to me.

We hadn't yet reached a stage where police had legal representation. In the Met., it was normal for police to deal with most of the hearings at magistrate's court. Remands, paper committals, even the odd not guilty trial for lesser offences. Giving officers the opportunity to present a case and cross-examine witnesses. Be Perry Mason for a while. In some ways it gave you an insight into how some lawyers worked. Attending court could also provide excellent intelligence; seeing which mates, girlfriends, boyfriends or anyone else for that matter who was turning up to support a defendant was good knowledge.

On our arrival, we were confronted with a confusion of solicitors, one for each defendant. All making daft suggestions relating to the terms on which they thought each of their defendants could get bail. Part of their assumption had been based on the prosecution seeking a lengthy remand in order to prepare for committal. During which time it would be unreasonable to expect their clients to remain in custody. Providing sufficient grounds for the magistrate to grant conditional bail. Thanks to our concerted efforts, we were already in a position to serve most of the statements, effectively nullified their application. The hearing took less than five minutes, with bail refused. It was just gone eleven when we got back to the office, just in time for the boss to call yet another meeting, only this time it was in the annexe. It wasn't yet midday but had the makings of an away-day.

As Mo had left a message to meet and afternoon drinking didn't normally go well with me, I left them to it and made my way to the tower.

Riley and the others had spent the night at his place, but should be on their way by now. Having gained their trust, he'd made an excuse to get out, which had been accepted. Something about not being able to leave his pitch for another day.

They were splitting up, going their own way for a month or two. Everyone had been given pocket money. He knew Riley was leaving London, heading down to the West Country to mingle with tourists, which is what he'd done before. He was getting a train from Paddington that afternoon. Riley didn't drive much and thought that stealing a car in London and then taking it down to the West Country was too risky, and it would probably be a bit of a giveaway. Mo gave me his description, saying he was juiced. Meaning that he was carrying a Jiffy bottle full of ammonia. A small plastic container shaped like a lemon, which could easily be filled with other liquids. It was possible to flip the lid and squirt the contents, all in a single movement. A good squirt could easily go fifteen to twenty feet, causing serious harm.

When I rang PeaSea, he could only spare two men. Who would meet me at Paddington Green, assuming I could go? Alan, having joined the others in the pub, was up for going when he heard. The boss less so. He would only agree to us going on the proviso we acted as backup, nothing more. Agreeing, and with Alan insisting on driving, we headed for the meet, giving me time to read Riley's file.

He was only five foot five, slim build, incredibly violent, with a big chip on his shoulder. Included in the file were several photographs, quite a few had been taken over a relatively short period. The information on how the photographs had been obtained had been withheld, implying they were from undercover operations as opposed to surveillance. Changes to his hairstyle, length, colour and the amount of facial hair made him unrecognisable from one photograph to the next. The differences were enormous. Both adding and taking years from his actual age. It was also clear he would do anything to avoid capture. The photographs told me that if we didn't get him now, it could be months, even years, before we had another chance. His was the first double-sided wanted notice I'd ever seen. With numerous references to him carrying weapons, mainly firearms and ammonia. He had a total disregard for the law, having shot at police on several occasions. Taking hostages and squirting ammonia at anyone who got in his way. He was a nasty little piece of work who hated authority, especially the police. An officer who'd dealt with him was of the opinion that the chip on his shoulder was because of his height or lack of it.

When we met up with PeaSea's men, one of them turned out to be the sergeant who'd undertaken the initial checks regarding the robbery, a DS Gray, who told us there could be a slight problem. It turned out that both he and his partner, whose name I didn't catch, were already known to Riley. And, if spotted, the situation was likely to get out of hand, potentially putting the public at risk. He thought we could easily find ourselves in a hostage situation. If we were going to get him, Alan and I would have to make the arrest. Either that or let him go. If we were to let this opportunity go. Who knew when there would be another chance or what might happen in the interim. We decided to look for him. If we saw him, we could take it from there. If we didn't, there was nothing to discuss.

The information board showed trains for Plymouth and the West Country, leaving from platforms six and seven. The platforms shared a single walkway. I spotted the little shit almost immediately. Partially obscured by a pillar, he was standing about half-way along the platform. Just beyond him, a set of stairs leading to a bridge, providing access to other platforms and an exit. His getaway should he need it. He was wearing the leather bomber jacket Mo had mentioned. A cigarette in his right hand, while his left remained in a jacket pocket. Trying to look casual, while constantly looking around, giving his eyes a treat. Assessing those coming onto the platform, looking for eye contact with anyone approaching.

There was no time to discuss tactics. If we were going to take him, hanging around would only give us away. It was here and now. I picked up a discarded ticket and while holding it in my hand walked along the platform, looking at my watch and the information board, as if hurrying for a train. Looking beyond Riley at the stairs, just as other passengers were doing. I didn't know where Alan or the others were, and I couldn't risk looking around. As he hadn't made a run for it, I assumed DS Gray and his mate were out of sight. As I got closer, I could see that he was actually leaning against the pillar. Still looking at the stairs, I marched past him. He'd given up on me, I'd been dismissed. He was now scanning others coming on to the platform.

Introducing myself, warrant card in hand, and telling him he was under arrest and then cautioning him was what I was supposed to do. It was undoubtedly a sure-fire way of getting sprayed or shot. I wasn't going to give him the chance of squirting me. Or anyone else, for that matter. A cigarette burn I would take if I had to. Having passed him, I turned, and when close enough, simultaneously grabbed his left wrist with one hand and a handful of head hair with the other, repeatedly pulling it back and forth smashing his face into the pillar while pushing his left hand into the pocket. It wasn't pretty or regulation, but I wasn't taking any chances. I'm not sure where it came from, but for the first time since leaving training school, I instinctively managed a judo leg sweep. Taking his legs away, getting him face down on the ground with me on top, I'd taken him completely by surprise. For a while, I continued trying to bury his head in the platform. Making sure his left hand stayed jammed in the pocket. His legs kicked away, unable to get any purchase, and neither did he seem to able to get his right hand far enough around to do me any damage with the cigarette. While continuing to struggle, I managed to get my legs into a kneeling position. Burying my right knee into the small of his back, just below the shoulders. He was now pinned to the ground and provided the Jiffy bottle stayed wedged in the pocket. I should be okay.

A few seconds later, Alan arrived. A Smith and Wesson Model 36 clasped between his hands, pointing it at Riley. Typically issued to CID officers on central operations, like Special Branch. The short two-inch barrel made it easy to conceal in the small of your back close to the coccyx. Accurate to about twenty-five yards and extremely uncomfortable should you sit on it. Alan shoved the revolver in Riley's ear and calmly said, "This doesn't half make a mess; you can be sure I won't hesitate to use it. Oh, and by the way, you're under arrest." The way he said it sounded as though he'd said something similar in the past.

While Alan had been talking, distracting Riley, I'd managed to manoeuvre myself a little more, getting my knee even closer to the base of his neck. Having let go of his head, I could now make a grab for the wandering right arm, pinning that to the floor too. I couldn't work out where Alan's revolver had come from. We hadn't had time to get handcuffs, let alone book out firearms. Riley's flailing legs began to slow. Whether he was running out of steam, had accepted the situation, or was trying it on, I wasn't sure. Apart from dealing with the ammonia we had to make sure that he wasn't carrying any other weapons. It was probably no more than a minute before DS Gray and his mate arrived. Handcuffs in hand. But instead of using them to handcuff Riley, Gray couldn't resist greeting him with.

"Hello Gerry, remember me? We're going to have a bit of a chat later, you little shit."

They had history. Something else we hadn't been told and winding Riley up the way he had wasn't clever. It simply made him struggle more.

"Fuck off, prick. I've got nothing to say to you or anyone else, wanker."

"Got his hands?" asked DS Gray.

I nodded.

"Keep hold."

What did he think I was doing? I'd been struggling to keep his left hand in his pocket. I don't think they realised just how strong Riley was. He reminded me of ex-special boat squadron guy I used to play rugby with. Small, strong, wiry, and bloody aggravating. I'm not sure whether DS Gray had foreseen the situation, but I was more than a little surprised when he produced a Swiss army knife, swapping it for the handcuffs he'd been holding. Using them to cut around the jacket pocket sandwiched between our hands. It wasn't long before we could clearly see Riley's hand firmly gripping the yellow Jiffy bottle. DS Gray and his mate then took hold of Riley's hand as I released my grasp. Gradually prising Riley's fingers away from the bottle. While he continually tried to flip the lid open with his thumb. It was a right old performance, causing a small crowd to gather. DS Gray's mate then took it upon himself to tell everyone that this was a dangerous police operation and that they should all piss off if they knew what was good for them. It wasn't the best of public-relations exercises, but it served a purpose. Having secured the Jiffy bottle and with Alan still pointing his gun at Riley, we now had to get the cuffs on. It was another struggle, but it was a good thing we did, as the little bugger had a tasty flick-knife tucked in his right sock. We then tried to get him to stand up, which only resulted in him trying to kick everyone. When that didn't work, he went limp, forcing us to drag him backwards all the way to the cars. Getting him in their car was yet another fight, during which Riley started spitting a mixture of blood and saliva at DS Gray. It didn't seem to matter what I'd done. He just targeted Gray. When we did finally get Riley handcuffed into their car, I saw Alan hand the revolver back to DS Gray's mate, with DS Gray saying he would keep us posted.

When we arrived back in the office, the rest of the team were still there, putting the world to rights, discussing anything and everything. It was also clear that the boss was already aware of Riley's arrest, with him saying, "Typical Flying Squad, beating up prisoners."

Chapter 11

Overnight three messages had been left in the office, the first read:

Book 66 Ref: HB/10148/83:
Item (s): One (1) Sony VHS Video Recorder
Person (s): Andy Cheng
Remark (s): found in lock-up.

The second told me that surveillance logs and photographs had been dropped off and were now in the station officer's safe. Finally, there was a message for me to call DS Gray.

The photographs were good quality. City's surveillance team were a lot better than some had given them credit for. Hopefully, we could identify those in the snaps. Sally offered to make copies. Leaving some with the collator, in the hope that someone in the station would recognise them.

The Book 66 reference was a ledger entry listing property believed to be involved in the proceeds of crime which couldn't been associated with a specific case. The station officer read out the entry and the contents of a note pinned to it.

"Andy Cheng stopped by police carrying video recorder. Unable to provide proof of ownership. Recorder originally found in a lock-up garage. Parents had told him to get rid of it. Address and story verified with parents. Recorder confiscated.

Entry made. No other suspicious items at H/A. Officer aware of interest in lock-up."

I advised the station officer that we would get the recorder collected as soon as possible, and that it needed to be preserved for fingerprints. DI Clarke overheard the conversation and volunteered to pick it up and then interview Cheng, taking Julia with him.

I then called DS Gray, who told me the investigation was going well. Riley was now cooperating. I was amazed, given his reaction to Gray at the station. DS Gray wanted to confirm certain information with Mo. And in order to do this needed his real name and address. There was no chance of that happening. I suggested he gave me the information, and I would get it confirmed. Gray didn't like the idea and tried telling me it was an order from PeaSea. That wasn't working. He didn't know how well I knew him. It wasn't the sort of thing he would do. Gray was either looking to take on Mo as an informant. Or give him up to someone else who could benefit from knowing what he was, looking to do himself a favour. He then tried another tack, saying that Riley had rolled over on a number of jobs, which would be good for me, especially if I was looking for a posting on the Squad. To get rid of him, I told him I would check with Mo first and then get back to him. I already knew the answer – it would consist of two words, and the second was 'off.'

The DI had taken a statement from Cheng and collected the video recorder. He was sixteen, neither he or any of his family were known to police. The story was that some weeks ago he and a couple of mates had been out on their bikes. And while waiting for another friend to turn up, had been riding around, occasionally riding up and down the ramp to the underground garages, where they would sometimes hide. Having ducked into one garage, he noticed something shiny in the corner, partially covered by an old carpet. The video recorder. Thinking it had just been abandoned, he took it home for his mum and dad. His parents didn't want it and had told him several times to get rid of it, which was what he was doing when he got stopped by the police.

Having taken elimination fingerprints, DI Clarke took Cheng and his mother for a drive, to point out the garages where the recorder had been found. The lock-ups were at the bottom of Heylyn Square, a stone's throw from the kidnappers' address. There was no way he would be prosecuted. We needed him as a witness. If for nothing else, he helped to corroborate Kerwin's version of events.

We then found that the home beat officer covering St George's Church occasionally helped at the youth club, something Brother Thomas had forgotten to mention. He identified the three faces in the surveillance photographs. Matthew Peters, Gabriel Baptiste and his girlfriend, Andrea Smith. The officer was also reasonably sure he knew the street Smith lived in and thought that Baptiste and Smith had been an item for quite a while, which was unusual for two so young. The mugshot of Baptiste bore little resemblance to the surveillance photographs.

PKW popped in, wanting to run over the submissions. He wanted to see how many results were still outstanding and whether there was anything he could do to hurry things along. While he was there, we got him to dust the video recorder. There were a couple of prints on the inside of the lid and a couple on the outside. He could make an initial comparison, which would be verified later. A partial smudge of someone's right thumb had been found on the top rear left-hand corner of the unit. Just the sort of place you would hold the recorder when picking it up. It looked as though one of the prints found inside of the recorder belonged to David Lacey, a resident of the squat, who'd been charged with kidnapping Pope. If that was right, at least it helped to prove that the recorder was from the kidnappers' address.

Having not been in Cranford Cottages, some of us, including PKW, thought it worthwhile going to have a look before handing the keys back. Going Sunday morning was favourite we could then be home for lunch. Ken Reeves wasn't happy. He thought we were checking up on him. He was right. What's more, he couldn't make it. To score some house points at home, he'd arranged a family gathering he couldn't get out of.

Having agreed to meet at the cottages and despite the drizzle, everyone had parked their cars in Cable Street, electing to walk the short walk to the Cottages. Realising that it would be much easier to leave from there when we were making our way home.

Once inside, it was obvious that someone else had entered the property since the examination. Items had been moved, and there were more empty cans. All very different from the photographs. With the padlocks and boarding still in place, there were no obvious signs to show how anyone had got in.

Alan and I went upstairs and to our surprise found Ramadi lying in his sleeping bag, pretending to be asleep.

"What the fuck are you doing here, you were told to keep out?" Alan said.

With our small torches shining at his head, Ramadi turned over to face us, his pupils dilated, high on drink or drugs. We searched but couldn't find anything. He just lay there, giggling.

"How long have you been here?"

He said nothing, continuing to grin like a Cheshire cat. He was so aggravating; it was a miracle he hadn't had the smile wiped off his face. Arresting him didn't suit our purpose. The paperwork, his attitude and the likelihood that it would only increase his notoriety were all good reasons. By defying the police, it gave the impression that nobody told Ramadi what to do. The only sensible option was to throw him out. Once we'd got rid of him, it took a while to work out how he'd managed to get in. The Cottages had a shared roof space, and he'd gained access to the space through one of the other cottages crawling through. Begging the question of whether it was worth continuing.

PKW's view was that while we were here, we might as well have a look. He wanted to do a couple of tests; he thought worthwhile, looking for blood. Having set up his lighting, he started going around with an ultraviolet lamp. Here and there odd blotches revealed themselves, splatter patterns. High on the walls. There weren't any references to swabs or samples being taken during the previous search. PKW concentrated on these. Taking small circular discs of paper, similar to refined blotting paper. He carefully folded them several times, ending up with a cone shape. The tip of which he dipped into a small bottle of clear liquid, which he then rubbed over the target area. A damp circle would appear when the paper was unfolded, which would change colour within thirty seconds, if there were any traces. Violet-blue was the colour we were looking for; human blood. Not wanting to get in PKW's way, Bob Clarke and Alan Harrison went upstairs to go through everything that had been left behind, while I moved around into the tiny kitchen area. Where, judging by the photographs, a few more cans had been added to those already there. What I hadn't noticed in the photographs were the black refuse sacks which sat on top of the dustbin were marked London Borough of Barking and we were in Tower Hamlets. The rolls were not sold to the public, being provided to householders for refuse collections in their respective boroughs. The cost of which was met through the rates. None of this lot were ratepayers, and we were in the wrong borough. Some bags from the roll had been used, but wherever they were, they weren't in the dustbin. Which to my surprise was almost empty, given the number of tins and old papers lying around.

PKW then started grunting, making strange noises.

"Something wrong?" I said.

"I don't think the kit's working."

"What do you mean?"

"None of the tests are conclusive. The paper changes to this faded, light blue. I've had the odd one or two like this before but not all the time."

"Got another kit?" I asked.

"No, just this one, it's less than a week old though. I've been too busy to stock up."

He then cut himself, allowing a few drops of blood to drip onto a small mirror he'd taken from his kit. Once the blood had congealed, he did a controlled test. The kit was working perfectly. Now, he couldn't understand why he was getting the results he was. There was nothing I could do to help, so I just carried on looking around.

Opening the cupboard under the stairs, I was surprised to find a large yellow tarpaulin stuffed inside – it was so big it took up most of the cupboard.

"Here, look at this."

PKW stopped what he was doing and helped to drag it out. It was too big to open fully indoors and as it was raining, we couldn't take it outside. PKW shone the UV lamp over the parts we could get at. The signs were good. He wanted to do a proper test. Opening up the tarpaulin a little more, some dark red stains were more evident, and even to the naked eye they looked like dried blood. The first test proved positive. Having checked the exhibits book, there were no records of a tarpaulin or the contents of the cupboard being examined, and neither were there any photographs. The cupboard had been completely overlooked.

The only way of examining the tarpaulin properly was to take it back to the station. It was far too big to get in any exhibit bag. All we could do was roll it up as tightly as possible and carry it under our arms. Behind the tarpaulin was a plastic carrier bag containing empty spice jars and part-filled bottles of cleaning fluids, which were also seized.

Bob Clarke and Alan Harrison hadn't found anything of any significance upstairs and neither were they very enamoured with Ken Reeves, given what we'd just found. It was a good thing he wasn't there, trotting out loads of implausible excuses. By the time PKW had logged his swabs and we were ready to leave, it was well past eleven. Sunday lunch was going to be late. Then, having made our way back to the cars. We found ourselves in the middle of the London Marathon, having parked on the course. And with hundreds of runners trundling by, all we could do was wait for numbers to dwindle.

As soon as we were back in the office, the DI rang the boss to bring him up to speed with regard to finding Ramadi in the Cottage and Ken Reeves' apparent lapse. The rest of us unfolded the tarpaulin, which was a huge yellow plastic-coated sheet. With eyelets spaced out around the edge. Most of sheet was covered in grime. Although, there were cleaner areas, which had been created by the tarpaulin continually being folded the same way. The sort of thing I'd seen being used to cover cargo, either on a barge or on the back of a lorry. There were no identifying marks or labels. PKW got to work taking photographs, including areas he'd identified and marked for testing. Confirming the existence of human blood, several times; taking samples for comparison.

We were trying to work out how it had been missed when the DI returned, saying that the boss wanted the U-bends from the property analysed too. We were keeping the property for now and needed to arrange for it to be guarded. He also insisted that none of us had a go at Ken Reeves. He would deal with the matter personally. It wasn't long before PKW had taken the samples he needed, and we were heading back to the Cottages to get the piping.

The following morning, Notso was assigned to assist Ken Reeves with exhibits. It was the boss's way of dealing with Ken. Ken interpreted it differently. Thinking that Notso had been assigned to deal with the exhibits relating to the kidnapping case. Notso's brief was, in fact, to go through all the exhibits looking for any glaring errors or omissions, without showing out. The boss didn't want anyone making waves. Consequently, I again found myself not mentioning Reeves' assignation with Hampton's Muppets.

It was exactly a week ago that Peters had met Gabriel Baptiste and Andrea Smith in the café. And I wondered whether this was a regular meeting and wanted to find out. As a precaution, I booked out to some spurious location and changed into clothes I'd previously used for surveillance. Becoming a painter cum decorator, dressed in a pair of old torn jeans and a casual shirt covered in paint. My garb complemented by an official London Borough of Hackney donkey jacket I'd acquired when working undercover on a case in Dalston.

I bought myself a copy of The Sun, seemingly the preferred choice of newspapers for painters and decorators, and made my way down to the market, which was part of a pedestrian precinct with access from both ends. There were rows of shops on either side, which were open most days. Above them, two floors of flats, their walkways provided vantage points from which you could see the whole precinct. Twice a week the shops would be joined by more traditional stallholders pitched in the centre. Today was not one of those days, the market relatively quiet. The café was at the Commercial Road end where a raised brick-built flower bed had originally been built. Now a dust bowl devoid of plant life, it had become an enormous ashtray. Full of cigarette ends dubbed out in the earth. The walls of the flower bed doubled as seating, where the men would sit and read their newspapers while others shopped. Able to see the café from there, I joined a couple of those sitting and started reading my paper.

The café was open and typical of most in the area, having a counter where people queued to give their orders. After which, they either took a seat and waited for their food to be served or stood while their take-away was prepared. There were eight tables, each with four chairs. On the tables, an industrial-size sugar pourer, salt, pepper and vinegar. A couple of tables were also adorned with those oversized tomato-shaped plastic squeezy containers for red or brown sauce. Only one table was occupied, an elderly man sitting alone, vacantly looking out of the window at passers-by. From my vantage point, I had a good view of the entrance. It was now just a matter of watching and waiting.

After a while, I found myself alone. The men, having been collected, were now heading for a bus stop across the road. I didn't really want to go into the café, but sitting alone made me feel exposed. So, I joined the others standing at the bus stops, lingering with a fluctuating group of people waiting for their buses. The time when Peters had met the others had passed, and I wondered how much longer to give it and decided to wait the time it took for each of the scheduled buses to come by, which I estimated this to be another forty minutes. I wasn't that far off, and by the time all the buses had passed, there was still no sign. Now thirsty and hungry, and with the old man gone, it was time to give the café a go.

They served pretty standard fare. The all-day, big boys' breakfast with variations. A variety of freshly made sandwiches, rolls and bagels. Fish and chips or a daily special. Today's offering, pie and mash without liquor – sacrilege. I went for a couple of bagels and a mug of black coffee. The food was okay, the coffee not so – someone had stolen the flavour. I was just finishing when Matthew Peters walked in. He was wearing exactly the same clothes he'd been photographed in. I could hear the person at the counter asking how he was. Peters bought a roll of some kind, a mug of tea, and sat two tables in front of me. Picking the chair which gave him the best view of the door and those passing. He glanced around briefly and then sat looking out into the market, as if waiting for someone. I kept my head down and read the paper for the umpteenth time. There wasn't anything in it, mainly pictures. Every so often, he would glance over to the door and then back outside. I braved another coffee, hoping Peters would meet up with the others in the photograph. What if he was waiting for Ramadi and the Parkes brothers? It hadn't occurred to me he could be waiting for them. I was trying to work out whether it was best to stay or leave when Peters glanced at his watch, got up, and left. He'd moved so quickly, trying to follow him was not an option. I left too, carefully picking up the mug he'd been drinking from as I left. I didn't try to hide it, I just picked it up. Holding it around the rim as I made my way back to the car. Emptying the dregs on the way and then carefully drying the inside with some tissues. Hopefully, PKW could get some prints to compare with those from the cottage.

It wasn't until the following day that PKW got around to lifting the prints from the mug. They matched one of the outstanding sets from Cranford Cottages. Peters had been there. Whether we could actually use this as evidence was up for debate, but at least it was good intelligence. I was now kicking myself that we hadn't done the same thing with Donovan Parkes when he was in custody.

DS Gray rang with another attempt to get Mo's details. An update and variation on his theme. According to Gray, Riley had confessed to twenty-three armed robberies and two attempted murders. With more on the way, naming all those involved. A total of seventeen individuals. Once all the statements had been prepared, other arrests would be made. With Riley offering to give evidence against them all, in return for a reduced sentence. Before papers were submitted to the Director of Public Prosecution. Gray wanted to know whether Mo was one of those named. If he was, he was prepared to help. Although he needed his real name now, otherwise it would be too late. We had another impasse. He wouldn't tell me the names of those Riley had given up and I wouldn't tell him Mo's. He wasn't getting the message and was another who was becoming frustrated with me. If Mo was one of those named, he would just have to take his chances.

Gray then told me that Riley was now officially part of the supergrass programme. I couldn't believe Riley had rolled over so easily and that they were getting on so well. Riley turning over a new leaf and allowing Gray to be his handler just didn't compute. Especially after what I'd witnessed at the train station. I just couldn't imagine him standing in the witness box, grassing someone up. If he did, he would live the rest of his life in fear. Constantly in danger, looking over his shoulder. There was always someone bigger and harder. I was just as surprised to hear that the powers that be had been swayed into approving Gray's application, given the history. At the end of the conversation, Gray offered to nominate Mo for a financial reward. Cheeky bastard. Naturally, he would need to know his true identity. Persistent wasn't the word. I wasn't sure of Gray's motives, but whatever they were, I didn't see them being good for Mo. Riley's supergrass status meant that he would now be moved to a dedicated police station in north-east London. Where he would be afforded additional privileges. While there, he would make statements detailing all those he'd named.

The station's entire cell area had been adapted into a single suite. Consisting of a cell, which was larger than normal, with a sleeping area, toilet and washing facilities. Next to this was a games room. During daytime, this gave access to a small secure courtyard. The games room had a television, table tennis table, a small card table, chairs, playing cards, and a few board games. Along with the cell door, the entire games area and yard were monitored by CCTV. The sleeping area remained private, with occupants, such as Riley being allowed conjugal visits. An armed guard for the facility was mandatory. Stories existed, where previous supergrasses who'd got on well with their minders had been taken out for walks in the local park, even the odd visit to the pub.

Gray suggested I pop over to see the facilities, where we could get to know one another a little better. There was no chance, and the more he persisted, the less I trusted him. And, in any case, I'd already been there, as back-up to a colleague with a previous incumbent, who'd been given the handle 'Brian'. A reference to the snail in the Magic Roundabout. Brian was a little slow on the uptake and was now holidaying in a special wing at Bedford Prison. From the few times I'd met him, he was by far the scariest. Another enforcer, just in a different league.; kneecapping a speciality. On one occasion, we did him a tiny favour. Making sure his mum got a birthday card on time. He wanted to repay us by offering a freebie. We could have anyone capped, provided we could wait until he got out.

JACOB DARR

Chapter 12

Alan and I spent a couple of days ringing around; going through records, looking for any information that might help identify and locate the girls from the youth club, as well as Gabriel Baptiste. The hope was that we might detain them at the same time we went for Peters. It proved a fruitless exercise, and while we were trying to decide what to do next, the DI rolled in, throwing a spanner in the works by announcing that he'd arranged for the two of us to visit Albany Prison; to go over Ramadi's prison record. As the prison wouldn't allow copies of confidential information to leave the prison and the DI couldn't take Julia. I was the next best thing, meaning I was driving. With a lot of the information being treated as highly confidential, containing psychiatric reports, decisions on parole, friendships and lots of hearsay, we could only read the records and make notes later.

The following day, while queuing for the ferry, the DI's pager chirped. Glancing at the display, he mumbled something. Then, having looked at his watch, made his way over to a call box next to the ticket office. When he returned, just out of courtesy, I asked whether everything was alright?

"Danny's care's gone up again."

"I didn't know you had kids."

"I don't, Danny's my sister's. It's a long story, best leave it. It will only wind me up and make me feel grumpy. One way or another, we've all got crosses to bear, just look at the boss."

"What about the boss?"

"Ignore that. I shouldn't have said anything, slip of the tongue. Just forget it, would you?" Instantly changing the subject by saying, "So, what do you think Ramadi's records will tell us?" I took the hint.

Ramadi's records showed a young man who had no visitors while serving his sentence. Who had systematically lost all his rights and privileges. No parole, television, radio, access to activities, nothing. He'd been involved in a series of what were described as unprovoked attacks on inmates, using improvised weapons, resulting in him being periodically segregated from other inmates. On one occasion, he'd managed to steal the blades from two craft knives, which he'd then attached to a pencil, binding them together with string. Creating a double-bladed knife with parallel blades just a few millimetres apart. On three separate occasions, he'd been able to slash the face of a prisoner without the weapon being found. Eventually, it was discovered being carried by another inmate, too terrified to talk. Ramadi had deliberately made the weapon to ensure the two blades were as close together as was possible. That way, when it was used, it would create two cuts that would need to be treated as one. Resulting in pronounced scars that would never disappear. An everlasting reminder of their meeting.

On another occasion, he'd used razor blades pushed inside a potato. Targeting the face of his victim, causing serious injury. He was another nasty piece of work. Confirmed by the fact that none of his victims had made a formal complaint. And with no complainant or witnesses there was no chance of there being a prosecution, leaving the prison with little choice other than to withdraw privileges together with any opportunity for early release. The file painted a picture of a cruel, hurtful, young man, who continually bullied others. With a total disregard for the law. To me, his fixation with blades and desire to be feared by all had the signs of a psychopath. Only no one had used that term or anything like it in any of his social behaviour reports. Riley and Ramadi would make an interesting couple.

The weekend when the French came to town had arrived, and as promised, I was making a rare appearance for my old rugby club. Dearly beloved had dropped me off before heading off to do some shopping, hopefully returning before things got to raucous. I'd got changed and was going through some warm-ups, which now included drinking a schooner of sweet sherry just before kick-off. Not for social reasons, it was now club policy before the start of all first team matches. One of the former players, a local GP, was convinced that there were properties in sweet sherry, which helped increase the levels of adrenaline during a game, supposedly improving performance.

Just as we were about to kick off, one of the bar staff came running out of the club, saying I had an urgent call from my wife. When I got to the clubhouse, she was shouting and screaming down the phone. I was having so much trouble making sense of her; I thought she'd had an accident. Once she'd calmed down, I said, "What on earth's the matter, tell me what's wrong."

"You've been seeing someone."

"No, I haven't. Don't be ridiculous. What are you on about, what makes you say that?"

"You've been seeing someone else."

"I haven't. Tell me what makes you say that."

"I've got the photographs to prove it right in front of me."

"Photographs, what photographs? What are you talking about? I haven't been seeing anyone, you're not making any sense."

"I've just picked up them up from the chemists. The film was in your camera."

"And?"

"There's a photograph of you with another woman."

"I don't know what you're talking about."

"There's a photograph of another woman. She's got her arms round your neck, sitting on your lap. How long has this been going on, I want the truth?"

"There's nothing going on, I still don't know what you're talking about."

"You're at a party, and she's sitting on your lap."

"Party, what party?"

I was trying to work out what she was on about when I realised that the only thing remotely close to what she was saying was when Sally Bowers sat on my lap to thank me for the helping Alan Harrison with Ricketts. What I couldn't understand was how a photograph of that had ended up on my camera.

"Okay, I think I might know what this is. It's not what you think. I can explain. If it's what I think it is, the lady in the picture just wanted to thank me for something I did to help her. There's nothing going on, I promise. If you come and pick me up, I can explain."

So much for the game. I had to get changed and walk home. It could only be Sally Bowers, but how did a photograph get on my camera? No one in the office had said anything. I now needed to convince my wife that nothing was going on. A photograph of me at a party where I was enjoying myself, with another woman sitting on my lap. That's what she'd said. Somehow, I had found myself in a bucket load of grief for nothing. When I got home, there, on the kitchen table, was a single photograph accompanied by a frosty silence. At least she was still there, waiting to hear what I had to say. It was a photograph of Sally Bowers sitting on my lap.

The only thing I could do was to tell her the whole story. I'd never lied to her, and I wasn't about to start. Having told her what had happened, I even offered to get either Sally Bowers or Alan Harrison on the phone. Even to meet them, I was that confident they would tell her the same story without being prompted. I got the impression she was prepared to give me the benefit of the doubt, and I asked whether there were any other photographs. There were four that had been taken, with Ken Reeves and the boss the only ones missing. It was the sort of thing I could see Reeves doing, thinking it would be funny, not caring about how much trouble it might cause. If the boss had taken them, I felt sure he would have said something. I was now rueing having left my equipment in the office for so long.

I was sitting in the office next to Alan, waiting for the obligatory Monday morning meeting to start, grateful my marriage was still intact, trying to decide whether it was worth asking the boss about the photographs or just confronting Reeves, when Notso approached the two of us, saying, "Have you got a moment. It shouldn't take long. I just need a word, privately preferably, before the meeting starts." Everyone heard him.

"Now?" said Alan.

"If that's okay. It would be better before the meeting."

The three of us then took a walk along the corridor towards Gold Control, where we could duck into a small alcove.

"When the boss gave me the job of shadowing Ken, he wanted me to check all the f'ing exhibits, which I've done. I thought I was losing my mind. I felt sure that when Cranford Cottages was initially searched, there were three plastic bags with clothes in, and I can only find entries for two."

"There were definitely three. I'm pretty sure we mentioned them in one of the interviews," I said.

"I know there were, just bear with me, I'm not quite sure how to say this."

"Come on, get on with it, we've got another bloody meeting in a minute," said Alan.

"To start with, I could only find two of the exhibits which have consecutive references and entry numbers. The thought then crossed my mind that the contents of three bags may have somehow become two. Somehow getting mixed up together. But the descriptions of the contents don't match, and neither do they mention any bloodstained clothing. So, I've physically searched through all the exhibits, making a separate list to compare with the exhibits that have been submitted to the lab and have been returned or are still here. Cross-referencing the physical exhibits with the entries, everything. The lab has a record of receiving three bags of clothing originating from Cranford Cottages and sending them all back, about a week ago. The description of one of the bags mentions the stained clothing, and the exhibit reference for that bag is the first in a sequence of the three. It's not recorded in any of the books, and up until about half an hour ago, I couldn't find it anywhere. I've just found it, together with the results of the examination, stuffed in the bottom drawer of Ken's desk. It's where he keeps his booze and is usually locked. I went to use the phone and noticed the drawer open. Inside was the exhibit, a report on the findings, and of course some booze. I've photocopied the report and put it back, I wasn't sure what else to do. Just to finish this off, the findings are that the blood found on the clothes matches the blood taken from the body at the post-mortem, and there's a note to say that the blood also matches with the stains on the tarpaulin. It's Pope's blood and I can't remember Ken saying anything, can you?"

"He hasn't said anything to me. What's he up to, it doesn't make sense?" said Alan.

"Tell me, with the exhibits book, the two entries are they the first in the book?" I asked.

"No, I don't think so."

"Are there many mistakes in the book?"

"I don't remember there being any. In fact, thinking about it, it's remarkably neat and tidy."

"He's rewritten the whole book; I wonder if he's said something to the boss, and he's told him to?"

"Let's try and decide what to do after the meeting. The boss will be waiting." As we made our way back to the office Notso said, "Talking about the boss, when I picked him up, I was surprised to see a ramp at the front of his house, what's that all about?"

"What do you mean, ramp?" said Alan.

"When I went to pick the boss up from home, you have to walk up this ramp."

"I've no idea," said Alan, not really paying any attention.

The meeting was just starting, and it soon became clear that it was a meeting for the sake of a meeting. The only thing of any interest was the boss saying we would soon be making more arrests without being specific. Matthew Peters the obvious choice. The boss's suggestion triggering a lot of interest from guess who, Ken Reeves, wanting to know who the targets were and when the boss was thinking of making the arrests, fishing for information. I knew it and the DI knew it. Again, telling Ken that he would know in good time. In earlier discussions, the idea of arresting Peters and then getting Baptiste and Smith while Peters was still in custody had been mooted. There was, of course, the possibility that Peters might even tell us where they were.

I wanted to know why the boss was being so coy about the target or targets, and the best way to find out was to ask the DI. His reply:

"What do you think?"

"You don't trust someone?" I said.

"We just need to be careful, okay."

"Ken Reeves?"

"What makes you say that?"

"A couple of things, something Notso has just told me about the exhibits, and—"

"What, that Pope's blood's been found on some the clothes from Cranford Cottages?"

"How do you know? Did Ken tell you?"

"No, PKW did. He saw the results at the lab and told me the other day."

"Notso's just found the report in one of Ken's drawers. He didn't know what to do."

"What's the other reason?"

"I know that on at least one occasion Ken Reeves has met with some of Hampton's Muppets."

"Interesting. Keep it to yourself for now. I'll let the boss know. Make sure Notso and Alan do the same. Tell them to do nothing, it's in hand and by the way, when we get Peters, the boss has decided we'll be interviewing. I might even do the writing if you're lucky."

"Yeah, right," I said.

"No, I will. You're probably in a better position to lead."

He then decided that it would be a good idea if the two of us just went down to Peters' address. To sit and wait for him, on the off chance of the others turning up. If they did, we would get back up. We'd been there for ages and the only activity had been his parents arriving home.

Mrs Peters answered the door when we knocked.

"Good evening. I am Detective Sergeant Lomax, and this is Detective Inspector Clarke. Is Matthew in?"

"He's upstairs, why?"

He'd been in all the bloody time.

"Can we speak to him?"

"What's it about?"

"We're investigating the murder of a young man whose body was found on waste ground not far from here. We believe the victim may have attended the youth club at St George's where Matthew may have met him, that's all."

She called out. "Matthew, you're wanted downstairs."

"Coming," said a voice.

A few moments later, Matthew Peters appeared and as he made his way downstairs, his mother said, "These policemen are investigating the terrible murder of that young boy."

His facial expression changed immediately, looking more than a little worried. His mother's facial expression changed too, sensing something was wrong.

"Mrs Peters, purely as a matter of course, we've been asked to look in all the bedrooms of everyone we speak to. We've been asked to check for bloodstained clothing and sharp implements. Would it be all right if we had a look in Matthew's room?" asked DI Clarke.

"Of course, look all you want."

We all went upstairs. It wasn't the stereotypical teenagers' room. Tidy. Everything in its place. No posters on the walls, just a raft of family photographs dotted around. On the walls, on the shelves, and on the top of a small set of drawers, where some hardback books were also stacked. On one wall, a wooden religious cross, above which, was a small placard bearing the words, "Jesus is the father of this house."

"We're going to take Matthew to the station so that we can write everything down and show Matthew some photographs, if that's okay. He might be with us for quite a while, possibly overnight," said the DI.

"You have to do what you have to do. Matthew, you make sure you tell the truth. The Lord will be watching."

Technically, he'd been arrested. We were just trying to be as tactful as possible. As much for his parents as anything else. By all accounts, they were good people, and they hadn't tried to interfere. Mrs Peters then started to pray or preach. I wasn't sure which and for a while we waited politely for her to finish. But she kept going and in the end, we had to usher Matthew out of the door and into the car. She was still going as we drove away. Our journey passed in complete silence. Matthew didn't ask any questions, so we left him to think about what else may have led to our visit, and as far as I could tell, he hadn't recognised me from the café.

As part of the booking in process, we got him to provide elimination fingerprints, putting him into an interview room as opposed to a cell, where, just to make sure he didn't wander off, he was guarded by uniformed PC. We needed to let the boss know Peters was here, as well as getting the elimination prints sent off for comparison. About half an hour later, we sat down with him for his first ever police interview. Yet another who didn't want a solicitor.

"Matthew, tell me a bit about yourself."

"Like what?"

"Well, what do you do for a living?"

"I'm not working at the moment; I'm looking for a job."

"What sort of thing are you looking for?"

"Anything really."

"Have you worked since leaving school?"

"I did some part-time work. Filling shelves at a supermarket until it got taken over by this Asian family, who said they were changing things and I wasn't needed anymore."

"Anything else?"

"Not really."

"What sort of things do you do during the day?"

"Mum, makes sure I get up. She won't let me lie in. She gives me jobs to do, cleaning, shopping, that sort of thing. It's for my keep, and I go to the job centre at least twice a week to see if there's any work."

"Your mum seems very religious?"

"She goes to church a lot."

"What about your dad, is he religious?"

"He goes on Sundays."

"Do you ever go?"

"Sometimes."

"What about the youth club, do you go there?"

"Sometimes."

"Who are your friends there?"

"Nobody really."

For the first time, there was hesitation in his answer.

"Honestly? That's not what Brother Thomas says."

He didn't say anything.

"What did your mum say when we were leaving. Something about telling the truth?"

"You mean, Gabriel, Andrea and Georgina."

I said nothing, waiting for him to continue, looking at him while the silence became almost unbearable.

Eventually, and in a reluctant sounding voice, he said, "Gabriel Baptiste, Andrea Smith and Georgina Small."

"There, that wasn't that hard, was it? What about the others?"

Again, he said nothing, with us again just waiting silently. He was becoming uneasy and began to fidget, shifting around in his chair. Until now, he'd been looking in our direction, he was now searching for a distraction, eventually saying, "That's it, no one else."

"Matthew, I know that's not true. There were more than just the four of you."

"That's it, I tell you."

"Let me ask you one more time. Who else did you make friends with at the youth club?"

For a while, he again said nothing, going back to looking around the room. I wanted to get him talking again and decided to revisit the subject later.

"Okay, tell me a bit about Gabriel?"

Immediately, he answered. "We used to go to the same school. Not in the same class, though."

"Were your friends at school?"

"Not really."

"So, how did you become friends?"

"Georgina, she went to the youth club."

"So?"

"Georgina and Andrea are good friends and go out together."

"Including the youth club?"

"Yes, including the youth club."

"Gabriel and Andrea are boyfriend and girlfriend, aren't they?"

"Yeah, Gabriel liked Andrea, and after a while they started going out together, seeing each other."

"And you fancied Georgina?"

"Maybe."

"Any luck?"

"What with Georgina? No."

"Do you know where she lives?"

"Near Luke House, I think. I'm not sure of the number, but I could probably take you there."

"What about Gabriel, where does he live?"

"I don't know where Gabriel or Andrea live now."

"Honestly?"

"Yes, honestly."

"What about the others?"

We were back to silence, with him looking around pensively. It was as though something was scaring him. We had a choice. Keep pushing and have him clam up or leave him for a night in the cells. Which could still make him clam up, but it could also help to concentrate the mind, getting him to talk. There didn't seem to be much to lose, letting him spend the night in the cell and on the way there. I had an opportunity to give him a bit of a pep talk.

"Have a think about what you're not telling us and why, we're just trying to establish the truth. What do you think will happen, if someone else tells us something you know or have been involved in and you don't? What will that look like? Remember what your mum said. You wouldn't want to disappoint her, would you?"

He said nothing while I took him into the charge room, where the station officer formally booked him in. The process of emptying his pockets, being thoroughly searched; with everything other than a handkerchief taken away. Then being asked some basic questions before being escorted to the cells gave him a jolt. A reality check, making him realise he was now a prisoner. As I closed the cell door, he turned and looked at me as if to speak. Troubled by something. A look of sorrow in his eyes. He said nothing, slowly bowing his head, as if in shame. In some ways, I felt sorry for him. I got the impression he knew about Adam Pope's death but was too afraid to say.

Having got back to the office, it soon became apparent that the DI had decided that work had finished for the day. Hurrying off for a shower. Julia loitered, having already changed into something more suited to a West End show. Only the boss and Ken Reeves were left. They were entertaining two other visitors. A local Beefeater and someone called Johnnie Walker. Even if I was invited to join them, I wouldn't be. I would only end up accusing Reeves of all sorts of things. As I left, I wondered who'd instigated the session. Whether it was the boss trying to elicit information from Ken, or Ken trying to pump the boss? Either way, it would take more than just the two bottles.

Chapter 13

Having made a conscious effort to be in early, the instantly recognisable smell of fresh cigar smoke told me I was not the first to arrive. As I got closer to the office, I could hear voices. Alan and a team from the Flying Squad, chatting. I was about to say good morning when I noticed DS Gray sitting at the back of the group. Jokingly I said, "What's happened, don't tell me, he's escaped?"

"How do you know?"

"Yeah, right?"

"I'm being deadly serious; how do you know he's escaped?" The tone of his voice even more severe. Still thinking it was a joke, and the team were more likely to be there waiting for the off on some job. It was only when I looked at the faces of the others, I had second thoughts.

"Get out of bed on the wrong side this morning, grumpy bugger. What's the matter, can't you take a joke?" I said.

"I asked you a question. How do you know he's escaped?"

"I'm not falling for it. What are you really doing here... Honestly?"

"Honestly, he's escaped."

"Really?"

"Yes, really."

"It's true," said Alan. "They've been waiting quite a while. The only reason I'm here is that I'm having an early night, so I thought I would get in early to go over the actions while it was quiet."

"Okay, go on then. Tell me what's happened?"

"He got out through the window in the leisure area, around two this morning. It's all on CCTV. I got a called about an hour later. PeaSea knows. He says we need to speak to Mo urgently. We've got twenty-four hours to get him back, or the shit's going to hit the fan. You can call him if you like, he tells me you've got his number."

It was only then that I began to take him seriously. But from memory, the window was tiny, making it hard to believe.

"I'm not sure what's the best way to get a hold of Mo at this time of day. It depends on whether he's working or not, and I don't know the answer to that. If he's working, he'll be at Covent Garden or Spitalfields and I should be able to get hold of him around ten. If he's not working, I could try his gaff, but would need to be careful as he might have visitors. So, what happened to Riley's guard, when all this was happening?"

"Well, the collator…"

"The collator! What's he got to do with it?"

"He was the one guarding Riley."

"Sorry, I'm not with this, what's the collator doing guarding Riley?"

"Well, because of a few manpower shortages, we've had trouble covering nights. So, we went through the list of authorised shots on district, looking for volunteers who wanted to do some overtime, and he volunteered. He's done it before. All he had to do was search and log any authorised visitors and monitor the CCTV."

"So, what happened?"

"Riley's been at the custody suite for quite a while, and his girlfriend's been visiting him every day. She turns up most evenings after dinner in shagwear. Stays for a couple of hours and then leaves. Visitors aren't allowed after ten, and we're interviewing during the day. So early evening is about the only time she can stay for any length of time. The collator says that last night, she turned up as usual with a change of clothes. Which he says he checked, searching her too. She wasn't wearing a lot, scantily clad, was how he described her. He's adamant that he searched her thoroughly, but we doubt it. She's only twenty-two and turned up last night wearing very little, as verified by CCTV. A white shirt tied up around the midriff, with several buttons undone showing a lot of cleavage. A light-blue neckerchief and an extremely short mini-skirt or wide belt, as someone put it, and high heels. We're sure she flirted with the collator, although he denies it. We've seen her flirting with others. Riley's probably told her to. She's even tried it on with us. Anything to distract you. She could quite easily have had cash and car keys stuffed somewhere and the collator would have never known. He wouldn't go anywhere near those places. As usual, she stayed for a couple of hours and left just after nine-thirty. It's all logged correctly and verified by CCTV. Once his girlfriend had gone, Riley moved the table tennis table. So that it was up against the wall and then started playing against himself. Hitting rebounds off the wall for about fifteen minutes. He then went into his cell and stayed there. Which again, is confirmed by CCTV. When the collator went to check on him around two-thirty, he'd gone. About an hour later, I got a call, and here we are."

"How the hell did he get out of a locked cell, and then the suite?"

"Having gone through the CCTV, his cell door wasn't locked. Riley closed it when he went back into his cell and turned his light out. Making it look as though the door was shut, and he'd gone to bed. He must have used a credit card or something similar to cover the recess. Stopping the door from locking but making it look as if it was. The collator didn't check, turning the suite lighting off from his panel in the control room. Leaving just the night lights. Just after one, Riley can be seen coming out of his cell, climbing onto the table tennis table and then clambering out through the window. We didn't believe it until we watched the CCTV. The window is just eighteen inches by eight, none of us could have got through it."

"And where was the collator when all this was happening? No, don't tell me, he'd gone for a dump?"

"The truth is, he fell asleep. With back-to-back day and night shifts, he thought he would be okay with Riley locked in his cell. He's just not used to it. He's got less than a year to go."

"Is this for real? I can just see the headlines, it won't be Sweeney Todd, Flying Squad, it'll be Sweeney Nod, Dreaming Plod. I bet PeaSea's well impressed?"

DS Gray cringed at the quip, which I didn't think was that bad considering how early it was.

"He knows, and you can probably guess his reaction, which is why we've got twenty-four hours before things go public. That's how long we've got to get him back. Otherwise, not only is the collator's job on the line, but a few of us could be on the move. PeaSea thinks it could jeopardise the whole supergrass programme. Finishing it off completely, especially if the D.P.P. gets wind."

"Does Riley think he's been bubbled?"

"Of course, he does."

"Has he said who he thinks it might be?"

"Not to my knowledge."

From what had been said, Mo could be in a spot of bother. And with Matthew Peters to deal with, I was trying to figure out the best thing to do. It was a bit too early to go down to Tower Hill, and I didn't want DS Gray or any of his mates joining or following me to Mo's. I still needed to protect his identity, irrespective of the situation. The phone then rang with Alan taking the call. Waving an arm about trying to quieten everyone down, saying in a loud voice, "Chris, I've got someone called Mo on the line for you." The room instantly fell silent.

"I was just thinking about you. I was going to pop down later and see how things are," I said.

"What the fuck's going on? I've had Riley at my place since four this morning. He scared the shit out of me."

Angry was an understatement.

"I've literally just been told he's escaped. You okay?"

"At the moment."

"Is he still with you?"

"No."

"Where are you?"

"Never mind, what's going on?"

"All I know is that last night he managed to kid his guard into thinking that his cell was locked and that he was asleep. Then, sometime between one and two, he squeezed through a tiny window and away. What about you?"

"I'm not sure what time it was, but I got woken up by this knocking noise. At first, I couldn't make out what it was or where it was coming from. Then there was a lot of banging on the front door. I peered out of the window and guess who, Riley. He saw me and wanted in. I didn't have a choice, so trying to act normal, I asked him what he was doing out. He said he needed a favour and wanted to stay for a few hours, and that he needed cash. He then told me this story, saying he'd been nicked at Paddington Station, by the Sweeney, who'd offered him a deal, meaning he could get banged up at a station instead of prison, taken for walks and his bird could visit him too."

Gray had said it was the other way around and that it was Riley who'd offered to turn Queen's evidence.

"Riley said he agreed to the deal. As being in the nick with his bird visiting gave him a better chance of legging it. And, telling the old bill about the blaggings they already knew about seemed easy. Apart from his bird visiting, he'd been taken for walks, which had given him an idea of the layout outside and where to head for. He just needed to get through a little window in the cell area. So, he stopped eating a lot of the food. Hiding it in his cell until his bird took it away in the evening. He was meant to meet up with her when he got out, but for some reason, she was a no-show. So, instead of hanging around, he'd headed my way, mumping a lift into town. He needed some cash to tide him over for a couple of days, as he didn't want to visit his stash. I ended up bunging him a monkey and taking him to King's Cross, dropping him in York Way."

"Do you know where he's gone?"

"No, the only thing is that in the past, he's mentioned a caravan site where he knew the site manager in Suffolk I think – Ipswich, Great Yarmouth somewhere that way."

"Has he said anything to you, about how he got nicked at Paddington?"

"He thought he'd been unlucky, and the Sweeney just happened to be at the station, looking for someone else, when he got spotted."

"So, he doesn't think he's been bubbled?"

"I don't think so. I don't think he would have come to me, if he thought I had anything to do with it."

Another variation on Gray's version of events.

"Did he say anything else?"

"He went on a bit about one of his minders. A detective sergeant he didn't like. He thought he was a bit of a prick who couldn't be trusted. Someone he wanted to meet in a dark alley one night, as he had a score to settle."

If it was who I was looking at. I didn't entirely disagree. I then asked what clothes Riley was wearing.

He didn't answer, saying, "See you around sometime, maybe." As he hung up.

What a complete cock-up this was turning out to be. It was looking as though I may have just lost a good informant. The collator was going to lose his job, and it was possibly the end of the Supergrass programme. Gray, I didn't care about. The only minor saving grace was that Mo's identity would remain confidential. I repeated some of what Mo had said, making it sound as though Riley could still be at King's Cross. Which is where they all rushed off to, leaving the two of us to figure what to do next.

Somewhere down the road, I needed to show Mo some goodwill and make a serious effort to sort out his street trader licences.

Even if it didn't lead to anything. It was just the sort of thing the boss might be able to help with. It was right up his street. He might even be able to use some of his contacts in the Fraud Squad, after all their police force was paid for by the Corporation of London.

The boss wasn't looking great when he turned up. Much the worse for wear after his whisky mission with Ken Reeves. Despite this, when I spoke to him about Mo's problem, he immediately got the drift of what I was trying to achieve. As far as he could see, the only stumbling block would be the name in which the licences were issued, which was likely to depend on whether he remained an informant or not? I just hoped that if Riley got in touch, Mo would contact me.

Due to the late arrival of my interviewing partner, it wasn't until early afternoon that were able to re-interview Matthew Peters. He didn't say why he was late, and neither did he try to come up with any lame excuses, heading straight for the shower and a change of clothes. Volunteering to scribe, as if in penance.

When I collected Peters from his cell, he didn't speak and there was little or no eye contact. With his head down, he constantly looked at the floor walking next to me. The night in the cell had definitely had an effect. The question was whether it had concentrated the mind sufficiently for a meaningful interview to take place. DI Clarke had prepared the interview room, with Peters sitting in the same chair where he continued to look at the floor, avoiding eye contact.

After the formalities I said, "Yesterday, I was asking you about the names of those you knew at the youth club. You mentioned Andrea, Georgina and Gabriel. What about the others?"

At first, I thought he wasn't going to reply, then still looking at the floor and with a tremor in his voice he said, "There wasn't anyone else."

"Are you sure?"

"Yes."

"Let's try that again, shall we? There were more than four of you, Brother Thomas has told us that. You know their names, so why not just tell us?"

"There isn't anyone else, I've told you."

"If you don't believe me, what about Adam, Adam Pope? You haven't mentioned him, and we know you two were mates, so..."

I didn't have the chance to finish before he began to shake. More and more, violently convulsing. It got so bad; it looked as if he was having a fit and we'd need to call a doctor. He was so scared. I couldn't remember ever seeing anyone react this way. Petrified, more than Donovan Parkes had been. Surely we couldn't be frightening him. It had to be someone or something else. It took several minutes, a drink of water and a lot of patience before he'd recovered enough for me to carry on. If nothing else, his reaction said he knew a lot more about Adam's death.

"As I was saying, we know you know, Adam?"

Still looking down meekly he said, "Alright, I know Adam."

"There, that wasn't very difficult, was it?"

"No... I suppose not."

"Okay, so why don't you tell us how you first met?"

"I don't really remember. I just remember seeing him at the youth club. He used to go there now and again. He was a bit of a loner, like me."

"Why's that?"

"I used to get picked for having to go to church. Adam told me he got picked on because of his size. If his dad found out, he'd been bullied he would beat him too, for not sticking up for himself."

"So, how long do you think you've known each other?"

"A year, maybe more."

"And how many times have you been to Cranford Cottages?"

The jitters returned and there was still no eye contact. It was another question that had hit a nerve. All we could do was wait patiently, hoping to get a response. As we again sat in silence, I was sure of one thing, I wouldn't be moving on anytime soon. For a few minutes we sat in total silence, not knowing which way the interview would go. He then raised his head and after another brief pause said, "A couple of times. I didn't like it."

"Why was that?"

"I just didn't... because of Ramadi, mainly."

His reply, immediate. As I went to continue, he started shaking again. His nerves again getting the better of him. Shaking and shivering, as if really cold. Again, we waited patiently. In the end I said, "Benjamin Ramadi?"

"Yes."

Then, to my surprise, DI Clarke interrupted.

"Matthew, we need to have a break. I'd like you to sign and initial the notes as you did before, if that's okay?"

I wasn't sure what the DI had in mind, and having made what I thought was a breakthrough, I didn't understand or see the need for a break, but had little choice. Peters agreed immediately. Visibly relieved at the possibility of getting back to his cell.

Taking him back, I said, "Matthew, whatever it is that's scaring you, we can't help if you don't tell us. Just remember what your mum said. Have a think and I'll see you later."

He just nodded, looking so troubled. Not crying, but almost inconsolable. I couldn't remember seeing anyone like it. He wasn't a hardened criminal, but without knowing what was causing his anguish, we couldn't do anything to help. I left him again, head down, looking at the cell floor. When I got to ask the DI why he wanted to stop, he said that getting Peters to sign the notes admitting he knew Ramadi was a big step forward. The bit I couldn't fathom was letting the rest of the team to know. I didn't agree, but it was too late.

I then found myself in a discussion about how long to wait before we interviewed him again and how long he could be detained. The boss was of the opinion that at present we could argue that he was at the station voluntarily. Being treated as a person at risk; kept at a place of safety. It would only be if or when further evidence of any involvement in a crime came to light that we would have to change our stance and the clock would start. Some of our paperwork would have to be modified to fit with the circumstances and provided he didn't ask for a solicitor or want to leave; everything should be fine. I wanted to get on with interviewing but was overruled. Matthew was set to spend another night in the cell.

The following morning, Matthew looked rough. With bags under his eyes, which looked sore. It didn't look as though he'd slept much, if at all. For the third time, I went through the interviewing formalities with one variation; getting him to agree that he'd been staying at the station voluntarily. DI Clarke then asked him to sign a declaration before we went any further, which he did.

"Yesterday, we were talking about Cranford Cottages, Benjamin Ramadi and Adam Pope and you referred to him using the word's, he was a bit of a loner, why did you..." But, before I could finish, Peters interrupted saying, "I can't do it anymore."

"Do what?"

"Keep quiet, it's killing me. I can't live with myself. I can't sleep, it's not right, and it's not fair."

"What is?"

"They made me do it."

"Do what?"

"I did something terrible."

"Who's they?"

"Ramadi and the brothers."

"Benjamin Ramadi and the Parkes brothers?"

"Yes, yes, yes."

"Anyone else?"

"No, just them."

"Is this to do with Adam Pope?"

"Yes."

"What do you mean?"

"It was horrible."

"Okay, calm down, take it slowly and in your own words, just tell us exactly what happened. We can't help if we don't know?"

"Ramadi, he made me do it. He forced me. If I didn't do it, I would be next. He would kill me too."

"You just said it was Ramadi and the Parkes brothers?"

"The Parkes brothers, Devon, will do anything. He just copies Ramadi. He's the leader."

It took nearly six hours for Peters to tell us what had happened, going over what he'd said. Getting as much detail as was possible, while looking for any discrepancies or ambiguities – there weren't any.

On two occasions, he'd been with Adam Pope to Cranford Cottages. Which he described as a bit of a squat, but as he said, "At least it was dry." The first time they went there was in March, when they could sit and talk by themselves for most of the time. Adam had taken him there one evening after the youth club, saying that he'd stayed there a few times with people he knew. Later, Ramadi and Devon Parkes turned up. It was the first time Peters had ever come across them. Peters said it was obvious that Ramadi was in charge by the way he spoke, where he sat and the way he issued orders.

Ramadi kept playing with a knife he had. A pencil with two blades at one end. He twirled it between his fingers, like a baton. He called it Baby. Later, he went upstairs coming back with a hatchet; he called Daddy. Which he also played with, twirling it around.

Peters didn't like the way they bragged about forcing others to do things. If they didn't do as they were told, he would slice their faces. Ramadi bragged about having done it lots of times. "It's the mark of The Axeman," he would say. He called himself 'The Axeman,' wanting to be known as 'The Axeman.' According to Peters, Ramadi and Devon Parkes started to boast more and more. With Devon Parkes bragging about making girls have sex with him. If they became difficult, he would rape them, and then cut their faces. The scars a permanent reminder of their meeting. He thought it would make them look ugly, so that no one would want them, and they would eventually end up old and lonely.

Devon Parkes had a fixation with Georgina Small. Peters didn't know how he knew her, but Parkes knew she went to the youth club with Andrea and was friends with Gabriel and Adam. Parkes said that, "One day, when he got the chance. He was going to have her one way or the other, willing or not, he was going to fuck her backwards, forwards, sideways, anyway, he could." Those were his exact words, which he repeated several times, convincing Peters he meant what he said. Another thing they boasted about was how they hardly ever paid for anything. Taking, whatever they wanted from the shops. Beating up anyone who tried to stop them. It was their way of life.

Also, during the first meeting, both Ramadi and Devon Parkes had ordered Adam around, telling him where to sit. Getting him to wait on them, being mean and nasty. Making him their servant, putting him in his place, looking small in front of a friend. The more Peters spoke, the calmer his voice became. As if a burden were being lifted. The first time he left the Cottages, someone else was making their way there. Peters was sure he'd seen that person from time to time at the youth club. It turned out to be Devon's brother – Donovan Parkes.

The second time Peters visited was in early April. Bored, he'd gone looking for Adam, who wasn't at the hostel. The first time they went, Adam had just walked around the back and straight in, which is what Matthew did, save knocking on the door as he opened it. Donovan Parkes was in the kitchen area and gestured for him to go through into the living space where Ramadi and Devon were sitting with something on the floor wrapped in yellow sheeting.

Ramadi asked if he was looking for Adam, repeating the question time and again, and while he did so, he kept looking at Peters and then down at sheeting, drawing Peters' eyes to the floor and the covered bundle.

The more he looked, the more he realised it was the shape of a body, the implication being that it was Adam. Peters said he was stunned and just stood and stared, not knowing what to do. As he did so, he was grabbed on either side by the brothers, who pushed him back against the wall, pinning him.

Ramadi stayed sitting in his chair, watching, casually twirling Baby. He then asked Peters what he was doing there and whether he was alone. The next thing Peters remembers is Ramadi telling the brothers to hold him still, resulting in them pushing him against the wall even more. Having got up, Ramadi got so close; their heads were almost touching, pressing Baby high up into Peters' cheekbone. Unable to move, he thought Ramadi was going to cut his eye. It was that close.

Ramadi then told Donovan Parkes to check outside, making make sure no one was there and then to stand by the door. As Donovan signalled, the coast was clear, Ramadi, still twirling Baby went back to his seat. Pulling back part of the sheet as he did so, revealing Adam's head and some of his chest. Peters felt sick. The sheeting still covered most of Adam's body, but from what he could see. His mouth was open with a cloth of some kind pushed down his throat and a cord around his neck. Which Peters described as the sort of cord used to tie curtains back in posh houses. Adam's eyes were open, staring.

The thought went through my mind that fibres found on Pope's back during the post-mortem could be from either the cord or the cloth.

Ramadi then told the brothers to make sure Peters didn't leave while he went upstairs, returning with Daddy. Peters had seen him playing with the hatchet the first time he'd been there. This time he was tossing it higher, catching it every time. He didn't drop it once, and when he wasn't throwing Daddy. He was running his thumb back and forth along the blade, intimidating Peters. Ramadi then started pacing around the room, going into the kitchen area; Stepping over Adam's body; continuing to pace. Staring at everyone, psyching himself up, he then started chanting, to the tune of 'Ring a Ring o' Roses'.

"Ring a Ring o' Roses, this is what a narc is, a pocket full of grasses, atishoo, atishoo, he fell down." He kept circling, repeating his poem. Then suddenly stopping, smashing Daddy into the windowsill near to where he'd been sitting. Daddy was embedded so far into the wood he had trouble freeing it. He then told Peters that if he wanted to live, the only way that would happen was if he were part of the gang. And to be part of the gang, he had to prove himself. Which meant helping to get rid of Adam. Cutting his head and hands off would do. If he did that, they might trust him. If he didn't, couldn't or wouldn't, he would join Adam on the floor. There was plenty of room for two.

Peters said that since his first visit to the Cottages, he'd heard stories, rumours about how brutal and vicious the three of them could be. They didn't seem to have the same values or care about other people's lives, just their own. Picking on those too scared to do or say anything. Peters said that he'd been told, but couldn't remember who by that Ramadi hadn't been in the area that long. He'd also been told some of the things they would do. Like walking into shops and helping themselves to whatever they wanted and then just walking out without paying. If the shopkeepers challenged them, they or their families would get targeted – intimidated by following them home. The shops or homes would find their windows getting smashed or torched. Horrified by what Peters had heard and by what he'd witnessed. He was convinced that if he didn't do what Ramadi wanted, he would be killed. Realising he might still be killed, even if he did. The choice was stark, and if proof were needed, it was lying right in front of him. Adam, his friend, dead. Wrapped up in some grubby yellow sheet.

He'd never seen a dead body before, and from what he could see Adam's skin was much lighter than normal, a greyish brown.

Ramadi told Devon Parkes to get the tools. Going into the kitchen area, he picked up a pack of kitchen knives and a meat cleaver, which he held in one hand while picking up another knife in the other. The pack and meat cleaver he dropped on the floor beside Adam. He then started tossing the other knife in the air – mimicking Ramadi. The pack contained several knives. Peters described the meat cleaver as a smaller version of what you would see in a butcher's shop. The knives had shiny black plastic handles. The handle of the meat cleaver was also black but made with duller material. With the pack containing a bread knife, a carving knife, and three smaller knives. The sort he'd seen his mum use to peel and cut vegetables.

Ramadi again told Donovan Parkes to sit in front of the back door, making sure nobody could get in or out. If they did, Donovan would find himself lying on the floor next to Pope. Ramadi got up from his chair. As he did so, he pushed the handle of Daddy inside his trousers, so that only the head of the hatchet was visible, hooked over the waistline of his trousers. Stopping it from sliding down. Peters said that he'd placed the hatchet with such ease, it seemed second nature. Then, taking Baby out of his pocket, he grabbed Peters around the neck, pulling him over Adam. Forcing him to stoop over the body, saying, "He deserved what he got. Do you want to go the same way? So easy, it was so easy, I could do it again, anytime... Watching the grass suffer was best. I made him suffer, really suffer. I wanted to make sure he remembered everything, everything until the end. Would you like to remember everything?"

Peters could tell by the way Ramadi acted and spoke; he got a real buzz from telling the story. Enjoying every moment. How he planned it. How it had worked, what they'd done, everything. With the brothers nodding in the right places, showing their approval.

"We set a little trap to get him here, didn't we? Then, when he came in, I was waiting behind the door and got him. Got him with a rope around his neck. Just tight enough to make him choke a little, making sure he couldn't talk. I didn't want to kill him straight away. There was plenty of time to play. We got him on his knees and forced that down his throat," he said, pointing to the gag coming out of Adam's mouth.

"He struggled a bit and made this gurgling noise. Then we hogtied him. Devon knew how to do that. I had him; he was at my mercy. Tied up, we got him kneeling on the sheet. He kept gurgling, trying to talk. I didn't want to hear any excuses; he was going to die. He knew it. I left him on his knees, looking at us, scared. He fell over a few times and got a jab for his pains, as we got him back on his knees. He was going to die. I told him so. It was just a case of when. Slowly cutting his shirt off. He was grass and grasses have to die."

Peters reiterated several times just how much Ramadi revelled in recounting the story. With Adam unable to speak, Ramadi said he cut him a few times across his arms, chest and legs, using Baby. Saving the face for later, he enjoyed watching the blood trickle from the cuts. When the blood looked to be stopping, Ramadi let the brothers have a go. Again, using Baby. Taking in turns to cut Adam some more. Gradually, Pope started to lean over. His head began to droop. He was getting weak, so weak they had to prop him up. For their finale, Ramadi had the three of them stand around Pope and, on the count of three, take it in turns to stab him repeatedly. Targeting the stomach, chest, his back and sides. According to Ramadi, when Pope then keeled over, he was probably dead, but he couldn't resist a few more hits, just to be sure.

Peters kept going back to the way Ramadi told the story. He loved it, relishing every moment. So much so, he was horrified at the thought of Ramadi looking forward to doing it again. Feeling sure that he would suffer the same fate. Devon Parkes repeated some of what Ramadi had said, mimicking him. Saying killing was easy and he would be next if he didn't do as he was told. For Peters, Ramadi was much more menacing. He knew Ramadi was more than capable of carrying out the threat. At one point, he said he shook so much he was convinced was going to be killed, even if he did as they'd asked. The only chance he had was to do what they wanted, in the slim hope that it would keep him alive. Adam was already dead; he was now trying to save himself.

Ramadi had again taken hold of Daddy. Donovan Parkes had moved away from the door; leaving a chair wedged against the lock. There was no chance of moving it and getting out before being caught. The place was just too small. Both of the Parkes brothers were now brandishing knives, closing in on him. He was having trouble plucking up enough courage to try. Feeling so threatened, he bent down over Adam's body. Close enough to move more of the sheeting that covered him.

It was only then that he saw the extent to which Adam's body had been mutilated. No longer tied up as they'd said. Cut marks covered his chest, the upper parts of his legs and arms. He could also see cut marks around one of Pope's wrists. Having both heard and seen what he had; he could envisage the wounds being inflicted, just as Ramadi had described. It was truly gruesome.

Peters still couldn't understand what Adam could have possibly done to have been treated so viciously. Tied up, gagged, strangled, tortured, and then slowly stabbed to death. It was awful. Peters managed to kneel beside Adam's body. The blood on the sheeting, not as much as he'd expected. Ramadi then told Devon to get some bags, which he did. Black plastic sacks, which he threw down beside Peters.

Ramadi then said, "What are you going to do first?"

According to Peters, Ramadi and Devon Parkes came closer, wielding their weapons more threateningly. So much so that Peters felt he had to do something, taking hold of Adam's wrist; to pick up. He was surprised at how cold and clammy it felt. He immediately let go. Parkes then slowly handed him the meat cleaver, saying, "Come on, chop, chop." Laughing as he did so. Taking the cleaver in his right hand, Peters then held Adam's forearm higher up nearer the elbow, aiming to cut higher up the arm. Taking a few practice swings, worried he would hit his own hand. The fear in his face must have been there for all to see as he struggled to maintain control. Staying knelt beside Adam, he tried to summon up the willpower needed to wield a blow that would sever the arm in one go. Worried he might struggle to do it more than once. There was now complete silence as the others watched and waited. Again, Peters tried to muster up the courage to have one good swing. Realising the longer it took, the more agitated Ramadi would become. Ultimately losing patience. Now with two hands on the cleaver, shaking almost uncontrollably, he drew his arms as far as he could, coming down, striking the arm with all the strength he could muster. It was enough to go through the bones completely. All that was needed now was to cut a small amount of flesh that had kept the hand attached to the arm. Peters wanted to be sick and kept retching, but nothing came out. He thought there would be quite a bit of blood. There was hardly any.

Devon Parkes got one of the rubbish sacks. Opened it, and nonchalantly picked up the severed arm, dropping it in the bag as if it were leftovers. As he did so, he said, "One, down, two to go."

Peters shuffled around to the right-hand side of Adam's body, getting himself into a similar position. Unsuccessfully, he tried to repeat the process. This time it took several goes before he'd managed it. Again, he felt as if he wanted to be sick, and again, nothing came out. He said his heart was pounding at an incredible rate. Sweating, struggling to control himself.

Devon Parkes again counted, "Two down, one to go." Picking up Adam's right arm and plopping it into the same bag. Devon Parkes had been the most animated and seemed to be getting the biggest kick out of the spectacle. Ramadi hadn't really said anything, he'd just watched.

For Peters, this was going to be by far the hardest part. He wasn't sure if he could do it. Removing Adam's head was a whole new ball game. His eyes open, still staring. Eventually, Peters said he plucked up enough courage to close Adam's eyes.

Touching his face, he thought it much colder than his arms, almost freezing.

Again, Peters closed his eyes, trying to summon enough courage to wield one more blow, when Donovan Parkes started rustling bags, deliberately distracting him. Again, he closed his eyes and again Parkes distracted him. This time by walking over to the knives, opening the packet, tossing him the bread knife, saying, "I think you should use this. What about it?" Parkes looked to Ramadi for approval. He just said, "Whatever you use, you'd better get on with it, I'm getting bored."

Peters then got one of the other sacks that were close to him and placed it over Pope's face, hiding it. Devon Parkes wanted it taken away, Ramadi let it stay. Peters said that not seeing Adam's face helped a little. Still using the meat cleaver, partly in defiance of Parkes but also because he thought it would be quicker. He started chopping at Adam's neck, and despite several attempts, failed. At first, he couldn't understand why. Thinking he no longer had the strength to succeed? It was getting messy, with pieces of flesh coming away. Peters then noticed the Jeye cloth, which was in the way. It had been shoved so far down Adam's throat it was acting like a spring against the meat cleaver. Preventing the blows from being effective. Much to Parkes' delight, Peters had to resort to cutting the rest of Adam's neck with the bread knife. The sawing motion, along with the sound, finally made him physically sick. With most of the vomit going over, some of the newspaper spread over the floor.

Having cut through the bone clearing the cloth, one more blow with the meat cleaver would do it. Just one more go and one way or the other, the ordeal would be over. He mustered as much strength as he could and, with a big swing, cut through what was left. Adam's head fell away from the body and lay on the floor. Ramadi then got Peters to place the head into a separate bag, telling Donovan Parkes that Peters had done a better job than he had.

Using the bag which had covered Pope's face. Peters then wrapped it around the head, placing both into another bag. Parkes then handed Peters some cut string, which he used to tie the bags. He was then made to wash the knives and meat cleaver with some water from a bottle before putting them into another of the sacks. After which, he was made to sit on the floor near the sheeting with his back to the wall. Donovan Parkes moved his chair, sitting closer to Peters. Nobody was talking or doing anything, they just seemed to be sitting in silence. As if, waiting for something to happen. He didn't know what was happening, too scared to ask. Sometime later, he wasn't sure how long it was. There was a knock on the door, which Ramadi insisted on answering. Peters heard him say. "You took your time, get everything?" Followed by, "Good, come in."

It was Gabriel Baptiste, who was clearly surprised to see him there. He was carrying a shopping bag, which he left in the kitchen space before going into the living area. As he did so, he stopped, staring at the sheeting.

"Bit different, Matthew's been helping, haven't you?" Ramadi said. Peters nodded. Ramadi, again in his element.

"It's nearly time for the 'grass' to say goodbye, but first me and Gabby are going to take a walk, while you three go for a ride. When we're done, we'll all meet back here, won't we?" he said, staring threateningly at Peters. Peters didn't have a clue what he was on about, but nodded. Ramadi then took Devon Parkes outside. When they returned, Devon Parkes said to Peters. "Get the bags, the ones with the hands and knives in, we're going out."

Peters was then taken by the Parkes brothers to a bus stop on the Commercial Road, where they waited.

"Don't try anything stupid. You know what will happen if you do," said Devon, flashing the knife he'd been playing with. "When the bus comes, get on it, go upstairs, and sit on a seat by yourself towards the front. Make sure the seat behind you is empty. Most of them will be, got it?"

They then waited for a bus heading to East Ham. Donovan Parkes followed Peters upstairs, while Devon got tickets from the conductor. Upstairs was completely empty. Peters did as he was told, sitting in the third row. Sitting by the aisle, he placed the bags beside him near the window. Donovan took a seat at the back, close to the stairs. His back resting against the window, with his feet dangling over the edge of the seat into the aisle. Sitting that way, he could keep an eye on Peters and block the way should he need to. Devon came upstairs with the tickets, sitting immediately behind Peters. He didn't say where they were going. They stayed on the bus for about twenty minutes, maybe longer, when Devon told him to get off. Having done so, he pointed towards some high-rise flats, which Donovan started walking towards. Peters, still carrying the bags, was told to walk a few paces behind, with Devon following at the back. Not far down the road they crossed a river and about half-way across, Peters was told to stop, while the brothers stood at each end. Peters was then told to throw the knives into different parts of the river, one by one. When he'd finished, he was then told to carry on following Donovan towards the flats.

Peters knew the design, typical of most council flats. Fairly square, with a communal rubbish chute in every corner of every floor. Occupiers or anyone passing could dispose of anything that would fit in the chutes. The rubbish would then fall into one of the large bins in the basement area. Devon Parkes knew the bins were emptied three times a week.

Having walked down a ramp to the large bins. Peters was told to take the hands out of the bag, putting each one into a different bin. Then doing the same with the bags. Again, he did as he was asked. He didn't know exactly where he was but felt sure he could show police, provided they followed the bus route. The three of them then made their way back to the Cottages. Again, sitting separately on the bus.

On the way back, Peters continued to do as he was told, making no attempt to speak to anyone or get away. When they got back, Gabriel Baptiste and Ramadi were already there, waiting. Ramadi asked Peters why he hadn't tried to get away or speak to anyone, like the bus conductor. Peters told him he knew the brothers would stop him and he didn't want to be killed trying. And even if he'd succeeded, they would have come after him and his friends, and he didn't want that. What he didn't say was that he'd prayed several times for forgiveness.

Peters was then taken into the living area by Donovan while Ramadi spoke to Devon. Gabriel Baptiste was sitting on one of the chairs, staring at what was left of Adam.

Ramadi came in, ordering them to get Adam's body tied up in the sheet. Peters said that he felt a little more secure with Baptiste there. Continuing to do as he was asked, they tied the sheeting around Adam. They were then made to carry Adam's body around to the waste ground. Donovan Parkes acted as the front lookout, with Devon Parkes walking beside them, carrying a fuel can, with Ramadi at the rear. Peters didn't know where the fuel can had come from, but assumed it had either been in the kitchen or backyard. They walked around the block to the gap in the fence, where Peters thought the sheet got caught.

With Adam placed on the ground near the middle. Ramadi got everyone else to look around for anything that would burn. Wanting it placed next to the body, which Peters said, wasn't that easy in the dim light. The pyre was made up of broken wooden furniture, pallets and plastic piping, laid out for a funeral. Peters and Baptiste were then told to get Adam unwrapped and put on top of the pyre. Ramadi wanted a sense of theatre, a ritual. He was sending a message.

Devon then doused the body with the liquid from the can. Passing two boxes of matches to Ramadi, he took a match from one of the boxes, struck it and then used it to set light to the two boxes. Creating two small fire torches, lobbing one to each end of the pyre. Almost instantaneously, the pyre burst into flames, producing a mini explosion. For a few seconds there was a flash of light, where the entire area was clearly visible, before quickly fading as the flames diminished. The pyre was burning, just not as fiercely or as brightly as Ramadi wanted. He wanted more of a show. Devon Parkes emptied the small amount of fuel left in the can over Adam, causing another momentary flare. According to Peters, parts of the pyre and body were burning, and it didn't look as though it would go out. Ramadi still seemed disappointed. The flames hadn't been high enough or lasted long enough. Donovan then pointed to the flats, where Peters could see people looking out of their windows. Ramadi smiled; the fire had been noticed. The Axeman's work was there for all to see.

Ramadi then ordered them back to the cottage, taking the sheeting. Leaving Adam's body to burn. When they got back, Ramadi told them to get everything from the living area outside. Which again wasn't easy with the only little light coming from the open door. They were then made to clean the downstairs using the materials Baptiste had brought. Bleach was put into a saucepan and mixed with a little water and vinegar. This was then used to wipe everything down using some of the Jeye cloths. Once this was done and before anything was put back. Devon Parkes sprinkled spices all over the floor. After that, the furniture was wiped and then put back, with more spices being scattered around.

The leftovers were chucked under the stairs, as was the sheet. The Jeye cloths were put in a plastic bag along with a load of newspapers, including the one's Peters had been sick on, placing it in the dustbin by the kitchen sink. As there didn't seem to be much else to do, Peters wondered what would happen next. Ramadi had repositioned his chair and was again sitting in the living area; as if sitting on his throne, looking over his subjects. Then with Baptiste and Peters flanked by the Parkes brothers and to Peters' astonishment, Ramadi said, "A word of this to anyone and I will not only kill the two of you, but your friends as well. I mean it, remember what I said, earlier."

Peters didn't understand the last part, but didn't have time to think about it, with Gabriel grabbing him. Getting him to move, getting out before anything changed. Peters couldn't believe it, finding himself trying to thank Ramadi as he left. Devon didn't agree, but there was nothing he could do.

Peters said that, having had some time to think about what had happened and the way Ramadi had sought attention. He now thought that letting them go had become part of Ramadi's plan, in the hope that it would help to get the bush telegraph going. He'd seen an opportunity to further rumours, making The Axeman more feared and more infamous. An image he craved and what his ego coveted most.

Now out of sight, the two of them ran as far as they could. When they did eventually stop, Peters asked Gabriel what had happened to Adam's head. He said that he'd been made to weigh Adam's head down by putting into another bag with bricks, which he'd then thrown into the Thames.

They then found themselves walking along Cable Street near Shadwell, where they parted company. Peters said he couldn't think what to do or where to go and started jogging aimlessly, eventually finding himself near the church. Ending up sitting in the dark behind a tombstone, trying to think. Looking at the mess his clothes were in, he wanted to have a bath, wanting to wash everything away. If he went home and had a bath at this time of night, his parents would ask questions. It was so out of character.

Home was the only place he could go, and eventually he headed there. It was in darkness and having crept in; he went straight upstairs. Getting undressed, he put the clothes he'd been wearing in a supermarket shopping bag, hiding them under his bed. He kept them hidden until his parents went to church. He could then burn the clothes at the end of the garden, sprinkling the ashes over the fence into one of next door's overgrown and unattended flower beds.

When the interview was over, DI Clarke couldn't wait to get back to the office, running off to tell the others what had happened. Leaving me to take sure Matthew was returned to his cell safely. back to his cell by myself. The walk along the few corridors was in complete silence. That is until, we were nearing his cell, when Matthew said. "Have you got a bible, I'd like to the read some, if that's okay... please." Appreciating the importance of religion within his family. I agreed without hesitation. Although there was something about how he asked, which worried me.

Not wanting to take any chances, I decided that save for his underclothes, I would get him to take all his clothes off. I didn't want him doing anything stupid, giving him lots of blankets made out of some odd material which looked like clumps of fluff stuck together. The blankets kept you very warm but fell apart under strain. He looked puzzled. I told him that his clothes were needed for examination purposes. It was bullshit. But I didn't want to say anything that might give him any ideas either, especially if he was thinking of taking his own life. The last thing we wanted was him to trying to take how own life. Having checked the wicket gate was closed, I left feeling that his request was more than just wanting to pray or having something to read.

He was finding it difficult to deal with the ordeal he'd been through. His confession was one thing, but he would have to face his parents and others. What would they make of it? It was something I needed to guard against, and removing anything he might be able to harm himself with was part of the process. The other was completing a form six forty-eight. The form used to notify station officers starting their shift of a person in custody who needed additional supervision to ensure their safety. Once completed, I photocopied the form, handing the original to the station officer, so that it could be added to the occurrence book. Giving him an account of what had happened, what Matthew Peters had done, the ordeal he'd been through, and his importance to the investigation. The station officer appreciated Matthew's importance, saying that he would place a guard by his cell in the corridor, leaving his door open.

The station had a variety of sacred books and texts relating to different religions, mainly used by interpreters who would on occasions would need to take an oath. I got a copy of the New

Testament and took it to him. Matthew seemed happy I hadn't forgotten, saying that I would be in his prayers. His comments put me on edge, convincing me I'd done the right thing. Matthew sat on the side of his bed, thumbing the pages. Before leaving him and in an effort to comfort him. I told him not to worry, saying that in my eyes he was the victim of circumstance and although he may have been involved in a terrible thing, there were extenuating circumstances. Which meant there was a distinct possibility he could be treated as a witness. He wasn't listening. My words weren't registering. He didn't look up, just nodded, as if on autopilot, aimlessly thumbing the pages of the bible. Looking vacant, lonely and very dejected. I felt genuinely sorry for him, but there was nothing else I could do, and as per the station officer's request, I left his clothes in a bag outside his cell, on which I wrote a large note, which read:

MATTHEW PETERS – Murder Squad
SUICIDAL TENDENCIES
SEE 648 – IN HANDOVER
RETAIN CLOTHES – DO NOT RETURN TO PRISONER
Signed. DS Lomax – Pope Murder Enquiry

When I eventually got back to the office, it was empty. The word "ANNEXE" again written in large letters on the board. At first, I wasn't sure that I felt like celebrating, but went anyway. The boss had a large 'doins' waiting, and it wasn't long before Alan came over full of excitement, saying, "We knew you must be getting somewhere, just because of the length of time you were with him. I kept coming down to see if you'd finished."

I didn't really feel like it, but before I realised what was happening, we'd been locked in. Mixed in with the merriment was a very brief discussion about what should be done next, including taking Peters for a drive, retracing his steps, hopefully recovering Adam's hands and the knives. The boss wanted to read the interview again, to make sure everything had been covered. Only then would a decision be made on whether Peters would or could be dealt with as a witness or a defendant. I got home in the early hours, only to find a message saying that I was to attend the Inner London Crown Court in the morning for an old rape case.

Chapter 14

Having rung in to say I would be late; I made my way to crown court for the case. Where it soon became clear that to everyone that had turned up we were wasting our time. The defence were applying to break fixture. Their key witness had been hospitalised and wouldn't be able to attend court for several weeks. Had the information been passed to the court earlier, the case would never have been listed. Instead, on the off chance of the trial judge insisting the case go ahead, we now had to sit around waiting for him to officially grant the application.

By the time I got back, it was nearing midday. Anne was alone, typing up Peters' interview. The boss along with some others were holding a meeting in the annexe, I was to meet them there.

When I arrived, they were sitting around a couple of tables which had been shoved together. Most were drinking coffee. Ken Reeves was speaking, and I heard him say,

"We should have the knives shortly. The hands, have gone, they're fish food, somewhere out in the North Sea."

As I joined the group, DI Clarke said, "Just to bring you up to speed, Ken and a couple of the aides have taken Peters out. He's shown them where the knives and hands were dumped, and one of the aides is waiting for the underwater search unit to recover the knives."

Turning to Ken Reeves, I said, "How was he?"

Shirtily, he said, "What are you, his fucking mother?"

"No need to get arsey. I just wanted to know how he was. When I left him last night, he was pretty wrecked."

"He's okay, all right?"

"I was only asking."

He was a grumpy git; we didn't seem to see eye to eye on anything. Whenever I asked him anything, he was always curt. Immediately putting my back up. Never mind his drinking, association with Hampton's Muppets, hiding lab results, and probably taking those bloody photographs. I was just about to have a pop when the boss said, "Now, now, children. Just to add to what Bob said, Barking Council has confirmed their schedule for the bins. By now, they would have been emptied several times since Matthew's visit. The rubbish gets taken directly to Thames barges, which are used to dump the rubbish somewhere in the North Sea. Chris, I want you and DI Clarke to interview Peters again to expand on the knives which went into the river. Anything to do with where they may have come from and get him to go over his trip to the river and the flats. Ask him where he thinks we might find Baptiste and these girls, Andrea Smith and Georgina Small. Where they live, the things they do, where they shop, anything that might help find them."

"We've checked with local social services and possibly need to expand to other places like East Ham and Barking. Which seem to feature more and more," I said.

The boss was ordering refills when the pub door crashed open, and a uniform PC burst in, shouting,

"He's dead, he's killed himself."

"Who's dead?"

"Peters, he's hung himself in the cell."

Before anyone else could move, Alan and I jumped up and sprinted back to the station. Rushing through the charge room and into the cell corridor, passing a PC who was just standing at the corner, staring. As we turned the corner, all I could see was the door to Matthew's cell open, with Matthew hanging from the wicket gate, motionless. Fully dressed. His hoodie anchored to the open wicket gate. The hoodie's arms around his neck. His legs splayed out in a 'V' shape. Had they been bent instead of splayed; his knees would have almost touched the floor. Throwing his legs out, away from his body to get the tension needed to hang himself, must have taken a lot of effort, let alone willpower.

I couldn't understand why no one had taken him down. Why was he still hanging from the cell door? His head slumped forward. If it hadn't been for the hoodie's sleeves, his chin would have been resting on his chest. Alan and I lifted him down, laying him on the floor, releasing the hoodie from the wicket gate. Alan loosened some of his clothes, checking for vital signs.

"I think I can feel a pulse," he suddenly said, starting to administer CPR.

I then remembered previously seeing a resuscitation device in the doctor's room and ran back to get it. The room was locked, but the station officer was there and had a key. While he was opening the door, he told me that an ambulance had been called. Within a few seconds, I had the device. It was sealed in a clear plastic container. According to the station officer, it was for single use. I ran back to Alan, who was still administering CPR. Pushing down on Peters' chest, giving mouth to mouth. The device had two tubes with what looked like a series of valves in the centre. What wasn't obvious was which way around it went. It was obvious one end went in the mouth, but which? There were no arrows, or any other indicators, and all the instructions were in foreign languages: Asian, Arabic and Russian. I frantically ploughed through the instruction booklet, looking for anything that would help. I didn't even see any European languages; let alone anything I could read. It was useless. I tried sucking and blowing through both ends, but nothing seemed to happen.

Alan kept plugging away. He wasn't giving up, and neither would he hand over. I felt so helpless, holding the resuscitation device, but not knowing how to use it. All I could do was watch. All our efforts, my words of comfort, in vain. It wasn't long before the ambulance crew arrived. Taking over from Alan, they quickly checked for vital signs and gave up. Matthew Peters was dead. A feeling of emptiness and failure swept over me. Despite suspecting he might, I'd been unable to prevent him from taking his own life. The divisional surgeon was next to arrive, who after the briefest of examinations formally pronounced life extinct. I was trying to make sense of what had happened when Hampton appeared. As I looked up, his face visibly lit up, seeing the two of us. Having looked at the others present, Hampton singled Alan and I out, pointing and saying, "You two, out, go straight to your office, do not leave, stay there and make duty statements. Is that clear? Oh, and you can tell your chief superintendent, that I will be the one in charge of this investigation."

He hadn't asked what had happened or what we were doing there. Already relishing the prospect of causing as much misery and mayhem to all those involved, and I was probably the cherry on top. The look on his face was a look I'd seen before. He didn't really care what had happened or why? All he cared about was what he could make of it and how much misery he could cause for others. It was an absolute disaster. We had no option but to do as we'd been ordered. With my feeling of sorrow and sadness for what had happened to Matthew, quickly turning to one of survival.

An internal investigation was all we needed, especially with Hampton in charge. Apart from the casework and exhibits, his team would now have access to all our diaries, notebooks and duty states. It was everything he could wish for. Crawling over every little detail, looking for crappy misdemeanours that had no bearing on Matthew's demise. The entire murder team and a fair number of the uniform officers were now at risk of losing their jobs. I didn't know what had happened, but the bag Matthew's clothes had been in was lying on the floor next to me.

With survival now a priority, my mind started asking questions it didn't know the answers to. Why was Matthew Peters still dressed? How did Hampton get there so soon? Had he spoken to the station officer? Did he know about the six forty-eight? If he did, it would be manna from heaven for him. It would give him all the ammunition he needed to cause carnage for almost everyone concerned with Matthew's detention. He would revel in the amount of grief he could cause. I picked the bag up as if it were something I'd been carrying and left. Notso and DI Clarke were in the charge room with others who'd been prevented from going any further. Everyone on the squad was to make a duty statement. Hampton was treating the custody suite as a crime scene, which was fine. It was just that we were his suspects.

The completed six forty-eight was now the main issue. Not necessarily for me, but certainly for others. If Hampton was aware of it, it was too late. Its existence was all the evidence he needed to show that all those involved with Peters' detention had failed in their duty of care. The cell it transpired hadn't been the place of safety it was supposed to be. All those who'd taken him out, the duty officer, station officer, the officers who'd monitored him in his cell, given him refreshments, together with most of the murder squad, were now in Hampton's sights.

Had any other senior officer been investigating this tragedy, the investigation would have concentrated on just the root cause. However, the way Hampton investigated complaints, there was absolutely no doubt he would broaden the scope, looking to find fault with the slightest thing. It was a bloody nightmare, and I was probably the one person who might be able to do something about it. Which meant getting rid of the six forty-eight before anyone else became aware of it. If I did nothing, we'd all be in the shit. If I got caught, we would still be in the shit, just a lot deeper. Destroying evidence, perverting the course of justice were only a few of the potential charges. Hampton would hang the flags out. Although someone else had screwed up, doing nothing wasn't really an option. As it would give Hampton all the ammunition, he would need to make others needlessly suffer. If I managed to get rid of the form, I needed to make sure the copy I'd made was safe, purely for self-preservation.

While everything was still pretty chaotic, I made my way back downstairs and found the station officer. He wasn't really sure what was happening. Hampton was still in the cell corridor, guarding the scene, waiting for his Muppets to arrive. He wanted to either move the male prisoners into the female section or to another station. I took the opportunity to mention the form, which station officer had completely forgotten. It was just as much in his interests as anyone else's that it disappeared. He, too, knew of Hampton's reputation. We had to be careful not to draw anyone's attention to it being removed from the OB. I felt like a naughty schoolboy placing the offending document between a couple of blank forms, and then venturing into the photocopy room, where the relatively new crosscut shredder whirred briefly, before I slipped back upstairs.

Having disposed of the form, I needed to do something with the bag Peters' clothes had been in. Hampton was sure to search parts of the station. Our cars, lockers, wastepaper bins and the confidential waste would be on the list. I mocked-up an exhibit. Hoping to hide it amongst others in the exhibits room. I just needed to get it mixed up with the other exhibits without Reeves knowing. I didn't want him with a bargaining chip.

Having left the main office door open, I could see anyone passing along the corridor. Ken was who I was looking for. I was waiting for him to leave the exhibits room. Hopefully, it wouldn't be long and only needed to be for a few moments. Even if he just went for a pee. It was as though my prayers had been answered when I saw him heading to the toilet a few minutes later. As quickly and as quietly as I could, I snuck into the exhibits room and hid the fake. The chances of it being spotted or singled out remote, and even if it were suspicion, would initially fall on Ken. Within a few seconds, I was back in the main office, completing my duty statement. Throughout, my heart had been pumping like crazy, scared at the thought of getting caught. Only now was it beginning to settle. Happy to have hopefully saved the careers of a few. I was surprised at how easy it had been to move around the station without being noticed.

Not long after, two of Hampton's team appeared. They'd been told to secure everyone's diaries, their duty sheets, our duty statements, the contemporaneous notes relating to or referring to Matthew Peters – it was just about everything we had. They were to stay while everyone completed their accounts.

While everything was being gathered together, one of The Muppets let slip that a team from the Complaints Investigation Bureau were on their way. Hampton would not be the investigating officer, after all. I wasn't sure whether this was a good thing. Depending on the team, they were likely to be far more thorough than Hampton's lot. But it would also depend on their brief; whether they were undertaking a surgical strike, to identify the primary cause or carpet-bombing, looking for anything and everything, Hampton's way. If it were the latter, they would be promotion hunters, seeking an opportunity to screw anyone for their own benefit - trouble for those involved.

When the team arrived, DI Clarke and I were split up and placed in separate offices. I had a supervisor and wasn't allowed to leave or communicate with anyone. Effectively, I'd been arrested. My gaoler, an ultra-clean cut fast-track inspector straight out of Bramshill. He looked down at me, as if with contempt, and I wondered what he'd been told. He'd probably spent no more than eighteen months as a PC, been on umpteen courses and attachments; had a degree in graphic design or some other God-forsaken useless subject. Had no practical experience or common sense and was now looking at becoming a chief inspector within the next twelve months. He had all the hallmarks of a person I could just imagine being at a party and someone asking, "And what do you do for a living?"

His reply, a well-rehearsed line with just the right amount of intonation along the lines of, "I work at New Scotland Yard. I investigate the investigators... or I detect the detectives."

Some glamorous-sounding load of bollocks. His type seemed to think that having a degree instantly turned them into

Sherlock Holmes. The job was breeding idiots at an alarming rate, and it wouldn't be long before the entire promotion ladder was completely clogged with inexperienced high-ranking imbeciles with nowhere to go and a long time to get there. The top of the pyramid would soon be full of officers with little or no practical experience. The die had been cast. Those with practical experience were seen as dinosaurs. Soon to be extinct. Within twenty years, they would all be gone. With everything being paper driven. Provided you'd ticked all the boxes and justified your actions, everything was fine. Solving cases becoming secondary, almost a by-product of the exercise. Intelligence in the police would have a whole new meaning. With real specialists the likes of PKW a distant memory. My detention was making me cranky, and I was getting angry. I hadn't done anything that warranted the way I was being treated. Of course, whether Hampton or those from C.I.B. saw it the same way was a different matter. After all, we'd only tried to save his life. I kept reminding myself that this was now a case of self-preservation. I'd been sitting in the room with no food, drink or conversation for nearly three hours, when two men entered, introducing themselves as DCS Aggers and a DI Ford. They told me they'd been appointed to investigate the death in police custody of Matthew Peters and that the investigation would be thorough, covering all aspects of the time during which Matthew Peters had been in custody. I was to be taken to Tintagel House for questioning. DCS Aggers then asked for my pocketbook. Having two, I gave him the one with no references to my informants. Aggers and his DI then left without saying anything or looking at my pocketbook.

Tintagel House was a large tower block on the southern side of the River Thames. It was the home of the Complaints Investigation Bureau. I'd been there once before as a young PC, when working as an aide to CID at Stoke Newington.

DCS Aggers and DI Ford gave me the impression of being uniform officers given the temporary rank of detective while posted to complaints. Either that or they were officers who'd transferred in from the constabularies. Whichever it was, it meant they'd volunteered for the posting, seeing it as a steppingstone.

I was taken to the sixth floor, searched and then ushered into an interview room where the guard said, "Please wait here, somebody will be with you shortly." It was a joke. As the door automatically closed, I could see there wasn't a door handle on the inside. I couldn't have gone go anywhere if I wanted to. Apart from the lack of a door handle, it looked to be a typical interview room. Two-tone grey, a table and chairs, a clock on the wall, no papers and no rubbish bin.

It was nearing nine-thirty in the evening. I'd now been held for getting on for seven hours, and still had no idea of what was really going on. I wondered whether DI Clarke was being treated the same way. Did they think we were somehow responsible for Matthew's death? And why hadn't Alan been treated the same way? Matthew had been the victim of circumstance. Calling round to Cranford Cottages when he did had cost him his life. I'd gone over everything in my mind countless times. My conscience was clear. What was taking so long, and why hadn't I been interviewed at Leman Street? Where was DI Clarke? Or were they interviewing him first? More questions I didn't know the answers to. When the door finally opened, Aggers and Ford walked in. I didn't give them the opportunity to sit or speak before saying, "I need a piss and a drink in that order. If I don't, you'll be wearing it. Seven hours without access to any facilities is taking the piss, literally. If you're looking for a complaint of false imprisonment and denial of access to basic human rights, you're going the right way." I couldn't help myself. I was so angry. It certainly wasn't what they were expecting. DI Ford escorted me to the toilet. A cup of water was waiting for me on my return. Also on the table, a telephone they'd brought in, it was their key, their way of getting out.

"As you are aware, I have been appointed to investigate the suspicious death of a prisoner in custody identified as Matthew Peters, who, until his death, was detained at Leman Street Police Station. A person you were responsible for," said DCS Aggers.

"I don't think I was responsible for him. I just interviewed him along with DI Clarke. Although, I did try to save his life. What exactly is suspicious?"

"The cause of death is as yet unexplained," he said.

"Are you saying that Matthew Peters didn't commit suicide, and someone killed him and then hung him on the wicket gate? You're not seriously suggesting that somebody murdered him and then made it look like suicide?"

"At the moment, we're looking at all possibilities, but I want to talk about something else. I understand that you have two registered informants and that you've been in contact with one of them recently. Tell me about that?"

The fact that I'd met with Mo would have been in the duty state.

"Sorry, I don't see what that's got to do with this investigation or Matthew Peters?"

"Perhaps, not surprisingly, a disproportionate number of officers with informants have found themselves being investigated by this department."

"I still don't understand what that has got to do with Matthew Peters?"

"Most of the investigations are because officers in your situation have succumbed to inducements."

"I'm not with you. You seem to be suggesting that I've been involved in some form of conspiracy with one of my informants. Which is somehow mixed up with the death of Matthew Peters?"

"How many times have you had a complaint made against you?"

"I don't see what that's got to do with Matthew Peters' death either. I would have thought you had access to that information, anyway."

"Are you being deliberately awkward? I should add that our investigation will be looking into both criminal and disciplinary matters."

"No shit, Sherlock. I wondered why I'd been stuck in this room for so long?" My anger was beginning to show, making me sound surly, which I knew would only put their backs up. I needed to calm down, and quickly, making sure I didn't dig a hole for myself. Aggers, Innis and Hampton were like peas in a pod. Complaints department, a magnet for their type. I wouldn't have been at all surprised if they'd met on some course or other.

DI Ford then chipped in, "Conspiracy to pervert the course of justice. Failure to take sufficient care of a person in custody or under your control. Unwarranted and or inappropriate behaviour with a fellow officer. Failing to take some action or other. Corruption. We'll find something, we always do." A veiled threat to fit me up. "Unwarranted and or inappropriate behaviour with a fellow officer." What the hell was that? I'd never heard of it.

"This is stupid. The last time I saw Matthew Peters was when I returned him to his cell last night. And then this morning when the PC turned up saying he'd been found hanging in his cell. I was at Crown Court all morning."

"This is no laughing matter. We are treating the investigation with the utmost gravity."

"Do I look like I'm laughing? If this is going to take a long time, I want to call my wife."

"She already knows, we told her when we searched your home."

"What? Did you have a search warrant?"

"We didn't need one. She gave her permission."

The way he spoke angered me even more. Mocking me, trying to wind me up. I was trying to work out what they were looking for? Whether they knew about the form, whether it was purely speculative or something Hampton had suggested. I needed time to work things out. I couldn't understand why they kept changing subjects. If they'd found something, why weren't they asking me about that? I was tired, struggling to think straight. It was time to shut up.

"You threatened Matthew, and when that didn't work, you put him under more pressure by leaving him alone for ages, didn't you?"

I said nothing.

"And when that didn't work, you systematically beat him. Forcing him to confess, didn't you?"

That definitely wasn't right, but I still said nothing.

"You made his life a misery. Deprived of him of his liberty, kept him in solitude for long periods. Deprived him of a solicitor, prevented him from being fed and wouldn't allow him any sleep. In short, you tortured him to get the confession you so desperately desired. That's what caused Matthew Peters' death. One way or another you killed him, didn't you?"

I couldn't help myself. "Have you read any of his interviews?"

They said nothing.

"This has gone far enough. If you're going to treat me this way, then you better serve me with a formal complaint, and get my federation rep. You haven't cautioned me; taken any notes and you're now threatening me. I've been held in custody for most of the day and want to leave. If you are not going to do this formally, I'm not answering any more questions. Alternatively, you can charge me with something you don't have any evidence for... fucking wooden tops."

I'd been doing so well until then. I'd let myself down with the reference to wooden tops. It just slipped out, and I wished it hadn't. It would anger them more than swearing. But I wasn't about to apologise. I could tell I'd hit a nerve. Aggers unable to hide his emotions. We were getting underneath each other's skin.

"I was asking how many complaints, had been made against you?" said Aggers.

Another change in direction. I said nothing.

"I'm ordering you to answer my questions."

He couldn't. Again, I said nothing.

"Did you hear me? I'm ordering you to answer my questions. How many complaints have you had?" he shouted.

I still said nothing.

"Matthew Peters' post-mortem will be taking place in the morning, and if there are any bruises, I'll be making sure you're charged with manslaughter, at the very least. Possibly even murder. Do you hear me? This is your one chance to put your side of the story."

Again, I said nothing.

They then sat, looking at each other. Ford then made a call asking to be let out. When the door opened, Aggers got up and stood by the door, holding it open while Ford leant over the table, getting very close to me, saying, "If you do get out, don't expect to find your wife and child at home. I wouldn't be surprised if they're long gone. Funny how the odd comment can unhinge a woman. Especially one that's left alone for long periods."

Then, without saying anything else, he leant even closer, close enough to smell his breath. I thought he was going to whisper something; he didn't. He was goading me. Looking for me to hit him or push him away, he nearly succeeded. Instead, I slid back on the chair, creating space between us. Joining Aggers, they left the room.

Alone, frustrated, angry, and tired. I couldn't think clearly and started pacing around the room, looking at what there was. The door, the power points, running my finger along the seam between the different shades of paint. The clock, anything. I needed to think straight, and sitting in the chair for so long didn't help. Having circled the room several times, I was again looking at the clock, which had a keyhole just below the hands. The thing was, I couldn't see anyway of opening the clock face which appeared to be mains powered. Then, looking at the keyhole from an angle, I could see the reflection of a small lens. A hidden camera, they'd been able to watch me, but why? Was that one of the reason's I'd been brought here? I then wondered whether there was a microphone? If there was, it had to be nearer to the table; the clock seemed too far away for audio. Why were they watching me? I didn't get it.

I was so tired and didn't want to make a mistake, saying something I might regret. I kept telling myself that everything would be all right and there was nothing to worry about, trying to convince myself. Until now, their interview hadn't any made sense. Not making proper notes, keeping a record of what had been said. The way the interview, if you could call it that, made any sense was that they were just trying to wind me up. Trying to get me to lose control. If they succeeded, any visual evidence would be enough to have me dismissed. Apart from references to Matthew's post-mortem, they hadn't asked me or made any real attempt to find out what had happened.

The bible! I'd completely forgotten about the bible. I hadn't seen it in the cell, but then I hadn't been looking. My heart sank. A feeling of desperation flooded over me, stuck in this room, unable to do or say anything. Was it still there? Had it been found? If it had, why hadn't anyone said anything? Matthew Peters had hung himself, with a bible in his cell. Surely that wouldn't go unnoticed. Why hadn't I been asked about Matthew's mental state? Had I given him the bible? If I had, then why hadn't I completed a six forty-eight? Did they know all that already and were just making me stew? That bible was now giving me more than just a headache. They could have found it and were submitting it for fingerprints. I was now trying to remember whether I'd said anything in the pub. I didn't think I had, but couldn't be sure. Now wondering whether it was better to say something. Even tell the truth. Just like Matthew, I had become a victim of circumstance. Come on, think straight. Work it through. In the end it came down to one thing. If I said something, it might make me feel better for a little while, but a lot of us would definitely lose our jobs. Which didn't appeal to me. And all because someone else hadn't done their job. If I said nothing, we might survive.

According to the dodgy clock, it was coming up to 2 a.m. when the door opened and DI Ford walked in. Another officer I hadn't seen before kept the door open. Ford said nothing. He just tossed a complaint form, listing several criminal offences and one procedural matter on to the table. Manslaughter, perverting the course of justice, conspiracy to pervert the course of justice, perjury and failing to notify General Registry of a search.

"When can I go?" I asked.

Leaning over and again getting close to me, he said, "Soon, maybe, but if I were you, I'd start looking for another job – solicitor's runner, store detective, security guard – you know the sort of thing. Corrupt bastards like you always get caught. And don't be surprised to find no one at home when you get there. I'm pretty sure she'll be gone. Living alone with a broken home is all you've got to look forward to, such a sad little existence."

He was goading me, seeing if he could get me to hit out. His futile efforts gave me a feeling of warmth, a sort of confidence. Not saying anything had been the right thing to do. DI Ford, in particular, was a disgrace to the job he was supposed to be doing. My fatigue now replaced by resolve.

"Any chance of a phone call?" I said.

"Sorry, no."

"Not getting what you want on camera?" I said, turning my back on him and walking towards the door, wondering what he would do. Nothing apart from instructing his colleague to escort me from the building. I then found myself walking along the Albert Embankment towards Vauxhall Bridge, where I could see the occasional cab crossing the river. Apart from that, it was quiet. When I reached the bridge, I managed to get one to take me to Leman Street. With hardly any traffic, I was back in the office for three. Immediately calling home, where my wife answered within a few rings. I could tell by the sound of her voice she sounded a little worried, having not heard from me, and wanted to know what was happening. I told her about Matthew being found in his cell, having taken his own life, and a little about being taken to Tintagel House. The police hadn't been to my house. The bastard had lied. What's more, they didn't have my copy of the six forty-eight. I hung up, saying I would call back in a few minutes. With calls being frequently monitored primarily looking to identify unauthorised long-distance and overseas calls. I wasn't taking any chances and as there was no possibility of the home phone being tapped, I went to a working call box nearby and rang home, telling her the whole story. Trying to convince her there was nothing to worry about and that everything would be okay.

I was curious to know what had happened to DI Clarke and some others, like Alan Harrison – who'd been in the cell area too.

Feeling a lot more relieved, I needed to clear up a few loose ends. For once I was grateful that the exhibits room was open. I could now get rid of the bag Matthew's clothes had been in. It was just where I'd left it. Tearing out the part which had been written on, I made another visit to the shredder. Then there was the New Testament and being so close to the station office, it was an ideal opportunity to have a look. It was sitting on top of some other books in the drawer. I had no idea how it got there and didn't care. They'd missed it, and the chances of it now being linked to Matthew Peters had gone. The feeling of relief, immense. Just for good measure, I flicked it to the back of the drawer with the back of my hand. Covering it with some other books, heading back to the office. There wasn't anything else I could think of that needed doing. With regard to any serious disciplinary offences, hopefully, everyone, even Ken Reeves, was out of the firing line. Whatever was left was purely procedural and hardly worth pursuing. With Hampton securing the cell area the way he had, one of his Muppets must have put the bible back and even if it had been photographed in situ, there was now no direct evidence to associate it with Matthew Peters. It could have been there for ages, or someone else could have given it to him. It just proved they didn't know what they were doing. Before getting my head down, I had another quick look at the complaint form; it was difficult to figure out where they were coming from.

Manslaughter – it didn't happen, and there was no evidence to suggest it had. Matthew hadn't been beaten. I was confident they wouldn't find any bruises to support that theory.

Perverting the course of justice and conspiracy to pervert the course of justice – I wasn't really sure what they were referring to. It was so vague and to conspire you had to agree with someone to do something illegal, so who was that?

Perjury – it just showed how little they knew. For a start, I couldn't remember actually telling any lies that could come back to me, and if I had, they certainly weren't on oath.

Failure to notify General Registry of a search – something everyone in the job who'd ever searched premises was guilty of. It was almost laughable, and if they were referring to Cranford Cottages, they'd have to discipline everyone else. It was nonsense. I was sure I could survive the allegation should it ever come to anything. Suddenly, I had another thought. I needed to check whether the station officer had made any mention of the six forty-eight and Peters' suicidal tendencies in the handover book.

That was all I needed. Leaving one small piece of incriminating evidence was worse than leaving lots. Effectively providing evidence of an attempted cover-up. Heading back to the station office, I found the assistant station officer sitting alone by the mini switchboard. Immersed in the sports pages of one of the early editions of newspapers that were delivered to the station. Everyone else was on a tea break in the canteen. Sitting at the station officer's desk, I started making small talk.

"Anything interesting?" I asked. He raised his eyes briefly, shook his head, and returned to the paper. He wasn't interested in me or what I was doing. Having found the handover book, I started flicking through the loose-leaf pages. Half expecting them to be photocopies, the originals still there. Matthew Peters' suicidal tendencies had been referred to just once by the station officer I'd originally spoken to. Which would have been enough to cause significant problems had it been found – more work for the shredder. It was another record missed by the investigators. C.I.B. wasn't usually that sloppy. I could only assume that The Muppets who initially seized the records had told C.I.B. they'd taken everything and that had been accepted by them – not knowing The Muppets.

I went through everything in my head one more time and was now satisfied that I'd covered everything. Feeling more relaxed, my tiredness returned. It was time to get some sleep. I nodded off in the boss's office chair, only to be woken a few hours later by the sunlight streaming in. It was only 7 a.m. but considering everything; I didn't feel that bad. I needed to freshen up and have a shower, finding some old soap and a towel mixed in with some smelly, unwashed rugby kit in the boot of my car. A small bottle of highly perfumed shampoo, which had to be the DI's, and the tiniest amount of toothpaste were in the shower room. I did the best I could. It was just a pity that I didn't have a change of clothes. As the canteen was open, I treated myself to a couple of bacon sandwiches and strong coffee. It was incredibly quiet. I then found myself just waiting for someone to turn up, wanting to know what had happened to the others? It was gone nine-thirty before I heard the lift rattle, signalling the arrival of Bob Clarke and Alan Harrison.

"You don't look too good," said DI Clarke.

"Thanks, I got locked up in Tintagel House until nearly three this morning and was then left to my own devices to get back. What about you?"

"Well, DCS Dopey and DI Grumpy tried to get me to make a statement basically dropping you in it. They wanted me to say you'd forced Peters into saying the things he had. Threatening him and beating him in the cell. They told me a uniform PC had seen you hitting Peters in the cell. All I was doing was corroborating what they knew, while looking after myself. They couldn't believe I'd written all the contemporaneous notes, you being a minion. I tried to explain that although I was the higher-ranking officer; you had a better understanding of the investigation and, given the circumstances, it seemed appropriate. Dopey couldn't get his head around it. Wasn't that the whole point of being a higher rank? If you didn't make use of it and get others to do the hard work, what was the point? He then suggested that you had some dirt on me, and that was the reason I wasn't saying anything. And if you did have something, I shouldn't worry, they'd be able to sort it. Really!

I wouldn't worry too much; they don't seem to be that bright and they've really pissed the boss off. He's going to sort things when he sees the A.C.C. on Monday. That's assuming they don't find anything at the post-mortem which, for your information, is just about to start. He's been taken to Walthamstow. Keith Thompson's doing it in front of a bunch of witnesses, mainly briefs. We're unlikely to hear anything until Monday."

Walthamstow mortuary wasn't that big. Mainly, made up by a series of small buildings. Some of which looked like a line of garages joined to together around a yard. With no dedicated viewing gallery or screened area, it would be an experience they were never likely to forget or want to repeat.

"They won't find anything, so there won't be an investigation. This leaves me with one unanswered question, which I think I can guess the answer to. How did Peters end up fully clothed in the cell? I left him in his underwear and blankets. His clothes were in a bag outside his cell with a great big note on it saying..."

"I can answer this, if you promise not to go mad," said DI Clarke.

"Okay, I promise."

"You know when you arrived in the Annexe, Ken Reeves was telling us about the trip to Barking."

"Yes."

"Well, it turns out he didn't actually go. Being a little worse for wear, the aides took Matthew Peters out. With one of them staying at the river while the other brought him back. Reeves was passing on what the aides said. We only found out when the underwater search unit rang up, wanting the name of the prisoner and a reference for their report. We've spoken to both the aides, Ken didn't go. When the aide collected Matthew from the cells, he said that he was already dressed. He didn't know about the clothes, and Ken hadn't said anything. The boss is aware of everything. He wants to get C.I.B. and Hampton off our backs before anything gets sorted. Doing something before then will only make them ask more questions, prolonging their investigation."

"You sure Reeves is not a flipping cat, the chances he's had?" I said.

"On a brighter note, we think we know where Baptiste will be Tuesday morning, and we'll be waiting for him. It looks as though he's been using Andrea Smith's parents' address. He could even be living there. The best thing for you to do is to go home and get some rest. No one else is coming in today and we won't be staying. The boss wanted us to check on a couple of things. It's all procedures and admin with him, which in some respects has been a godsend."

Chapter 15

There'd been two post-mortems over the weekend, and the solicitors supposedly acting for the Matthew Peters family weren't happy with either. Professor Thompson had found no evidence of foul play. The few bruises he'd found consistent with hanging. Hiring another pathologist, the solicitors were convinced they would find bruising which couldn't be accounted for, and to be sure nothing was missed, had insisted on Matthew being skinned. According to one of the mortuary attendants, this had been against the family's wishes, causing more pain and anguish, but with the solicitors insisting had reluctantly agreed. With the second pathologist finding nothing untoward. His conclusions mirrored Professor Thompson's. Matthew Peters had asphyxiated by hanging himself from the wicket gate. With the results of both post-mortems now acting in our favour. It left the internal investigation with nowhere to go. We just needed to get complaints out of our hair and our papers back.

Given the limited period between Peters being found and our documents being seized. The boss was insisting on any minor infringements found not being investigated. Simply because there hadn't been a reasonable amount of time between the events occurring, and the records being seized for entries to have been made in the normal course of events. The A.C.C. agreed. C.I.B. now knew that even if they carried on with their investigation, it would amount to nothing.

Matthew's suicide did present other problems. The main one being that the evidence garnered from his interviews could no longer be used in court. Hardly anyone would ever know of the harrowing experience he'd been through at the hands of Ramadi. His confession, now nothing more than intelligence. We couldn't use it for corroboration or make mention in any interviews. We just had to move on and do the best we could.

"So, where do you think Baptiste will be tomorrow?"

"At the Jobcentre in Barking, signing on. You were right, we needed to expand the search area," Alan said.

"Is it my imagination but hasn't Barking cropped up a lot in this job?"

Anne, normally fairly quiet, suddenly piped up, rattling off a list of connections.

"Ramadi lived there. Most of his previous convictions were committed there. The refuse sacks found in Cranford Cottages came from there. The knives and hands were dumped there. The Parkes brothers knew which buses to catch to get there, and Baptiste and Andrea Smith appear to be living and or signing on there."

I was just starting to check some more statements when the DI came in, saying that boss wanted to see me in his office, but wouldn't say why. It turned out that the boss was becoming increasingly concerned about how I seemed to be the one who was continually being singled out for unfair treatment. And that in his mind there was a good possibility that Hampton was probably the one causing the problems. He knew we had history but didn't know what, and wanted to know more. As I had nothing to hide and told him everything.

"About eight years ago, Hampton was Chief Inspector on 'N' District. At the time, I was a PC working in plain clothes on the crime squad at Stoke Newington with my partner Russ. We got on really well, we worked, socialised, played rugby together and our partners got on well too. We'd been together for over a year and were attending the CID office's Christmas party. It was a three-line whip, no exceptions. For some reason, Russ had decided to drink spirits, which wasn't normal. He was a beer drinker who could drink pints, lots of them with little or no effect. He wasn't good with spirits and had got into a bit of a state. I was going to take him home and had been looking after him. That is, until he went to the toilet and disappeared. When I realised he'd gone, I went looking for him and found that his car had gone. The following morning, we were meant to be at Crown Court, when I got a call from his wife asking if I could pick up the papers and meet Russ at court, which wasn't a problem. A little later, I got another call to say he'd collapsed, and an ambulance was taking him to hospital. Because Russ was fully bound and the defence wanted to cross-examine him, the case ended up being remanded, with Russ off sick for a couple of weeks.

I didn't get the chance to visit him at home with all the work, but had kept in contact. When he returned to work, he was in a different car. It was only then that he told me about that he'd pranged his car on the way home from the party. It was the first I knew of it. Russ didn't want to talk about the accident, so the subject got dropped. Four or five months later, Russ got interviewed by Hampton. It turned out that the accident had been reported to police and was being treated as a failing to stop. Apparently, a witness thought there were two people in Russ's car. It had taken Hampton an absolute age to identify Russ as the owner of the vehicle. But once he had, he was convinced I was the passenger. I wasn't, and to this day, I honestly don't if there was one and if there was, who it was.

Hampton interviewed both of us several times, with Russ eventually being disciplined and required to resign. Hampton was so angry he couldn't prove I was the passenger; he became obsessed. Having convinced himself that I was not only the passenger, but that I was also involved in some sort of organised crime. He'd gone to extraordinary lengths to prove I was involved in something untoward. Searching my address and getting on to my bank were just two of the things he did, which is probably the real reason he hates me so much.

At the time, I was living with my parents. It wasn't ideal, but it allowed me to save a little. You should also know that my father and I have the same first name and we bank at the same branch. He'd taken me there when I was sixteen to open an account. On top of which, the car Hampton is likely to have seen me using was his. With him being away a lot, he didn't use it that much. It was a brand-new Ford Cortina two litre Ghia. A nice car. Everyone at the station who knew me knew it was my dad's, and if he'd asked anyone, they would have told him. Hampton must have done a PNC check and assumed it was mine because the name and address tallied. Pay branch presumably provided him with my bank's address and sort code. And I know now that he bullied someone at the bank to provide him with information about my account. Over time, he'd asked for balances, deposits, including details of any foreign transactions. Unfortunately for him, the information he was getting related to my father's accounts. He was a director for a plastics company, with factories in the UK, USA and Europe. As a result, he would make frequent trips abroad, so currency exchanges were commonplace. This led to him mentioning a couple of things 'off the record' to the bank official, thinking it might get him more information. Given the activity, account balances, car etc., he was convinced I was living beyond my means and kept contacting the bank for updates, implying I was suspected of being involved in the illegal importation of goods. The bank assumed this to be drugs. Hampton's persistence worried the bank and thinking they might end up losing all the company's business, contacted the finance director in confidence to tell him what they'd been told, which is when this all came out. Ending up with my father complaining about Hampton's conduct, forcing the job to apologise. All of which can't have done Hampton's promotion prospects any good. Something he's obviously not forgotten."

Once the boss had listened to the story, he wanted me to take a step back. At least for a few days, while we regained control of the investigation. He also suggested I clear my desk in the main office and give up my locker, removing the possibility of anyone planting anything suspicious. It was more writing, but I was grateful for the advice and support, and did as suggested. Behind the occasional blustering and odd thoughts, the boss's heart always seemed to be in the right place. He was giving me a welfare visit, trying to do the right thing.

Just after lunchtime, the others returned with Baptiste. He'd been arrested leaving the Jobcentre. Notso was booking him and would now be doing the interview with Alan. I was trying to keep myself busy, but my mind kept drifting back to Matthew. I kept wondering whether I could have done more. Had I been responsible for his death? I couldn't really think of anything, but it was becoming a recurring theme. Loafing around wasn't doing me any good, either. I would have been better off having something meaningful to do. Instead, I'd got this weird feeling in the pit of my stomach, which I didn't like and wanted to go away. Somehow, I'd become emotionally involved, which wasn't supposed to happen.

Den the Pen, as he was known, had joined the bosses for lunch. C.1's commander, the boss's boss. Nobody knew whether it was a social visit or something more serious, given the timing. My first thought was that it was to do with Matthew Peters. The commander wasn't known for making house calls. Usually, you went to see him.

It wasn't long before I found myself in the office alone with Anne. Everyone else was either out or busy with Baptiste, when the front desk rang, saying that two females had turned up asking for him. As usual, the front counter was pretty chaotic with lots of people milling around waiting to be seen. There was no privacy or queuing system – we'd gone continental. A PC pointed towards two young women in their late teens or early twenties, standing towards the back of the crowd, their arms linked together.

I beckoned them into the interview room at the side of the front counter. The taller of the two was white, with a very pale complexion. The other, light tanned and of afro Caribbean appearance. As they came into the room, they were still holding hands. The shorter of the two sat at the table, while the taller stood beside her, placing a hand on the shoulder of the one sitting, as if to comfort her.

"Can I help you?" I said.

"We've come to see Gabby, Gabriel Baptiste," said the taller.

"And you are?"

"Andrea Smith."

"And?"

"This is Georgina, Georgina Small."

I couldn't believe it. The two girls we'd been looking for had just walked into the station.

"And what makes you think he's here?"

"We saw him being taken away."

"Sorry?"

"We were waiting outside the benefits office when the police took him away, and this is where Adam Pope's murder is being investigated, isn't it? And you are one of the detectives, aren't you?" Andrea Smith was doing all the talking. Georgina Small looked apprehensive, timid, even frightened. As if she didn't want to be here.

"He didn't do it," Andrea continued.

"Do what?"

"Kill, Adam Pope, that's what. Are you being deliberately stupid?" she said.

"How do you know?"

"He told me, he's my boyfriend. He tells me everything."

Andrea Smith was a small, yet feisty-sounding individual. Georgina Small, even more petite. She'd just sat by the desk and said nothing, occasionally looking dolefully up at Andrea.

"He didn't have anything to do with Adam's murder. We know he didn't cos we saw the body."

"Whose body?"

"Adam Pope's body, that's who. You're being stupid again."

"Where was this?"

"Cranford Cottages, come on, where do you think?"

"Do you know when this was?"

"I can't remember exactly. We ended up going there looking for Adam. We were meant to be going ten-pin bowling. He wasn't at the hostel and having been there before we called round. Adam's body was on the floor, wrapped in this yellow thing, it was horrible."

The more Andrea spoke, the more vacant looking Georgina seemed to be. As if nothing was registering. I couldn't believe what I was hearing and was trying to figure out what to do. Saying to myself "Don't screw this up, we need this." When Andrea Smith blurted, "They raped her, the bastards."

"Who did?"

"Devon and Donovan Parkes, Ramadi, they were all there. The bastards. I hate them, I hate them all for what they have done. I bloody hate them."

It was easy to see just how upset Andrea was, and as soon as she mentioned the word rape, Georgina just burst into tears. Sobbing, she pushed Andrea away, as if she were to blame. Putting her head in her hands, she just wept. Andrea then tried to console her, but Georgina kept on pushing her away. Eventually, Georgina's renewed desire to be comforted changed things as she held out a hand. As they cuddled, Andrea kept apologising. Georgina's emotions had been on a rollercoaster, as she clung on to Andrea for all she was worth; within the space of a few minutes, she'd gone full circle.

Speaking to Andrea I said, "If you want to help Gabriel… and Georgina, don't say anything else. Not until I find some lady officers who've been trained to deal with this sort of thing. Okay?" She nodded. I then got a PC to stand by the door, making sure they didn't leave.

Georgina Small was eighteen or nineteen, pretty and petite. She had light golden skin, and, despite the circumstances, looked as though she cared about her appearance. She wasn't covered in jewellery, wearing the latest clothes or carrying the latest designer handbag. Her clothes were well co-ordinated and for someone her age, she looked sophisticated. Nothing tacky, just very well presented. Assuming we could get her to talk and give evidence at trial. I felt sure it would impress any jury.

Andrea Smith seemed to be the complete opposite in terms of appearance. Slightly taller, with a very pale complexion. She too was quite good-looking and spoke with a strong cockney accent. The amount of jewellery she wore made up for Georgina. A ring on every finger. A cluster of gold bracelets around her right wrist, and a sparkly watch on the other. With a couple of golden studs in each ear and several gold chains around her neck. One of which I noticed had a small gold cross pendant. All rounded off by a Gucci shoulder bag, which I assumed to be fake. There was so much jewellery, I didn't notice the clothes she wore. She gave the immediate impression of being forceful and not easily intimidated. And, because of the way she spoke, she too had the potential of making an excellent witness. And credible civilian witnesses were something we were desperately short of.

I managed to get hold of both Sally and Julia and having told them what had just happened. Julie said she'd been trained to deal with the victims of rape and could deal with Georgina. Saying that the best thing I could do was just disappear while they got on with things. Having introduced them, I was about to leave when Andrea said, "Gabriel won't talk, you know. He doesn't like the police. I could get him to talk if you want. But you would have to let me see him first."

"I'm not sure we could do that at the moment." The way she spoke sounded as though she genuinely wanted to help.

"Why are you doing this?" I asked.

"He's not like the others."

"Who?"

"Ramadi, and those brothers who just follow him like sheep. They'll do anything he says and make others do things they don't want to. They're just evil. I just want to see Gabby and make sure he's all right. He's got mixed up with the wrong lot."

"Do you mean he's been stupid?"

"No, doing what they wanted. Helping to get rid of Adam's head."

If she knew that, the chances were, she knew a lot more. Even if some of what she knew was hearsay, we needed it on paper. Just like buses, you wait ages for one and then two come along together. It was the first remotely humorous thought I'd had in ages.

"Stop there, don't say anymore," I said. "We need to put this in writing, and you'll have to make a statement before anyone is likely to let you see Gabriel. And the statement needs to be the truth, not what you think we want to hear or what you think will get you in to see Gabriel. Just the truth, understand?"

"Okay… I'm not stupid, you know."

"Even then, I can't promise it will be enough. It will be up to my boss to make that decision. But if you play ball, I'll do my best, okay?"

"I've had enough of hiding, looking around, wondering what might happen next. I just want this over. Then me and Gabby can move on."

"Do you love him?"

"What do you think?"

"Tell me, were Georgina and Adam an item?"

"More or less, they were getting there. Two shy, nervous people, Adam hadn't had much luck. Georgina initially felt sorry for him and then fell for him."

I didn't want to, but had to leave Sally and Julia to take the statements. I was back to hanging around. When I got upstairs, Anne was still the only one in the office.

"Do you know where the bosses went?" I asked.

"Sticky Elbows, I think?" she said.

Sticky Elbows was the name given to a local Asian restaurant just a few minutes' walk away. Reasonably priced, where most customers were Asian. If you leant on a table, your elbows would stick, hence the name. I thought about letting them know, then realising that it would be better to wait until we had something in writing. Hoping that by then, they wouldn't be too drunk.

It wasn't long before Alan Harrison and Notso returned to the office.

"Any joy?"

Notso looked at Alan Harrison, his eyes rolled into his head.

"He hasn't said a bloody word."

"So, what's taken so long?"

"I've asked every question I could think of more than once. I thought I would try the long-winded approach to see if that had any effect. Poor old Notso's had to write it all down. I've no idea how many times he's written no reply. I even tried the do you have a legitimate reason for the not-answering-my-questions routine. He just sat there in complete silence."

"We might be able to remedy that."

"What do you mean?"

I then told them about Andrea Smith and Georgina Small coming to the station looking for Gabriel, and that Georgina had been raped. I then mentioned the proposal Andrea had made. As far as they were concerned, it would depend on what was in the statement and what the bosses thought. The girls were likely to be a few hours and with Baptiste saying nothing; I took a walk to Sticky Elbows. The bosses weren't there, and neither were they in the annexe, they'd gone.

It seemed to take an age before Sally emerged with Andrea's statement, wanting us to go through it to make sure nothing had been missed.

She'd been to Cranford Cottages four or five times. The first time she could remember was when she and Baptiste were walking along Cable Street and Gabriel saw a person who she now knows to be Ramadi. Initially, Gabriel had asked her to wait where she was while he went and had a quick chat. After that, they all walked to the Cottages where Gabriel asked her to wait outside while he and Ramadi went in. Gabriel didn't talk about what had gone on inside and because of his behaviour, she thought it dodgy, but didn't ask.

The last time she went was just before Easter. They had gone to get Adam. As the four of them were going ten-pin bowling. Having been once before. It had been fun and hadn't cost too much. Adam wasn't at the hostel and when they got to the Cottages, the back door was open, so they went in. Ramadi and the Devon Parkes were sitting in the living room looking at something wrapped in yellow sheeting. Devon Parkes, who'd been upstairs, came down. As he did so, Ramadi said. "This is what happens to grasses," pointing to Adam's head, which Andrea could see in the sheeting. As he did so, Devon got up, grabbing Georgina, pulling her away from the others. Then with the help of his brother dragged her upstairs, covering her mouth to muffle her screams. Georgina looked terrified as she tried to resist, but wasn't strong enough. She was no match for the brothers.

Andrea said she felt so helpless unable to help. Petrified the same thing would happen to her, she clung onto Gabriel even more tightly. She wanted to run away but couldn't. Georgina and the brothers had reached the top of the stairs and were just out of sight when Ramadi said to her, "If I were you, I'd let them have their bit of fun. Why don't you take a seat?" Pointing to the floor, on the other side of Adam's body. Scared, Andrea slowly let go of Gabriel and did as he asked, walking around the yellow sheet, being forced to look at Adam as she did so, not wanting to touch or catch the sheeting.

Ramadi then said, "Gabriel, why don't you join her." According to Andrea, Gabriel looked a little surprised, but again, did as he was asked. Sitting together, they held hands.

"Relax... if you can," Ramadi said, as if smiling to himself. Ramadi was getting a kick out of what was happening. The muffled screaming that had been coming from upstairs had all but stopped. All Andrea could hear was the occasional sound of something scraping along the floor. In her mind, it was at least half an hour before Donovan came downstairs. Followed a few minutes later by Devon, grinning like a Cheshire cat.

"Finished?" said Ramadi.

"For now," said Devon. "Nice arse," he continued.

"Is she alright?" said Ramadi.

"She's not dead. If that's what you mean."

"You've had your fun."

Ramadi then turned to Andrea and said, "You better go and get her."

Andrea didn't know what to do, wondering whether it was his way of getting her upstairs. In the end, Gabriel gave her a nudge to go, telling her she would be all right. Petrified, she slowly made her way upstairs. There she saw Georgina cowering in the corner of one of the bedrooms. Curled up in a protective ball, too scared to move. Her tights torn, what was left around her ankles, her bra and pants lying close by on the floor. Her skirt bunched up around her waist, with her shirt and pullover up around her neck.

Andrea said she pulled the shirt and pullover down to cover Georgina's body, trying to sort her skirt out while sitting next to her. Putting her arms around her, comforting her, saying sorry. Georgina had a look that Andrea could only describe as complete desolation, vacantly staring at her while they cuddled together. The small amount of make-up she'd been wearing had either run or been smudged. Andrea told Georgina a few times that if they wanted to get out of there, they needed to get downstairs sooner rather than later. Andrea didn't want to stay upstairs any longer than she had to, she didn't feel safe. It took quite a while to coax Georgina out of the corner. Eventually, getting her to stand, leading her downstairs, picking up her bra and pants on the way.

Having got downstairs, they stood next to Gabriel, not knowing what was going to happen, when Ramadi said, "We've got better things to do. If it wasn't for Gabby, you wouldn't be leaving. Just remember this is our little secret, not a word to anyone. If you do say something and I find out, you know what will happen."

Ramadi looked in their purses, taking a letter from Georgina's, after which he let them leave. Andrea said that not long after this, she thought more about the comment Ramadi had made. "If it wasn't for Gabby..." She started pestering Gabriel, wanting to know what Ramadi had meant, threatening to end their relationship. At first, he wouldn't say, but Andrea wouldn't let it drop. In the end, he told her that while she'd been upstairs looking after Georgina, he'd done a deal with Ramadi. In return for letting them go, he'd agreed to help get rid of Adam's body along and any evidence from the Cottages. He knew somebody who would know what to do.

The day after they'd been let go, he'd gone to this friend he wouldn't name who'd told him what to do and what he would need; giving him a list of things to get from different places. Baptiste went back to the Cottages to tell Ramadi, wanting to know what he was about to do next. Ramadi, having listened and looked at the list, told Baptiste to get everything except the blades, which they would get.

Gabriel told Andrea that he'd then had second thoughts and wasn't going to go through with it. Then, realising that if he didn't, he would put the girls and himself in more danger. He had no choice. She knew there was more to the story and wanting to know everything kept on at him. Eventually, he told her that by the time he got back to the Cottages, Matthew Peters was there and that Ramadi had forced him to cut Adam's head and hands off. This was part of his friends' plan and was something he thought he was going to have to do. Ramadi didn't go along with the entire plan. Insisting on burning Adam's body. He wanted to show off, making an example of Adam. Gabriel ended up throwing the head in the river and moving the body to the waste ground where it was burnt.

As far as we were concerned, Sally had covered everything. It was an excellent statement. We now needed to sort out the possibility of her seeing and speaking to Gabriel. There was still no sign of the bosses, and nobody seemed to know where they were. It was looking as though they'd gone for the day. Andrea didn't care how long we took; she was prepared to wait.

When Julia Meadows emerged with Georgina Small's statement, although fragmented, her version largely mirrored that of Andrea's. The one significant difference was what went on upstairs. Every time Julia had broached the subject, Georgina's emotions got the better of her. Clamming up, getting very upset. She was trying to block it out of her mind, as if it had never happened. Julia ended up leaving it. She didn't want to risk upsetting Georgina so much that she wouldn't make the statement. She thought it best to deal with the rape at a later date. If she was going to come to terms with the trauma and prosecute those responsible, we needed a specialist to help her. Hopefully getting her to open up and tell the entire story. Apparently, blocking out such an awful experience was quite common, especially when it came to the victims of sexual assault.

Rape was one of the few cases where hearsay evidence was allowed. Particularly where the victim had relayed their story or part of it to a third party at an early stage. Any forensic examination of Georgina after all this time would have been both invasive and fruitless. Although the evidence Andrea gave would compensate for that. With no underwear and no prospect of any forensic evidence from the scene, such as semen, hairs or fibres, the only things that might help were the clothes she'd been wearing. Our problem, Georgina wasn't speaking, and we didn't know where to find them.

Before giving Andrea the chance to speak to Baptiste, the guys decided to have one more go at interviewing. Only this time they would be letting him know Andrea was there, providing him with some information only she knew. Telling him Andrea wanted him to tell the truth, and that this was his opportunity to make a clean breast of things a fresh start.

When they returned, Notso said, "It wasn't an interview it was a monologue. We'd have got more out of Harpo Marx."

We now had to decide on whether to allow Andrea access to Baptiste or not. On the face of it, there seemed little to lose, providing Andrea agreed to be searched and police were present when they met. The station officer wasn't so happy but agreed purely on the basis that we would take the blame should anything go wrong. Baptiste was then moved to the witness interview room on the first floor. It was a much larger room than those in the incident suite, with more natural light and not as drab as others. The meeting was supervised by Alan and Sally, while I hung around outside to see if I could make out what was going on. It went on for nearly an hour. I couldn't help clock watching. Occasionally, I could hear Andrea raising her voice, as if she was trying to get through to Gabriel who was continuing to being stubborn. I got the impression that the longer it went on, the more likely we were to miss out on the evidence he could provide. When the meeting finally finished, Alan opened the door to take Baptiste back to the cells, giving me a thumbs-up on the way out. Sally took Andrea back to the waiting room where Georgina was waiting. According to Julia, they hugged, whispered, and cried a lot. She then heard Andrea tell Georgina that Gabriel was going to tell us everything.

In terms of evidence from a prisoner, a statement under caution was considered the best evidence you could get. It was their version of events, usually written in their hand and signed by them. That was followed by a question-and-answer session. An interview with contemporaneous notes being made and then signed by the prisoner. Finally, notes of an interview. These were unsigned and often alleged to have been made up. Corroboration of what Baptiste said would go a long way to providing the necessary evidence to convict Ramadi and the Parkes brothers. It would also vindicate the decision to allow Andrea and Gabriel to meet prior to him being further interviewed, and was something the loophole lawyers would no doubt look at.

Gabriel, it turned out, was not the brightest tool in the box, and didn't do himself any favours. During both the interview and when he made his statement under caution, he fully admitted his part in the disposing of Adam's head. Saying that, a Jamal Ahmed had told him how to dispose of everything and how to clean-up the scene using specific cleaning agents and spices. His confession also included conversations with Ramadi and the Parkes brothers, in which they'd described how they'd plotted and planned to kill Adam Pope. Conning Adam into going to the Cottages, on the basis of taking him to another house to break into, being part of the gang. Then trapping and killing him. Where things had gone slightly wrong was that despite lots of hints he hadn't once mentioned the reason for cooperating or that he'd feared for the lives of Andrea, Georgina, and himself. He hadn't once taken any of the opportunities offered to him, not even in his statement under caution.

Gabriel had gone to see Jamal; someone he'd known for a long time. He was involved in drug trafficking, heroin in particular. They hadn't seen each other for a while because Baptiste didn't believe in hard drugs. But he'd remembered Jamal bragging about the police, never finding anything when they searched his place, even with the sniffer dogs. One of his chemists had come up with the idea of using certain cleaning products and spices to sanitise the room at the end of a session. The combination would remove any traces of drugs, blood, almost anything. As well as masking any scent. Having been used successfully on many occasions, it was now part of their routine.

Ahmed had also suggested how best to dispose of the body. Cutting Adam's head and hands off, smashing his teeth into pieces, pouring hydrochloric acid over the head, hands and any other parts of the body with scars or tattoos. Dumping the knives in the river Roding, and then getting rid of the body; by dumping the head, hands and torso in different parts of the Thames where they would drift out to sea. And even if any were discovered, no one would know where they'd originated from. Ahmed had also mentioned seeing spices being used in a film called Cool Hand Luke. Apparently, there was a scene in the film where bloodhounds were put off of a human scent by spices. Gabriel told Ramadi what Jamal had said, but as no one knew where to get the acid from, Gabriel had been told to just get the bleach and spices. When he returned, Matthew Peters was there.

As part of the clean-up, Ramadi had made Gabriel throw Adam's head into the Thames. Walking behind him while he carried the head the short distance to a nearby disused jetty. Ramadi wanted to make sure that Gabriel didn't just dump it somewhere else. So, he followed him, always staying a few steps back. Having arrived at the jetty, he made Gabriel walk out to the farthest point, where the water was at its deepest. And although it was dark, Gabriel knew the tide was out, because he could see some of the riverbed below the jetty close to the bank. Further out, he could see the water shimmering as it reflected the light coming from the opposite bank. As he neared the end of the jetty, he could hear the water lapping beneath him. Ramadi had told him to throw the head as far downstream as he could. So, picking a point in the river, he swirled the bag around a couple of times before lobbing it as far as he could. After that, he'd been made to help Matthew carry Adam's body to the waste ground. Here, they were told to get anything that would burn and put it in a pile. Adam's body was then put on top, with Ramadi setting fire to it. Once they'd cleaned the cottage, they were let go.

Ramadi had gone on several times about Pope being a grass, convincing Gabriel that Adam must have said something untoward. But Ramadi didn't say who or what might have been said.

Where Baptiste and Matthew's stories coincided, they were almost identical. Ramadi and the Parkes brothers had devised a plan to lure Adam to Cranford Cottages. Because Donovan got on with Adam the best, he'd been given the job of going to the hostel and convincing Adam they needed his help to do another job. The story was that they'd come across another house which looked good and had louvre windows, which only he could get through. If he agreed, the two of them would go back to the Cottages to get the others. All four of them would then go to the address, where the others would act as lookouts while Adam got in.

We knew from interviewing the kidnappers that Adam hadn't grassed on anyone, which made us wondered whether Ramadi knew or just didn't care. What Ramadi really wanted was a fall guy, someone he could justifiably kill. He would also need to justify the killing to the brothers. His continual accusations were aimed at doing just that, convincing them that Adam had grassed and needed sorting. Adam getting caught when he'd gone back to steal the TV, hoping to prove himself a worthy member of the gang, had effectively sealed his fate. With Ramadi seizing the opportunity, he'd finally been able to convince the brothers.

Planning his death, including the torturing, the burning had all been part of the show and was for one purpose and one purpose alone, to create fear. When Gabriel and the girls called round, Ramadi saw another opportunity to spread rumours about The Axeman, hopefully enhancing his reputation. Being able to force Matthew into cutting up Adam's body would only increase the level of fear others would have for him. It was just what he wanted.

It was getting late, but there was just enough daylight for Gabriel to show us where he'd thrown Adam's head. Directing us to a jetty on the south side of The Highway, almost directly opposite Schoolhouse Lane. Probably not more than a three-hundred-yard walk to the Cottages; shaped like a capital 'T' extending from the bank. The jetty had been built when the wharves were at their busiest, but had now fallen into disrepair, having not been used for years. The shaft of the jetty extended into the river some forty or fifty feet to a platform, which again was about forty feet wide. More recently it had been used by local anglers, but the Thames was now so polluted there weren't any fish. Several planks on the jetty had rotted away, while others creaked as they took the weight, making the journey out to the platform more than a little treacherous, even in daylight. I dreaded to think what it must have been like in the dark. I was better off walking along the edges, where more substantial beams which made up the framework existed. When we reached the eastern tip of the platform, Baptiste said, "It was just about here, this is where I was when I threw the bag, that way." He said, pointing downstream towards Newham, the Thames Estuary and eventually the North Sea.

"How sure are you?" I said.

"I'm certain."

"Show me how you threw the bag."

Baptiste then swung his right arm around in a circular clockwise motion to the side of his body. I made a rough sketch of the jetty and where we were standing. On our return, as a gesture of goodwill, we allowed Andrea Smith and Baptiste more time together.

Chapter 16

The next day I arrived early, thinking I would be one of the first, only to find the office heaving. Everyone except the bosses and Reeves were there. Anne had already typed up several pages from one of the interviews. Feeling a little paranoid, I ventured down to the cells just to make sure Baptiste was okay.

All we had to do now was re-arrest Ramadi and the Parkes brothers. We knew they were due to sign on at the Jobcentre in Settle Street. It was less than half a mile away and would open at nine. Within a few minutes, everyone who was in the office was on their way, leaving Anne to explain what was going on should the bosses turn up before we got back. We managed to scoop up some extra bodies from the crime squad, arriving about fifteen minutes before the Jobcentre opened. Notso, having been there before, knew which of the side doors the employees used. It was our best chance of getting in early, and as luck would have it, as we were made our way there, a member of staff arrived, allowing us to tailgate. Once inside, we introduced ourselves to the manageress, taking the unusual step of not only being very specific about the people we were looking for, but why. She was all too aware of the incident and more than happy to help. The problem we now had was that most of our faces would be known to many of those signing on. If word got out that the old bill were waiting, we would be wasting our time. We needed to stay out of sight until the very last moment.

Looking at past records, the manageress was able to tell us that the three of them normally signed on within a few minutes of each other, between ten and eleven, and they'd been signing on at the centre for some fifteen weeks.

Martin Page, one of the officers from the crime squad, had found a vantage point on the first floor, from which he could see along the street outside. Allowing the rest of us to get out of the way, sitting in the staffroom. Just after ten, he came rushing in. He'd seen them walking along the street. As soon as the manageress gave the nod, some of the team went back outside and around to the main entrance. A few moments later, those left entered the foyer via a staff door. It was all over within a few seconds. There was no resistance. When we searched them, they were all found to be carrying weapons. Ramadi had Daddy the hatchet tucked into his right trouser leg, just as Matthew Peters had described, with Baby in one of his coat pockets, wrapped in kitchen towel. Devon Parkes had a large lock knife with a four-inch blade hidden on the inside of his jacket's right-hand sleeve. Which had been suspended by trapping the lining in between the blade and handle. The way the knife was held, he thought he was being clever and in normal circumstances if he'd been stopped in the street, he would have most likely got away with it. Donovan Parkes was struggling to conceal the knife he had. A carving knife, which was so long that the handle and a couple of inches of blade continually poked from his trouser pocket. With no protection, he must have held on to it when walking. If he hadn't, he'd have done himself a mischief.

Even though I'd technically arrested Devon Parks, I was long past needing to show figures, which was something the aides and those on the crime squad needed to do. As Martin Page had shown some initiative, I gave the arrest to him. Telling him exactly where and how the lock knife had been found, and that Parkes had made no reply when arrested. Page was more than happy. It wasn't every day that a PC got to show an arrest for murder in the back of their diary. It would give him something to talk about on a CID board, were he to get that far.

Once the formalities had been completed, the three suspects were placed in cells as far apart as was possible. We then made our way back to the office, where the bosses were waiting. Having collectively updated them on developments over the past couple of days, the boss, smiling, said, "I don't think we're needed any more. Leave you lot alone for a while and look what happens. So, what do you want to do now, what's the plan?"

It was agreed that we interview them, telling them a little of what we knew; seeing whether that would encourage any of them to talk, while giving them an opportunity to tell their side of the story, should they want to? Given what we knew, the likelihood was that they would all now be charged with murder and we would be moving on to the next phase. No longer was it about finding those responsible. It was now about getting them to trial and doing everything possible to ensure the best evidence was put before the court.

A decision was also needed on how best to deal with Gabriel Baptiste, whether as a witness or defendant? If he were to be a defendant, it would make sense to have them jointly charged, effectively ensuring they all appeared in court, were committed and stood trial together. His confessions would form a significant part of the evidence. It would also improve the chances of other defendants running a cut-throat defence. Where defendants blamed each other for what had happened, effectively convicting themselves. If he became a witness, a statement would be needed along with some assurances that he would turn up to give evidence. Being a witness reduced the chances of one of them running a cut-throat defence. But it would certainly increase the chances of Andrea and Georgina giving evidence. And it was common knowledge that having civilian witness giving evidence significantly increased the chances of a conviction. Whichever option was chosen, there were advantages and disadvantages to both.

With the bosses having not been seen since disappearing with Den the Pen, there'd been speculation about what they'd been up to and as there was no sign of them saying, I tried sowing a seed.

"How was Sticky Elbows, I've heard mixed reviews?"

"Alright, usual bowl of shit. Meat Bhuna, can't beat it. It's the best around. Come on, let's get on with the interviews. The sooner they're done, the sooner we can have a proper drink," said DI Clarke, as if deliberately avoiding the subject.

Alan and I were back to doing the interviews, which, if the last lot were anything to go by, shouldn't take long. The pecking order was as before. The Parkes brothers, Donovan then Devon, with Ramadi last. When I went downstairs to get Donovan Parkes, the station officer told me that the duty solicitor had been called, with them all now wanting a solicitor. We had no idea who the solicitor might be. And unfortunately, the vast majority of duty solicitors were not particularly objective, their primary concern maximising their fee. Getting legal aid forms signed, their first priority. Advising clients came later, and we already knew what that would be. "Say nothing." Irrespective of whether it was in the client's interests or not. Saying nothing meant the solicitors had a better chance of earning more money – it was as simple as that, never mind the truth. To demonstrate they were on their client's side, some would offer to pass messages to others, including those involved in the crime. Irrespective of whether they were in custody or not. It was in their interests, as it could provide further opportunities for work. Given the circumstances, and that it was unlikely that any of them would answer questions. And we would be better off if they each had their own solicitor, as opposed to one solicitor representing all three. It might aggravate the solicitor who'd originally been contacted, but with calls made, it wasn't long before three solicitors from different practices were privately consulting their clients.

As expected, we were subsequently advised that they would all be making no comment interviews, despite which we were obliged to go through the motions. The Parkes brothers said nothing.

With Ramadi's desire to be in control, and that he revelled, almost craved having an audience. I was going to try a different approach, verbally putting him in his place. Suggesting he wasn't the one in control. Goading him, trying to wind him up to see where that would lead. Just as DI Ford had tried with me.

As before, we went through the motions and as expected Ramadi didn't respond. Going with the 'I'm bored routine.' Leaning back, feigning a yawn, closing his eyes as if he wasn't interested, pretending not to be paying attention. I got the impression Alan thought I'd gone nuts when I started repeating some of the questions. The only difference was that I'd changed from referring to Adam Pope by his full or last name, just using his first, making it more personal. At which point Ramadi's expression gradually changed to a scowl. I was beginning to annoy him. He still wasn't answering any of the questions, but I felt sure that I was getting to him. He then tried staring me out, wanting a contest, looking to stare me down. Occasionally, his nostrils flared. He then started hissing, forcing air through a gap in his front teeth. Until then, neither the solicitor nor Alan had taken any notice, they'd been too busy writing. I then went on to ask questions about the original burglary, something we'd largely glossed over in previous interviews. It gave me the chance of mentioning Adam's name, while swapping roles, suggesting that Adam was the one making the decisions with Ramadi doing his bidding. After all, Ramadi hadn't gone back to the address. Was that because he either didn't have the bottle or wasn't up to it? Ramadi was still trying to stare me out while I waited for Alan to catch up with the notes. Then, without warning, Ramadi jumped up, grabbing his side of the table, throwing it over and shouting.

"Pope's a nobody, a fucking nobody. He's a nobody, he didn't decide nothing."

The slight head-start I'd had on the others had allowed me to push my chair back, just enough to get my legs out of the way of the table as it fell. Unfortunately, the same couldn't be said for Alan, with the table scraping down his shins as he tried to move. The solicitor just sat there, mouth open, shocked and scared. With papers going everywhere. Ramadi stood there, arms bent, fists clenched, pumped. He groped for Daddy. Like a cowboy going for his gun, it wasn't there. He then stood glaring; in a pose, as if transformed into the Incredible Hulk. He was eyeballing the two of us, ready, wanting to fight. He wanted to show that he was in control. Violence his only option. He couldn't just back down. I simply looked at him and smiled inanely. It was our turn to say nothing. While keeping an eye on Ramadi, we slowly righted the table, collecting up the papers. All without saying a word, we were really pissing him off. Finally, we'd got a reaction. We'd found the psychopath's button and had managed to press it. His solicitor, having gathered himself together, immediately requested a break, which was politely declined, we'd nearly finished. I repeated my last question while Ramadi remained standing, staring all the while. Alan was writing away when the solicitor took hold of Ramadi's wrist in an attempt to get him to sit. Ramadi just turned his head and glared; the solicitor, immediately letting go. While he remained standing, we just looked and waited. For a while he remained defiant, continuing to pose. Then, with nothing being said, he slowly sat back in his chair. Still staring, still trying to look menacing. I left it a while and then asked a couple more questions, more in devilment than anything else. I just wanted to see whether I could goad him again. Regrettably not. It was no surprise when he declined to sign the notes. It didn't really matter; his solicitor had witnessed everything.

The way Ramadi had acted during the interview convinced me even more that he was either a sociopath or a psychopath. I didn't know which. Adam's slaughter, his dismemberment and the way he'd been burnt were all aimed at one thing: getting Ramadi, a reputation he so desperately craved – wanting to be known as The Axeman.

On the way back to the cell, rightly or wrongly, I gave him a piece of my mind. His reaction told me everything. When I mentioned Matthew and Adam, he didn't care. He cared more about Daddy and Baby, who after the trail would meet their maker. Angry with the system and his attitude and before doing something I might regret, I shoved him into his cell, slamming the door shut and immediately walking away, not giving him the chance to respond.

Ramadi and the Parkes brothers were jointly charged with murder. Rightly or wrongly, a decision had been made to deal with Gabriel as a defendant. Resulting in all of them being charged with preventing the lawful burial of a body and perverting the course of justice.

The boss had half a dozen bottles of scotch waiting in the office, and having been joined by some of the crime squad; he was insisting on a small celebration. Later, the boss took Alan and me aside to say that when the team reduced in size, no matter what, we would be the ones remaining. It wouldn't be long before the team would be down to just a few. The girls, Ken Reeves, Notso along with others would be back to normal duties. At least I would still be away from the main office and Hampton. It might even give me the chance to resurrect communications with Mo. He then said, "Bob and I have been talking. We've been trying to decide what to do about Adam's head, and whether it's worth looking for. If we do nothing, we could be criticised. So, we've decided that something needs to be done. If for nothing else other than to cover our backs, we need to be seen searching the river."

This'll be fun. How in hell's name are we going to do that? The boss was suggesting we look for something not much bigger than a football, which had been thrown into a large, fast-flowing, muddy, polluted river months ago. I couldn't quite work out how we were going to do it or why they were telling us. Having already dealt with some floaters, I doubted whether the visibility in some parts of the river was more than a foot. And it wasn't as if we could use a metal detector, had sonar or some other underwater scanning equipment.

"I've been onto the underwater search unit. I didn't realise just how busy they were or how long searches can take," the boss continued. "Anyway, the upshot is that with their current commitments they can search a single stretch of water of our choosing. One day this weekend, assuming of course, we cancel their leave and authorise their overtime. And for your information, a stretch of water is approximately one hundred yards by fifteen yards. That's how much of the Thames this far down, they can do in a day."

"Are we actually going to do it? Surely the head could be anywhere by now?" Alan said. "And what difference will it make if we find it?"

The boss ignored the question, saying, "Chris, you're the Wapping Liaison Officer, aren't you?" It was a question he already knew the answer to.

"Boss, with all due respect, you know I am."

"Then it's up to you to pick where we search."

"But I don't know anything about the river, its tides, currents, nothing."

"That's what you get for being the Wapping Liaison Officer. I don't really have a choice. Let me know where you decided by close of play tomorrow. I need to tell the underwater search unit and cancel their leave. Can I suggest that after court you spend time on the river and make a go of it?"

"You're joking, we might as well throw a dart or stick a pin in a map for all I know."

"No, I'm serious. If for nothing else, we need to be able to demonstrate that we tried, and that there was at least a chance of finding it wherever we look. Justification, it's all about justification, which is why I'm picking you. You're the Wapping Liaison Officer. Your title is my justification for getting you to pick where we search. It doesn't really matter what the title means or what the job entails, it's the perception. What others think. Don't worry too much if we don't find anything. From what I'm told, the chances are negligible. I'm not really expecting us to, we just need to be seen to be trying, that's all. I'm sure you'll have a good time. Just remember it's all about justification."

"Come on, boss, let someone else pick. Why me?"

"No, you do it. I've just told you why. Have a go at picking the place. Talk to the guys at Wapping. Do whatever you need to. Take a trip down the river, anything you like. Just remember justification. We just need to be able to justify our actions, it's as simple as that. Right, it's time for me to be getting going; I need to be off." And with that, the boss left, leaving the rest of us to carry on.

Chapter 17

Getting the remand in custody at the first court appearance was a breeze given the serious nature of the offence. A carefully planned, premeditated killing. The only thing of note was the stipendiary magistrate intimating that he expected the prosecution to be able to serve papers within four weeks. It was a bit tight, but just about doable.

I then spent the rest of the day trying to work out where to search the river. Having spoken to Thames Division, they were willing to help, suggesting I look at some of their charts, which showed the estimated depths and shallows at certain points. Having looked and not really understood them, I went back to the jetty where the tide was out, trying to visualise how far Baptiste might have thrown Adam's head. Despite the jetty's condition, it had lasted longer than most. With the tide out, weathered stumps could be seen protruding from various parts of the riverbed. The footings of former piers and jetties that had once existed close to ours.

Still unsure what to do, I headed back to the station to mull over how to justify choosing a location to search. If the boss was justifying his action by selecting me because I was the Wapping Liaison Officer. Somehow, I needed to justify selecting one small patch of water over another. Sitting in the canteen stirring my coffee gave me an idea. To justify my selection, I could hopefully apply a limited amount of science. Taking all the wooden coffee stirrers from the dispenser, I was going to take a trip down the river for a game of Poohsticks near the jetty.

As we made our way downstream, my pilot told old me about the tidal flow, and how incredibly strong the current was in certain places. With cars going into the river being discovered more than four miles from their point of entry. Bodies would frequently travel further. The jetty was close to a bend in the river. He told me that the current tended to be stronger on the ebb tide. From his description, this meant that objects would get out to sea quicker from the northern side of the river. Apparently, the water had always been deep enough there for boats to dock. He also said that the waters there were too dangerous to wade in unaided. It didn't take long for us to arrive alongside the jetty. The driver knew exactly where to go. When we arrived, he was able to hold station using the engine, without the need to lower the anchor. I threw some sticks into the water across a distance of a few yards. Some whizzed off at a rate of knots, while others went at a much gentler pace. I was surprised at the variation given the relatively short distance between them. Watching as they moved downstream, they all fell into line. Following the same path, line astern, elephant file or one behind the other. I'd run out of ways to describe what I saw, but it did make me think. I asked my pilot if we could have a go at drifting across the river from the other side. Turning the engine off once we had some impetus. I could then throw sticks in at greater intervals, widening the angle, and with the engine off we would further minimise any outside influences. We had several trial runs, so the pilot could work out where to start from on the opposite side of the river and when to stop the engine drifting across my imaginary line. He eventually worked out where to start, and we drifted across. I threw the sticks across a span of about thirty yards along my imaginary line. Hopefully, this would include where Adam's head had entered the water. Again, I was surprised to find that after fifty to sixty yards, all the sticks had converged and were now following one another along the same path.

When Baptiste threw the head into the river, there must have been a small amount of air in the bag which would have taken time to dissipate. After which, the weight would have forced the bag down to the riverbed. Was there the remotest possibility of finding the head after all? Then, with the help of the driver, I suddenly found myself taking things a lot more seriously. Making mathematical assumptions based on a number of factors, including what I thought the estimated weight of the bag was, and the likely depth of water at the time the bag was thrown in, while allowing for an element of drift. At the same time, I was trying to imagine where the head would end up, like a golfer visualising pitching a ball onto the green. Imaging the shot and where it would roll to, it was all very surreal.

We only had one shot, and I couldn't see where any other useful information was going to come from. I hadn't had anything resembling a sensible suggestion from any of my colleagues, who just took the mickey.

My best guestimate was to search an area starting fifty yards downstream from the jetty, with the centre of the platform acting as the mid-point for the width of the search area. Our start point was well beyond where all the sticks had converged, which at least would justify the location. If pushed, we could now demonstrate that a certain amount of reasoning had been used to select the location selected, and that we hadn't simply stuck our finger in the air, closed our eyes and hoped for the best.

The officer on the launch then told me that any searches would have to start close to low tide, which was around four in the morning at this time of year. We would have to be on site at daybreak around five. He then insisted on describing the search procedure. It would take the entire unit the whole day to cover this tiny patch of water. Despite helping me, he obviously didn't hold out a lot of hope for finding the head. He was probably right. Topping things off by saying that as far as he could remember, apart from cars, the search unit had never actually found anything this far downstream from Tower Bridge. He now didn't get that I was doing as I was told, and by trying to find Adam's head, we were hoping to avoid any criticism. Nothing was going to stop him from continuing his description of what was going to happen. Firstly, they would have to rope off the area, dividing it into grids using weight-bearing ropes. This would allow for a systematic search of the area square by square. As the tide was very strong, the divers needed to be anchored in place, attached to both the grid and the launch as they moved around. Other members of the team would ensure their safety, preventing vessels from entering the area... I got the message. We all had jobs to do.

Having got back to Wapping, we went and saw the inspector in charge, showing him the location on the map. He said he would let us know whether Saturday or Sunday was best. He wanted to check both the weather and tides before making a final decision. By the time I'd got back to the office, he'd already been on the phone. We were on for Saturday. The unit would be on site from about 5.30 a.m. I needed to be there to confirm the location. Others, including the boss, would be turning up later. The inspector anticipated it would take a couple of hours to lay the grid. The search would probably start in earnest around 8 a.m., giving them until approximately 3 p.m. to complete the exercise.

Until then, the boss wanted us to do paperwork. What I wanted was to find Ahmed, the last piece of our jigsaw. Since Ramadi and the others had been charged, the bosses kept overlooking him. The problem was that if we took too long, we could have difficulties getting all the defendants tried together, meaning more than one trial. Unfortunately for me, admin ruled with paperwork the order of the day.

Saturday morning, I drove straight to Wapping. According to the weather forecast, it looked as though it was going to be a pleasant day. Jumping onto one of the two launches being used, we made our way down to the site. The pilot who'd taken me down river previously was again my driver. Once I'd pointed out the location and was happy the correct area was being marked out. I was taken back to Wapping to await the boss's arrival. With the pilot, or whatever the correct terminology for him, continuing his journey upriver towards the Tower of London and HMS Belfast. It made a pleasant change to be out in the early morning sun, even if it was a little chilly. I'd been standing on the quayside for a couple of minutes when another officer emerged from the station, asking if I was with the murder squad? When I told him I was, he said, "You can get on the launch if you want, I shouldn't be long. I'm your helmsman for the day." As I pointed towards the only launch moored on the quayside, he shouted, "Yeah, that's the one. The big green thing, make yourself at home, the others shouldn't be long." We were using the commissioner's launch.

Others? The way he said it, I wondered how many were coming. The commissioner's launch was about three times the size of the others; painted green, as opposed to the usual dark blue and white. It wasn't designed for normal river police work. It was designed for entertaining and conveying dignitaries up and down the river on a gentle cruise, showing police-related high-flyers and other dignitaries the sights of London. With a covered area that had a couple of fixed tables with small ornate guardrails, to stop things from sliding off. I could just imagine them being used for posh drinks and nibbles. There were bench seats, both under the covered area and out towards the back. All were covered with a white waterproof fabric adorned with loose cushions embroidered with the Metropolitan Police logo. I wondered how many had been lost to trophy hunters and privileged guests. The logo was also emblazoned on a small plinth fixed to the roof of the covered area. Apart from a small area for preparing food, there was a sizeable functioning toilet too, something none of the other launches had. All very classy.

It was getting close to eight when others began to arrive, and it soon became clear that the entire team had been invited. As they made their way along the jetty, laden with slabs of beer, spirits, mixers, thermos flasks, cooler bags, picnic hampers, everything you would need for a riverboat party. Waiting on the quayside, I went to join them. Not long after the boss arrived, saying to one and all, "I'm not sure who it was, but someone suggested we make a day of it. By the way, I've been told that our hosts are extremely sociable, and they've also been known to play the odd trick or two on their guests, so be careful."

The boss didn't hold out much hope of finding anything, deciding to make a day of it without telling me. The plan was to go downriver and have a few drinks while watching the search, with everyone returning to Wapping for drinks with the search team after. Finishing everything off with a trip upstream to the Houses of Parliament and beyond. It was the boss's treat. An end of term party, a way for the boss to thank everyone. It didn't take long for the food and drinks to be stowed, and with the helmsman enjoying a quick snifter, we were off.

Not long after setting off, I found myself standing at the back of the launch next to the boss when Sally came over with two cups. She was serving pre-made black coffee laced with rum. Everyone was getting the same starter. The journey was taking longer than before, with quite a few of the team wanting to steer. Tacking downstream, completely ignoring any river etiquette. For a short while, I found myself alone with the boss. It was an opportunity I'd been looking for, to ask him something personal, saying. "Boss, can I ask you a question, you don't have to answer if you don't want to, but some time ago, DI Clark said something which made me think you had problems away from work, and if you were, I just wondered whether there was anything we could do?"

He looked at me for a moment and I wondered whether I'd said the right thing.

"Bob mentioned he'd inadvertently blabbed, I wondered how long it take."

"I haven't said anything, it's just a comment he made, along with a comment Notso made having picked you up from home."

"I don't think anyone can help, not now. It's my wife, she's been in a wheelchair for nearly six years, now. She fell five feet out of a bloody pear tree she was pruning. That's all, five feet. That's how far she fell, fracturing her spine. She so loved the garden. I can tell you one thing, I know my way to Stoke Mandeville, that's for sure. Two and a half years of toing and froing. Anyway, things could be worse. At least it wasn't her neck. Come on, let's enjoy the day."

"Sorry boss, I had no idea, I won't say anything, but if there is something I can do just ask." I was now wondering whether I'd put my foot in it and spoilt the day, and whether his drinking on occasions was a way of escaping.

"She just loved gardening," he repeated, his thoughts drifting home. The wash of a passing water bus buffeted the launch making him smile, saying, "Come on, let's watch the show."

We'd dropped anchor downstream from the divers' launch. The search looked to be well under way. There were two divers in the water, and I could see another on deck. They were using what I thought was old-fashioned deep-sea diving equipment, with air pipes, lead belts and boots to keep themselves weighed down. Over the radio, we were told that so far nothing had been found, with the riverbed described as being 'as smooth as a baby's bottom'. Staying anchored to our spot, we watched, chatted, ate, and drank. Occasionally, a diver would come up and swap places with the one on deck; the changeover taking forever. It was early afternoon, and everyone was well oiled when one of our lot started pointing at the divers. They were waving and crossing their arms. The helmsman said they were finishing. Thankfully, no one had taken the mickey, and everyone was still having fun. The only downside was the toilet, which had been in overdrive. And with the gentle rocking, things had got a little messy. The intake of both compulsory and voluntary drinks had taken its toll. The one genuine surprise was Anne. I'd never seen her so animated. Whatever she was drinking, she was enjoying it. Getting more than a little tipsy. Ken Reeves had either fallen asleep or was comatose, wedged in a corner at the back of the launch. Thankfully, I wouldn't have to work with him much longer. With one of the divers recovered, we were almost ready to leave, when the helmsman suddenly said, "They've found something, they've actually found something. It's being brought up now. That's why they've stopped searching." Repeating himself a couple of times.

With what the boss had said earlier, everyone thought it a hoax. We waited for the diver to appear, to give him a round of applause, cheering, playing along with the ruse. I was half expecting an arm to emerge from the water in dramatic style; holding something aloft, akin to the legend of the Lady of the Lake, where a sword initially emerges from the water. It wasn't quite like that. At first, a helmet emerged from the murky waters with the diver being unceremoniously hauled onto the launch. In his right hand a dark grey object. Everybody still thought it was a hoax and played along, shouting and chanting "Good effort. A bag in the hand's worth two in the river" clapping all the while.

"It's not a wind-up, it's for real," the helmsman said, becoming animated. And with the divers recovered, he hauled up our anchor and moved closer. Eventually, drawing alongside the other launch, I could see the bag the diver had brought up was a refuse sack. The white lettering had gone, but I still could just make out the outline of some of the lettering "...ough of Bar..." It wasn't a wind up; it was for real. Slowly it dawned on everyone, they'd actually found the bag Gabriel had thrown in the river. Adam's head.

"What a result, I don't bloody believe it," said Alan as he started slapping everyone and then jumping on everyone's back, continuing with. "This'll bring the fucking pains on, big time." While struggling to light yet another café crème.

I couldn't quite believe it. It was hard to imagine that after all this time and with what had been said. We'd actually found Adam's head in the river.

It was a sobering thought, and trying to get back into work mode was a real problem. Deciding what to do? Whether we were going to open the bag or not? If we were. We needed to photograph what we were doing, and we didn't have any equipment. When Alan tried to wake Ken Reeves, he was out of it. The underwater unit had some rubber gloves we could use to feel the bag.

It was a strange sensation, feeling the contents. I was surprised just how cold it was, even with the gloves on. The chill went straight to my bone. I could make out three distinct objects. The head, a brick and another lump of concrete or something similar. As we scrambled back onto our launch, the others were still celebrating. The diving unit ecstatic, they'd broken their duck. Their first real find in that part of the Thames, and what a find it was. I still couldn't quite believe it. Despite the fact that I had seen and felt the bag myself, if it hadn't been for the words on the side, I would still be thinking it was an elaborate con. With the bag tied up, it wasn't much bigger than a lumpy basketball, and we'd found it in this vast stretch of water. Although happy, I didn't feel like celebrating the way the others were. Celebrating finding someone's head so exuberantly just didn't seem right. Especially someone so young.

With the DI chanting 'Justification, that's justification' to the tune of 'It's just an illusion', a song which had been in the charts not that long ago, the others started joining in bouncing to the beat. It was as if they'd just won the final of some tournament. The actual contents of the bag seemed to pass them by. It wasn't the prize at the end of a long cup run. We weren't champions. It was the head of a young man, a human being, Adam Pope.

I was wondering what Adam's head would look like after all this time, when the diver who'd recovered the bag, a PC Philips, called over, saying he found the bag snagged on a wooden stump. If it hadn't been for that, the bag would have been long gone. We'd been lucky. If finding someone's head could be described that way.

A decision was made to photograph and document the opening of the bag. Assuming we could get all the necessary paraphernalia together. In order to do that properly, we had to make our way back to Wapping. Our helmsman arranged for a message to be passed on to Leman Street to get the kit we needed to be brought over. The journey back was a lot choppier, going into the breeze, against the tide, and quicker than before. The combination of food, alcohol and diesel fumes having an adverse effect on quite a few. With some being sick over the back of the launch, which just happened to be where the diesel fumes were coming from. When we got back, the kit was already there, sitting outside on a bench that was mainly used by the unit for cleaning equipment. Which was partially covered by an old shelter, with a butler sink and hosepipe at one end.

On one of my previous visits, I'd been told that the bench had also been used for dealing with contraband seized from vessels on the river. Wapping frequently undertook joint operations with Customs and Excise. Occasionally, damaged contraband needed to be dealt with. Normally, spirits being smuggled in, where excise duty hadn't been paid. Damaging the odd crate ensured that part of the consignment would no longer be the subject of excise duty, having to be destroyed in the appropriate manner. In other words, divvied up amongst the team. The bench was now going to be used for something completely different. With our bag placed on the bench, we were ready to confirm its contents.

There was no possibility of getting PKW at such short notice, and Ken Reeves hadn't moved. Notso was stepping up. Apart from confirming the bag's contents, we needed to take whatever steps were necessary to preserve everything until examined.

Not everyone wanted to witness the debagging, but for continuity purposes someone had to. In the end, the boss, DI Clarke, Alan, Notso, and I would be present. Along with Anne, who was desperate to see the bag opened, truly excited by the prospect of being present for part of the investigation. For those actually involved in the exercise, the effects of alcohol were wearing off fast. Notso got me to check the camera's date and time, after which he was ready to go. As I'd been to the scene and formerly identified Adam's body at the post-mortem, the boss thought it best I open the bag for continuity purposes. It would also save someone else dealing with elements of the body's identity at court. With little choice, I gloved up and got ready to make a start. The outer bag had been knotted by tying the two ends of the neck, using a granny knot. Having gently pulled the lower part of the bag apart, the words London Borough of Barking could now be made out. Notso snapped away. He wasn't leaving anything to chance, taking photographs from every angle. So much so that I wondered whether we had enough film. The bag had faded from being in the water and was now dark grey rather than black. Inside was another faded refuse sack, again tied with a granny knot. The white printed lettering loose, but present. The other thing that was noticeable, the smell, more pungent than it had been. Inside this, a brick, and a piece of concrete about the size of a large grapefruit, together with another bag tied differently from the first two. This time string had been used to tie the bag further down from the neck. Having felt the bag, there wasn't room for anything else. What was left had to be Adam's head. The knot was so tight; it was impossible to undo and had to be cut. Once I'd managed that, I slowly opened the bag, immediately being hit by this awful smell. The reactions of the others was to step away. For a while, it didn't seem to matter where you stood. The smell was there, clinging to your clothes. And although there were similarities, it wasn't the same sweet, sickly smell you got from a naturally decaying human body. It was more pungent, more putrid. Opening the bag further, I could see Adam's head, partially covered by another refuse sack. Bloated, but not as much as I had expected. Eyes open, despite what Peters had said, staring. The glint in his eye faded, as if covered in film. His mouth full of Jeye cloth. Having pushed the sides of the bag away, we could now see most of Adam's head lying on its side. It was only then that I noticed cloth poking out from where the neck had been severed. Matthew Peters had told us about the difficulties he'd had severing Adam's head. And, despite seeing it with my own eyes, I still couldn't believe just how far down his throat it was. Looking at it now, Adam must have had real problems just breathing. His face, whether it was or not, looked anguished. I couldn't imagine what it must have been like. No one deserved to be treated the way he had. There was no justification. I could only describe those responsible as savages. Nobody said anything, and an extremely sombre mood quickly replaced the joy of the discovery.

Professor Parker had left a message to say that the head was to be placed in a lidded container filled with water from the Thames. Making sure everything was covered. It could then be taken to the mortuary and left with one of the technicians. The rest of the body was currently being stored at a much lower temperature, which needed to be raised before any examination could take place. Monday was the earliest anything could be done. The underwater search unit found a large bucket we could use, in which everything was carefully placed. Slowly filling the bucket with water from the river, Ken Reeves finally managed a brief appearance, stumbling over to join us, only to be sick on the way. Unable to keep his balance while trying to wipe the vomit from his clothes, he collapsed over one end of the bench. He was a mess, an embarrassment that needed sorting.

The London Hospital was less than a mile away, a few minutes' drive through the back streets. The PC who'd brought the camera had offered to take one of us to the mortuary. Notso obliged. Ken hadn't moved by the time he got back. Asleep on the bench, lying in the remnants of muddy water the from the bags and some of his own vomit. It wasn't going to be pleasant when he came round. One of the diving team offered to hose him down, suggesting we take him with us. We just left him. It was self-induced. He was over twenty-one and could make his own way to wherever he was going.

The boss was now eager that we get back on the launch to carry on the celebrations. Finding Adam's head hadn't been in his plans, but it didn't take too long for the party to get going again. With everyone making an effort to enjoy what was left of the day, taking it in turns to steer with one hand while downing a pint, the favoured challenge. By the time we'd passed the Houses of Parliament, everyone who'd wanted to have a go had. Anne was continuing to shock with her newfound confidence, talking freely to anyone and everyone. I couldn't remember ever seeing such a transformation. She'd changed beyond recognition. Going from this shy, solitary individual who spoke little and didn't mingle to someone eager to join in and with so much more confidence. The photographs, descriptions of horrific things we'd come across, together with what she'd read and typed, hadn't fazed her at all. She'd relished it if that was the right word. Physically seeing and experiencing the sensations that went with finding Adam's head, the icing on the cake, as far as she was concerned.

On our way back from Westminster, the boss insisted on saying a few words.

"Firstly, let me thank everyone for all their hard work. I have enjoyed working alongside you all. I'm sure you must realise that it is unlikely there will be many. If any other opportunities for us all to socialise together..."

Here we go. We all knew what was coming. It was just unfortunate he'd decided to announce it now. Soon, there would just be the two of us. Then before we knew it, we would all be back on general duties with only a watching brief. He went on to thank everyone associated with Thames Division and today's operation. Then adding, if we didn't already know that the commissioner's launch was in fact available for hire, to those in the job. With fees consisting of a couple of slabs of beer, plus a score for charity. It was his way of saying goodbye to some and see you around to others.

When we arrived back at Wapping, Ken Reeves was nowhere to be seen. The mess had gone. We now had to make our way to wherever we were going. Those driving, including me, ran the risk of the black rats. There was no alternative from where we were, and despite all the drinking that had gone on during the day, I felt decidedly sober. Driving home, I looked back on what had been an extraordinary day. More than a little satisfied that at least two parts of my estimation for finding Adam's head had been right. The tide had carried the bag in the line of the Poohsticks, and the bag had sunk to the bottom within the predicted range. The fact that it had taken an old jetty stump to stop it from disappearing out into the North Sea was neither here nor there. And with the head having now been found, I doubted whether anyone cared how it had been discovered, just that it had.

In the mortuary, the bucket had been placed on the first of the three slabs with the lid removed. Adam's body was lying on the middle slab. The slice of the neck previously removed beside it. With the head still submerged, there was little of the stench we'd previously experienced. For now, bleach and cleaning agents dominated. The professor, having removed the head from the bucket, spoke into his Dictaphone, initially comparing it with the slice of neck he'd previously removed. Trying a mechanical fit. Then, with the help of wooden supports, he put the pieces together in a line. Photographs were taken, and even to the naked eye, apart from skin discolouration and charring, everything looked proportionate and appeared to fit together. But more conclusive tests would be needed to confirm they were once all part of the same body.

He then removed the Jeye cloth from the mouth, only to find there were two. These would also be sent for analysis. Arrangements were then made to have dental records checked. Assuming any of the tests proved positive, it would be further evidence Adam Pope was the victim.

The team would only be together now for a few more days, with the boss wanting one last away-day: a trip to see the film Cool Hand Luke was favourite. Anne was first with her hand up, eager to join in, volunteering to help with arrangements. How was she going to cope with returning to the typing pool, and what would her colleagues make of the new Anne? In the past, she wouldn't have gone anywhere near the trip, let alone volunteer to help with the organisation.

Knowing the right number to call at the cab office gave you access to every type of contact you could ever hope for within London's theatre and cinema world. Occasionally, you could even get extremely cheap tickets. A charitable donation of just a pound could get you four tickets for a top London show. Very GTP or good to police, although it was potluck what you saw. Cab office could put me in touch with a someone at Elstree Studios, who arranged a private viewing of the film for the coming Wednesday afternoon. Another call and a police coach and driver were laid on. It was up to others to decide on refreshments. It was just what the boss wanted. He'd gone into holiday mode, celebrating the fact that he'd just been told he would be getting his old job back at the Fraud Squad; penance served. I had no doubt the more regular hours would be welcomed at home. The following day there was cause for further celebration. News was filtering through that Hampton was also on his way back to complaints. Surely his last posting before being put out to pasture. I didn't really care where he was going or who was going to replace him. They couldn't be any worse. It was as though the clouds were lifting. Hopefully, those in the main CID office would remember how to smile and enjoy their work. It could even see the end to The Muppets and their privileged status.

We'd reached a point where the bosses had effectively left us to get on with clearing up any loose ends, which was fine. But before everyone disappeared, there was still the minor matter of Ahmed. He was like an itch I couldn't scratch, which kept bugging me. Some of the other loose ends were also proving difficult, such as locating Adam's dental records. It was beginning to look as though there weren't any.

I then had the idea of trying to link the refuse bags together forensically and wondered whether it was possible, and if so, how it could be achieved. If it was possible to prove a scientific connection between the bags found at Cranford Cottages and those the head had been in, it would help to link the head, body and Cranford Cottages together. There must have been millions of bags printed with the borough's logo on during any one year. And while bags with the same printing on was evidence, it wasn't conclusive. A call to the lab told me that the only way of proving an association was by comparing characteristics within the bags. Typically, striation marks, and to do that effectively we would need control samples. This meant identifying the manufacturer, the factory where they were made, and then getting samples of bags produced at specific intervals, using the same machine and manufacturing process that had been used to make the bags in our possession. An analysis of these bags would tell us how rapidly the characteristics within a run changed from bag to bag during production. This would then provide a basis on which our bags could be compared.

After a series of phone calls to Barking council, I managed to establish that the bags were manufactured by ICI at their factory in Stockton-on-Tees. A few more calls and an appointment had been arranged to go there with a scientist from the lab. A Dr James Cutler would accompany me to the factory, making sure the appropriate samples were obtained.

Jamal Ahmed had yet again fallen into the too-difficult tray, with nobody wanting to do anything. I could hear my mother-in-law's voice in the back of head chirping, "If a job is worth doing, it's worth doing well." We knew where he lived, slept, and what he looked like. And it wouldn't be long before there were just two of us, making things a lot harder. Finally, after a lot of nagging and cajoling, Alan and Notso agreed we should try. A couple more calls and Barking's Crime Squad agreed to help. Four PCs and a sergeant, who were more than willing to deal with any drugs found. They would also arrange for local uniform back up to be available for the hit at 2.30 a.m. Hopefully, getting some nets in drains before the knock. If a lot of drugs were found, they could be a very useful bargaining chip.

When we arrived, our uniform assistance was already there. They'd also managed to place nets in some drains and had eyeball. The lights had been on in a ground floor room until about twenty minutes ago. It was time to go, and with the usual feather knock, which nobody ever heard, we invited ourselves in.

Having a pretty good idea of the layout, it wasn't long before we were in control. And, despite our best efforts, someone had still managed to get half a dozen bags down an open sink. They'd been caught in one of the nets, and contained a slightly off-white light tan coloured powder. Probably heroin. No dabbing your finger in it, to have a taster. It could just as easily be rat poison, and it wouldn't have been the first time a drug dealer had sent a dummy down the drain. Just to make those searching think they'd got the stash. Subterfuge, it was just like the old the war films where submarines would send up life jackets and oil slicks to give the impression they'd been sunk. We would have to wait for proper analysis.

A shopping bag full of bottles of bleach and spices was found in the back of a wardrobe in Ahmed's bedroom. An odd place for that sort of thing. At first, he tried to say it was shopping he'd forgotten to put away. He still had the receipt in his wallet, which showed more than what was in the bag. The rest, in the kitchen, along with a roll of refuse sacks marked London Borough of Barking. Some scales and empty bags, similar to those containing the powder, along with a stack of used notes were found under the floorboards in his bedroom. If this was normal, he'd been sloppy. And assuming the drugs were confirmed, it was enough for a charge of possession of a class "A" drug with intent to supply. He was looking at stir, whether he talked or not. Ahmed immediately asked for his solicitor to be present. Unemployed with his own solicitor, who said crime didn't pay? Alan Harrison and Notso were going to do the honours, and despite consulting privately with his solicitor and undoubtedly being told to say nothing, Ahmed decided to pick and choose questions to answer, trying to be clever. After about twenty minutes, he must have realised he wasn't doing himself any favours and should have taken the advice he'd been given. During the interview, he'd suggested that packets of powder were somebody else's. Then changing that to 'they'd been planted.' The spices and cleaning stuff were for cooking and cleaning, nothing else. Strangely, he decided not to answer any questions regarding his friendship with Gabriel Baptiste. Which seemed pretty stupid, given that the spices and cleaning fluids on the shopping list were almost identical to the empty containers found at the Cottages. Something he would find out later.

He was charged with assisting in the disposal of a body, taken to court and remanded in custody, which surprised him immensely. Wrongly, he'd assumed he'd get bail while the powder was analysed, giving him the opportunity to disappear.

Chapter 18

I met Dr Cutler at King's Cross Station for the journey to Stockton-on-Tees. As I was travelling with a scientist, we could travel together in first class. I got the distinct impression that initially; he didn't seem that enamoured either with the assignment or his company, and had no idea why? As we sat on opposite sides of a table in the sparsely populated dining car. Hardly speaking for the first hour, immersing himself in The Daily Telegraph's cryptic crossword. Having already had a dabble at the quick puzzle, which I could see because of the way the paper was folded. Periodically, he would read a clue aloud, and in an effort to engage in conversation, I occasionally proffered a potential answer. I wasn't sure what else to do but had noticed that the answers to the first across and down clues in the quick puzzle weren't complete. I didn't know whether the good doctor knew that the answers to those clues were always a play on words, mentioning the fact, while suggesting he look at yesterday's answers, to give him an idea of what I meant. He didn't know, and my knowledge of that small fact appeared to gain a little respect, with him putting down the paper and asking me to tell him about the case.

He hardly knew anything. All he'd been told was that we needed to establish a link between a group of plastic bags. I then realised part of the fault was probably ours. Submitting the request had been one of the last things Ken Reeves had done. It was basic to say the least, and didn't really say anything, with hardly any background to the case, just what was required. It was my chance to elaborate not only on the investigation but also on the significance of the bags and how they potentially tied everything together, so to speak. Explaining both the logical and scientific approach that had been taken in searching for and finding the head in the river. Trying to impress him, glossing over our stroke of luck.

Until now, the vast majority of Dr Cutler's jobs had been traffic cases. Traffic cops were a completely different breed, which was probably why his perception of the police appeared so warped. The intricacies of this investigation and lengths to which we'd gone to genuinely surprised him. Changing his perception, making the rest of the journey a whole lot more enjoyable. It turned out that Doc was a bit of a wine buff, and as a gesture of goodwill promised him, we would try whatever wine he fancied the hotel had to offer. Courtesy of the commissioner. Our journey also included changing trains at Doncaster. It was the first time either of us had ever been on a train that consisted of just two coaches and a conductor selling tickets. It wasn't long before we found out why. When we arrived at the station, I saw what looked to me to be one of the longest platforms I'd ever seen. The main reason, there was absolutely nothing on it. Just a bridge to get over the track. No ticket office, waiting room, toilets, employees, nothing. My assumption that there would be a taxi rank had also been badly misplaced. We couldn't even find a working phone box. The vision of the two of us standing outside the station suited and booted, figuring out what to do, reminded me of a scene from the film Butch Cassidy and the Sundance Kid where the trio disembarked at a deserted and crumbling railway station in Bolivia. This was the modern version of that, we'd been dropped into an urban void. I had to walk for ages to find a call box, and with the help of directory enquiries, managed to get a number for a cab.

While making our way to the hotel which had been and arranged by the local police, I asked the driver where the town centre was.

And in this broad northern accent he said, "You've missed it."

"I didn't notice, anything," said Dr Cutler.

"No, you've missed it by about ten years. We haven't had a town centre for at least that long." Comedian.

"Sorry, I don't follow," said the good doctor.

"Don't worry, I'll explain later. Any decent watering holes?" I asked.

"The hotel you're staying in is about as good as it gets. It's always busy at weekends, nearly everyone goes there."

Dropping us off, I booked him for the morning, not wanting to be late for our appointment. With the hotel being arranged by the local force and validated as one of the better hotels in the area by the cabbie, Stockton-on-Tees must have seen better days. The rooms were quite large, but that was about it. There was no ensuite, no television or hot drinks and the telephone didn't work. Both rooms were similarly furnished with a bed, a wardrobe, with a large mirrored door, a lounge chair, a small round coffee table and wash basin. The only other item in the room a Sony Digimatic radio alarm clock. A shared bathroom was down the hall. Apart from the clock radio, it was all very fifties, early sixties.

Meals were typical bar food – steak, fish and chips, pie, gammon, that sort of thing. And it didn't look as though the wine selection was going to be that great either. While the Doc mused over the limited menu, he asked for a list of wines.

"Red or white?" was the response from the lady taking our order.

"The red wine list, please," said Doc.

"No, that's the choice, red or white wine."

That didn't go down well with either of us. With Doc settling for a few very large gin and tonics. Having eaten, he fancied a cognac and coffee to take to his room – Asbach was as good as it got. The Scarborough Arms at the back of the nick was top drawer compared to this. I couldn't work out what the appeal of the hotel was or whether we'd been tucked up by the locals. Once Doc had gone, I found myself chatting to the barman. Having the odd nightcap or four, he told me the place was usually heaving from Thursday to Saturday, quiet the rest of the time. Normally there would be entertainment, a band or disco, along with a comedian. It was only when he mentioned rooms being booked by the hour that I realised the hotel doubled as a knocking shop and the local police were either turning a blind eye or participants. I didn't dare tell Doc and was now hoping we were staying for just the one night.

The factory was an enormous complex, primarily producing agricultural products. There was also the continuous production of refuse bags. Made from poor quality leftover plastics which had been turned into granules of differing colours, depending on their origins. The entire process automated. The only variation during a run was whether any printing appeared on the bags. Unfortunately, the man I'd spoken to over the phone and who I'd arranged our meeting with wasn't actually there. And the manager we did meet wasn't entirely clear on what we needed. I briefly explained the nature of the case. He was quite excited to be taken away from his normal work for a murder investigation. After which he was able to provide some documentary evidence relating to the production of the bags. During a run, every bag had a batch code punched into the bottom seam. The batch codes on ours related to a huge consignment of bags delivered to the London Borough of Barking. It was a good start, but we needed scientific proof and an understanding of the manufacturing process. We needed to know how the striation marks were created and how quickly they changed during a run. The striation marks were effectively lines created during the manufacturing process as the plastic was extruded. From our point of view, it depended on how many consecutive bags the lines could be traced through? Would it be possible to link bag one to bag two, three, five, ten, twenty or even further down the line? The fewer bags it was possible to trace the lines through, the better it was for us.

The Tailor's Dummy

The manager was happy to show us the machinery in action. It started with a large hopper at one end containing the plastic granules: the cast-offs from other products. Millions of granules the size of small lead fishing weights sat in a huge hopper, which was automatically replenished when the volume dropped to a certain level. At the other end, the rolls of folded black bags, ready for distribution. The granules, together with a black dye, were fed into a heating chamber where they were mixed, becoming a warm black goo. The goo was then pushed through a tube, where it cooled slightly, turning into a continuous pliable strand which then had air forced into it. Creating one very large open-ended continuous moving balloon that was pulled through a series of guides, stretching the balloon to more than twice the width of the sacks. As its journey progressed, the bag cooled. It was then fed through a series of rollers, pressing the balloon together, with the centre of the balloon being cut and sealed, making two parallel runs. Effectively creating left and right-handed bags. These were then pulled through more guides. Where, if required, any printing would be applied. The train of plastic then went through a device which added folds, pressing the train together. After which, another heated element repeatedly opened and closed. It had several functions. Firstly, creating a seal which would become the bottom of the bag. Just below that a series of perforations, which would allow for the bag to be torn from the roll. The unique batch number being stamped between the two.

Stopping and starting the machine several times to collect samples was a big ask and beyond our manager's authority. We now had to find a director. The machine ran constantly. If it stopped for any significant length of time, the plastic would solidify, requiring some parts to be completely cleaned down before it could be restarted. Each clean down took over an hour. After a lot of negotiating, pleading, and promising to be quick, the director allowed us to collect our samples. Two groups: one for the scientists to play with and a spare. To be kept as another control sample should the results of any examination be challenged. Each bundle contained groups of consecutively produced bags attached to each other. They were in twos, threes, fours, fives, tens, twenties and fifties. What surprised me was that if you held the side of a bag up to the light, they were so thin you could see some lines with the naked eye. When the bags were forensically examined, the striation marks could only be traced through a maximum of three bags.

We could now scientifically prove that the bags Adam Pope's head had been found in came from the same roll of bags recovered from Cranford Cottages. Provided we could overcome any problems with the initial search of Cranford Cottages and Ken Reeves. It was another significant piece of evidence.

Chapter 19

We'd been a team of two for a couple of weeks. Although on paper DI Clarke, in his supervisory capacity was still a frequent visitor. In reality, the only supervising he was doing was with Julia. To assist with his deception, he'd started hanging a spare jacket on the back of a chair in the bosses' office, with an open briefcase containing reports he'd minuted and a newspaper on one desk. Making it look as though he was in the station, but away from his desk, should anyone ask. From time to time, the contents would be updated.

The four lovebirds would regularly go out together, leaving me to my own devices. Occasionally they would ring in just to check that everything was okay. I didn't really mind, and to some degree; it suited me. Just so long as it wasn't all the time.

Having served a raft of statements on the defence, Ramadi's solicitors were the first to request an old-style committal with the others following suit.

An old-style committal was more like an actual trial where witnesses the defence wanted to test, or challenge would be called to court to give oral evidence. The answers they gave could then be compared with any answers given during the trial. Old-style committals were often testing times, particularly for civilian witnesses, significantly increasing anxiety and stress. A tactic used by some defendants and certain firms of solicitors. The more unpleasant they made it, the greater the prospect of a witness not wanting to go through a similar ordeal at trial, potentially increasing the likelihood of an acquittal or even the trial not taking place.

With little to lose, certain firms would invariably put the victims of rape and sexual assault through the wringer hoping to get the case discontinued. Our case was no different.

The list of witnesses the defence wanted to test was considerably more than we had envisaged. We could come up with two reasons for such an extensive list. Firstly, it was a poor attempt to mask their actual targets, namely Andrea Smith and Georgina Small. Or more likely, it was the number of witnesses the defence felt were needed to justify the time they were suggesting the committal was likely to take. Knowing that the longer it took, the harder it was to find a court capable of hearing the case anytime soon.

For some reason, it fell to the prosecution, or more accurately, the police, to sort out. With the defence teams predicting that the committal would take a minimum of twelve days. They knew that finding a court that was both big enough and able to hear the case in the foreseeable future was remote. And just to add a little extra pressure, they were now collectively writing to the magistrate's court, asking for the case to be heard as a matter of urgency. Suggesting that any delay would unfairly result in their clients being held in custody longer than was necessary. It was all part of a ploy, designed to cause the prosecution more work while laying the foundations for a potential bail application. Not being able to have an early hearing would provide the defence with a reason for making such an application. And again, as part of the ploy, we knew the defence would soon be providing the police with the details of a raft of supposedly suitable sureties that would need checking. And it wasn't unknown for the defence to deliberately provide the details of individuals knowing the prosecution would deem them as inappropriate once the checks had been made. Testing to see how thorough the police were. If some of those passed muster, either because the checks hadn't been done or were inadequate, you could find yourself accepting sureties that were just as likely to abscond as were the defendants. If they didn't pass muster, other potentially suitable sureties would then be provided.

Sorting out the hearing was becoming a headache, which of course the defence would seek to exploit. We couldn't find a court or a magistrate that had anything like the slot we were looking for in the foreseeable future, increasing the possibility that if things didn't change, the defence might be able to make a successful bail application. Something we couldn't afford to let happen. As it would increase the possibility of defendants disappearing, which would undoubtedly result in more trials. Assuming they were recaptured. Creating more work, while increasing the number of times witnesses might be required to give evidence. As well as putting the likes of Georgina and Andrea at greater risk. We didn't just need a magistrate; we needed a court too. As things stood, the earliest date we could get was ten months away at Highbury Corner Magistrates Court. Which we knew would be unacceptable. Having done the rounds of all the other magistrates' courts several times, one of the clerks suggested the possibility of convening a temporary court using the old town hall. Part of the building had previously been used as both county and coroner's court. The building was no longer in use, having been mothballed about a year ago. The local council gave us permission to use it, assuming it was suitable, and having been to look, it would just have to do. Part of it needed cleaning along with some utilities that needed restoring. It was all a little déjà vu, reminding me of the first days with the incident room. Having convinced a recently retired stipendiary magistrate to sit and hear the case, and with no other alternatives, the venue was agreed.

Once we'd successfully sorted out the court with an earlier date for the hearing, the defence amended their list of witnesses, reducing it to just civilians. The dustmen, a couple from the hostel, and as expected, Georgina Small and Andrea Smith. One of the other notable changes was that all the defendants were all now represented by firms better known for adopting procedural defences as opposed to actually challenging the evidence or proffering plausible alternatives.

Having the opportunity to make witnesses suffer without the possibility of influencing a jury or pissing off a judge was effectively a freebie for the defence. Most didn't have scruples. The stock answer from any defence lawyer wanting an old-style committal was that 'they needed to test the evidence to the best of their ability. After all, it was their job.' It would also give them an indication of just how good the witnesses were likely to be at trial. With Georgina Small and Andrea Smith, their prime targets, being able to discredit or debunk either would be their primary aim. Anything else, a bonus.

As the committal got underway, Alan and I didn't see the need for both of us to be at court all the time, especially as Sally and Julia had been assigned to look after Georgina and Andrea.

The hearing opened with the usual addresses, counsel weighing up their opposition, the prosecution taking the high ground, majoring on the serious nature of the offence, with the defence casting doubt over the validity of witnesses – suggesting there was no case to answer, the usual bollocks. For a couple of days, everything went pretty much as expected, except for everything being so slow. The only issue to arise was with one of the dustmen who threw a wobbler when the defence started questioning him on his previous convictions. It was something he hadn't expected and something he hadn't told his employer.

We'd reached a point where Nicola Saltmarsh was slowly going through her evidence, which just left Georgina and Andrea to give theirs. During the morning break, I was asked by counsel to arrange for Georgina Small to be available after lunch. Defence counsel had intimated they would finish their examination of Ms Saltmarsh just after lunch. Pleasantly surprised, I left the messages for Georgina and the girls to be at court for 2 p.m.

Our makeshift court, as with most others, had an area outside where witnesses waited before being called. As the afternoon session kicked off, I found myself with one of the solicitor's runners, waiting for Georgina to arrive. It wasn't that long before I saw her walking along the corridor. The runner immediately disappearing to pass on the news. Georgina looked more than a little pensive, which was to be expected. I reassured her as much as I could. She didn't want to read the statement she'd made, saying she could clearly remember everything. The more we talked, the stronger her voice seemed to become. I had to let counsel know she'd arrived, while making sure everything else was all right. Before going back into court, I gave her a quick rundown of what was likely to happen. Leaving her before either Sally or Julia had arrived, saying that one of them should be with her shortly.

Our counsel looked bored to tears listening to one of the defence barristers carrying on. He seemed to be constantly going over the same ground, re-phrasing the same questions. The sticking point, if there was one, was how often Adam stayed away from the hostel. I couldn't see the relevance, but they kept plugging away. I passed counsel a note saying that Georgina had arrived. After reading it, he handed it to the defence. They already knew.

Our counsel then had me going through both Georgina's and Andrea's statements, highlighting certain aspects he wanted to draw their attention to. It was something he should have already done. While going through the statements, I then noticed some of the defence's runners periodically popping out of court for a few minutes. I assumed they were going for a smoke and with everything else going on; it was something I hadn't previously noticed.

We'd been going for at least an hour and neither of the girls had poked their heads around the door to announce their arrival. I had to assume that Georgina was still sitting alone. With the defence counsel continuing to drone on, the chances of Georgina actually giving evidence were quickly diminishing. We were now reaching a stage where the magistrate would be reticent about starting such an important witness so late in the day. A witness being part heard while still giving their evidence in chief could complicate matters. Easily leading to allegations of a witness being coached or them conversing with others about the case whilst still giving evidence, which wasn't allowed. I then wondered whether getting Georgina to court early and making her sit outside was the defence's way of increasing pressure on her. Having finished counsel's bidding, I needed to make sure she was okay. When I got outside, I could see one of the runners standing in front of her. As soon as he saw me, he headed off, as if to leave court. As he moved, I could see Georgina was upset, she'd been crying. Her emotions had clearly got the better of her. Consoling her as much as I could, I asked what had happened. She then told me that people had been coming out of court and just staring at her without saying a word. Making her feel uneasy, threatened. Sometimes they would pace up and down in front of her, staring all the time. After a while, they would just disappear. Not knowing what to do, she'd just sat there. I needed to tell counsel. Poking my head around the court door, I managed to catch the usher's eye getting him to come and sit with her.

Instead of telling the magistrate, our counsel asked for a recess so that he could discuss 'an urgent matter' with the defence. Predictably, they denied any knowledge of what was going on, suggesting Georgina was exaggerating. So much so, she was effectively lying. I asked counsel which of the weasels had asked for Georgina to be at court so early. He took exception to the term weasel, saying he couldn't remember. The barristers were sticking together. I wanted him to tell the magistrate. He didn't see the need to trouble the magistrate with such a paltry matter, refusing to accept that members of the legal profession would stoop to or engage in such activity.

With the delay and Nicola Saltmarsh still giving evidence, there was now absolutely no chance of Georgina starting hers. And there would be even less if I took her home. With everything that had happened, I felt sure that getting her to court so early had been on purpose. Georgina was still in a state, and I found myself apologising for the girls not turning up, trying to reassure her nothing like this would ever happen again. Dropping her off, I offered to have her collected the following morning. She declined, saying that she would get her dad to bring her. I just hoped she would be all right.

When I got back to the station, no one else from the team was there and given what had just happened to Georgina, checking on Andrea to make sure she was okay seemed appropriate. Although I wouldn't be mentioning the ordeal Georgina had just been through. I wanted to be sure that should she become concerned or suspicious of anything or anyone; she was to call the police immediately. The meeting was brief. She wasn't aware of anything untoward. Although one thing was very apparent, she still hated Ramadi and the brothers and wanted to do everything she could to help Gabriel. She was ready.

Alan was surprised to see me at court the following day. I wanted to know where Sally and Julia had been and why they hadn't got my message. He would know. It was only when I told him what had happened; he realised that I wasn't exactly enamoured at being left high and dry. And that if I didn't get the truth, it would jeopardise more than just a friendship. The truth was, they didn't think they would be needed for a few more days. So, the four of them had gone off for the day without telling anyone.

While I'd been taking Georgina home, Nicola Saltmarsh had finished giving her evidence, meaning Georgina would be first up. Ten-thirty came and went with no sign of her. The later it got, the more it looked as though yesterday's antics had been too much and she'd got cold feet. With every passing minute, it was easy to see the defendants' optimism growing. It was now too late to mention the yesterday's antics to the magistrate, counsel had seen to that. With no one answering Georgina's home phone, something had to be done. Our counsel got a short adjournment, during which we were to make enquiries regarding Georgina, whilst arranging for Andrea to attend. I called the station to explain our position, with officers being sent to both addresses. I was hoping that getting Andrea to come to court would convince Georgina to change her mind. Andrea wasn't too impressed at the short notice she'd been given but had made it and was now sitting outside court while we waited for news on Georgina. Andrea did not know where she was, having not seen her for a couple of days.

Not long after leaving court, the officer who'd delivered Andrea returned. He'd received a radio message from the officer attending Georgina's address. Georgina was dead, she'd been found in her bedroom by her parents, earlier that day. Several empty pill containers had been found close to her; the case was being treated as suicide. Her parents had gone to wake her and, having found her dead, were so distraught they hadn't done anything. They'd just sat looking at her, laying where they'd found her. The officer attending was now helping to make the arrangements with the divisional surgeon and coroner's office. Given the circumstances, there would have to be a post-mortem, while another internal investigation couldn't be ruled out.

Shocked and saddened was an understatement. Devastated was nearer the mark. Alan, speechless. He didn't know what to do or say, either to me or anyone else. If only they'd said something. It was taking a while for the ramifications to sink in. We had to inform others, not just counsel and the court. I couldn't imagine what some would say or do, particularly Andrea, and couldn't believe that yet another young life had been taken. Another unnecessary death, the sadness and misery this case was causing; incredible. I could have accepted Georgina, not wanting to go through with giving evidence after what had happened in court. The more I thought, the more my sorrow turned to anger. Anger at the runners, my colleagues, the legal system, all of which had contributed to her death. The prospect of yet another internal investigation wasn't helping either. Wondering what Andrea's reaction would be? What the hell was going on, I'd never been involved in a case like it.

I had to get out and go for a walk, to collect my thoughts. The legal system had done this, and there was nothing I could do. I felt so useless. The system had taken her, killed her. Reminding me of when I saw her sitting outside court yesterday, vulnerable and alone. The look on her face. Our conversation. Had I missed something, could I have done something better? The vision of Matthew Peters, when I turned the corner of the cell corridor, seeing his body hanging from the wicket gate, returned. I couldn't seem to shift it. Georgina's face and then Adam's swollen head in the refuse bag joining in. The images merging and morphing between themselves. It was the weirdest of feelings, having these images swirling around while still being able to see and hear everything around me. Suddenly blown away by the sound of a fire engine's two-tone horns nearby. As I returned to court, I wondered how I'd become so emotionally involved. What was it about this case that had caused so many young people to needlessly lose their lives? Leaving friends and relatives to pick up the pieces, and for what? All because of a lousy video recorder worth little more than twenty quid. The waves this pebble had caused were immense, and we hadn't even got to trial.

As soon as I entered court, my anger with the legal system returned. With the court reconvened, our counsel simply got up and informed the court that Miss Small would not be giving evidence due to her untimely demise. It was so matter of fact, there was no emotion in counsel's voice. Cold as if he didn't care. As he made the statement, there were gasps of dismay, followed by utter silence. The defence counsel looked at each other, slowly realising there was now an opportunity to derail the entire case. If Andrea didn't give evidence, that would probably do it. It was something else all counsel had in common, so detached from reality. The defence counsel happy one of the major pieces had been removed, not caring how, with the runners looking anywhere and everywhere, except our way.

We were in a hiatus, while some of our sharpest minds continued to look at each other, deciding who was going to take the lead and what, if anything, they were going to say. Were any of the defence going to publicly express their sorrow at what had happened? Was the magistrate going to comment, call a recess, or even adjourn the case?

The first to react, Ramadi. Shouting "YES... die bitch, die..."

Except for Baptiste, who genuinely looked shocked. The others began to appreciate the possibilities of what this could mean as they started clapping and cheering. Having total disregard for everyone except themselves. What was even more galling was just how long defence counsel allowed their clients to carry on. The magistrate, now struggling to restore any semblance of order, threatened to hold the defendants in contempt if they didn't behave. Which was hardly a threat, given their circumstances. With the magistrate rising until order was restored. One by one, the defendants were slowly taken to the mobile prison van to calm down. Until now, the few local stringers that had been the following the case hadn't seemed that interested. But were now scribbling away furiously. It wouldn't be long before they were sending copy to their editors.

As soon as the magistrate had left the court, our counsel came over saying, "Well, unfortunately, it looks as though Miss Small wasn't able to cut the mustard. Do we think Miss Smith will do any better? If not, we may have to consider our position."

Callous git. I couldn't believe what I'd just heard. Looking at him in disbelief. A few graphic expletives, along with administering a little gratuitous violence, was what was needed. He was as bad, if not worse, than defence counsel. His crass attitude made sure of one thing: assuming we got to trial, he wouldn't be involved. He didn't seem to care for the well-being of witnesses, just what they could provide. Any platitudes now primarily aimed at self-preservation. He wasn't a team player. The welfare of witnesses didn't seem to enter his mind. I had to back Andrea, who'd been sitting with Julia. I just wasn't sure how much she knew or how she would react to the news? When I went outside, they were by themselves. We needed to speak privately and away from the court. Finding a suitable room on the other side of the building where there was no possibility of being overheard. I wasn't sure what her reaction would be when she was told. She could just walk out. If she did, I wouldn't stop her. It was her choice. It wasn't worth trying to coerce her. Andrea guessed something was wrong, just because of where we were; now standing in a dusty, unused office away from the court. Initially, I didn't know what to say. It was never easy breaking the news of someone's death. Especially when it was a good friend or close relative. What had been obvious from the very first time they came to the station was that they'd formed a closeness. In the end, I just said, "Andrea, I have some bad news. I've been told that Georgina has unfortunately passed away. I don't know the exact details, but I'm told they think she may have taken her own life."

Andrea sat quietly for a few moments. "Was it suicide?"

"We think so. I haven't been told anything about a suicide note. Just that a number of empty pill bottles were found by her parents when they went to wake her this morning. I don't know anything more, sorry."

She again sat quietly, presumably taking in what I'd said, before saying, "Well, at least she can be with Adam," pausing, then saying, "that bastard, he did this. Ramadi, the bastard, him and the others, they did this. I hate them. I bloody hate them." I was astonished at her resolve, her strength of character, having expected her to dissolve into floods of tears. Not a bit of it, there'd been a change in the tone of her voice and a steeliness in her eyes. When Julia went to comfort her, she shrugged her off, wiped an eye, looking incensed and driven.

Quietly I said, "Do you think you'll be able to give evidence?"

"Yes, why? I'm not letting them get away with this. Ramadi's got even more blood on his hands now."

"Okay, but you need to try and keep calm. Defence counsel are likely to ask some difficult questions. In an effort to unnerve you, trying to get you riled. Even suggesting you're lying. That you've made things up to help Gabriel. Whatever happens, you must try to stay calm, okay?"

She nodded. She despised Ramadi. Hated him, more than any of the others, despite what the Parkes brothers had done to Georgina. Somehow, they were incidental to Ramadi. In her mind Ramadi had taken Adam, Matthew and now Georgina, and she held him solely responsible for their deaths. She also held him responsible for the predicament Gabriel now found himself in. Realising that it might be a very long time before they were together again. She was going to have her day in court and make Ramadi pay, whatever it took. Her attitude told me she would cope. She'd become a time bomb that was about to explode in Ramadi's face. Determined to tell the truth and prepared to suffer the consequences. It would have been so easy for her just to walk away, and no one would have blamed her. She now appeared not only ready to give evidence, but desperate to do so.

The faces of those in the dock soon changed when they saw her walk into court and heard the tone of her voice when taking the oath.

Given what had just happened and with her boyfriend a defendant, I got the impression they thought she wouldn't give evidence. Gabriel knew differently. Giving her evidence in chief, she was both clear and concise. Even better when the defence started. At every opportunity she would point at Ramadi and the Parkes brothers. Ramadi tried staring at her to put her off. It was all he could do. She just stared back, pointing more, and for longer. If she gave evidence at the Central Criminal Court like this, we couldn't ask for more. She didn't seem to be intimidated by anything. I felt sure the defence cut their cross-examination short because of all the finger-wagging and pointing she was doing. She'd single-handedly screwed them. The outcome, a foregone conclusion. Only Ramadi's counsel made a futile attempt at suggesting there was no case to answer. With them all being committed for trial.

While I packed the case papers away, I looked across at the runners doing the same, wondering whether Georgina's death would have any effect on them. They knew I held them responsible.

It had only taken a matter of days for the investigation into Georgina's death to be completed. During which time, the boss had been made aware of an approach by C.I.B. to take over the investigation. Instigated by guess who, Hampton. Somehow, he'd found out, and he just couldn't resist the opportunity to interfere. Our saving grace was that the post-mortem had been undertaken at the London Hospital, as had the toxicology, speeding up the results, confirming an overdose as the cause of death. The investigating officer had found no other suspicious circumstances. On top of which, Georgina's parents had praised the police in relation to the treatment Georgina had received. Which included the appointment of female liaison officers. If only one of them had been at court on the fateful day, things might have been so different. But with no suicide note or evidence to suggest any wrongdoing, the internal investigation had nowhere to go, and the case was closed.

Chapter 20

A couple of weeks after the committal, my first wish had been granted with new lead and junior counsel being appointed for both the kidnapping and murder trials.

As with all trials, there was a need to correspond with everyone in the case, especially the witnesses. One of the first things to do was to fix dates for the trials. Finding out dates to avoid was key and with an expected length for the murder trial of between five or six weeks, we'd been given a proposed start date of the 7th of November. With cases like this, it was neither feasible nor practical to have all your witnesses either at court or constantly on standby. To avoid this, we needed to work out a potential running order. Which was accomplished after a couple of conferences with counsel. This then allowed us to estimate how long each witness was likely to take. Then taking into consideration legal arguments, swearing in a jury, opening speeches, and a little wiggle room, we could guestimate which weeks the witnesses were likely to be required. Having done this, we could then write to the witnesses, informing them of when the trial was due to start and at what point during the trial we thought they would be needed. Asking them to complete and return an acknowledgement form. We normally allowed three weeks for the replies to turn up before chasing the witnesses. The one I was most interested in making sure we received was, of course, Andrea's. There was a sense of relief when it turned up. Attached to the form was a brief note, which read:

"Please address any further correspondence to Mrs Baptiste."

I wasn't sure how to interpret the message. Did it mean to send all correspondence to Baptiste's mother, or had she married Gabriel? Initially, I dismissed the idea on the basis that we hadn't received any notification of an application to marry from the prison. If Andrea had married Gabriel, the implications were huge. A marriage between the two would mean that she was now no longer competent or compellable to give evidence against her husband. The knock-on effect of that would be that she wouldn't be giving evidence against any of the other defendants. I then wondered whether we had in fact been conned or whether she was having second thoughts and was now looking for a way out. But she'd been so convincing at the committal proceedings, I couldn't quite believe it. The quickest way to find out was to see her. As a precaution, I needed to take someone with me. If she had turned against us, I didn't want to give her the opportunity to make any accusations of impropriety.

Having seen Julia Meadows arriving for work, I managed to get her away from her duties to join me. Andrea appeared happy enough to see us, inviting us into her home. It was another fairly small, terraced council property where the front door led straight into a living room. Similar to Cranford Cottages, it had stairs and another door, which presumably went to the kitchen. The room was sparsely furnished with an old three-piece suite, television, coffee table and a couple of framed prints on the walls, copies of which I'd seen on sale in the local market. Everything had seen better days, but it was immaculate, extremely clean, tidy and very well kept.

"Should I be saying, congratulations?" I said.

"Thank you," she said.

Bollocks.

"It's true then, how long have actually you been, married?"

"Gabby and I have been married for three weeks and three days."

"You realise, you might have some time to wait before you're together, don't you?"

"I don't care, I'll wait. I love him."

I genuinely believed what she was saying. "Is this going to affect you giving evidence at trial?" I asked.

"I don't think so, is it?"

"Are you sure?"

"Yes, why?"

I told her about the legal position. I felt sure that if I didn't, someone else would, putting their slant on things, looking to take advantage.

"Because you are now Mrs Baptiste. That means you don't have to, and we can't make you give evidence against Gabriel. No one can. As things stand, it's now unlikely that you'll be giving evidence at the trial. The likelihood is that when the other defence solicitors find out, they will want confirmation that you are not going to give evidence. They might even challenge your right to give evidence or try to influence you by threatening Gabriel. Getting him to talk to you, suggesting that something might happen to him if you do give evidence. Has he spoken to you?"

"No, he hasn't," she said indignantly. "But it may explain this." She continued.

Getting up, she fetched a letter from the kitchen. It was from Donovan Parkes' solicitor, addressed to Gabriel's mother, asking to interview her in relation to an impending court case. It was suitably vague; they knew they were not allowed to contact prosecution witnesses directly. But there was nothing to stop them from contacting a defendant's mother, which could be an indirect way of applying pressure on Andrea.

"Andrea, do you trust me?" I asked.

"I think so. Why?"

"Well, I'm going to trust you. I'm not supposed to, but I have a proposal for you. Which, if successful, would mean Gabriel not spending so much time in prison as he might do. Interested?"

"Go on."

"I'm trusting you. If anyone finds out, I could lose my job. And if you do say something, not only will I deny it, but I won't be able to help Gabriel and he could end up being in prison for a very long time, possibly in the same prison as Ramadi and the brothers."

"I'm listening."

"Now that you're married. For you to have your day in court giving evidence against Ramadi, we need to sever the trial. Which means having two trials, one for Gabriel and one for the others, and for that to happen we need to convince our counsel it's worthwhile. The prosecution will have to consider the best way to proceed based on whether you do or don't give evidence. If you don't give evidence, the prosecution case will be strongest if everyone stands trial together, with Gabriel's interview implicating the others. It would form a large part of the evidence against them. If you were to give evidence and did so, the way you did at the committal, then I think the prosecution's chances of getting a conviction would be higher. However, as I have said, we would need to sever the trial, which in effect means we would be swapping Gabriel's interview for your testimony. Something prosecution counsel may be reluctant to do. So, the deal is. If you promise to give evidence and carry it through, I could arrange for the most serious offences Gabby's charged with to lie on file. Which means they would never be tried in court, assuming he keeps his nose clean, that is. This can be done in a couple of ways, but only after the others have been tried. One way is by writing to our solicitor's department suggesting the case is not proceeded with, due to mitigating circumstances. Having Gabriel being viewed as a victim, emphasising that he was forced to do what he did and that it was no longer in the public interest to proceed. If that didn't fly, Gabby would need to plead guilty to a minor offence and get a reduced sentence. We could do this by registering him as an informant, which would then allow me to get a letter written to the trial judge giving the reasons why either a short or non-custodial sentence would be in the interests of the Crown. I've done it before, and it works. Either way, it could mean Gabriel being home for Christmas. If you don't give evidence and he's convicted, he'll probably be looking at ten to fifteen years in prison. If you want to see Ramadi and the Parkes brothers go down for what happened to Adam, Georgina and Matthew, your giving evidence and telling the truth is our best chance. Lastly, have you thought of what might happen should they walk? Coming for you, Gabby, other friends, even family. Do you understand what I'm saying? If not say so?"

"I've got it completely."

"Okay, so what do you think. Are you up for it?"

"If Gabby could be home before Christmas, that would be brilliant. Do you think there's a real chance? You're not just saying it to get me to give evidence, are you?"

"I can't promise, but I think there's a good chance he could be home for Christmas. What I do know is that if we don't have a go, there's no chance. The evidence against him is compelling. Which is partly due to finding Adam's head in the river. Not that far from where Gabby said he threw it in."

"You've found Adam's head?"

"Yes, didn't you know?"

"No, Gabby didn't say."

"Well, we have, but let's get back to Gabby, can we?"

"Okay."

"Right, just so that you don't think that I've had you over, you need to be aware that if the trials are severed, we need to make sure the main trial is dealt with first, and we won't be able to make any applications in relation to Gabby's trial until then. If we tried to do anything before, it would be a complete show-out which would cause problems. Even telling someone you think you can trust could screw everything. We need to be smart. Still up for it?"

"Definitely. I'll never forgive Ramadi. The bastard. The grief he's caused and taking Georgina."

She was beginning to get upset.

"Okay, well firstly, we need to convince counsel that severing the trial is worth doing. If they don't go for it, we're stuffed."

"That should be easy. Just tell them if they don't, I won't give evidence," said Andrea.

"Unfortunately, it's not that easy. As I said, it's a trade-off. One of the main reasons for Gabby being linked to the others, is that his interviews and confession go against all the others. If the trial is separated, his evidence won't be read out, so it won't be heard. Counsel has to make a choice of risking you turning up and doing your thing or the police reading out what Gabby said, with him sitting in the dock. Which would you choose?"

"If I was in their shoes, I'd probably pick you, the police."

"Normally, so would I. But you're a good witness who comes across as being both honest and genuine. Which can be very powerful. Whereas the police can always be portrayed as being bent in some way, irrespective of whether we are or not.

If you gave evidence with your boyfriend, sorry, husband, as a defendant, the other defendants would make it look as though you were giving evidence against them for his benefit. So, to put it simply, we need to convince counsel that your giving evidence without Gabby in the dock is better than Gabby sitting there."

"I'm sure you can do it."

"We'll see. By the way, we need details of the marriage – have you got a copy of the certificate?"

"No, not here. It was at Tower Hamlets Registry Office, three weeks and three days ago, you can work the date out."

"I'll get a copy. You must promise me you won't say a word to anyone. Not to Gabby, not to your mum, no one, not even to Georgina in a prayer. This is our secret. If anyone finds out, it will be trouble for all of us. With Gabby ending up in prison and me looking for a new job, and I don't want either of those things to happen, clear?"

"Yes... I've got it, I have."

"Finally, it might take quite a while to get this sorted. With any application unlikely to take place until a week or so before the trial is due to start. Don't worry if you don't hear anything. As soon as I know something, I'll let you know, I'd ignore that letter if I were you. Don't reply, don't do anything. You never know, something similar might turn up from one of the other solicitors. If it does, let me know. If you need us, you know where we are."

She nodded, and with that, we left. Julia had sat in total silence throughout. I wasn't sure whether she agreed or disagreed with what I'd said or done.

On our way back to the car, I said, "Julia, it goes without saying that no one else can know about this, including Bob."

"I know," she said.

She wasn't happy at being put in such a position. I didn't push it. And in any case, if she did say something to Bob Clarke. Given his postings and previous experience, particularly with the Flying Squad, he would understand and could well agree. If he didn't, and things got tough, there was always the possibility of their liaison becoming a lot more public, making things difficult for both of them.

"I'm only trying to do the right thing and get the right result. Do you want to see them free? Walking around, terrorising everyone, killing someone else? Which is what's likely to happen."

She just looked at me disapprovingly. I couldn't make her out and decided it was best not to carry on. After all, until this case, she'd never been involved or experienced a major investigation. Although there was little doubt that given time, she would begin to realise that not everything was black and white. And when she did, I was sure she would make an excellent detective if she wanted to.

Counsel would be only too aware of the options and would have their opinion. However, as the police instructed counsel on behalf of the Crown, we could effectively force them to take a particular course of action. To do that, the boss, DI Clarke and

Alan, would all have a say and would need to agree that severing Baptiste from the main trial was the preferred course of action, which would then have to be sanctioned by the boss. It would also be a lot better for me if one of the others thought it was their idea. The only way that was going to happen was to have a meeting and get them drinking. I was trying to work out how to achieve this and was obviously overthinking things. When all I really needed to do was to tell them that Andrea Smith had married Gabriel. The first part of the plan worked like a dream. Within a couple of hours, DI Clarke called to say they would be over for a meeting in a couple of days. It was the earliest they could do with the boss being away with his daughter visiting universities.

When we did get to meet, I didn't need to do any cajoling subliminally or otherwise. Bob Clarke and Alan Harrison were in favour of severing the trial from the start. They instantly understood the options. As far as they were concerned, the alternative of just the one trial with all the defendants and Andrea not giving evidence wasn't the best way to go. In their minds, that scenario would allow the defendants to effectively gang up on Baptiste, suggesting he'd lied having played a much larger role, while diminishing theirs, demonstrated by pointing the finger at him. Saying he was the one with the knowledge who went and got the chemicals. He was also the one who knew how to clean-up the scene, and he was the one who threw Adam's head in the Thames, muddying the waters. After a while, the two of them turned to the boss, wanting his thoughts. As I hadn't really said anything, the boss looked at me. Seeking my opinion. I just nodded and with the three of us agreeing. The boss wasn't about to go against us. Bob Clarke offered to sign off the paperwork. Giving him a legitimate reason for coming over for the next few weeks. In reality, it just meant him popping in to sign reports when ready. A ten-minute job at most, but it would give him more time to be with Julia. On one of those days, I was waiting in the office. When the door opened, with

Bob Clarke standing there with a young lad, saying, "I hope you don't mind. This is Danny. Danny, this is Chris."

Danny was four and by the look of him quite shy, hiding behind the DI or Uncle Bob. Then after a few minutes of him getting used to his surroundings, I managed to make friends, providing him with drawing paper and loads of coloured felt-tip pens. Setting him up at his own desk at the far end of the office, where he could play detective for a while. The DI's sister had called looking for a favour. She'd been given the opportunity of a last-minute cancellation for a scan she'd been waiting for, but needed someone to look after her son, Danny. Having agreed, the DI thought it would be a good idea to bring him to the office. So that when Julia finished work, they could all go off to the tower for a bit of a surprise.

Once the reports had been submitted, and various queries dealt with, the solicitor's department agreed that severing the trial was the preferred option, which just left our new counsel to agree. It took a while, with them only agreeing after they'd spoken to the idiot who'd represented us at committal. Thankfully, he confirmed how good a witness Andrea had been. It wasn't until late October, just two weeks before the trial was due to start, that we received written confirmation counsel were making the application. I made a copy of the letter to show Andrea. I was sure that it would have more credence than me simply telling her, hopefully, keeping her on board, which it did. Along with being able to see the application for herself from the court's public gallery. The hearing took no more than five minutes, with the application going through unopposed, clearing the way for Andrea to give evidence. The only reason we could think for the application not to be opposed was that the defence now knew they wouldn't have to deal with Gabriel's confession. Optimistic that one way or another, Andrea wouldn't be giving evidence. It was only then that I again had second thoughts, wondering whether we'd done the right thing. If she didn't give evidence, it would mean the jury not hearing the evidence of Georgina or Andrea or the confessions of Gabriel or Matthew Peters. The prosecution would be relying almost entirely on forensic evidence, which itself could end up being excluded because of Ken Reeves' ineptitude. It was too late now. I just hoped we hadn't misread Andrea.

Chapter 21

The day before the trial was due to start, we had our final conference with counsel. Michael Cromber, QC was lead; getting on in years, untidy greying hair similar in colour to the fading wig he wore. He walked with a slight stoop, while his mannerisms could easily lead you into thinking he was a little absent-minded. Every time we'd met, he seemed a little flustered, his gown off the shoulders half-way down his back; gathered in at the elbows, his arms never straightening. The way it was worn was more akin to a ladies' fur stole or wrap, creased and faded over the years with odd stains of port or red wine that had been taken over many lunches in chambers. This was the old-style way of wearing a gown and reminded me of my old headmaster and Latin teacher.

Nicholas Reece, our junior, a much younger, brighter speed merchant. Dashing everywhere, a bit of a flyer whose was going places. He'd gone through the papers with a fine-tooth comb and was definitely up to speed. By comparison, his gown looked as though it was regularly cleaned, even pressed occasionally. He was from a more modern school. Whenever his gown slipped off the shoulder, he instinctively put it back, even when walking at a pace, with the gown trailing in his wake.

Having gone over such things as running orders, exhibits, checked that both handwritten and typed copies of statements were available in both alphabetic and chronological order, we were pretty much ready to go. It was only then that counsel told us we'd been listed in number one court, the most famous of all the criminal courts at the Old Bailey.

The following day we arrived at court early, only to find we'd been bumped and were now listed in court seven. Preparations for the murder trial of Dennis Nilsen, The Muswell Hill serial killer, were being made, which was due to start in a couple of days. The media coverage alone demanded his trial took place in court one, where the Recorder of London presided. In a way, I was quite pleased with the move. Having previously had cases in court one, it was quite pokey and would have been really cramped given the number of defendants we had. One of the other problems the court had was that if you were sitting in the well of the court looking up to the judge, all you got was a crick in the neck, along with the occasional glimpse of a wig bobbing around. Court seven was in fact the second highest court, where The Common Sergeant of London was currently presiding. His Honour Judge Campbell-Porter.

At some point in the Central Criminal Court's history, the original building had been extended with new courts being built beside the old. The two elements joined together by a large, long, flowing staircase and several lifts that were used to get around both old and new. The lifts were some of the smoothest and quietest lifts I'd ever been in. Orange rings of light illuminated the floor numbers as they silently moved up and down. Regular visitors were likely to use the very gradual main staircase next to lifts. It was a much quicker way of getting around, and with some offices being midway between floors made more sense. The entrance to the Metropolitan Police room being one. If the wheel was coming off, it was one of two bolt holes where police officers could seek solace away from counsel and witnesses alike. It was also where officers checked in and where messages were left for those attending court. The other bolt hole, the City of London Police canteen. If you knew how to get there, that is. On the top floor, through a warren of corridors with no signs to guide you, the only sign you were getting close was a row of coat pegs so high up the wall you had to be nearly six feet tall to reach them. A subliminal statement of the additional height requirement needed to join that force.

Court Seven was the furthest of three courts from the lifts and staircase on its floor. Outside the courts, a cavernous communal area where the majority of seating had been judiciously placed away from the court entrances. Long orange sofas were placed back-to-back at intervals in the centre, with similar sofas spaced out along the outer walls. A few individual seats judicially placed close to the entrance of each court. On the far side, floor-to-ceiling windows looked out onto Old Bailey. Covered by bomb blast net curtains, significantly reducing the amount of natural light. They, along with a large shard of broken glass embedded into a pillar because of an IRA bombing, acting as a constant reminder to be vigilant.

The majority of newer courts were similar in design. Fairly square with the usual raised areas for the judge, clerk of the court and defendants. To actually get into court, you had to go through double doors into a small vestibule, at the end of which was another set of double doors leading into the courtroom proper. Within each vestibule a tiny conference room where barristers could take final instructions. In our court, the judge sat to the right of the entrance. Opposite him the dock, with enough space for our defendants and guards. In between, seating and desks for the various legal teams. Along the wall opposite the entrance and separated from the rest of the court, two rows of six chairs for the jury. The sort of folding chairs you would see in a university auditorium. Close to those, another chair set slightly apart. The jury usher's chair. In between the judge and jury, the witness box. It was quite a distance from the entrance and walking in front of everyone could give you the feeling of running the gauntlet. A separate entrance to a mezzanine floor above the court's entrance provided access to the public gallery, under which there was a table and chairs reserved for the police. Mainly used for going through statements and sorting exhibits that would be needed when a particular witness was giving their evidence. Close by, another small table and chair. Reserved for the court usher. Behind the two tables, a small row of chairs pushed up against the wall, close to the entrance.

The first few days of a big trial could be pretty stressful, particularly with a case like ours, given the number of defendants and with space at a premium. Just finding somewhere for your legal team to set up camp could present problems. So much so, that on the first day of any big trial, as soon as the court building was open, defence runners would manoeuvre for position; waiting outside their nominated court for an usher to unlock the door. Once inside, they would quickly assess the layout and attempt to claim a pitch which they thought best suited their team. Something the police and prosecution counsel didn't have to do. Their success could, to a degree, be measured by where counsel sat, allowing them to silently interact with the jury. Catching the occasional eye of a juror at an appropriate moment and then being able to visibly show their approval or disapproval without being spotted by the judge. Being able to grandstand, addressing judge and jury alike, also important. It was up to the runners to assess what was best for them. Finally, the runners had to make sure that they, their solicitors and counsel, could also communicate with their defendants while the trial was in progress without causing any disruption.

No witnesses were required for the first day, with everyone expecting it to be taken up with formalities. Pleas, swearing in a jury, opening speeches and the inevitable legal arguments. Our team for day one consisted of the boss, the DI, Alan and yours truly. Alan and I would be permanent fixtures for the duration, with others coming and going as needed. With just a few minutes to go before the kick-off, the boss thrust a piece of paper in my hand, his new pager number.

"I've joined the modern world but keep it to yourself, just in case you need me."

I guessed that with his daughter now at university; he needed to spend more time at home, and in all honesty, we were probably better off without him. Senior officers could be a liability at court, especially if they weren't concentrating.

It was exactly ten-thirty when M'lord entered court. Everyone stopped what they were doing and stood in silence as the usher started his morning interjection.

"Oyez, oyez, all persons having any business with the court, draw near and give your attendance. God save the Queen."

Everyone bowed, taking the judge's lead as he slowly sat, fiddled with some papers, searched his pockets for glasses. Then with a pair of half-rimmed specs perched on the end of his nose, he looked down at the clerk of the court, and with a gentle nod of the head indicated he was ready. The defendants were asked to stand while the clerk began to read the various counts, asking for their pleas. All the counts related to the death of Adam Pope. Murder, preventing the lawful and decent burial of a dead body and assisting an offender. The drugs recovered when Ahmed was arrested would be dealt with separately, and presumably, if convicted of this and receiving a substantial custodial sentence, would lie on file.

Normally, after the clerk had read out a count, the defendant was asked whether they pleaded guilty or not guilty, with the defendant replying one way or the other. Not our lot. They all stayed tight-lipped. It was in total defiance of the court, resulting in not guilty pleas being entered on their behalf.

After this, Mr Cromber, the prosecution's lead counsel rose and in line with tradition, began to introduce his peers.

"May it please, M'lord, I appear for the Crown along with my learned friend, Mr Reece." Mr Reece duly rose a little, bowed and sat.

"Mr Nichols appears for the defendant, Benjamin Ramadi."

Mr Nichols rose slightly, nodded, and then continued to rise. Before other counsel could be formally introduced, we had our first application. Mr Cromber was obliged to take a seat.

M'lord peered over his glasses, looking unimpressed at the early intervention and break in tradition.

"A little early for legal argument, Mr Nichols?"

"M'lord, this is purely an administrative matter, which I believe my learned friends would support. I wonder whether M'lord would make a ruling on bail being granted for the defendants during breaks in proceedings. As it would greatly assist the defence with taking instruction. Ultimately saving the court valuable time. Of course, this would be on the understanding they remain within the confines of the court?"

"Mr Cromber, any observations?" said M'lord.

"I'll have to take instructions. Perhaps Detective Chief Superintendent Simmonds could deal with the matter."

The boss stood up, looking awkward, and started to make his way to the witness box. And as soon as he'd stepped into it, Ramadi's counsel was at him.

"Chief Superintendent, you wouldn't have any objections to my request, would you?"

We'd only been going a few minutes, and already defence counsel were testing the boss. Seeing if he was up to speed. Trying to work out what liberties they might get away with.

"Yes, err... I think that would be..."

We'd been caught hopping and before he could finish and without speaking, the three of us stood in unison. A reflex action, the sound of our chairs moving back automatically attracting everyone's attention.

"Chief Superintendent, from the reaction of your colleagues, I believe they may have a view on this, perhaps you should consider..."

M'lord didn't finish the sentence, he just left it hanging as the boss turned and looked in our direction, where we were all shaking our heads, mouthing the word "No" as clearly as we could. Hoping he could lip-read everyone else could. All this did was aggravate the remaining defence counsel, who, not wishing to be outdone, had also risen, wanting to raise their objections. There were now more people standing than sitting. This is going to be fun, I thought. As Mr Travis, Donovan Parkes counsel won the race to address the court, and with an appropriate degree of disbelief condescendingly said.

"Never have I ever seen the head of an investigation. A detective chief superintendent no less, be countermanded by colleagues. Surely M'lord is not going to allow for answers to be a consensus. I wish to voice my immediate objection in the strongest possible terms. I feel sure that I speak for my learned colleagues."

Defence counsel were like a pack of nodding dogs sitting on a parcel shelf in the back of a car, bobbing up and down. They wanted the boss and had immediately smelt blood. The boss gestured to Bob Clarke to take his place as he stepped down. It was all becoming a bit of a shambles. We hadn't started well. Already my fears of having a senior officer in court a reality. The likelihood was that the last time he'd stepped inside a Crown Court for a fight was years ago. And the last time he would have dealt with a bail application even further back in time. As a result, he was completely out of touch. The defence had suspected as much. Now they knew and were seeking to take advantage. As we were standing there, my mind went back to one of the earlier hearings where the boss had stepped aside, leaving me to deal a fairly straight-forward remand. I wondered whether this was the reason. The boss then continued his retreat; turning and making his way to the back of the court where he sat close to the exit in complete solitude, distancing himself from everyone, looking more than a little embarrassed. The three of us now looked at each other, wondering what to do. I'd never seen or experienced anything like it. DI Clarke then whispered, "You do it. You dealt with the bail applications and the committal. Use that as an excuse for going up, taking the boss's place." Immediately sitting down, leaving the two of us standing, and with Alan looking at me, I started to make my way towards the witness box. This time Mr Ritchie, counsel for Devon Parkes, was up like lightning, determined to beat everyone else, wanting his turn, voicing more objections.

"M'lord, firstly, I would like to say that I concur with my learned friend's views regarding Detective Chief Superintendent Simmonds and would like to add that never before have I ever witnessed such a situation. This is not some sort of football match and neither should it be treated as such. Substituting a detective chief superintendent for a sergeant."

The pack nodded, but by the time he'd finished I'd made it to the witness box and said, "M'lord, should I take the oath?"

A chink of light in the gloom. Thankfully, M'lord was on the same wavelength. The break in tradition regarding formal introductions and the excessive gloating, a little too much. Not that we'd covered ourselves in glory. The nodding dogs stopped, realising the mistake. In counsel's eagerness to land an early blow, the boss hadn't actually got to take the oath before he'd started on him. Consequently, he hadn't formally given evidence, and neither could he perjure himself. As a result, it was still possible for him to be substituted. As the defence had put it. A fact that M'lord dwelt on for some time. With bail applications being refused, it was an indication of what was to come, and it hadn't been our best start.

Mr Travis then rose again, stating he had several points of law he now wished to raise, and whilst those matters were being considered, he wanted the police to be excluded from court. The case had been going no more than twenty minutes and we now found ourselves sitting outside, like the four wise monkeys. It turned out that this was where we would spend most of the week.

I wasn't sure whether we'd done anything to upset or offend our counsel, but while we'd been outside, conversations had become extremely limited. "Back at two," was about as good as it got at lunchtime, with counsel walking straight past us on their way to chambers. Having quizzed the usher, he told us that most of the legal arguments were about exhibits, such as which photographs were going to be acceptable to put before the jury. With the way the case had started, the defence probably didn't want to agree on either the number or content of any photographs. The extreme nature of some would undoubtedly have an impact. There was no doubt the defence would want to limit the numbers to as few as possible, with the prosecution wanting the opposite. Arguments about each one presumably now taking place. A representative balance needing to be achieved. M'lord would also have to ensure that he didn't give the defence grounds for an appeal. It was a delicate balance. There was little doubt that other exhibits were likely to be challenged when the trial really got under way.

So much for a five to six-week trial. Week one was nearly over, and we didn't even have a jury.

At the end of day four we were summoned to a pow-wow with counsel. Mr Reece did most of the talking. He gave us a brief account of what had been going on. There'd been arguments about all sorts of things, not just the photographs mentioned by the usher. The main ones being our presence in court and the severing of Gabriel Baptiste from the trial. After that, they then went onto other evidence they were seeking to have disallowed. Such as the knives recovered from the river Roding. Which had been found as a result of what Matthew Peters had said during interview. And as the interviews were no longer admissible, the defence was now making the argument that not only should his interviews be excluded but also any evidence deriving from them. With a similar argument being put forward in relation to the discovery of Adam's head. Where the suggestion was that as Gabrielle Baptiste was no longer a defendant in the trial, any evidence emanating from his interviews should also be excluded. The judge, having heard the various arguments, had deferred making a ruling on all matters until the morning.

During some of the arguments, our counsel had also become concerned about how well prepared the defence appeared to be. They seemed to have a response for almost every counter argument prosecution counsel put forward. It wasn't the first time something like this had been said during the investigation, bringing back memories of office meetings. Mr Reece confided that he'd unintentionally overheard Ramadi and Devon Parkes counsel discussing elements of the case during which they'd used terminology found in some of the police reports. Counsel wanted to know how they may have come to possess such information. Police reports had a limited circulation. Ours were initially written by Alan and I, typed by Anne, checked by us, and then read, agreed and signed off by one of the bosses. Six copies. Three for the police, with the others being forwarded to solicitor's department. All the remaining handwritten drafts and working copies destroyed, in accordance with the boss's instructions. Raising the question of how the defence may have obtained copies. More importantly, what impact might it have on the trial? It also answered the question of why counsel had been behaving the way they had, believing one of us to be responsible for the leak. The DI told counsel about some of the issues we'd previously encountered. This, together with his assurances, seemed to convince counsel that none of those present were responsible for the disclosure.

Moving on, Mr Reece went on to say that he hoped it wouldn't be too long before the jury would be sworn in, and that police may actually be allowed back in court.

When it came to prosecution witnesses giving evidence, the defence would normally have their spies out, the runners. It was part of the game. They would be checking to see which witnesses were waiting to give evidence, trying to make sure there were no surprises. With what had gone on, some of our civilian witnesses wouldn't be coming through the main entrance or be waiting outside court for too long. We would be bringing them into court using the staff entrance in Warwick Square. Using this entrance would avoid any unnecessary contact with others, allowing you to get a witness to a nearby waiting room without being seen.

According to counsel, it looked as though most of the day would now be taken up with jury selection. The defence were trying to load the jury with as many men as they could. Just after lunch the usher came over, handing me a note from the police room. Ken Reeves wanted someone to give him a call. I felt sure the number he'd left was for Arbour Square. A call to the switchboard told me it belonged to one of their exhibit rooms. Ken wasn't exactly known for initiating calls and apart from wondering what he was doing there, I wondered what he wanted? When I called, the number was answered almost immediately.

"DC Reeves, Leman Street," said the voice. It was Ken, sounding sober.

"It's Chris. You left a message for someone to call?"

"Oh… yeah… Hi. I just wanted to make sure everything was okay and to see if you guys needed anything doing? Any exhibits needed for court?"

"Not that I know of. As it happens, we've just finished a con and nothing's been asked for."

"When do you think the witnesses will be starting? Tomorrow?"

"I've no idea, we're not allowed in court. All I've been told is that we hope to start swearing in the jury later today. We haven't been told to warn anyone."

"Still dustmen first?"

"Well, they found the body, that's where it all started, so I guess so."

"Okay. Well, if anything changes, just let me know."

"Thanks."

And with that he hung up, probably wishing someone else had been given the message.

What was all that about? In all the time, I'd known him. Apart from collecting money for a drink, I'd never known him to offer or volunteer to do anything. And what was all that Leman Street rubbish, who did he think he was fooling.

Day two of week two and still no live witnesses. The first was about to be called, and we were still sitting outside, having been joined by two of the three dustmen. Mr Reece then came out saying that due to the amount of unrest and the issues around officers being allowed in court, there had been a change of plan. Counsel was amending the running order. In most cases, officers nominated to oversee a case such as Alan and I would be allowed in court from the beginning. Effectively, we would act as the prosecution's runners, primarily responsible for ensuring witnesses were at court at the right time, and the exhibits they referred to were available. Following through a witness's statement while they gave evidence, making sure nothing was missed, being part of the team, generally helping with the smooth running of the case wherever possible. Once a witness had given their evidence, they could stay in court should they want to? The only way of ensuring police were in court was to change the order. I needed to be ready to give evidence in ten minutes. Alan would follow the two dustmen. The defence weren't ready for the switch; all standing in a huddle, having been told as the court reconvened. The jury must have been wondering what was happening with M'lord cajoling them to return to their places.

Having taken the oath, I said, "Detective Sergeant Christopher Lomax, attached to Leman Street Police Station, M'lord" wondering how many times I'd said that or something similar before giving evidence, hundreds.

I had time for a quick look around the court, including the dock. Looking to see who was sitting with who. Were there any signs of discord or disagreement? Was anyone sitting alone? It was difficult to say, although Ahmed looked a little detached. I didn't recognise anyone in the public gallery, and the defence teams were still in the same order they had been from day one.

My evidence became a little disjointed. Primarily due to Matthew Peters death and the severing of Gabriel Baptiste's trial, as neither could be mentioned. With the jury not being aware of their existence or what they might have said or done; any mistake by me was likely to be jumped on, potentially leading to a retrial, which was something we wanted to avoid at all cost.

Our counsel rushed me through my evidence, including the final interview with Ramadi. It was really unusual. Instead of plodding meticulously through all the evidence in a chronological order, he only went over three elements: searching Cranford Cottages, the various interviews of defendants in the dock, and my part in finding Adam Pope's head. Counsel had obviously won that legal argument, so long as Gabriel's name didn't get a mention. After which, he said, "I understand that you have been involved in various other elements of this investigation?"

"That's correct, M'lord."

"Just wait there, my learned colleagues may have questions for you." And with that, he sat down.

The defence hadn't expected or didn't appear to be prepared for me giving evidence. It was their turn to be in a bit of a shambles, working out who was going to question me first. Their cross-examination turned out to be really tame. Things like why was evidence found during the second search of Cranford Cottages and not the first? Like I knew, that was something they would have to ask the officers present at the first search. There was a pathetic attempt to suggest that during Ramadi's interview, I'd misheard him. He hadn't said, "Pope was a nobody." He had in fact, said, "I don't know nobody." With a suggestion that I hadn't asked some of the questions in the notes, implying they'd been fabricated; glossing over or forgetting that the interview had been in the presence of his solicitor – something I took delight in reminding counsel. Including Ramadi's antics with the table, the jumping up and posing like the Incredible Hulk. It couldn't have gone much better. None of them went anywhere near the finding of Adam's head. It had been a breeze. I could now sit in court and with the dustmen and Alan giving their evidence, counsel had achieved their objective.

The only disappointment was that we were now unable to play one of our court games. Frequently played, when quite a few police officers were giving evidence at trial. The object was really simple. All you had to do was get a particular word or phrase into an answer during cross-examination. If you failed, there was the inevitable forfeit, normally involving the purchase of alcohol. One of the most embarrassing and entertaining of these had been at Inner London Crown Court when the term "higgledy-piggledy" had been picked. Getting it into cross-examination was pretty easy. With those involved in searching the addresses typically describing one of the rooms or areas as being "higgledy-piggledy." Where things got sticky was that by the time the fourth officer had said the same thing. Others were beginning to catch on, with both prosecution and defence counsel now getting "higgledy-piggledy" into their questions. Saying things like, "It seems to have been accepted that... was higgledy-piggledy." Forcing the officer into replying along the lines of, "That's correct your honour, the... was very higgledy-piggledy." It got so bad that even the judge joined in. At one point, interrupting counsel and saying, "I believe I know where my learned friend is going with this. Officer, would you describe... as higgledy-piggledy?" By which time the jury had cottoned on, with some starting to snigger as the witnesses reached that stage in their testimony. Knowing what was about to happen, the trial descending into pantomime.

Chapter 22

I wasn't sure what had happened overnight, but there appeared to be a cessation of hostilities returning to some sort of normality. How long it would last was anyone's guess. The prosecution now calling witnesses in a more logical sequence, with the defence having had a change of heart. Relenting on the number of fully bound expert witnesses they now required to physically attend and given evidence in court. With some of the witnesses' evidence now being accepted, their statements could be read to the jury, meaning the witnesses would no longer have to attend in person.

Having been provided with a revised running order, we now needed to make sure all the necessary exhibits would be available in court when the witnesses came to give evidence. Counsel gave me a list of the exhibits needed, which I faxed through to Ken Reeves, as per his earlier call. Everything was to be at court well before kick-off in the morning. Counsel wanted to familiarise themselves with some of the exhibits before formally producing them. I was pleasantly surprised to find that Ken had not only left a message confirming receipt of the list. He also promised to have them at court in ample time for counsel.

The following morning, Alan and I had arrived early, primarily to sort out the witnesses due to be giving evidence, allowing them the opportunity to read their statements, refresh their memories, making sure everything ran smoothly, making sure any of the exhibits they produced or referred to were ready and available. The bosses would be turning up later. Despite yesterday's promises, we were getting close to kick off before Ken arrived, puffing and panting. Carrying a refuse sack full of exhibits, which he placed beside our table.

"Sorry I'm late. Got held up in traffic."

There wasn't time, and this wasn't the place to have a go. "Everything here?" I said.

"Yes, I've checked it," he said, in that what-do-you-think-I-am-stupid-or-something kind of voice.

We were so tight for time. Having untied the knot, I started to go through the bag. Looking for the exhibits counsel would need first, trying to get everything in some semblance of order. The bag was almost full, with lots of bags and bags within bags. All of which made a dreadful noise as I rummaged through the sack. Even before we'd started, everyone was looking in our direction. The various knives, Daddy and Baby, I could feel at the bottom. For some reason, several unedited photograph albums had been shoved on top, now so creased they were unusable.

As with most major investigations, there were lots of exhibits and not all would be produced. Counsel had planned to read some of the now accepted statements, while holding up the relevant exhibit or exhibits for all to see. After which, they would move on to live witnesses. Once an individual's exhibit had been produced, it would be allocated a court exhibit number, which would then be used throughout the trial. I was still fumbling through the sack when I heard the usher say, "Oyez, Oyez, all persons..." I stopped and stood along with everyone else, bowing as M'lord entered. Mr Reece, having seen Ken Reeves with the sack, glanced in our direction, giving us the thumbs-up. Looking for confirmation the exhibits had arrived, I nodded, and the message was conveyed to Mr Cromber. By the time M'lord had taken his seat, Ken Reeves had disappeared, leaving me with a sack of unsorted exhibits. Trying to get them out without disturbing everyone was impossible. I had to stop and was now hoping that we could get to the comfort break, which was normally around 11.15 a.m. before any exhibits were needed. If we could get there without causing too much of a disturbance, we should be able to sort things out.

Had our resident alcoholic managed to get to court as promised, everything would have been really simple. The exhibits would have all been neatly laid out on the table, in the order they were likely to be needed. Then, when counsel asked for an exhibit, we would have been able to immediately hand it over via the usher, looking relatively professional instead of ill-prepared and amateurish.

For an hour or so counsel hadn't needed any exhibits, confining himself to reading statements and ploughing through a succession of uncontentious photographs, mainly relating to the waste ground and surrounding area. Giving the jury a sense of the location and surrounding area. Given the way most of the jurors were dressed, I doubted whether many, if any, were from similar areas. Sadly, we didn't quite make the comfort break before the first of the day's live witnesses was called; the SOCO who'd originally attended Cranford Cottages with Ken Reeves. At some point, counsel was going to ask the witness to formally identify the bags and clothing found there, and after a few minutes, Mr Cromber said, "Would you please take a look at your exhibit PH/28, a plastic bag?"

It was the usher's cue to make his way over. While I rummaged through the sack, looking for the exhibit which I eventually found. It was a clear plastic bag sealed within a clear plastic exhibit bag. Having handed it to the usher, he took it to the witness, who glanced at it and then formally identified the exhibit as the one referred in his statement.

"Thank you. If it pleases, M'lord, may this be court exhibit twenty-two?" Mr Cromber continued with counsel, asking a few questions about the bag. While the usher wrote out the court reference on one of his pre-printed sticky labels.

"Moving on, would you now please look at exhibit PH/29. Another clear plastic bag."

The usher collected PH/28 from the witness applying the sticky label with the court's exhibit reference, which he then passed to me. I then placed the bag on the floor beside me, while continuing to go through the sack looking for PH/29. It wasn't there and with everyone waiting and, in an effort to save any embarrassment, I turned PH/28 over, hiding the label and handed it back. Without realising, the usher passed to the witness. Who again glanced at the bag before formally identifying it as exhibit PH/29.

"Thank you, court exhibit twenty-three, M'lord," said Mr Cromber.

Again, the usher wrote out another court label while counsel asked the witness the similar questions to those he'd previously asked, getting similar answers. Both bags had now formerly been produced in evidence.

Mr Cromber then asked the SOCO to look at one of the items of clothing which had been found in court exhibit 22, the first bag. Resulting in the usher going through the same process of collecting the exhibit and sticking exhibit label twenty-three on the other side of exhibit twenty-two. Then for some inexplicable he turned the bag over, stuttering to a halt on seeing the other court exhibit label, then looking at me. I beckoned him over as inconspicuously as I could and whispered, "I know, I can explain, I'll have it sorted by lunchtime, I promise." Not quite sure what to do, he handed me the bag, taking the next exhibit, carrying on. We'd been lucky. I had no doubt that other ushers would have just dropped us in it. During the comfort break I told Alan, who'd been blissfully unaware of what had happened. As usual, he went ballistic and while I checked the other exhibits, he got hold of Reeves, ordering him to get the missing exhibit to court before lunch. As soon as we'd risen, I went to the police room. The missing exhibit was there, having been dropped off by a uniformed officer. Reeves couldn't face coming himself. Before reconvening, and with the usher supervising, we made the necessary modifications to the exhibits, explaining what had happened. As the two bags looked remarkably similar, no one was any the wiser.

Over the next couple of days, PKW and Professor Parker gave their evidence which, although protracted, went without incident. What I found strange was that with the evidence they'd given together with Dr Cutler's provided conclusive proof linking the head, the body and Cranford Cottages together. It was as if the defence didn't appreciate the significance of Dr Cutler's evidence, which in some ways gave some credence to the suspicion that the defence were utilising the police reports where they could, when assessing the witnesses, they were looking to challenge. Dr Cutler had taken a very long time to provide a formal statement, resulting in his evidence being served with an NFE or Notice of Further Evidence. Consequently, neither his statement nor its significance had featured in any of our reports, potentially resulting in the defence not realising its relevance.

As the trial progressed, we were fast approaching one of the points I was dreading, Ken Reeves giving evidence. We were bracing ourselves, waiting to see what would happen. What would be made of the tarpaulin and spices not being found during the first search? Readying ourselves, looking at what sort of damage limitation exercise we might be able to do when Notso gave his evidence. It didn't happen. Alan and I just sat looking bewildered. The defence gave him an extraordinarily easy ride. None of them went anywhere near the exhibits he'd missed. We were convinced he would get hauled over the coals and have great difficulty in trying to explain how the cupboard under the stairs with the tarpaulin and spice jars had been missed. It was something else we couldn't make sense of. As far as we could work out, there were possibly two reasons. Either they didn't want to draw attention to tarpaulin and spices. Or it was bent, and some kind of deal had been done. With the defence asking so little, it was left to the judge to ask Ken some questions. Should the case reach the point where he was required to sum up, M'lord needed to be clear on certain aspects of his evidence. He wanted to be sure there was no possibility of him misleading or misdirecting the jury. His questions caused Ken more discomfort than any the defence had asked. There was no doubt Ken would have been a complete mess had the defence got stuck into him.

An opportunity to score some house points at home had arisen, with some of those from the hostel giving evidence. Dearly beloved had often wanted to come to court, to see what really happened, and here was an opportunity to come to the Old Bailey. Having arranged a babysitter, namely mother-in-law, everything was sorted. We arrived quite early, giving me time to do a small tour, pointing out some of the murals on the ceilings of the older courts. Then, having personally escorted our latest witness into court, I found Alan and the bosses already there, going over statements. I introduced dearly beloved and gave her a quick rundown of the court's layout. She'd heard their names and my opinion of them, which it was true to say, had varied from time to time. As the session was about to begin, she sat on one of the chairs behind me, near to the exit where others from the team would occasionally sit. She could see everything, and it would be easy for her to leave, if needed.

There were a couple of statements to be read, and then we would be onto live witnesses. Counsel had just started reading one of the statements when Sally Bowers came in, sitting next to my wife. She immediately recognised Sally as the person who'd sat on my lap at the infamous office party. When an opportunity arose, Sally got up to pass Alan a message. I could see Alan whispering to Sally. Doubtlessly telling her who she was sitting next to. I was now hoping this wasn't all going to blow up in my face, opening up old wounds. I didn't realise the message Sally was passing on related to our first no-show. Cathy Kerwin was no longer willing to give evidence. Too scared of what might happen to her if she did. She wouldn't say whether something had already happened to make her change her mind, just that she was no longer willing to come to court and give evidence. It wasn't worth trying to force her. Having to deal with a hostile witness was fraught with potential problems. We couldn't make our minds up whether someone had got to her or the thought of giving evidence was just too much, given what had happened to Matthew and Georgina. In reality, her evidence was more important in the kidnapping trial. Hopefully, she might turn up for that.

It took counsel longer than expected to finish reading statements, and when he went to call Ms Saltmarsh, the judge intervened. It was time for one of his comfort breaks. As the judge left the court, I caught a glimpse of Sally and my wife in conversation. Although I didn't get the chance to join them and could only guess at what was being said. Counsel wanted to confirm a couple of matters regarding the hostel before any other witnesses gave evidence. By the end of the day, Nicola Saltmarsh had finished her evidence, and Claire Laker had started. Very little had really been contested. It was more background stuff about the hostel and how people, including Adam Pope, became residents.

On a personal note, the day had been a success. Dearly beloved had enjoyed the experience. She was also very surprised to see just how much paperwork there really was. All very different from dinky reports waved around on television. Best of all, "Lapgate" had been put to bed.

We were now reaching the point in the trial that everyone had been waiting for. There were just a few police officers who'd been involved with arrests and searches to give evidence, and Andrea Smith. Assuming she gave evidence, and it held up. Counsel had decided to leave her until last, believing the impact on the jury would be far greater than a gaggle of plods at the end of the prosecution, all saying the same thing. Something along the lines of, on day, date, time and place, I was present when Joe Bloggs was arrested and cautioned. To which he made no reply. He was then conveyed to blahdy, blahdy blah police station. Where he was searched and later interviewed. After which he was charged and cautioned with x, y and z. To which he replied, dah dee, dah dee, dah – boring.

With the changes in running order, we were now getting a bit of a buzz out of the fact the defence knew that traditionally police would normally be last to give evidence. And with those officers now giving their evidence and there being no sign of Andrea. It raised the defence's expectations that she wouldn't be giving evidence and the prosecution had in fact lost their best witness.

Martin Page was the last of those officers dealing with the arrest of Devon Parkes. On the face of it, his evidence was a formality. I wasn't really paying attention, thinking more about Andrea and how things would go. When Parkes' counsel asked for the jacket, he'd been arrested in, to be produced in court. The jacket hadn't been on any list, and we didn't think it would be needed. Wanting it brought to court as soon as was practicably possible, and while PC Page remain in court. M'lord had no option other than to grant the application.

Getting a copy of PC Page's statement, I took it to the police room to read while making the arrangements for the jacket to be brought to court. In the statement, PC Page had said that the knife Parkes had in his possession had been found in a hole in the lining of his jacket and not trapped in the lining, as I'd told him. Obviously, the defence now wanted to see the hole PC Page was referring to. Unsurprisingly, we couldn't get hold of Ken Reeves and ended up speaking with the station officer who said he would get it sorted and if there was a problem, he would let us know. I told him to make sure the jacket was dropped off in the police room, and that under no circumstances was it to be taken straight into court. Less than an hour had passed when an officer from the police room came into court, passing a note – the jacket had arrived. Alan and I went to examine it before it was brought into court, making sure a hole was where Martin Page said it was. The jacket had arrived in another of Ken's black sacks, and it wasn't long before the jacket had a hole in the sleeve, just as PC Page had described. We then arranged for one of the officers from the police room to bring the jacket into court after a suitable delay. It was more than ten minutes before the jacket made its appearance, and with the jacket now in court, the session and PC Page's cross-examination could continue. Parkes' counsel insisted on examining the jacket before handing it over to PC Page and had just started his examination when the dock erupted. There was an almighty rumpus. With Devon Parkes trying to climb into the court. The prison guard struggling to control him. Parkes kept looking in our direction, shouting, "Raasclaat, Babylon."

Over and over, he kept shouting, hissing and spitting. The clerk of the court kept saying, "Order, Order." We were totally bemused, as was everyone else as to what was going on. His guard was then joined by a second and between them, they managed to restrain Parkes. With M'lord rising, saying he would give counsel plenty of time to find out what had caused the outburst. We were then left wondering what the hell was going on. About twenty minutes later the court reconvened, with Parkes' counsel apologising for their client's outburst. Then taking great joy in telling the court that the jacket which had been produced wasn't his client's. It was the wrong jacket. Ken Reeves, the idiot, had sent the wrong one and with the jacket having arrived in an unmarked open bag, with no exhibit labels or description, we had no way of telling. The judge rose again, while counsel looked to resolve the matter. Ken Reeves was again nowhere to be found. We needed to not only find the right jacket, but come up with a plausible excuse for the cock-up. While counsel argued, the only solution was for the two of us to head to the station and sort things out ourselves, with PC Page remaining in court.

When we arrived back at the station, there were half a dozen sealed bags sitting on the desk in the exhibits room. All contained jackets seized during both investigations. Amongst them Devon Parkes' jacket. At least we knew where it was. What we couldn't work out was, what were all the jackets doing just dumped on the desk. And how was it that the jacket we needed hadn't made it in the first place? There wasn't time to work things out. All we could do was make sure the jacket had a hole in the appropriate sleeve, and then get it to court as quickly as possible, without Ken Reeves knowing what we'd been up to. We also needed to make sure that after our inspection, any modified exhibit was all nicely bagged up as per the exhibit book, ready for inspection. Because of all the cock-ups Reeves had made, we were now committing all sorts of breaches of discipline and daft criminal offences just to keep the case on track. It wasn't as if there was anything seriously wrong or corrupt. It was just another mistake which could prove embarrassing and could help to sway any jurors that were anti.

With rubber gloves, it was time for our Blue Peter skills to come to the fore. Armed with a similar exhibit bag, adhesive labels, Sellotape and pen, we locked ourselves into the room and did what was needed. Ken Reeves' signature was a doddle to trace. There wasn't a hole in this sleeve either. A waft of our magic wand and one almost identical to the first instantly appeared; coincidences do happen. All that was left was to tidy up and securely dispose of the old exhibit bag. I left Alan tidying up while I got rid of the bag. Hampton's old office had been left open and still wearing the rubber gloves. I could make use of one of his secure burn bags. Normally used for confidential waste, authorised for destruction without further examination. A few crumpled sheets from a report Hampton had left out, strategically placed on top. One dodgy signature later and the bag was ready for incineration. Quite fitting, given the trouble Hampton had caused. As I placed the bag in the designated tray, I noticed the latest tenure list sitting in the tray next to it, waiting for whoever was taking over his role. It was a list of all the officers on district, with their length of service and the amount of time they'd served. Anyone who'd been on district for more than five years would be coming to the end of their tenure. The list was in warrant number order. DI Lambert's was just four less than Ken Reeves. That one fact pretty much provided the answers to everything. The two of them had joined together, gone through training school together, and were now working at the same station. It was how Reeves had survived for so long, how he'd been recommended as the exhibits officer and how his record had been removed from the admin office. Making me wonder why he hadn't been involved with the other crappy domestic murder? Looking back through the duty states, it didn't take long to get an answer. He'd been on leave for two weeks when the murder broke. Reeves had been spying on us in return for protection; keeping the DI up to date. What the DI was doing with the information was another matter. Presumably, Reeves had been able to copy the police reports. I then wondered whether that was the reason for the easy ride he'd had when giving his evidence? With about a year to go until he could retire on full pension, he needed help to make sure he got there. His prospects outside the job didn't look great, and being forced out early would cost him dear.

As we headed back to court, I told Alan what I'd found. It didn't seem to register. He was more concerned with coming up with a story to cover Ken's cock-up. The best we could come up with was that DC Reeves appeared to have found the jacket, but it looked as though he may have been taken ill and whoever had taken over the responsibility had got the bags mixed up. And in any case, our search of the exhibits room had identified the correct jacket, which was still sealed in its original bag, as per the exhibits book entry. So, it couldn't have been tampered with. That was the story we were going with. The sealed bag and exhibits book were immediately seized and examined in great detail by the defence. The court then resumed without the jury, with the bag being discussed and externally examined by all. Even M'lord had a quick gander. After which, the jury were recalled, and the case resumed with the usher being selected to open the bag in front of everyone and reveal all. It was an odd piece of theatre, adding a little drama, and quite unusual. Once the bag was opened, the jacket was then passed around, being inspected by everyone except Martin Page. Who'd been sitting silently, in or near in the witness box for hours, and was still none the wiser. Devon Parkes was not a happy bunny, gesticulating with counsel. Anyway, provided PC Page kept to his story and didn't look too surprised when he got to see the hole, we should be back on track.

I wanted to have a look at the court's CCTV. To see if it was possible to identify who'd dropped the first jacket off. And, having been to various offices, I found that I would have to wait until the end of the day before being able to look. On my return to court, I was surprised to see PC Page still being cross-examined; the jacket lying over the corner of the witness box. What was taking so long? Had there been another cock-up? Alan told me that PC Page was having trouble describing both the lining and the hole in which the knife had been found. The defence had stopped him from looking at the jacket lining. It wasn't great, but eventually he muddled through. Alan Harrison was also interested in knowing who'd dropped the jacket off and joined me going through CCTV footage. Timed at 12.22 p.m. We saw one of the Met's general-purpose cars pull up outside the court's main entrance, stopping on the double yellow line. From the angle of the camera, we could see at least two occupants, possibly three. The driver placed the logbook on the car's dashboard for all to see. It acted like a free parking ticket for police.

The front passenger then jumped out of the car, carrying the black sack and a piece of paper. I didn't know his name but recognised him as one of Hampton's lot. They'd somehow morphed into a crime squad and were still working from Arbour Square. On entering the court building, our man could be seen from an internal camera getting into one of the lifts and then returning to the car empty-handed about five minutes later. We were both sure the GP car was from Arbour Square. This sent Alan into what I was now describing as Rickett's mode, as opposed to rocket mode. With a flurry of expletives, he just wanted to head over to Arbour Square and beat the crap out of someone, anyone. I wasn't sure whether it was a good thing or not, but once he'd calmed down; I told him about some of the other things I was aware of regarding Reeves, including his earlier meetings with The Muppets. Initially, he was disappointed that I hadn't trusted him. I said that wasn't the case. The main reason for keeping things to myself was that I wanted to be sure of my facts, and I didn't want him going off on one, reacting the way he just had. With that, a small grin emerged, accepting what I'd said. With DI Lambert and The Muppets still working out of Arbour Square and now knowing of the relationship between Lambert and Reeves, there was more than a good chance that this was where Reeves had been disappearing to. Unfortunately, we didn't have time to find out. Andrea would be giving evidence in the morning.

It seemed as though the world and his wife had turned up. Knowing that the prosecution case would either finish, and if it did, there would be legal argument or there would be just one more witness, Andrea. All the legal teams appreciated how important the prosecution's final witness could be. Should she materialise? All the seats were occupied, with some unfamiliar faces amongst them. We too had a full complement, with the DI and the boss sitting at the back of the court. Julia Meadows and Sally Bowers had gone to collect Andrea, with explicit instructions to use the rear entrance, taking her straight to the Met. Police room. With runners and possibly others looking for her, we weren't going to give anyone the chance of putting her off. Although Andrea didn't seem to someone who would be easily intimidated. As a further precaution, I walked around to the witness box to look in the public gallery. It too was full. There was only one person I recognised, Mrs Pope. The regular court junkies conspicuous by their absence, replaced by others, here specifically for the trial. I knew that Mrs Pope had attended from time to time, sitting quietly, not talking to anyone. I didn't see her acknowledge anyone. She was just looking around at others, probably wondering who they were and why they were there. Despite the gallery being full, she looked lonely. I wondered whether anyone knew or cared that she was the victim's mother? Whichever way this trial went, it was going to have an enormous effect on everyone connected to it.

I needed to remind Andrea that she was doing this for those who were or had been close to her – Gabriel, Georgina, Adam, Matthew and most importantly, herself. Provided she told the truth, excluding our little secret, everything should be fine.

When Sally Bowers popped her head around the court door, it was the signal to say Andrea had arrived. I picked up a large bundle of papers, including a copy of Andrea's statement, and I made my way to the police room. As none of their runners had reported in, the defence would still be assuming Andrea hadn't arrived. With the police room being out of bounds, no one could follow me, not that I think they tried. When I saw her, she was sitting beside a table in the locker room, opposite the main office, with Julia by her side. She'd taken a leaf out of Georgina's book and looked a different person. Dressed in a sophisticated grey suit and white shirt, with little of the jewellery she normally wore, her gold chain with the small cross, watch and wedding ring were all that remained. Her hair had been combed or styled in such a way that it made her look demure, even innocent. As far as I was aware, no one had told her what to wear or how to look. It was perfect.

I wanted her to be clear and not say anything which could be misconstrued. It was time for a small pep talk. I felt sure that I'd detected the slightest glimmer of a smile when she saw me. She was going to have her day.

"Good to see you. How are we doing?"

"Been better."

"How's Gabriel?"

"Not so good, he's been moved and is being kept away from everyone. He doesn't know why. He hasn't got anyone to talk to, he's worried Ramadi will get to him."

"Tell him not to worry, there's absolutely no chance of that happening – we've made sure of that. Trust me, there's absolutely nothing to worry about on that score. Just remember, if things go well, he could well be home for Christmas. This is for the five of you. It's about your future as much as it's about the past. I'm sure it will all be worthwhile. I know it's difficult. You just have to tell the truth one more time. At times it will feel like you're the one on trial. If that happens, just remember you'll be the one going home tonight. They won't. Before I forget, do you want to read your statement to refresh your memory?"

"Not really, I don't think I'll ever forget what happened."

"Okay, a couple of other things. At the moment, the jury doesn't know about Gabriel, and neither do they know about Matthew. Their names haven't been mentioned when the jury's been in court. Depending on how things go and how desperate the defence gets, they might mention Gabriel, suggesting that he is the one benefiting from you giving evidence. They may even suggest that you've done a deal. As I've said, all you have to do is stick to the truth. Tell them exactly what's in your statement. What you saw and what you did. Just leave out what we've talked about."

"I get it, I'm not stupid. I hate them so much more than you can imagine. What they've done to me, my friends, my life. I just want Gabriel back. I want the others back too, but I know I can't have them. This is the best I can do. I've been waiting for this."

As she spoke, her voice had changed. A characteristic I'd heard before, sounding more determined. Reminding me of how she'd been at the committal. If she could stay as focussed as she was now, the defence were in trouble. She wanted to get even, or as even as it was possible to get. Hoping for a future without fear for Gabriel and herself.

"Okay, just to let you know the public gallery is full. There are likely to be some people you recognise."

"That's fine, they can do and think what they like."

"If there is someone there that worries you, when you get the chance, let me know who they are, what they look like and, if possible, roughly where they're sitting. Just a couple more things. You could be in the witness box for most of the day, possibly even tomorrow. Don't worry about it. I always think the longer you're giving evidence, the better you're doing. Just speak normally, there's a microphone. Everyone will be able to hear you. Finally, the barrister who speaks to you first is on our side. He will lead you through your evidence. He may phrase some questions in such a way, so as to avoid using people's names, like Georgina, Matthew and Gabriel. If any of the others use their names, that's fine. You can do the same. But until then, be guided by what our guy says."

"I understand, I think."

"You'll be fine. I have to go back in to court now. So just wait here a little longer, say ten minutes, then make your way to court and sit outside with Julia until you're called. It won't be long, and the girls will be with you, okay?"

"Okay, okay," she said, as though I was starting to nag.

Before leaving, I wrote a quick note to pass to counsel, letting them know Andrea had arrived, and we were good to go. I was feeling more confident having spoken to her and made my way back to court. One of the runners was still hanging around outside court, watching and waiting. I was feeling quite smug. The defence wouldn't know she was here at until the very last moment. When I got into court, the proceedings had already begun with Ahmed's counsel addressing the judge about something. I had no idea what, and didn't really care. I handed my note to the usher who passed it on to counsel. The smirk on Nick Reece's face said it all. Reading the message, he then passed it to Mr Cromber. It was as though he was getting a kick out of the cloak and dagger stuff, too.

In my absence, the boss had promoted himself and was now sitting at the table next to Alan. I'd been in court for about ten minutes when the runner, who'd been waiting outside, came in. Andrea had just appeared and was now sitting outside with her escort. I still had no idea what Ahmed's counsel was on about. All I could think of was how the rest of the day was going to go.

When Mr Cromber finally got to call Andrea, there was an audible intake of breath from those sitting in the dock. Until now, I felt sure they were convinced she wouldn't turn up. As soon as she stepped into the witness box and gave her name. I got a sense that things were about to change. The jury immediately becoming more attentive. Her height, or lack of it apparent, with the microphone having to be lowered to accommodate her. The combination of the way she was dressed and size immediately giving the impression we were looking for. As someone who was prepared to stand up to the defendants. A little hesitant at first, but who wouldn't be? It wasn't long before her voice became stronger and clearer. Mr Cromber led Andrea through her evidence. Slowly, step by step. It was oh-so-slow, and because of the speed, I felt sure that some of her evidence lost its impact. She was still giving her evidence in chief at the end of the day, and whether she liked it or not, there would be a police car and a uniform presence outside her house all night. Prosecution counsel had been impressed by her clarity. With Mr Cromber happy to have lost a private bet between the two on whether she would turn up or not – barristers, what do they know?

Similarly dressed and just as confident, she continued giving evidence the following day. It was almost lunchtime before Mr Cromber said, "Just wait there, would you, these gentlemen may have some questions."

Time for the cross-examination. Would they press her? If so, how far would they go? They had a problem. Her evidence, although slow, had been so descriptive it was difficult to argue with. And the more they laboured a point, the more likely it would stick with the jury. Ramadi's counsel was first.

"Miss Smith, sorry Mrs Baptiste. Do you know what perjury is?"

M'lord's piercing eyes stared at counsel over the half-rimmed glasses that seemed to be glued to the end of his nose. The ill-conceived Freudian slip visually admonished, silently letting counsel know that was far enough.

"I think so."

"Please tell the court in your own words what you think perjury is."

"It's not telling the truth, isn't it?"

"Well yes, put simply, it's telling lies under oath. You swore on the bible to tell the truth before giving us your testimony, didn't you?"

"I affirmed. I don't believe in God anymore. Is that the same?"

Ramadi's counsel looked at the pack, seeking confirmation she'd affirmed. The pack nodded.

"Yes, it's the same..." deliberately stopping. As if thinking of what to say next. He was deliberately letting Andrea stand silently, trying to get her to fill the void. Cognitive interviewing in action at the Central Criminal Court. A technique frequently used by detectives when interviewing prisoners, but it seemed a strange thing to be doing in court. So much so that M'lord interjected, saying, "Mr Nichols, is everything, all right? Do you need some time?"

"No... Thank you, M'lord," was the rather curt reply. M'lord, having unwittingly broken the silence, and with it the tension Mr Nichols had been trying to create. M'lord was now the one being silently admonished by Mr Nichols for spoiling his cross-examination.

"Mrs Baptiste, your husband was originally one of the defendants in this case, wasn't he?"

M'lord again glared at Mr Nichols but said nothing.

"Yes."

"And he is now no longer a defendant in this case, is that correct?"

"Yes."

"Which means you are now free to give evidence against these defendants, is that correct?"

"Does that make a difference?"

"It would have been difficult for you to give evidence, if he was still a defendant?"

"I don't know, is that right?"

Ramadi's counsel didn't answer, continuing with, "What sort of deal did the police offer you?"

There was no messing about. No trying to lead her gently down a cul-de-sac, trying to catch her out. It was full bore, jugular or nothing.

"Deal, I haven't done any deal. I'm not sure I know what you are talking about." She was good, I believed her.

"The deal you have done with the police. To give evidence here today, what have they offered you?"

"I just said, I haven't done any deal. I don't know what you are talking about, I haven't been offered anything."

"If your husband had been a defendant in this case, you wouldn't be giving evidence?"

"I don't know, is that right? It wouldn't matter to me whether my husband was a defendant or not. I would still give evidence."

"I would like to remind you that at the beginning of my cross-examination, I asked if you knew what perjury was?"

"Yes."

"I'll ask you once again. What sort of deal you have done with the police?"

I was becoming concerned at counsel's persistence, whether he was fishing or actually knew something, wondering whether Andrea had said something to Gabriel, which had been overheard, or Julia had inadvertently said something. Before Andrea had a chance to answer, M'lord interjected, he too becoming concerned. In a way, I was pleased. Our counsel had done nothing.

"Mr Nichols, I'm concerned that we may be heading into dangerous territory. I'm going to ask the jury to retire for a short while, so we can deal with this matter."

Now was a good time to for me to disappear, which I did, taking Julia with me, heading for the sanctuary of the City of London's Police canteen. As I left, I could see our counsel looking at the boss. I had no doubt that the boss and possibly others would soon be being quizzed over the severing of Baptiste's trial, in an attempt to establish whether a deal had been done or even suggested. Counsel would also want to know who'd suggested the idea. They might even be given access to police reports and other relevant correspondence in which my name would hardly warrant or get a mention. And with the two of us out of the way, there would be little chance of that changing.

"Do you think this is going to work?" said Julia.

"Providing you haven't said anything to anyone, including Bob. Hopefully, we'll be all right. Have you said anything?"

"No, I haven't," she said sounding suitably aggrieved, putting on the snootiest of voices. How impertinent. How could I have ever dreamt of such a thing?

"I believe you, it's just with Ramadi's counsel banging on the way he has. I'm wondering whether he knows something, or he's just good at fishing, that's all. None of the others know. So, they won't be lying when they tell counsel they haven't done a deal."

"Do you know? It was only when Andrea gave her evidence. I realised just how tough things have been for her, and how strong and courageous she is. She deserves a medal sticking with Baptiste."

"Well, if everything works out, hopefully, Gabriel will be home for Christmas, and that will do."

"Are you really going to try and get him out?"

"If everything goes to plan. Yes, why not?"

"It's just that I thought you were taking her for a ride, that's all."

"I'm not like that. Like you, I think she needs and deserves a leg up, with what she's gone through. She didn't exactly bring this on herself. And, if you boil it all down, Gabriel is just as much a victim of circumstance, as Matthew was – well, almost."

Mildly embarrassed by her gaff and not wishing to dig a deeper hole for herself. Julia just looked at me and said, "What's the Magpie and Stump like?"

"It's okay. It's where a lot of the court reporters go. I try to avoid it, there's a couple of watering holes up near suicide bridge, which aren't bad."

Julia just wanted to change the subject and talk about something else, and I was more than happy just to be out of the way. We sat and drank coffee for over an hour, with Julia eventually getting off her high horse, talking about all sorts of rubbish. By the time we thought it was safe to venture back, the court had reconvened with Mr Nichols moving on with his cross-examination. I sat at the back, trying to pick up his line of questioning. It was about her past life. Friendships intermingled with questions about the youth club. At first, I wondered where he was going. He seemed to be leading up to suggesting that she and Georgina were party girls who slept around. It turned out that Andrea was smarter than Mr Nichols had given her credit for. Every time he looked as though he was getting close to implying that she was or had been promiscuous, she would end her answer with a question which in some way he was obliged to answer, occasionally, pointing at the defendants in the dock for good measure. She was playing him as much as he was with her.

Eventually, he gave up and sat down, giving way to the others who were also looking for a chink in her armour. Going over the same ground, time and again. Andrea consistently gave the same answers, so much so that towards the end, everyone knew the answer before she gave it. They were digging a hole for themselves. The prosecution counsel were obviously very pleased with the way she had given evidence. She'd covered everything and as a result, there was no need for any re-examination.

Everyone who'd listened to her must have been impressed. Again, she'd been clear and concise. Hadn't been rattled and had done more than her fair share of finger pointing at Ramadi and the Parkes brothers.

As she left the court, I managed to get a quick word. Letting her know how pleased we were and saying that I would be in touch with within a week of the trial ending, reminding her to keep our little secret.

Not long after M'lord decreed, there was a case to answer. It was now the turn of the defence.

Chapter 23

Problems on the Central line meant I was running late, but with the defence about to start I wasn't that bothered. Alan should be there, getting bored, listening to them pontificating about some rubbish.

When I arrived, I was surprised to find the court in recess, with all the defence counsel clustered together in the far corner of the court. With our counsel sitting alone in the opposite corner. Everyone else had been excluded from court, with me immediately being told to wait outside. Not knowing why, I went to look for the rest of the team, who were nowhere to be seen; they weren't outside, in the canteens or police room. I then found myself sitting alone, wondering what was going on. I'd been there for quite a while when the usher walked by.

"Any idea what's going on?"

"Not really. All I know is they're looking at a letter from Andrea Baptiste, the lady who gave evidence yesterday."

"I wonder what she's been writing about?"

"No idea, sorry." And with that, he carried on, making his way towards the lifts. What could she be writing about? All I could think of was our secret. Had she suddenly decided to let on? I couldn't think of anything else. If she had, I needed to come up with a story, but without knowing what had been said, it was impossible. The longer I sat, the more flustered I became, trying to work out what was going on and whether it was better to stay or go, when Mr Reece poked his head around the corner of the courtroom door and on seeing me, beckoned me into court. I wasn't sure I wanted to go, but had no choice. When I entered court Mr Reece simply said, "Just sit there would you." Pointing to the chair I'd sat on for most of the trial. I had no idea what was happening with the defence teams still huddled together in the corner. Occasionally, one would look round, swivelling his head like an owl looking for prey, surveying the court, checking they weren't being listened to.

"Can I ask, what's happening?" I said.

"We don't know exactly, we've been kept in the dark, pretty much. All we do know is that the defence asked the judge to delay proceedings this morning. We think one of them has a letter from Mrs Baptiste. Whatever it is, it shouldn't be long before we know more, as the defence have now asked for the judge." My nerves started to go into overdrive. For prosecution counsel not to be included, it had to be serious. With the huddle breaking up, the judge entered court. Mr Nichols, Ramadi's counsel, remained standing, holding what looked like a letter in his hand.

"M'lord, firstly may I take the opportunity to thank the court for the additional time. On arrival at court this morning, I was handed a letter. A letter from Andrea Baptiste. Your Lordship will remember she was the last witnesses to give evidence for the prosecution. Her testimony, their mainstay." He then started waving the letter around for all to see.

"The contents of the letter are compelling," he continued, "and cast serious doubt on the validity of testimony given."

"May I see the letter?" his Lordship asked. "Can you tell me, Mr Nichols, have counsel had the opportunity...?"

"Defence counsel, M'lord yes," replied Mr Nichols, as he handed the letter to the clerk of the court, who in turn passed it onto M'lord. I was desperate to know the contents, if only for self-preservation. As the judge read the letter, there was total silence, with everybody studying him, looking for clues that might give an insight as to his thoughts. Now and again, he would pause and look up, mulling over what he'd read, while scanning those in court. Every time he got to me, whether rightly or wrongly, I felt he lingered a little longer, making me feel even more uncomfortable. The not knowing was doing my head in. On top of which, where were the others? Their absence wasn't helping. What was in that bloody letter?

It then occurred to me that whatever its contents, if there was a suggestion that a crime had been committed, the letter would need to be forensically examined. Irrespective of whether it was for or against me, the Crown or someone else, it would still need to be analysed. It was a bit of a gamble, but it wasn't the first time we'd done something to draw the judge's attention. Having got an exhibit bag from under the desk, I stood up, deliberately pushing the chair back while holding the bag out. I had everyone's attention. Even M'lord stopped reading and stared. Despite his head hardly moving, he was looking straight at me as if annoyed at the interruption, and that his concentration had been broken. He then said, "Mr Cromber, Mr Lomax may very well be able to help with this matter. Have him take the stand, would you?"

With everyone now looking at me, I slowly made my way to the witness box, wondering whether I'd done the right thing. My initial thought had been that if the letter was about me, the defence would object, which would at least give me a clue. But with the judge asking me to take the stand, I was having second thoughts, wondering whether he was going to quiz me about the contents. Standing in the witness box, with so many thoughts going through my head, I was struggling to concentrate, when M'lord said, "Mr Lomax, the court has received a letter from Mrs Baptiste, the contents of which, if true, will undoubtedly have a significant bearing on this case. Not only in relation to the evidence given, but it would also cast a shadow over the entire investigation and how it has been conducted. We have a need for Mrs Baptiste to return to court and be available for questioning as soon as is possible and I'm going to charge you with that duty."

I'd got so wound up, I wasn't really taking in what was being said, when I heard the words "I'm going to charge you..." my heart skipped a beat.

Then Mr Cromber barked, "Mr Lomax. Can you get Mrs Baptiste here?" continuing with, "Is there anything else? M'lord."

I was still processing what was going on and must have looked more than a little gormless when I blurted, "But shouldn't it be examined?"

M'lord, realising he'd been handed the original, put the letter down and started scanning the line of legal beagles. As if viewing an identification parade, looking for the culprit who'd sold him a pup, realising the majority of defence counsels' fingerprints along with his own had potentially contaminated the evidence. Although I was still desperate to know the contents, I was beginning to feel much calmer. I couldn't imagine the judge giving me the responsibility of getting Andrea to court, as well as potentially dealing with the forensic submission of the letter, if I'd been mentioned.

There was then a relatively quick discussion on the types of analysis which could be accomplished within twenty-four hours, which was all M'lord was prepared to adjourn the case for.

Ninhydrin fingerprint analysis was the only one we had any chance of doing in that time. For all those who wanted and were entitled to read the letter, copies were made, and the case was adjourned. Andrea would have to be there when we next sat.

M'lord then ordered all those who'd touched the letter or envelope to provide their fingerprints for elimination purposes before leaving court, including himself. They'd screwed up, so they were the ones who would now have to hang around while we found the necessary equipment. The judge had made it very clear; he wasn't about to just let them disappear. If he wasn't leaving, then they neither were they. There were at least eleven sets of fingerprints to take, possibly fifteen, depending on whether any of the runners had been able to get their grubby little paws on either.

Given the judge's ruling, irrespective of the logistics, cost or personal inconvenience, someone had pulled an all-nighter. Others would soon be dashing around to accomplish M'lord's wishes. It would happen, M'lord had decreed it so. Once I'd taken all the sets of elimination prints, I made arrangements to get them to the lab.

I was certain the letter was a forgery. It just didn't read the way Andrea thought or spoke, and from memory the signature didn't look much like hers either. Before leaving, I was able to dig out Andrea's original statement, and having compared the signature, I was even more convinced that she wasn't the author. I just needed to hear her say it.

On the way to the lab, I read the letter properly, deciding to call on Andrea personally later. The lab wasn't very impressed with the judge, but had little choice. It was the only chance of getting any results in the time allowed. Blood, saliva and handwriting analysis all needed a lot longer. If the fingerprint tests were inconclusive, these might still have to be considered, and if things went wrong, we could find ourselves with the judge being forced to order a retrial. Having got this far, it was the last thing the prosecution wanted.

The letter was an apology to the court for the evidence she'd given. According to the letter, the police had made her say the things she had. It went on to say that if she didn't give evidence, the police would make sure Gabriel spent a very long time in prison, and that splitting the trial was part of their plan. Done to make sure Andrea did what the police wanted. Everything she'd said about the defendants was a lie.

If we couldn't prove who the author was, the letter could cause problems, even with Andrea being recalled. We just had to hope that identifiable fingerprints other than those of England's greatest legal minds were developed. I left a list of the defendants along with all the associates I could think of with the lab. Andrea had already provided her fingerprints for elimination purposes. All we could do now was wait, hoping we would have news before the judge's deadline.

It wasn't until early evening that I finally got to see Andrea. She'd been working late, doing overtime, trying to take her mind off the trial. She was surprised to see me so soon, thinking I was there regarding Gabriel. I was, but not in the way she thought. She categorically denied writing the letter, showing me some of her handwriting. It didn't look anything like the letter, and neither did her signature. She was more than willing to come back to court, anything to help to stick the knife into Ramadi, sounding just as vengeful and having gone through the ordeal of the past few days, was now relishing the prospect of standing in the witness box to have another go at him.

While there, I asked her whether she'd been able to look at the public gallery. She had, saying that apart from Adam's mother, there were a couple of the other faces she thought she recognised but couldn't remember where from.

In accordance with the judge's instructions, I arranged for her to be picked up so that she would be at court in plenty of time.

Unusually, when I arrived, instead of being in court, everyone was waiting in the vast area outside. The legal teams huddled together in groups. The sound of muffled conversations echoed throughout. I couldn't remember ever seeing so many people waiting in the space and despite the number, it still looked empty. Andrea and Julia were sitting by the entrance with the rest of the team not far away.

Yesterday, when the team had arrived, they too had been kept in the dark, being told to go away until after lunch. As a result, they'd all gone off to one of the early houses in Smithfield Market. By the time they got back, court had risen, and everyone had gone.

I wasn't sure whether it was just this case, but the boss had been getting himself into a bit of a state. The thought of having to get in the witness box and deal with questions surrounding the letter and depending on the results, having his leadership called into questioned was really playing on his mind. Consequently, we made Nick Reece promise that should anything crop up Bob Clark would be the one dealing with it. The boss was definitely better equipped to deal with fraud cases; which were more gentlemanly affairs, just as devious, but done with a smile.

With our deadline approaching and with no word from the lab, everyone seemed to be just hanging around, waiting for a miracle to happen. As now one else seemed to be doing anything, I made a visit to the police room to see if there was any news. The reception area temporarily unmanned, but I could see a fax lying in the receiving tray on the other side of the counter. The logo on the cover page I recognised as being from the laboratory. It was a statement from the fingerprint examiner assigned to our case. Looking at the timestamp, the fax had been there for close to an hour, which was really unusual. Normally the police room was pretty hot on fax messages.

The statement consisted of three pages, together with copies of all sides of the letter and envelope after it had been subjected to the ninhydrin, revealing the fingerprints developed. I had originally been told this process normally took up to twenty-four hours. Somehow the lab had been able to do the lot in quick time. All the marks and smudges that had come to light could be seen. Some of which had been circled and numbered. I immediately went to the last page. There was a template for the format of fingerprint statements. Where, if successful, one of the last paragraphs would start with the words: "In conclusion and as a result of my analysis, I am able to say that the fingerprints found on exhibit JBD/123 marked and circled with the number(s)... belonged to..." and there was the name – Frederick Ramadi. Ramadi's father's fingerprints had been found. Almost as an afterthought, there was another paragraph confirming Andrea's fingerprints had not. It was about as good a result as we could have hoped for. Four of Frederick Ramadi's prints had been found on the letter and one on the envelope. The ninhydrin had revealed a myriad of other smudges, prints and partial prints, mostly near the edges where our sharpest minds had made their mark. The thumb and forefinger prints of both Mr Ramadi's hands had been found on either side of one page around the midway point.

I had to take my hat off to the lab, they'd done a fantastic job given the circumstances. Not only in getting the task done but also in providing a formal statement, which could be served immediately, getting us out of a sticky situation. The question was how best to use the information and what to do with Mr Ramadi. He must have been in court and was one of the few people we hadn't been able to find or interview. Admittedly, we hadn't gone to the ends of the earth trying. As far as I could remember, we'd been to his last known addresses and that of a previous employer without any joy, but that was about it.

From the stories we'd heard, he'd disowned his son and wanted nothing to do with him. If that was the case, what was he doing in the public gallery? Were the stories true, or had there been some sort of reconciliation? It would be useful to know, as it could have a bearing on how he was dealt with. Attempting to pervert the course of justice was a serious crime, particularly when it related to a murder trial.

The question was what the best way to deal with this. We didn't want Frederick Ramadi's name being made public, and I had to let the bosses and counsel know. So, neatly folding the fax, I put it in my inside jacket pocket and walked back to court, passing the various huddles. When I reached our team, I beckoned the bosses and counsel into the court's cramped conference room. There was complete silence as everyone squeezed in, waiting for me to speak. Instead, I handed the statement to the boss and said, "The last page, page three, is what you want."

He went straight to it and, having read the page, silently passed it to Mr Cromber. The statement was then systematically passed around in complete silence, eventually coming back to me, after which the boss said, "Okay, that's good, so we just carry on?"

"I don't want to sound funny, boss, but have you actually read the letter?"

"No, do I need to?"

"Well, the way it's written. He or someone he knew was in the public gallery when Andrea gave evidence. Obviously, the judge needs to know and I'm assuming we don't want his name being bandied about, do we?" Then, looking at counsel, I asked whether it was something that could be dealt with In-camera?

"My thoughts exactly," said Mr Cromber. "Nick, when we've finished, would you be kind enough to inform the others?"

"Of course, Michael, pleasure," said Nick Reece.

"Smart arse" was what I got from the DI.

My reward for making the suggestion was to get photocopies of the statement. Two unedited copies and a load with Ramadi's name redacted. It was my understanding that counsel needed to seek the judge's permission to have this element of the hearing held In-camera. As part of that process, we needed to find the usher so that he could pass on one of the unredacted copies of the statement to the judge prior to sitting. Which meant a trip to the ground floor. On the way there, one of the lifts opened, and I jumped in, only to be joined by Ramadi and Devon Parkes's runners, heading for the lower ground floor, which was where you gained access to the cell area. The journey took place in complete silence. The runners seemed remarkably happy. I didn't know why. Having passed on my message and a copy of the statement, I headed back to court, where counsel were readying themselves.

As I entered court, I got the impression there was a little more banter between counsel. Not long after, the defendants were brought up and instead of taking their seats, started showing off. With Ramadi and Devon Parkes staring in our direction, trying to catch an eye, and when they did, delivering a rude hand gesture, either a two-fingered salute or wanker sign. It was all rather strange.

Once the redacted copies of the statements had been handed over, the mood immediately changed, and as soon as M'lord had sat an application was made to have the police excluded. It wasn't long before we were again sitting outside, waiting.

We had no idea what was going on or the reason for our exclusion. It wasn't until 3.30 p.m. when we heard the tannoy summoning us back to court that we found out why. Two things had emerged. Firstly, the defence were crying foul. Alleging the prosecution had misled them into believing Andrea Baptiste's fingerprints had in fact been found on the letter. And that this was the reason for requesting the session to be held In-camera; their belief being that the prosecution needed to seek directions from the judge on how best to proceed, which then explained why the defendants were acting the way they were. As we hadn't been responsible for informing them, I wondered what Nick Reece had said. That would give rise to the misunderstanding?

The second thing was that our counsel had successfully argued that only redacted copies of the statement be provided to the defence, showing that Andrea's fingerprints had not been found and somebody else's had. Withholding the identity of the culprit from the defence was something they had argued vehemently against, saying they had a basic right to know, and the information should be disclosed. It was this element of the argument which had taken the longest to deal with. The letter was now the subject of yet another investigation we would have to deal with.

There was another short recess while the jury were summoned. When the court reconvened, someone had been searching through our papers, presumably looking for the name. It wasn't there, they'd wasted their time.

Given the general lack of goodwill throughout the case, our counsel told M'lord about the search. He was not amused, warning the defence in no uncertain terms that if they or members of their team were found to be engaged in any such activity, they would be immediately locked up. Even threatening to stop the trial while all the police's papers were examined for fingerprints – the gloves were definitely off.

Finally, it was the turn of the defence to make their case, and it soon became apparent that neither Ramadi nor the Parkes brothers were going to be giving evidence. Not allowing themselves to be subjected to being cross-examined. Which left Ahmed.

It still took most of the day for the various counsel to outline their defendant's cases. Going through various elements where they saw potential weaknesses, questioning its validity and attempting to raise doubt in the jury's mind. Throughout, there was a lot of duplication. The jury must have been bored to tears.

Alan and I had again decided to share duties. We were just as bored and would have to listen to longer versions of the same twaddle during closing speeches.

It was during one of these exhilarating sessions I thought I would amuse myself by giving the prison staff something to do. Wandering down to the cell area, I was curious to know whether Frederick Ramadi, or anyone else for that matter, had visited any of the defendants during the trial. Given that no one had visited Ramadi while he was in prison. It was better than sitting in court.

The prison officers not assigned to specific courts were just as likely to be hanging around with little or nothing to do until trials started finishing for the day. Having told one of the prison officers who was sitting at the counter what I was looking for. He looked to defy physics, leaning as far back as he could in his chair and stretching out an arm to grab a log file from one of the many pigeonholes, predictably falling off. Having waited patiently while he recovered from the mild embarrassment. He then started leafing through the pages, while repeatedly asking me to either say or spell Ramadi's name. In the end, I wrote it down.

"Apart from his legal team, he's had one visitor," said the screw.

"His father?" I asked.

"No, someone called Desmond Griffith, a friend." A new name that meant nothing.

"What address did he give, I'm guessing somewhere in Barking or East Ham, maybe?"

"No, Dalston Lane."

I almost choked. "Say that again."

"12 Dalston Lane, Dalston. Do you know it?"

"It's the address of The Four Aces, a nightclub," I replied.

The address indelibly imprinted in the mind of anyone who had worked in that part of London. The Four Aces was a notorious little haunt known for drugs, weapons, stolen goods, rapes, fights, stabbings, reggae, ska, Red Stripe and excellent patties. It was not in Ramadi's normal circle of activity, and I doubted he'd ever been there or knew where it was. More recently, the area had begun to be influenced by Yardies. It was one of their meeting places – something we hadn't anticipated.

The address was one of three locations in the area where the police didn't go unless mob-handed. They were dangerous places. The others were Phoebes, a similar nightclub not far from The Four Aces, in Amhurst Road. The main difference being that Phoebes was on three floors; playing different types of reggae and ska on each floor. Previously known as the Regency Club. The haunt of Jack "The Hat" McVitie and the Kray brothers. The Three Crowns Public House, the other. A pub which had seen several drug-related stabbings. Desmond Griffith's address was definitely false. As no doubt was the name. His visit had coincided with Andrea beginning her evidence. Yardies were more violent than other gangs I'd come across. I was aware that on one occasion, they'd emptied an entire magazine from an Uzi submachine gun into a jeweller's shop. A drive-by, nothing more. Just to announce their arrival in the area. A shop assistant had lost her life. She hadn't been shot; she'd been cut to shreds by the shards of glass created by the gunfire. From the photographs, the place was a bloody mess, and it was all just for show, pure bravado. They didn't stop or take anything, picking the shop at random.

Yardies were definitely capable of nobbling a jury, if they put their minds to it. Ramadi could have come into contact with them while on remand. The fact he was standing trial for such a gruesome murder involving torture could make him recruiting material. Even in prison, he could be used as an enforcer.

Only relatives and a few known friends had visited the others. The screw then thought it amusing to tell me that their CCTV hadn't worked for some time, so there was no point in asking. Wondering what to do, I rang the DI. He was more likely to know what, if anything, could be done. He was horrified and unsure whether anything could be done regarding witness protection at this stage. Saying that he would make some enquiries and for the time being, we were to keep the information to ourselves. He didn't want the boss or counsel knowing. There would be a whole load of red tape to go through, for the names and addresses of the jurors to be made known to a protection unit. If any of the jurors had or were to mention being approached, it would be a different matter, with the judge making an order, even placing them in protective custody.

It was difficult to know how much longer the trial would last, so I asked counsel for their opinion, saying I was thinking of taking some time off when the trial finished. Their estimate was four or five days before the jury went out. Then another two or possibly three days for deliberations. So, anything after that should be okay. We had just over a week to work things out.

Having told Alan, he thought it worthwhile getting a couple of aides to watch the court's main entrance. Joining us for the afternoon session, the two aides sat behind us, concentrating on the jury, trying to memorise them as best they could. They were to stay for an hour or so, before making their way over to the first floor of the overflow courts, which were located the other side of Old Bailey, close to the Magpie and Stump. From there, they would have a very good view of the court's exit and surrounding area. Should anyone ask, they were here for the experience, part of their training. The other problem we had was that Dennis Nilsen, the serial killer, had just been found guilty of six murders. As a result, outside court was a lot busier than usual, with the media coverage and outside broadcast crews attracting additional crowds, making it easy for anyone looking for a juror to mingle.

Rightly or wrongly, we'd decided that should anyone be spotted following a juror, then the spotter would follow the follower, making it obvious they were being followed. Trying to put them off before they reached any address. If that wasn't working, they were to be arrested, and we would sort out what for later. It was all we could think of.

The other thing that was causing a certain amount of angst was there was no way of knowing whether they'd already selected potential targets. All we could be sure of was that they would need to influence at least three jurors to be certain that a majority verdict couldn't be reached. We then started playing pick the vulnerable juror. Studying them more intently than at any time before. I had this sense of desperation, helplessness. Unable to confide in anyone and not sure whether everything we and others had gone through would be in vain. With all the time and effort that had gone into the case, the number of lives lost and the extraordinary circumstances, we were now possibly at the mercy of others. We'd done our best to keep the case on track. The feeling was that if the defendants walked away, it would be a complete travesty. I'd become so distracted by my thoughts and feelings. Trying to assess the jury was a complete waste of time. I could only hope the aides were doing a better job. While I was moping around, feeling completely useless, one of the officers from the police room appeared, passing Alan a note addressed to me, which read:

"Urgent – Meet usual place before five. Mow – A/DC Page."

He'd misspelt Mo, but I got the message.

"You better go. I can look after this," said Alan.

I hadn't seen Mo for ages. The message was totally out of the blue. I thought he'd given up on me. Gerry Riley was another who had a lot to answer for. Maybe I would feel a little better after seeing him. I couldn't feel any worse. Mo was working a new pitch, right by the entrance to the Tower of London near Lower Thames Street. Still selling fruit and presumably still without a street trader's licence. By the looks of things, he was making a go of it. He had someone else working his old pitch, and they'd told me where to go. Mo with an employee, whatever next. I was greeted with the usual banter. It was as though nothing had happened and while he carried on serving the odd punter. I said, "You wanted to see me?"

"Yeah. Still looking for Gerry?"

"As far as I know. I haven't heard anything to the contrary, do you know where he is?"

"Well, sort of. I might do."

"What are you looking for?" I asked.

"For it not to come back to me, to start with."

"And?"

"To be left alone. I want out. I've had enough. I'm giving this a go, nothing more."

"Mo, on the straight and narrow, what's really going on?"

"Straight up, honest. Since I've been doing this, I'm not looking over my shoulder so much. Things are easier, and to be honest, I'm not sure I can do another long one, not even a handful. All I've got to do is square my pitch and everything is sweet. You know, topping Paddy, made me realise it could have just as easily been me. I could have been part of the hit. On top of that, there's a new order. Others are fighting to take the old patch, which gives me the chance of stepping away. If Gerry keeps popping round tooled up, he's bound to bugger things up, and I can't just tell him to piss off. If I can get him sorted, without it coming back on me, that would help, and if I could get the licences sorted too, that would be even better. What do you reckon?"

"What's the real long-term plan, then?"

"Do this, honest, nothing else. Since I started, I've made a few shekels, legit too. If I can get the pitches sorted, that would be really sweet, the landlord can't do anything." Which I took to mean sorting the street traders' licence.

"I reckon I can do seven months and then get on the piss somewhere warm for the rest of the year, if I fancy it. Gerry's putting all that at risk, and as I said, I can't just tell him to sling his hook. He wouldn't take any notice. If I did, he would just want to know what's going on. He's becoming a nuisance. He keeps popping around with some mate he's got, called Dave. They're always tooled up, having just hit somewhere. They stay for a couple of days and just get on the piss, wanting to party all the time. Hitting the clubs, you know the sort of thing. Bugger's my day right up, what with going to the markets for three in the morning."

"What sort of guns?"

"Pistols, not exactly sure what. Gerry's looks a bit like the ones you see in old war films. The ones, the German officers have, with a black handle. Dave's is smaller, stumpier, looks a bit like a starting pistol. Both 9mm though. I've seen them swapping loads. Gerry couldn't stop talking about one job. Which he thought was a nice little tickle. Turning over some old didicoy. He said, he got ten grand in readies with no old bill to worry about because the Didi wouldn't be reporting it. Meaning, the readies couldn't have been Kosher, could they?"

"What about his girlfriend?" I said.

"Hasn't mentioned his old lady. Come to think of it, neither has he mentioned going anywhere for it either, so she might still be around."

"So, where is he, then?"

"He's staying on a caravan site in Felixstowe. I don't know the exact name of the place. But it's got the word 'sands' in it and it's close to where the ferry docks. Dave's not there, he's in town somewhere. Gerry still won't drive; they meet up at Liverpool Street Station.

A couple of weeks after he legged it, he turned up back at my place. At one point he was fishing around in his pockets, looking for his lighter, taking stuff out. Bits of paper, odds and sods. There was a leaflet for this caravan park. It was folded, but I could see the letters "sands" and part of a phone number I can't remember. He said it was ideal for him. He could walk there from the station, it's somewhere at the end of a long straight road. Where he reckons it's impossible for him to be followed without knowing. Even if he's pissed, he says he just heads for the lights or cranes at the docks which can be seen for miles, and he's there. It's been a few weeks now, so I reckon I'm safe saying."

"Does he turn up on a particular day?"

"Normally the back end of the week, Thursday or Friday."

"Wage's days." I said, thinking aloud. I needed to speak to PeaSea and get an idea of what was going on. DS Gray would just give me a load of crap. I knew the Supergrass programme had been suspended and was now the subject of a review. If the review was about what went wrong, DS Gray was in the firing line and would jump at the chance of trying to put things right. He wouldn't give two hoots about anyone else, just so long as he could save himself, and there was no way I could just pop off to Felixstowe for a few days. I needed help and wouldn't be looking to Suffolk for it. Having already had a bad experience there. After all this, I needed to be sure Mo wouldn't be in any danger. The thought of him ending up dead in a ditch somewhere worried me.

"You mentioned your landlord not being able to do anything, what's that all about?"

"Yeah, I needed to get a nod of approval, making sure the pitches would be insured against any damage, if you know what I mean. Which meant an unscheduled meeting with the man. I had to meet him and his minder in the Anchor Tap, a couple of weeks ago. He was in the saloon bar, all suited and booted, which was a bit unusual. Anyway, while we were discussing things, I mentioned needing to get the licences sorted. Saying that, I might know someone who could help, meaning you. Which is when he said he was actually waiting for someone to arrive, who he thought could get things sorted, and as they were due fairly soon, he told me to wait in the public bar. Not long after, these two tame coppers rolled up in monkey suits. I don't think the man realised I could see them from where I was sitting. I've seen one of them before, drinking alone in the Artful Dodger, scruffy bugger normally, certainly likes a drink."

"Stocky guy, late thirties, Scottish accent?"

"Your joking, tall skinny git, quite old, with bloodshot eyes and those rosy cheeks vagrants get from drinking all that Emva or QC."

It had to be Ken Reeves. The Artful Dodger was definitely one of his haunts. Mo's description of the other tame copper sounded like DI Lambert.

"Could they sort the licences?"

"No, according to the man, they didn't have an in with the Corporation, so he's left it with me. So, you know what that means, don't you?"

"No, what?"

"If you can sort it, I'm sure he'd be interested in meeting you, he'd certainly make it worth your while."

"I don't think so, and if you've described who I think it is, you better be careful. If any of them link the two of us together, we could be deep shit. Proper trouble, I mean it. Just be careful, be very careful. I'll be in touch." He knew I was being serious as I left him to carry on.

In some ways I had a sense of relief, thinking how much Mo trusted me. He could have easily gone elsewhere about Riley. But the news that Reeves and Lambert were involved with the Adam's family or whoever was running the show, both surprised and scared me. We needed to be really careful. The people they were mixing with were in a different league. My mind then drifted to Andrea. The trust she had shown in me, and the risks she'd taken. If either Ramadi or Devon Parkes were released or were seriously involved with Yardies, her life and Gabriel's would be in grave danger, even in prison. And at present there was nothing we could do to protect them.

When I got back to court, the aides hadn't spotted any likely suspects and would be coming back for another go.

Donovan Parkes' counsel was hypothesising about possibilities of how the murder could have occurred and what the police had got wrong. Counsel for three of the defendants had bored me to tears. Four days of hot air. When he'd finished, it just left Jamal Ahmed, the summing up and closing speeches. Then the jury would be out.

Jamal Ahmed was risking being cross-examined, giving evidence from the witness box. If he got it right, he might have a better chance of being acquitted. With only one defendant risking being cross-examined, our counsel had been given more than enough time to prepare. As Ahmed gave evidence, his counsel carefully asked questions aimed at getting answers that were part of a well-rehearsed script. Fitting the answers as best they could to the answers he'd given in interview. It was high risk; he was definitely a gambler. His initial explanations for the cleaning products were that he and some friends were planning on giving the house a spring clean. The spices, or at least some of them, were going to be used for cooking a meal for all those who'd helped. Once he'd finished giving evidence and the cross-examination started, it was clear that he'd been able to rehearse answers to the more obvious questions he would be asked. Anything outside those, and memory fade kicked in, he couldn't remember. Ahmed was still being cross-examined when we rose for lunch. We'd been going around in circles and I couldn't see that he was doing himself any favours.

Cross-examination had already started when I got back from lunch. Although I wasn't sure what had happened, with exchanges being a lot more animated. After a while, I realised Ahmed was off script and was getting himself into trouble. The 'cooking a curry for some mates' scenario had somehow morphed into being some kind of culinary experience. Experimenting, creating new dishes. It was so implausible; Ahmed's counsel didn't seem to know where to look or how to intervene. There was no way back. Nick Reece just kept turning the screw, making him squirm. Just enough to make sure the jury got the message. But not so far that they might end up feeling sorry for him.

We were still studying the jury, while closing speeches were given and the judge summed up, looking for any signs which might give an indication of a change. Distraction, fidgeting, anything. It was difficult, and I was buggered if I could see anything. They all looked the same. Alan Harrison hadn't picked up on anything either. My ears pricked up when I heard M'lord say, "Tomorrow, members of the jury, I will be asking you to retire to consider your verdict."

Having passed the information on to the bosses so they could be in court for the verdict. It soon became apparent that they had told others from the team. Win or lose, we would all be going for a drink. The defence teams also appeared to be at full strength. Surely, they couldn't be thinking of celebrating, could they? Most of our lot were waiting in the canteen. Ken Reeves hadn't made it, thank God. To be honest. I wasn't sure he'd actually been told, and I didn't really care – bent bastard.

It only took M'lord forty minutes in the morning to complete his summing up, before giving the jury the usual blurb about trying to reach a unanimous verdict. If that was not possible, other avenues may be available. That was it. The jury usher took her oath to maintain their seclusion and led them away.

Once the judge had left court, everyone started packing up: collecting up case papers and any stray exhibits. With the usher refreshing the carafes of water, while replacing any used glasses. A new case, one of the floaters from the list, would be starting in court within the hour. By the time we'd made a couple of journeys to and from the police room, I found myself alone with the usher who was still tidying and refreshing the carafes as he moved around the court.

"You might as well go home, there won't be a verdict today." He said.

"Is that what your crystal ball's telling you?"

"That jury, there's no way they'll reach a verdict today."

"What makes you say that?"

"Do you want a bet?"

"Not really, but I'd like to know?"

"Simple, they've all turned up with overnight bags. It's obvious they want a night in a hotel. If they're still deliberating much past six, the old judgy-wudgy will call 'em back and ask whether they think they will be able to reach a unanimous verdict given more time? They'll say yes, job done. He'll have no option other than to put them up in a hotel. Think about it, they must have all been boy scouts or girl guides to court be so well prepared!"

"I thought the jury would normally be sent home?"

"Not with a trial like this. If they're still in there after six, it'll be a hotel. Sure, as eggs are eggs."

"Does anyone else know?"

"Just the jury usher. She's the one who told me in the first place, she overheard them talking."

Having collected the last of the papers, I found the others sitting in the canteen. We were still sitting there at 6.30 p.m. when a voice over the tannoy blurted, "All parties in the case of Ramadi and others to court seven."

Apart from a few court staff, the place was deserted, with the cavernous public areas echoing more than usual. Just as the usher had predicted, M'lord asked the foreman a couple of questions and then ordered the jury be taken to a secret location where they could continue their deliberations. Ramadi caused such a commotion looking up at the public gallery, shouting angrily, "Too fucking late, man, you're too fucking late, shit, fuck, fuck, fuck." Carrying on while the prison warders dragged him and the others away. I tried to get across the court to see the public gallery.

Everyone had heard him, including the jury. I wondered whether they realised why and who he was shouting at. His final chance of getting at the jurors gone. By the time I'd got across the court so that I could see the public gallery, whoever

Ramadi's comments were aimed at had gone. Apart from Pope's mother and some of the older incumbents, the gallery was pretty empty. When I got back to the desk, the boss said, "What's going on, what's happening?" The way he said it was priceless. Oblivious to everything that was going on around him. He didn't have a clue, bless him.

"Just curious. I thought I might be able to see who Ramadi was shouting at, that's all."

"Any joy?"

"No, looks as though they've gone."

"Any ideas what all the commotion was about?" he said.

"Not really."

A white lie. I wasn't certain whether the boss had even heard of Yardies and trying to explain everything would only end up with him causing a fuss and counsel getting involved. It wasn't worth it, not now. Some of the other groups looked as though they were having similar discussions, wondering what all the fuss had been about. Those who knew said nothing.

Just before lunch on the third day of the jury's deliberations, another tannoy announcement calling everyone to court. It looked as though a verdict had been reached, which was confirmed by the usher as we entered court.

As everyone gathered and the public gallery filled, reporters were now trying to squeeze themselves in, wanting to see and comment on the verdict. Andrea Baptiste among them. The word had spread and as the court filled, not only did the tension grow, but the quieter it got despite the numbers. And despite their previous antics, even Ramadi and the brothers sat quietly, awaiting their feat. The strain had finally begun to show.

Everyone was now waiting for M'lord. I couldn't remember feeling so nervous before a verdict. It had been an extraordinary ride and the longer the judge took, the more I wondered whether we'd done enough and whether the jury had been listening. The tension palpable, almost unbearable. All anyone could do now was wait and look at the judge's empty chair. The waiting was almost unbearable, and despite my experience of being in court, I, probably along with others, began to this knotting sensation in my stomach. Similar to the feeling I got when Matthew Peters was discovered having committed suicide. When the judge did finally enter, everyone stood and bowed for what would be the penultimate time. With the jury summoned, the defendants were made to stand while the clerk of the court went through his ritual. With the jury foreman standing, he asked whether they'd reached a verdict? They had. He then started to go through the various counts, saying, "In respect of count one, murder, how do you find the defendant Benjamin Ramadi, guilty or not guilty?"

"Guilty."

There was an audible gasp of air from all around. Even Ramadi looked shocked.

"And is that the verdict of you all?"

"It is."

Having gone through all the counts against all the defendants, it was a clean sweep with them all being found guilty of everything.

As the judge handed out four life sentences, Ramadi finally looked beaten and alone. The blood visibly draining from his face as he swayed, looking as though he could faint. His face a similar colour to that of Adam's head on the day it was recovered from the Thames. Moments later the four defendants were led away, with only Devon Parkes showing any sign of defiance. I caught a glimpse of Andrea, who I could see crying, the emotion too much for her too. As the seconds passed, the sensation in my stomach receded.

It was over time to regroup and relax with a small celebration, which, once again, the boss had arranged, this time at the Inn of Court. By the time we'd gathered, the entire team was there, along with others the boss had invited. Amongst them, prosecution counsel and Den the Pen, who'd turned up with a couple of others I didn't know.

With the majority staying on, small groups formed, with everyone enjoying themselves, socialising, mingling between the groups. At one point I was sitting with Alan and when the boss came over accompanied by one of those who'd arrived with Den the Pen.

"Let me introduce you to Detective Superintendent Maguire. Soon to be Detective Chief Superintendent Liam Maguire. An old friend and colleague. And whether you like it or not he's going to be your new boss, and do you know what one of the first things he's going to do is?"

"Sort out The Muppets?" I said.

"Not quite, let's just say KR will no longer be of this parish."

"Yeah, right, he's only had nine thousand lives, and you'll have DI Lambert to contend with," I said, possibly a little too sarcastically.

Mr Maguire then said, "He'll be in January's police orders, I can promise you."

He was so emphatic; I believed him. Guilty verdicts, no more Hampton, the end of Ken Reeves and hopefully The Muppets. It couldn't get much better, could it?

All I had to do now was sort out Mo, Gerry Riley and, of course, Andrea's Gabriel, but that would have to wait for another day. I was leaving Frederick Ramadi for someone else.

About the Author

Jacob Darr is an investigator and novelist who joined the Metropolitan Police in the 1970s, initially serving in London's east end.

Whilst serving as a detective, he was fortunate enough to be posted on to differing operational units at New Scotland Yard. Giving him the opportunity to develop a wide range of investigative skills and techniques which remain current today.

As a result, he has provided expert testimony in the UK, Europe, the USA, the Middle East, and Asia for private, corporate, and government clients. Examples of the investigations include blackmail, asset tracing (on-shore and off-shore), fraud, intellectual property, deception and unexplained deaths.

Happily married, Jacob lives in the UK, where he occasionally enjoys the odd glass of malt.

The Tailor's Dummy is his debut novel, which draws on personal experiences, combining a true story with a little poetic licence.

Find out more at jacobdarr.com

Printed in Great Britain
by Amazon